# THE VANISHERS

## Donald Hamilton

FAWCETT GOLD MEDAL • NEW YORK

The little .22 High  was comfortable in my hand. It was the only thing in the world, in my shut marksman's world. The fact that my knees were weak and I was beginning to have trouble with my breathing didn't matter a bit. When I squeezed off the first round I found that the agency silencer was really very good these days, with that low-powered target ammo. I'd have made more noise pulling a wine cork.

Well, three wine corks. I quit shooting when the pistol started becoming oddly unsteady in my hand, or maybe it was my hand that was becoming unsteady. There was no sense in just making stray holes in the premises.

Three should be enough to get the job done. . . .

# THE VANISHERS

# CHAPTER 1

I was driving from Chihuahua, Chihuahua, Mexico, to Washington, D.C., U.S.A., because, I'd been told, a car such as I'd been given to use in the Southwest was now needed in the Northeast and our current budget forced us to make the most of our limited rolling stock.

Furthermore, I'd been told, a few days of relaxed freeway driving would give me time to recuperate from the terrible strain of trying to *habla español* with my limited Spanish grammar and vocabulary. Never mind what the assignment down there had been. It was finished and wouldn't worry me, or anybody else, again.

What did worry me was that I was being used as a delivery boy. Please understand, it wasn't a question of status. I've been with the outfit longer than most, but if somebody needs a vehicle driven somewhere and I'm going there, hell, I enjoy driving; and I'm not too proud to play ferryman. The Matthew Helm Auto-Transport Service, at your service. However, I couldn't help realizing that any kid with a license could have done the job. I could have flown back directly from Ciudad Chihuahua, or driven north only as far as El Paso, Texas, just over the border, turned the fancy little turbocharged Ford compact over to somebody else, and taken the plane from there. I could have been back in Washington by now, ready to do battle once more for the nation I serve and the small federal agency by which I'm employed—which I won't name since it doesn't exist, officially.

1

I didn't buy all that nonsense about the badly needed car; we're not so hard up we can't pick up a baby Ford, even a loaded one, when and where we need one. It wasn't as if the heap in question were a priceless Rolls or Mercedes, or a unique all-terrain vehicle constructed to our specifications at great expense. As for the relaxing trip, the last time Mac worried about my mental health was when an airplane crash left me with a touch of amnesia; and that was quite a while ago. I came to the conclusion that he'd ordered me to drive north and east by easy stages, instead of flying, because he simply didn't want me in Washington, at least not yet. He wanted me out on the highway for a few days, an elusive target, reporting to a recording device at a special number to say where I was spending the night so he'd know where to make contact when he needed me.

The callback came when I was only a day away from my destination. It caught me after breakfast. I'd already thrown my bag into the car in preparation for leaving the Holiday Inn—well, one of the Holiday Inns—in Knoxville, Tennessee. If I hadn't stepped back into the room to make sure I hadn't left anything behind, and to kill the last couple of minutes before the specified departure time, I'd have missed it. You always wonder, in a situation like that, if you might not be better off pretending you didn't hear anything and slipping away quietly, letting the damn' thing ring; but of course you never do.

"Eric?"

"Yes, sir," I said.

There was supposed to be some textbook ID stuff in here, in spite of the fact that he'd used my code name and that we were pretty well acquainted with each other's voices. However, he bypassed the normal procedure, which was significant in itself.

He said, "I'm glad I caught you. We have a slight problem."

2

I winced. It was a trigger phrase and I didn't like it. I mean, if he'd mentioned a serious emergency, or even a total disaster, okay. It would have indicated merely that things were normally screwed up in Washington, no sweat; but after a previous occasion when home base had been threatened by somebody who'd considered us, rightly, as an obstacle to the attainment of certain undemocratic political ambitions, a new emergency-alert signal had been arranged between Mac and his more senior operatives, active and retired; an elite group of fairly nasty characters of which I was the ranking member. "A slight problem" meant that the ship was sinking and it was time to order the lifeboat crews to their assigned stations.

"A slight problem," I repeated, to let him know the message had been received. "Yes, sir. How would you like me to go about solving this slight problem."

Solving our slight problem involved for a start, I was told, carrying out the standing orders applicable to such a situation. Afterwards, as I'd been planning to do anyway, I should drive up Interstate 81 through the beautiful Shenandoah Valley between the Appalachian and Blue Ridge Mountains; but I should refrain from turning off on I-66, the main route to Washington some seventy miles to the east, as I'd intended.

Instead I should continue on to Hagerstown, Maryland, up near the Pennsylvania border. There I should stop at a certain motel—coincidentally another Holiday Inn—and check up on a certain female person in whom we were interested, who'd wound up in the local hospital a couple of days ago for reasons that were not entirely clear. I was supposed to make them clear to myself first and then report my findings to the same contact number, the one we were using now.

Mac said, "You will, of course, keep in mind that you'll probably be under observation from the moment you appear at the hospital and ask for the lady. You will behave

3

in a normal manner and make your normal telephone reports to me at the office number you normally employ. We'll both be full of concern for the patient, of course. We'll discuss her symptoms and treatment at length. You may use the word 'tachycardia' to describe her condition if you wish, and any other medical jargon you happen to pick up at her bedside; but please reserve the word 'arrhythmia,' meaning irregularity, to indicate that you've actually discovered something irregular and I should check the recorder here for details. I don't want to draw attention to this number by using it unnecessarily. Understood?''

"Arrhythmia equals irregularity, of a noncardiac and nondigestive variety. Yes, sir, I think I've got that.''

I hesitated. The question uppermost in my mind was why he'd saved this nursemaiding job for me. I mean, it's only some sixty miles from Washington to Hagerstown; and he undoubtedly had agents within easy reach of his office who could have been at the Hagerstown hospital within an hour or two of the time the lady in question stumbled into the emergency room. But he'd let her wait two days on her bed of pain while I made it up from Mexico—hell, I still had five hundred miles to go. Obviously there was some reason he considered me more suitable for holding the invalid's hand than whatever talent he had available in Washington.

I didn't ask the question because if he'd wanted me to know what made me so special, he'd have told me. All I'd get for asking would be a slap on the wrist.

However, I was entitled to request information about the subject: "Who is this sick dame who requires a male nurse, anyway?''

"The patient's name is Watrous, Astrid M. Watrous. Mrs. Watrous.''

I didn't bother to try to visualize the lady. Astrid was a good Scandinavian girl-name, but it didn't necessarily mean that the lady was a blonde and blue-eyed Norse beauty. If

4

you're dumb enough to bet your life, these days, on all Kathleens being Irish, or all Juanitas Spanish, or all Rachels Jewish, or all Astrids Swedish, you're not likely to live very long.

"Never heard of her," I said. "Under what name do I approach her?"

"Since Mrs. Watrous is using her own name, you might as well give an innocent impression, for the benefit of probable observers, by using yours. You can discard the cover we constructed for your Mexican assignment. I presume that, after returning to this country, you retrieved your own documentation in El Paso as instructed. We'll play it in the open, at least up to a point. It's no secret that, after the disappearance of her fairly prominent husband, Mrs. Watrous, unable to get satisfaction elsewhere, came to us for help. Under the circumstances, we'll be expected to send somebody to the hospital to check on her condition."

"Exactly what are the circumstances, sir?"

Mac said, "For various reasons we, like his wife, are unconvinced by the evidence indicating that Dr. Watrous vanished voluntarily."

"I never heard of the guy," I said. "Wait a minute. *Doctor* Watrous, Dr. Alan Watrous? Oceanography, or something, right? Head of a well-known scientific institute, I forget the name. Took off with a dame who wasn't his wife—that was before I went to Mexico. And a wad of the institute's dough. Big scandal."

"Yes, the newspapers made quite a thing of it. But it was never proved that any money was missing; that was just a rumor."

"But his wife's convinced you that the newspapers, and presumably the cops, are all wet? You both think Watrous was vanished?"

"An unfortunate use of the word, Eric; but we consider it a strong possibility. And suspecting foul play in the case

5

of the husband, we would naturally look very hard at any accident or illness affecting the wife who's been making so much trouble about his disappearance."

It was beginning to make a little more sense. It was a real problem, not just a question of keeping a sick woman happy. But while I'll cheerfully admit that I'm the best little problem-solver he's got, I still wasn't convinced I was good enough to justify the delay involved in getting me on the job. I sensed that there was another reason why my presence was required; a reason I wasn't being given.

"And I'm the man elected to do the hard looking?" I said. I grimaced at the phone. "Would I be looking for anything beyond the cause of her medical troubles, sir? Would I perhaps be looking for her husband, also?"

"Yes, as soon as Mrs. Watrous is released from the hospital, you will give her all the help you can in finding Dr. Watrous. And you will endeavor to keep her alive, and preferably healthy, in the process. If there should be other odd diseases going around."

I said, "You're obviously assuming that she'll survive her present illness. What if she doesn't recover from her attack of tachycardia, whatever that may be?"

"It's very unlikely, barring complications. The condition is seldom life-threatening if treated in time; and Mrs. Watrous is making a good recovery. However, in the event that she should be lost to us for any reason, you will still make every effort to locate and liberate Dr. Alan August Watrous."

I frowned at the inoffensive phone. There were more questions that needed answers. The one I asked was, "Can you give me a quick rundown on Mrs. Watrous' mysterious disease?"

"The only mystery is how she managed to contract it," Mac said. "There's no mystery about the condition itself. You could call it the opposite of a heart attack. Instead of faltering or stopping, the heart begins to beat much too

6

rapidly. Mrs. Watrous' pulse was over two hundred when she reached the emergency room. The ailment is not uncommon. There are several drugs that will control it. One of them, curiously enough, is quinine, which is what she's being given at present, quinidine to be exact. It seems to be doing the job. Her heartbeat is completely under control. There have been no more episodes; and she's merely being retained in the hospital for observation, to make certain her condition is stable.''

I said, ''As you say, sir, it's quite a coincidence. The husband disappears. The wife acquires a sudden heart ailment which, I gather, she's never shown any signs of previously. I presume that if she were to have another attack under conditions where help wasn't available, she could die from it. That could be convenient for somebody. Particularly since, after this incident, it would undoubtedly go down as a natural death.''

''The thought had occurred to me, Eric.'' His voice was dry; I was pointing out the obvious.

''Well, you'd better give me the priorities,'' I said. ''In case I have to make a choice, do I save the wife and let the husband go, or vice versa?''

Mac said calmly, ''While we would, of course, prefer to have Mrs. Watrous preserved, she's merely a means to an end.''

''I see,'' I said. ''And Dr. Watrous is the end?''

''No,'' he said. ''I am.''

I sat there for a moment listening to the traffic on the nearby freeway. ''You'd better spell it out for me, sir,'' I said carefully at last.

Mac said, ''It's quite simple. Dr. Watrous is not the only prominent citizen to vanish in the past year. Other important people—businessmen and politicians as well as scientists—have also disappeared, always with plausible reasons. To take just one example, a certain highly placed lady in the computer industry named Janet Beilstein, is supposed to have run off with a handsome young man and company funds, although the embezzlement angle seems to have been merely a vicious rumor. That's pretty much the same story, you'll note, that was circulated about Dr. Watrous. It's been used, with variations, in other instances as well; but there have also been supposed nervous breakdowns and other explanations. I can't give you the total number of cases, but it's impressive, even if allowance is made for the fact that, in spite of the bureaucratic paperwork that rules our lives, surprisingly many people do manage to pull down the curtain each year and are never heard from again." He hesitated, and went on: "In the time we've been on the case, we've come up with only two promising leads. Mrs. Watrous is one. I am the other."

I frowned at the phone in my hand. "It's one of my dull days. I'm still not following you."

He spoke carefully: "Let us say, hypothetically, that there is an organization devoted to abducting selected citizens for purposes still unknown, always with a suitable cover story to minimize the resulting publicity."

"Kidnapping doesn't seem to be exactly what's planned for Mrs. Watrous, if we're right about her having been drugged with the idea of eventually making it permanent."

"But Mrs. Watrous is not a principal in this affair, Eric. To these people, whoever they are, she is merely a peripheral nuisance. Unlike her husband, she's not well known, and she carries in her brain no valuable scientific information. She is merely a threat, not a possible asset."

"Then where do you come in, sir? I'd think you'd fall right into the same menace classification as Astrid Watrous."

I heard him sigh sadly at the other end of the line. "A bitter thing it is to be unappreciated by one's own associates! I've served as head of this agency for a good many years. I hope I have some value to my government; and I know I have accumulated knowledge that could be useful to somebody. To be sure, I was probably not considered a primary target; but when Mrs. Watrous involved me in the case, I came under observation. It was realized that, taking the lady seriously, I had to be eliminated before I learned enough to be a real threat. However, it would be wasteful to have me killed. Because of my position I could be quite valuable.''

''You seem to have a real pipeline into this abduction outfit, sir. An informant?''

''No, just a commonsense interpretation of certain things that have been happening around me.'' Mac laughed shortly. ''If you were going to cause me to vanish, what explanation would you leave behind to make it seem as if I'd disappeared voluntarily? At my age I'm not, I hope, a plausible candidate for amorous entanglements. Our operational funds are, unfortunately, quite limited, so I don't have access to large sums of money. My doctor informs me that for a man in my position, I show few signs of stress; a sudden breakdown would hardly be convincing. So why would I choose to go missing?''

He waited for my answer. I hesitated, but it was no time to be tactful. I said, ''Well, I can make a guess. Patriotism and loyalty are corny words these days. Patriots are out of fashion. Faith and trust are out, lie detectors are in. It's the time of the fink and the snitch and the traitor, sir. If I were planning to vanish you, I'd first send some known Commies to see you, on one pretext or another. I'd plant a few bits of evidence here and there to establish your subversive associations. It doesn't take much, these suspicious days. After that, when you went AWOL, nobody'd believe you hadn't defected, even after a lifetime of patriotic service.'' After a moment, when he didn't speak at once, I said, ''Well, nobody'd believe it except a few naive and trusting characters in this outfit, who're also suckers for Santa Claus

9

and the tooth fairy. It's amazing how gullible some folks can be."

"Thank you, Eric." After a moment, he went on: "Your guess is quite correct. After certain rumors had come to my attention, I investigated discreetly and learned that I'm currently supposed to be very depressed and angry at the scanty recognition my work has received over the years and the way our organization is forever being slighted, financially and otherwise. Furthermore, some peculiar characters have presented themselves here for interviews in recent months, supposed journalists, informants, and job applicants. I've made a point of taking on a couple of the last-named in spite of their questionable records. Very incriminating, for me. I've sent them out to the Ranch for screening and indoctrination with, of course, the special cautionary code in their induction papers."

The Ranch is our agent training, maintenance, and rehabilitation center in Arizona. It's a fairly tough place, and I wouldn't want to arrive there with that little watch-this-guy mark on my record.

Mac went on: "I'm afraid they won't be made very happy, and there will have to be a couple of training accidents after this is over, very bad for our safety record. However, at the moment their presence reflects unfavorably on my judgment or, if you want to be suspicious, my loyalty—the fact that I've admitted such dubious individuals to a highly classified government training area under my control." He paused, and went on: "Not to mention letting an obvious tap on my office telephone go unreported and unremoved."

"That's why we're using this elaborate communications system?"

"Yes."

"You're planning to let yourself be defected, then?"

"Your grammar is still deplorable, but the answer to your question is yes. I have sent a good many agents down

10

similar rabbit holes in the past. This time I am the logical ferret. You'll point out that it's a long time since I've operated in the field. Well, that leaves it up to Joel and you to look after your helpless superior, doesn't it? You remember Joel; you worked with him once out West."

"Yes, sir. I remember Joel."

"I thought you would. A good man. I know you won't mind working with him again."

"No, sir."

He was throwing it at me fast. The fact was that Joel wasn't a very good man, in my opinion. While technically competent enough, he was one of those scheming characters, ambitious for preferment, who'd hog the credit for success any time he could manage and try to slip out from under the blame for failure. I can work with anybody I have to, and there had been no blowup to jeopardize the mission; but I'd let Mac know how I felt afterwards. For him to now tell me calmly that I wouldn't mind working with Joel again was another clear signal: this line, too, was bugged, and we had an audience somewhere that we were trying to impress with the brotherly spirit pervading our undercover organization.

He went on: "Actually, the two of you will be operating independently. He will be covering me, rather carelessly of course. After he's lost me, however, he'll pull up his socks and do his best to find me. Maybe he'll succeed. But in case he doesn't, you'll be working at it quietly from the Watrous angle. Let us hope that at least one of you picks up a reasonable trail leading to a place being used as a detention center for all these kidnapped people, soon to include me."

I said dubiously, "You're making some rather optimistic assumptions, aren't you, sir? What makes you think all the kidnappees wind up in the same place and, if so, that it isn't just a large grave with room for one more? You."

He had an answer to that, of course. Once he's got a

11

plan made, he's got answers to everything. He'd never admit that he was betting his life on a hunch. Well, he often plays his hunches, and often they're very good; but I was glad it was his life he was gambling with, for a change, instead of mine.

A little later, picking up gas just off the freeway farther north, I called him openly from a pay phone, using the normal office number. I let him give me my Hagerstown directive officially, for the benefit of whoever had made arrangements to listen in on that phone, maybe the same snoopy character who'd bugged the other, maybe not. Life was getting very complicated. It happens any time you get near Washington, D.C.

CHAPTER 2

LIVING at seven thousand feet, as I did for many years out in Santa Fe, New Mexico, you tend to get snobbish about your mountains. I mean, snowcapped two-mile-high peaks are a dime a dozen out there; and they kind of spoil you for appreciating the puny geological formations people like to call mountains east of the Big Miss. Still, I've always considered the Shenandoah Valley to be a pretty fair scenic experience, even if it's on a somewhat smaller scale than what you get out West.

The weather was sunny and springlike. The Interstate was in pretty good shape, which was more than could be said for some I'd driven on during the past week. The traffic was moderate except for a bit of congestion near the Washington turnoff, which didn't delay me greatly. I had plenty of time to let the little car drive itself on cruise control while I considered what I'd been told over the phone; and particularly what I hadn't been told.

First there was the case of the two tapped telephones. Clearly Mac was playing one of his clever games, letting somebody know he'd discovered the bug on the office phone and set up an alternative contact number; but carefully giving them the impression that he thought the second number was still secure so the snoopers would believe what they overheard on that line. Just what information he wanted to feed them convincingly, and for what purpose, remained to be seen.

Then there was the interesting case of the lady named Janet Beilstein, which Mac had thrown at me, ostensibly, as just one instance of what we were up against—but why had he selected that particular disappearance as an example? After a good many years of interpreting his instructions, I knew that he didn't often talk at random. What had he been trying to tell me here without tipping off whoever was listening in? Well, there was a clue of sorts: when a healthy gent of any age makes a point of informing you that he's too elderly and decrepit to be a plausible candidate for amorous entanglements, that, as far as I'm concerned, is when you check to make certain the local maidens are all locked into well-fitting chastity belts. . . .

I'd already, at a morning coffee stop, made the emergency call to Doug Barnett in St. Petersburg, Florida, to set the disaster routine into motion. Doug was supposedly retired and building a new boat in his palmy back yard to replace one he'd recently lost in the line of duty. The agency was paying for the replacement. In return Doug was supposed to hold himself available in times of real crisis. The fact is that nobody really retires from our outfit. There are quite a few old, scarred agency warhorses grazing in quiet pastures in various parts of the country, waiting,

13

maybe even hoping, for the battle bugle to blow once more. Well, I was blowing it.

"Barnett here."

Using his code name, and mine, to make it official, I said, "Abraham, this is Eric. A slight problem in Washington. Contact: 325-3376. Code: arrhythmia. Pass the word. Do you want a repeat?"

"A slight problem in Washington. Contact 325-3376. Code arrhythmia."

"You've got it. Good luck, amigo."

"Shit, I was just going to varnish the brightwork around the cockpit."

"Why varnish? Use teak and let it weather, nice and salty." There was something I had to ask, and I went on: "How's Amy doing?"

Doug Barnett's daughter and I had spent some time together, having become acquainted on the mission on which he'd lost his boat. However, she was basically a nonviolent girl, and in the end, like others I'd met of that persuasion, she hadn't been able to resist trying to reform me; a sure way to kill a pleasant man-woman relationship.

"Amy's doing fine," Doug said. "Got herself a new boyfriend much younger and better looking than that ugly tall bastard she was seeing for a while; I forget his name. Schelm or something like that."

"Good for her," I said. "Well, keep your whistle wet and your powder dry. Eric out."

That had been in the morning. After hanging up, I'd returned to the car and concentrated on making miles without catching cops or, more correctly, being caught by them. One would think grown men would have better things to do than hiding in the bushes and jumping out to say "boo" at honest citizens. In the afternoon, an hour from my destination, I stopped to fill up again, and to make another call before entering the Hagerstown danger zone.

This call also went to Florida, but to the other side of

the state. I wanted to talk with a reporter on the *Miami Tribune* who'd helped me out before, when I was operating down in that part of the country. I'd tried for him at my earlier phone stop, but he'd been out. It took them a while to track him down this time; then his voice came on the line.

"Meiklejohn." When I'd identified myself, he said, "Oh, it's the Jack Daniels man." I'd given him a bottle by way of thanks the last time I'd consulted him. He went on: "What do you want now?"

"Beilstein comma Janet. An executive-type lady in the computer business, missing. Can you look her up for me?"

"What's the matter with your Washington sources?"

"They're in Washington," I said. "It's a very nosy city, or hadn't you heard?"

"Beilstein?" Spud Meiklejohn was silent for a moment, presumably searching his capacious memory. "I remember the story. I'll have to look it up if you want her under-graduate and advanced business degrees, and her complete employment record before she wound up at Electro-Syn-chronics, Inc., where she worked her way up to executive vice-president. But if you're satisfied with learning that she's fifty-two years old and ran off with her twenty-four-year-old tennis pro, and maybe a couple of million, al-though that's not been confirmed, there you are."

"The pro's name?"

"Emil Jernegan."

"Had he been around for a while, or did he just appear one day out of the blue, pretty much the way he disap-peared? In other words, could he have been planted on her?"

"Well, he'd been on the job for only about six months before he zeroed in on the lady executive who'd started taking his lessons, very charming and attentive. But there seems to be no real mystery about him. Just another good-looking young tennis bum who couldn't make it competi-

15

tively and settled for a country-club job. But there seems to be a slight mystery about the Beilstein woman herself."

"Give."

"She'd take a few weeks' vacation a couple of times a year," Meiklejohn's voice said in the phone. "She'd come back tanned and tough and healthy, they say, ready to lick her weight in financiers; but she'd never say where she'd been. Or with whom, if anybody. Not really normal for a single woman—well, she'd been married years earlier, but it didn't take. But most dames back from a glamorous vacation in the sun can't wait to tell the other girls in the office all about it. Not Mrs. Beilstein. No glowing holiday reminiscences from her."

"She didn't take the youthful tennis-playing Tarzan along on these mystery trips?"

"No. The times he was out of town don't synchronize at all with the times she was."

"Maiden name?"

"Janet Rebecca Winterholt."

I said, "Okay, thanks. That'll hold me for a while. One fifth of Daniels Black coming up."

Meiklejohn hesitated; then he spoke slowly: "Funny the way people have been disappearing lately, Helm. Not really big important people who'd throw the country in an uproar if they went missing. Just kind of medium-prominent citizens good for a few stories; and always with a plausible reason for vanishing."

"What are you trying to say?"

He said, "To hell with the thanks and the booze. Just remember me if you come up with something I can use."

"You're at the head of the list, amigo."

The Hagerstown Holiday Inn was expecting me, having been alerted by its opposite number in Knoxville to the fact that one unit of business was heading its way. No mystery about that Helm character. He'd received his marching orders, and he was reluctantly making a detour on his way

16

home to look in on a sick dame in whom his agency was interested. The motel was on the far side of the picturesque little city from the Interstate exit, and I had to buck a long string of traffic lights to reach it; but it turned out to be within a few blocks of the Washington County Hospital, as Mrs. Watrous' temporary, we hoped, residence was called.

I could have walked over, it was that close, but I didn't. Nobody followed my car as I drove away from the hostelry that overlooked a four-lane boulevard with a grassy median wide enough to boast some scattered shade trees that were just about to put out leaves. It had been late spring in Mexico and Texas, I remembered; but I'd come a long ways north as well as east. To make sure I was unescorted, I stopped at a shopping center and bought a handful of flowers at an exorbitant price—six tulips at four bucks apiece—and then I got myself lost, not quite accidentally, so that I had to circle around through a maze of little one-way streets to find the hospital. No surveillance yet. It made me feel quite lonely.

I passed up the parking garage across the street and found an open space along the curb a block and a half away. A little walk wouldn't hurt me. I entered the hospital by the front door, flowers in hand, asked my question at the information desk, and was directed to the third floor. Room 357. I didn't ask permission there. I just walked in and looked at the woman in the bed, who was a mess. Well, in a hospital they mostly are, otherwise they wouldn't be there. But this didn't look like a patient who was making a fine recovery.

Astrid Watrous turned her head to look at me. "Platelets!" she whispered bitterly.

"What?"

"Red blood corpuscles, yes, those I know. White corpuscles I know. But *platelets*?"

"What's the matter with your platelets?"

17

"I do not have them. Only a few hundred per . . . per something, and one should have thousands. The quinine, it killed them. It happens sometimes, so they say. But why is it that everything that sometimes happens now happens to me?"

"I know," I said without expression. "It isn't fair, is it?"

She winced. "Now you are cruel. But it is deserved. I am sorry to be so cowardly, but I am not accustomed to illness. It frightens me terribly."

The accent was intriguing, and she had the mannerisms of a woman accustomed to admiration; but she was under terrible handicaps here. I judged that under favorable conditions, properly dressed, she could have appeared quite youthful and handsome, but in the ugly cotton hospital gown, lying in the mechanized bed hooked up to the usual intravenous plumbing, she looked thin and plain and middle-aged.

The bones of the face were good, but they were much too prominent under the drawn gray skin. The brown eyes were dull and sunken. There was a considerable quantity of fine blonde hair spread over the pillow. It was probably spectacular hair in good times; but it was matted and un-cared-for–looking now. I wondered if it was real; true brown-eyed blondes are scarce. Her lips had the dry cracked look that goes with serious illness. They looked as if they didn't fit her mouth very well, and as if she were very conscious of having picked up the wrong size by mistake.

She licked the ill-fitting lips and moved them around in her face as if trying to get accustomed to them. She whispered, "Over six feet. Bony. Sarcastic. You must be the man called Helm. Washington said you were coming to help, but how can you help?"

"I'm the man called Helm. Is there anything you want that I can get for you?"

"I want to be out of here, but can you get me that? I

18

want to be out before they ruin me completely with their medicines! The runaway heart, that was frightening enough, but . . ." She drew a ragged breath. "I woke up spitting blood; I must have bitten the inside of my mouth somehow. Just a little, but it will not coagulate properly without the platelets. Who ever heard of those things? They invent strange new small particles all the time! From school I remember only electrons and protons; and look what they do to the atom now; nobody can understand it! And all the idiotic microscopic things they are finding in the blood! But not finding, not enough, in my blood. . . ." She swallowed hard, clearly on the verge of tears. "Look at me! I have the tiny red spots all over me, small hemorrhages under the skin. And they do not know where I may be bleeding inside. Instant hemophilia, all on account of their quinine and their platelets!"

I gestured towards the drip apparatus connected to the needle in her arm. "What are they pumping into you?"

"It is only glucose solution now. They do not want to make a new hole in me if I need another transfusion, so they leave the apparatus in place. They wait to see if I start making my own platelets again or if they must shoot more into me. . . . Are those flowers for me?"

I took a chance on kidding her a bit. "If I can't find a prettier girl to give them to."

After a moment, she drew a long breath, pulling herself together with an effort. She made a small, feminine gesture towards ordering her hair, and laughed ruefully.

"No problem," she said. "Just reach out and take the first female person who walks down the corridor. I am a very stringy and unattractive specimen today; you should have no trouble doing better." She watched me uncover the flowers; then she grasped the wrist of the hand with which I offered them to her, and drew me closer. Her voice dropped to a whisper. "If I do not live, look around Lysaniemi. Somewhere around there, up above the Pole Circle,

19

the Arctic Circle. Remember Lysaniemi. Say Lysaniemi. But softly, someone may be listening."

I formed the word clumsily. "Loosanaymie."

She shook her head impatiently. "Lysaniemi."

"Leesanaymie."

She said irritably, "It is terrible, your pronunciation. I thought, from your name, that you were of Swedish descent."

"Leesanaymie isn't Swedish."

"All right, it is Finnish, but most Swedes can pronounce it better than that. You have been in America too long."

"Hell, I was born here."

"Some of us keep the old ways, the old languages, nevertheless." She shrugged, and dismissed my linguistic deficiencies. "Lysaniemi. I heard them talking about it, all snow and ice. They were boasting that it was a place no one would think to search for anyone. But you must find them without me if I never leave this bed. My Alan who is not mine any longer, and his new woman, his dark woman, Hannah Gray. Perhaps he was weary of blondes, and I do not blame him. Find them, help them, set them free. Please. Oh, and investigate Karin Segerby, please."

"Karin Segerby?"

"You have heard the name. You live in Washington, I was told; and it was in all the Washington papers."

"I don't spend much time in that town. The apartment there is just a place I hang my hat between assignments."

"The newspapers were very cautious, of course. It was about a year ago, when her husband was murdered. She was released on a technicality, but there's really not much doubt. . . . And no doubt at all, in my mind, that she is the one who gave it to me when we had lunch together in Washington before I started on this trip; gave me the poison that made my heart behave so crazily that very night. That is why I stopped driving early, here in Hagerstown,

20

because I was feeling very strange and had to get off the highway. Remember Lysaniemi. Remember Segerby."

I nodded. There were a great many questions to be asked, and answered; but she seemed to think the room was bugged, and maybe it was. And maybe she just liked to dramatize things.

I asked in normal tones, "Where were you driving when this cardiac thing hit you?"

"To see my parents, in Indiana. To be with them for a little, while I waited to hear about Alan. If there was anything to hear. Your chief said it was all right, I needed to relax, he could reach me there."

I nodded. "What are they giving you for the heart now?"

"Well, if it means anything to you, they gave me a steroid last night, Solu-Cortef, to build me up, I suppose, after tearing me down so badly. But for the heart they are trying something called Procaine or Procan. Yes, Procan SR." She drew a long breath. "The flowers are very beautiful, Mr. Helm. We must give you a medal for valiant floral service beyond the call of duty. Really, it was sweet of you. I will call and have something brought to put them in. . . ."

After the tulips had been cared for, we talked a little longer. Quite steady now, completely under control, she asked me to do something about her car. It was in the hospital parking lot that wasn't supposed to be used by patients, just staff. However, sick and frightened in the middle of the night, with her heart going crazy, she'd just left the car in the nearest vacant spot a few steps from the emergency entrance and stumbled inside to get help. She'd been told that the physician whose space she'd taken would like it back.

She also asked me to settle up for her at the motel. She'd asked them to hold the room for her when she headed for the hospital. After giving her directions, the night man at the desk had offered to find somebody to drive her, she said, but she'd thought she could make it by herself since it was so close, and she had. But now, with this stupid reaction, it looked as if she was going to have a long siege here, so she'd like me to check her out and pack her things and bring them to her, not forgetting her coat in the closet and her toilet things in the bathroom. I said I probably wouldn't find it too much of a strain, since, not quite by coincidence, it was the motel in which I was staying.

Then I went out to find a doctor. The general-type physician in charge of the case referred me to the heart specialist, who, fortunately, was in the building. I had to pull a little rank before, a busy man, he'd stand still for my questions; but after seeing the impressive ID we carry, designed specifically to be brandished at such moments, he became quite pleasant and cooperative.

"Yes, it's possible," he said in answer to my question. "Melodramatic, of course, but possible. An overdose of thyroid might do it, but I think the effect would be hard to predict. However, there are other medications. . . . I'd rather not commit myself until I've checked some authorities, Mr. Helm. Do you really suspect, shall we say, foul play?"

I said, "I'll grant that it seems a clumsy way to commit murder. But our organization does make enemies, Doctor; and we like to investigate any mysterious accidents or illnesses involving anyone associated with us, even temporarily."

A lean dark gent in a white coat, he studied me shrewdly with cynical brown eyes. "I didn't catch exactly what your organization is."

I grinned. "You weren't supposed to. But if you're worried about my credentials, I'll give you a number to call in Washington and let my chief reassure you."

He regarded me a moment longer, and laughed shortly. "I guess that won't be necessary. We're not dealing with

22

state secrets. I'll do a little research and let you know what I find out. You'll be around for a few days?"

"Until Mrs. Watrous is released."

"We want to keep her long enough to make certain there aren't any more surprises and that she's recovering well from this one. And that the new treatment is doing its job."

"If her attack was artificially induced, will she be able to stop taking pills eventually, or is her pulse-rate mechanism, whatever you call it, permanently screwed up?"

"If a cardiac accelerator was used, the patient should be able to come off the medication fairly soon. But frankly, Mr. Helm, I'm not taking the possibility very seriously. It seems pretty cloak-and-dagger to me."

"That's the name of the game, sir." I hesitated. "There's no way somebody could have given her a fake quinine reaction, I suppose. Or a real one?"

He looked shocked. "Here in the hospital? I think your melodrama is running away with you! But I'll look that up for you, too, just to set your mind at rest." He smiled sourly. "And mine, now that you've made the suggestion."

I found Astrid Watrous' car in the staff parking lot. A dignified maroon color, it was a plushy Buick sedan that, although smaller than the impressive barges that used to wear the name, felt like an aircraft carrier after what I'd been driving.

But I wasn't too preoccupied with driving the unfamiliar car to note that a white Honda had been behind me from the moment I left the hospital. On that short run, it could have been a coincidence, but I wouldn't have bet a lot of money on it.

Mrs. Watrous' room had, of course, been tidied up. The beds were made and the loose clothes that weren't on hangers were folded on a chair. Her nightie hung on a hook behind the bathroom door, presumably the work of a conscientious maid, since it seemed unlikely that she'd have

23

taken time to dispose of it so neatly, herself, when the heart-flutters hit. It was, I noted, being that kind of a guy, quite a pretty nightie. Packing it away in her suitcase, I saw some other intimate stuff that also looked sexy and expensive. A satin-and-lace lady after my own heart, I reflected; but I wished I were as sure of her motives as I was of her lingerie.

With her smart brown spring coat over my arm and her suitcase in my hand, I left the room. I made my way to my own and managed to work the key in spite of my burdens. Entering, I turned to set the suitcase back by the door where it would be out of the way.

"Just stay like that, right there!" said a strained voice behind me. "I have a gun! Don't straighten up! Don't move a muscle!"

"Is it okay if I breathe?" I asked.

CHAPTER 3

THE shaky voice told me that I had an amateur behind me, and a female amateur at that. Under the circumstances, there were various actions I could have taken with some hope of success. Although we're taught that docile submission to a firearm is seldom an acceptable option, Hollywood and the cops to the contrary notwithstanding, I could have played along a bit, hoping to get close enough to disarm her. Or I could have slung the suitcase at her legs and flung the coat at her head and dived aside, pulling my own gun to shoot her dead.

Dealing with a man, I would probably have done one or

the other, gambling that, although I might incur some damage in the hassle, it wouldn't be fatal. However, the fact that there was a woman behind me made it, I decided, unnecessary to take the risk. A man, particularly a novice, holding a gun on another man, expects to have the situation under control. If his control is challenged, his pride is hurt, and anything can happen. The Wild Bill Hickok syndrome. With a woman, you don't have that kind of macho pride to contend with. Maybe.

All this went through my mind almost instantaneously as I crouched there. After all, the mental computer was programmed for situations like this, we'd been here before. The girl behind me—at least she sounded young as well as scared—started to speak again; but she had nothing more to say that I needed to hear. I released the handle of the suitcase and straightened up very slowly.

"I told you not to move!"

The voice was shrill; I hoped the trigger finger was less nervous. I reached out deliberately and grasped the knob of the door, which had closed automatically. I opened the door.

"Stop or I'll shoot!"

Moving with infinite care so as not to startle her, feeling very vulnerable in the spinal area, I stepped away from her, one deliberate step at a time, out into the Maryland spring night—it had got quite dark outside by this time. No bullets followed me. The door sighed closed behind me.

I drew a shuddering breath and told myself angrily that a stupid young bitch who'd never learned not to brandish a firearm she wasn't going to shoot ought to be turned over somebody's knee and spanked; and if nobody else would correct the serious flaws in her upbringing, I might even take her in hand myself, as a public service. It occurred to me that, dumb as she seemed to be, she might actually be foolish enough, now that the ambush had failed, to flee the joint heedlessly, weeping bitter tears of frustration. I moved to the side and waited by the door, holding Astrid Watrous' nice brown spring coat in both hands like a bullfighter's cape.

I'd judged the idiot female correctly. I didn't even have to wait very long. Soon the door opened cautiously. Seeing the coast apparently clear, a smallish, white-clad blonde girl sidled out, or started to. I noted that her hands were empty, but the right was steadying a large white shoulder-strap bag. I didn't waste time carrying the inventory further; I simply stepped out in front of her and wrapped the coat, and my arms, about her head. I marched her, blinded and stifled, backwards into the room, and hooked a heel behind her ankle, and slammed her to the rug, letting my two hundred pounds—well, I might have picked up a little additional weight on that Mexican food—land heavily on top of her. I heard the door close automatically, and the latch click.

It took me a tense moment or two to get a grip on the purse. I yanked it free and slung it across the room. The girl was getting back some of the breath driven out of her by the fall. She'd liberated herself from the smothering coat, and she was starting to fight me, but although she was strong enough to cause me trouble, she didn't really know how. I clamped a grip on her neck, knuckles digging into a certain pain center under the ear in a certain way. I heard her gasp in agony. Her resistance ceased. I rose to one knee and, shifting my grasp to take her by the scruff of the neck like a puppy, hauled her across the other knee, facedown. Pinning her there left-handed, I raised my right hand to warm her bottom as she deserved. Then I dropped my hand again.

I mean, it was getting through to me at last that this was a very female little body with which I, a male, was wrestling. The rump was particularly delicious in snug white slacks. Even though I don't go for dames in pants as a rule, I've been known to make exceptions. And for a gent my age to convince himself that he's walloping the shapely ass of a girl her age strictly in the interest of education and discipline, with no irrelevant biological considerations whatever, isn't easy. I stood up abruptly, dumping her to the floor. She sprawled there for a moment, clearly afraid to make a move lest it be the wrong move. At last, finding herself unraped, unshot, unwhipped, and unkicked, she sat up, regarding me warily through a veil of white-blonde hair.

"Get your purse," I said. "Get the gun out of it and put it over there, on the table by the window. Anything else you care to do with it, or try doing with it, be my guest. But remember, I'm just looking for an excuse to shove it up your anus, butt first."

She remained sitting for a moment longer, waiting for her breathing to subside. Then she got to her feet, a little awkwardly. She moved across the room and picked up the shoulder-strap bag. Showing a gleam of intelligence for a change, she turned to face me so I could see what she was doing, before opening it. She took out a tiny black pistol, neither a revolver nor an automatic, but a two-shot derringer. She crossed the room and placed it on the table as directed.

"Now let's try you on something hard," I said. "The coat. We can't leave a nice coat lying on the floor getting all wrinkled, can we? Hang it up neatly over there in the closet corner by the bathroom. Oh, and there's a nice little twenty-five caliber automatic right there in my open suitcase. By all means go for it if you like. I haven't had a good gunfight all week."

She wanted to protest against being ordered around so rudely and sarcastically, but a little common sense seemed to have fought its way to the surface through the thick layers of stupidity. She contented herself with a resentful glare, and picked up the coat. While she was taking it across the room, I examined her weapon. Two stubby black barrels; actually a solid, gun-shaped little block of metal bored with two holes, one above the other. A small curved butt that, with a hand of any size, wouldn't accept a full complement of fingers. If you held the gun normally, the pinky would be left waving in the breeze; but you don't shoot a derringer normally. You lay your trigger finger along the barrels, and point it at the cheating sonofabitch across the poker table, and pull the trigger with the middle finger.

The old-time gamblers wore them up their sleeves, or maybe in special leather-lined pockets of their embroidered waistcoats. The best-known specimens came in .41 caliber, throwing a big blob of lead without much velocity or accuracy; but how much do you need across a pile of marked cards? However, this was a modern job in .22 Magnum, an oddball rimfire cartridge that has considerably more punch than the standard .22 but still not enough to loosen the fillings in your teeth when you fire it. Incidentally, the derringer was first invented or at least popularized, we're told, by a guy named Deringer. Nobody seems to know where the extra *r* came from.

"May I . . ." On the other side of the room, having put Astrid Watrous' coat on a hanger, the girl hesitated, embarrassed. She spoke stiffly, avoiding my eyes: "I would like to use the toilet, if I may."

I refrained from grinning. After the suspense of waiting for me to walk in so she could wave her horrid gun at me, and the shock of being roughly manhandled, she undoubtedly did need to go. And while it was necessary for me to bully her a bit to keep her from getting independent and doing something else stupid, there was no need to humiliate her about a simple call of nature.

"Help yourself," I said.

She disappeared into the bathroom. Waiting, I finished checking the diminutive weapon in my hand. It broke open like a double-barreled shotgun, but reluctantly, with the stiffness of a brand-new weapon. Two brass cartridge heads showed in the twin chambers. I picked out the loads, closed the gun, and tried the trigger pull. The old-time derringer had a hammer that had to be cocked before each shot. Since the hard work was done with the thumb, the trigger finger had a relatively easy job. With this modernized, hammerless version, however, you simply hauled back on the trigger, cocking and firing the piece in a single operation—a very tough operation. It was the longest, roughest, heaviest double-action pull I'd ever met on a weapon, well over twenty pounds. It made me feel a little foolish. I'd really been in no danger. Even if she'd managed to fire the little monster, using both hands, the chances of her hitting anything while struggling against that incredible mainspring were practically nonexistent.

I reloaded the gun and dropped it into my jacket pocket. I looked into the big purse she'd also left on the table. There was a box of .22 Magnum cartridges inside, full except for the two in the gun, no practice rounds missing. I pocketed that as well. There was also, among the standard feminine junk, a passport. I examined it quickly. It was Swedish, issued to a female person born twenty-four years ago next June—a female person named Karin Agneta Segerby.

I stood for a long moment looking down at the little book in my hand. I had to hand it to her, she took a good picture. Any girl who can look pretty in a passport photo ought to grab the first plane to Hollywood. She looked cute and bright. Karin Segerby. The girl I was supposed to investigate if Astrid Watrous died. The sinister female who'd probably murdered her own husband and poisoned Astrid Watrous. According to Astrid Watrous. I grimaced, and dropped the passport back where I'd found it, and checked through her wallet quickly, finding nothing that didn't agree with her identity as a Swedish girl temporarily residing in

29

Washington, D.C., U.S.A. She seemed to be employed by a firm called Nordic Textiles, Ltd.

She emerged from the bathroom and came across the room and stopped in front of me in a challenging way, letting me know that, having dealt with her most urgent problem, she was now prepared to endure some more of my petty harassment. We faced each other like that for a moment. She wasn't actually tiny, I realized. She just had the kind of compact female body that's so nicely proportioned that it looks smaller than it is. Her waist was slim enough to keep her from appearing sturdy. She had a tomboy face without looking the least bit boyish, if you know what I mean, with a short nose and a generous mouth. Her eyes were very blue, shading to violet. Her complexion was breathtaking. If you could have bottled and sold it, you'd have made a fortune. Her hair, as I'd already noted, was pale blonde. It was cut moderately short, and it was reasonably tidy again. Well, with that kind of a hairdo, a shake of the head will do it.

Her close-fitting white cotton trousers terminated above the ankles, displaying sheer nylons and high-heeled white shoes. Above, there was a short white zipper jacket over a neat white shirt, or blouse, with a round collar. Although carefully casual, the costume wasn't inexpensive; it had a smart but slightly foreign look. Judging by the magazine covers I'd seen along the road, American ladies were still, that year, being stylish in baggy pants. I put her purse into her hands.

"I'm keeping your gun and ammo," I said. "If you want to take another crack at me, you'll have to find yourself another weapon. Incidentally, when you acquire a gun right out of the box, it's customary to take it out somewhere and fire it to see where it shoots."

She disregarded the expert advice. "You have no right to rob me of my gun! It cost . . . It cost me a hundred and sixty dollars!"

Her momentary hesitation told me that, whatever she'd paid for the little pistol, it wasn't the list price she'd mentioned. Either she'd got it free from an accomplice, or she'd given a premium price for it on the black market.

I said, "It almost cost you your life, Miss Segerby. I could have shot it out with you instead of taking the chance of just walking away from you."

"How do you know my name? Oh, you sneaked a look in my purse and saw my passport."

I said, "You speak English very well for . . . for having been born in Uppsala." I'd almost made a mistake; I'd almost told her she spoke English very well for a *Svenska flicka.* Male chauvinist linguistic pride. There was no need to show off and inform her that I knew even two words of Swedish, any more than there had been any reason to let Astrid Watrous know that I could pronounce a certain Finnish name perfectly well if I cared to. In the business, we try not to pass out any more information about our capabilities than we have to. I said, "While we're on the subject of names, mine is Matthew Helm."

"Yes, I know. Astrid told me you were coming here, when I saw her in the hospital early this afternoon. Astrid Watrous."

"I know Mrs. Watrous. That's her suitcase; she asked me to take care of it for her. That's why I'm here, to help her."

"Yes, that is what she said. She told me many things about you."

I said dryly, "She told me things about you, too, Miss Segerby."

"Yes, I can imagine what she said!" Curiosity got the better of the blonde girl before me. "What did she say?"

"Among other things," I said, "that you were a sneaky poisoner, slipping deadly heart stimulants into people's lunches."

31

Karin Segerby grimaced. "Yes, she made that accusation to me, too. It is perfectly ridiculous, of course."

"Is it?" I asked. "Considering what seems to have happened to your husband, if I've got the story right, and the way I almost wound up with a couple of twenty-two Magnum slugs in the back, it doesn't seem too unlikely you'd put something into somebody's soup. Of course murderers, and murderesses, do tend to stick to the same modus operandi, but it's not an ironclad rule."

"I'm not a murderess!" Her face was pale. "I didn't shoot my husband, and I had no intention of shooting you!"

I said, "It's a little hard to read minds from the wrong end of a gun, Miss Segerby, particularly when your back is turned."

She ignored that. "And I didn't poison Astrid; that is crazy! Where would I find a dangerous medicine like that?"

I patted my pocket. "Where would you find a dangerous weapon like this, an innocent girl like you?"

She hesitated, and shrugged. "I couldn't have bought anything in Washington, of course; they're totally against the law there. Here in Hagerstown the sporting goods store had some, but the man wouldn't sell it to me without impossible red tape and waiting. But there was another man listening; a rather unpleasant-looking little man. I was disturbed when he followed me out of the store; but what he wanted was to tell me that if I really wanted it, if I really needed it and was willing to pay . . . I gave him five hundred dollars. I made him throw in the bullets for that price."

Her firearms terminology was lousy, but it was no time for semantics. "You paid five C's for a gun you weren't going to shoot, and made sure you had ammo not to shoot in it?" I said cynically.

"I . . . I needed some protection!" the girl said angrily. "Astrid told me you were coming to fix me. She said you would find out just how I had managed to make her so

32

sick. And even if you could not discover the proof, you would arrange for me to be punished anyway, since nobody else had had the opportunity to poison her, so my guilt was clear. You represented a ruthless government organization that was helping her find Alan, that's her husband who's disappeared. . . ."

"I know who Alan is."

"Yes, of course. And you would make me pay for what I had done to her and find out why I'd done it. I think she actually suspects me of kidnapping her husband on top of everything else. Or wants me to think so. I think her sickness must have affected her mind. She sounded quite crazy. Paranoid crazy. She frightened me."

"So you got yourself a cute little black-market pistol and came here to my motel room to deal with me before I could make trouble for you."

She licked her lips. "When one has been harassed for months, when one is lonely and afraid, one does foolish things. I just couldn't sit quietly waiting for you to . . . to frame me. 'Frame,' isn't that what you say? I had to learn, at least, what kind of a man you were."

"What did you find out?"

She was silent for a little, studying me; then she spoke quietly: "I discovered that you were a brave man who would risk being shot in the back by a stupid girl rather than create a situation in which you might have to kill her. A gentle man who couldn't even bring himself to strike her afterwards." Karin Segerby drew a long breath. "Keep my silly little gun, Mr. Helm. It is better with you, and it has served its purpose. I have learned enough. I think I can trust you to find the truth, which is that if that woman was really poisoned, and did not simply bite herself and contract hydrophobia, it was not done by me. And I did not kill my husband."

After a moment, she walked to the door. The set of her shoulders under the little white jacket let me know she was

33

waiting for me to try to stop her. Perhaps she was even hoping that I would, but I didn't. Without looking back, she disappeared into the night, and the door closed behind her.

Well, it was nice to meet somebody who considered me a brave and gentle man. The opinion is not universal.


CHAPTER 4


WHEN I called the regular office number to make my evening report on the Hagerstown situation, after putting certain information onto the tape at the special phone, I got through to Mac immediately. I was aware of being relieved, which disturbed me. After all, I wasn't really a kid agent dependent on Big Daddy in Washington; I'd been tying my own shoes and zipping my own pants for a good many years now, professionally speaking. I should have been disappointed that the hypothetical vanishers we'd been discussing hadn't grabbed him yet. That would have proved that he'd been theorizing along the right lines. It would also have put the operation on the rails and running. As it was, we still had to wait for the other side, whoever they were, to demonstrate that Mac had read their tricky little minds correctly.

Nevertheless, I was glad we remained in contact. After all the years, I'd feel odd reporting to anybody else. I brought him up to date on the most recent developments, as I'd be expected to do by anybody who'd seen Karin Segerby leave my motel unit. Somebody driving a white Honda, for instance, assuming it wasn't hers. I also reported my earlier hospital-room conversation with Astrid Watrous, pretty much as I'd read it into the recorder at the special number but with certain critical details missing, like the name Lysaniemi. A very complicated operation, and I was having a hard time remembering who was supposed to hear what on which phone.

"Mrs. Watrous' reaction to her medicine is most unfortunate," Mac said, sixty miles away in the nation's capital. "You say it appears to have been quite a violent one."

"She was a sick lady when I saw her an hour ago, and apparently she had been a lot sicker," I said. What with one thing and another, it seemed longer than an hour, but that's what my watch said. "I was told by the doctor that she's coming out of it and beginning to manufacture her own blood platelets again, whatever the hell they may be. The last count was encouraging, well up in the thousands. And they do seem to have the cardiac arrhythmia under control. She's had no episodes since the night she was admitted. Let's just hope she tolerates this new medicine, Procan, better than she did the quinine."

"Yes, well, keep me informed," Mac said, showing nothing but normal interest in the subject under discussion, but I knew he'd caught the key word I'd thrown him in the middle of all the medical jargon. He would run the stuff on the tape and get me the information I'd asked for there. And if he disappeared as expected, Doug Barnett would take over and do it for him.

I ate my lonely dinner in the motel dining room, wishing I'd thought to invite my pretty, pistol-packing visitor to join me, for company and because I needed to know more about her. But she was probably stuffy about accepting invitations from strange men she'd pointed guns at. Amateurs tend to make these big distinctions between friends and enemies, never understanding that in this business whom you eat with or sleep with has absolutely no bearing on whom you shoot.

In the morning, since my own car was still parked at a sidewalk meter near the hospital, unless the cops had impounded it, I hiked over there, after breakfasting in the same booth in which I'd dined. Neither Karin Segerby nor the white Honda showed, giving me no chance to determine whether it was her car or somebody else's. In her hospital chamber, Astrid Watrous was sitting up and taking nourishment. Her long blonde hair had been brushed back to life. In the absence of a satin ribbon, it was tied back smoothly with a neat little bow of gauze bandage. There was color in her face and a touch of lipstick on her mouth.

"Well, you look a little better," I said.

"Such outrageous flattery, I cannot stand it," she said. "If I had looked any worse, the undertaker would have charged extra to prepare me for burial. Did you bring me something nice to wear? I am very tired of these ghastly hospital gowns."

"It was such a pleasant morning that I walked over just to see how you were getting along," I said. "I'll bring your coat and suitcase next trip."

Astrid Watrous gave me a rather intimate smile. She was obviously one of the handsome ladies who has to go to work on everything in pants that passes by. Well, as long as it's male.

"The sooner you do, the sooner I can look pretty for you," she said. "It's hardly worth making an effort for a man in these laundry bags they make us wear."

I said, unsmiling, "I'm adequately compensated for my work by the U.S. government, thank you, ma'am. Private incentives, financial or otherwise, are not required."

She looked at me hard. "You are angry with me. Why?"

I said, "Cut it out. You know why. I had a visitor last night. With a gun."

She started to speak quickly, perhaps to say that she couldn't imagine what I was driving at, but she thought better of it. She frowned instead.

"A gun? Karin Segerby? I can assure you that I never dreamed . . . Where would a child like that get a gun?"

"Child, hell," I said.

She was studying me shrewdly. "You sound as if you had done some research on the subject of her maturity, Mr. Helm."

"We had a little wrestling match while I was disarming her," I said. "I can assure you that is a fully developed, fully adult, female of the species. But next time please warn me when you sic one on me, whether it's a puppy or a full-grown bitch. We're supposed to be cooperating here, remember?"

She licked her lips. "I am truly sorry. I never dreamed . . . I think I was a little delirious yesterday when she came to see me, and so frightened by what was happening to me that I just had to blame somebody. I couldn't bear to admit that my own body was failing me; do you understand? Much better to tell myself I had been poisoned by somebody who hated me and that, having survived, I would soon get over it and be a normal person again. So there she was, and I'd never liked her, really, and she *had* had the opportunity. I convinced myself that it was all her fault and screamed my accusations at her, although weak as I was, it was a rather feeble scream. And I heard myself telling her that a very dangerous man was coming to punish her for what she had done to me, but I never dreamed she would *attack* you. . . . And please remember that I did give you her name and tell you to watch out for her, even though I couldn't bring myself to confess to you what an irrational, hysterical creature I had been."

I regarded her for a moment, frowning, wondering how much of this to believe, if any of it. "So this morning you don't really think you were poisoned, by Karin Segerby or anybody else?"

She shrugged. "All right, I am being inconsistent, but now that I am not so sick and feverish and frightened, it does seem rather implausible. I mean, even if she did kill her husband, even if she knows I suspect her, why should she take the dreadful risk of killing me? I can prove nothing, and she can hardly expect to get away with two murders barely a year apart.''

It was hard for me to think of the pretty, healthy young woman I'd encountered last night as a murderess, although I should know they don't come with labels on them. And the fact that Mrs. Astrid Watrous said so didn't necessarily make it so.

I said, ''Well, your heart specialist is checking it out for me, to see if it's even a possibility. Have you got a passport?''

The change of subject startled her. ''Well, yes, and your chief, or whatever you call that man in Washington, thought it would be a good idea if I kept it with me, so I got it out of the bank. It is in my purse, right over there. Do you think we will need . . . I am afraid that it will take a little time before I am strong enough to travel abroad.''

I said, ''I wasn't thinking of an immediate Grand Tour. I just wanted to know what country.''

''Why . . . why, I am a United States citizen!'' She sounded shocked that I would have to ask. ''I was born here!''

''Very odd,'' I said without expression. ''Karin Segerby carries a Swedish passport, but she speaks English as well as you do, if not better. You claim to be a native-born American, but most of the time you sound like Greta Garbo vaahnting to be ahloane.''

She said stiffly, ''I am not responsible for the fact that my parents were Finnish. Finnish immigrants. But I am very proud of it.''

I said, ''Hell, everybody's ancestors were immigrants around here, and that even goes for some of the Indian tribes. The Athabascans—Navajos and Apaches—immigrated to this continent from Asia not too long before Co-

38

lumbus started the big rush from the other direction. My parents came from Sweden and I'm proud of that, sure, but I like to kid myself that I can stumble along in English without sounding too much like a transplanted squarehead. Thanks to my folks, who made a point of not speaking Swedish around the ranch except, I suppose, when they were in bed together. Since they'd made the big switch, they wanted us all to be good Americans and talk good American. Of course they never got rid of the accent, but they made damned sure it didn't rub off on me.''

Astrid Watrous shrugged. "Some people are proud of their ethnic heritage, and some aren't.''

I said, "Sometimes I think the world would be a damn' sight better off if we'd all forget this ethnic crap.'' I grimaced. "Well, that's an argument nobody ever wins. So you're Finnish? I thought a Finn was a dark, mean gent who cast spells and conjured up storms at sea. . . . The old square-riggers wouldn't let a Finn aboard ship, if I remember right. He was considered very bad luck, a sure guarantee of adverse winds and vicious gales. But you don't look like a black Finn sorceress.''

"A great many Swedes settled in Finland after the Crusades.''

"Crusades? You mean to the Holy Land?''

She said stiffly, "Apparently you don't even know the history of the land your own people came from. There were other crusades, Mr. Helm. Your Swedish kings, having embraced Christianity and renounced Odin and Thor, then marched heroically into Finland and brought the Cross to the backward Finnish heathen. Three times, as a matter of fact. Each one was called a *korståg,* a crusade. Naturally, to be certain the conversion was permanent, the Swedes had to take over the benighted country. They stayed for seven hundred years. Some of them still remain, like my parents before they came to America, and consider themselves Finns.''

"I should think so," I said. "I consider myself an American, and I barely managed to get myself conceived here. I should think seven centuries ought to qualify anybody for citizenship." After a moment, I went on deliberately: "So that's where the blonde Viking hair came from; but the mysterious cheekbones and the dark, haunting eyes are presumably gifts from an ancestral Finnish witch or warlock."

She smiled slowly. "I could get hardened to your wicked insults. Mysterious cheekbones and haunting eyes. Very nice, Mr. Helm. So I will tell you a secret. I am not ashamed of my accent, but I do exaggerate it occasionally. I do not know why it is, but many American men seem to be taken by an attractive woman—if I may flatter myself—who speaks somewhat less than perfect English, if the accent is foreign. Some kind of snobbery, I suppose. They might not look at me twice if I spoke good Hoosier American."

I grinned. "Now you want me to flatter you and tell you that you're selling yourself short and they'd flock around even if you talked Brooklynese." Astrid Watrous stuck out her tongue at me daintily, and we laughed, and I said, "Tell me about your relationship with Karin Segerby. How long have you known her, how and where did you meet her, and why did you have lunch with her if you hate her guts?"

"I do not hate her guts, I am merely bored by her," Astrid said. "I have known her for several years, ever since Alan had to go to Washington on behalf of the Institute and I went with him. . . ."

But at that moment the door opened and the doctor came in, the heart man to whom I'd spoken the day before named, if you'll believe it, Hartman. It must have been something to learn to live with after he'd decided on his profession; and I remembered that he'd introduced himself with a wry grin that had had lots of practice. There was a nurse with him. He sent me out of the room while he did his stethoscope thing; then he emerged and came over to where I leaned against the corridor wall, waiting.

"She's doing very well," he said. "Of course it will take some time for her system to return to normal after two such shocks, the cardiac episode and the quinine reaction. I would like to keep her under observation until the weekend. After that, she should take it very easy for several weeks, preferably within reach of good medical facilities in case of an emergency. Not that I really anticipate any further trouble if her condition remains stable over the next few days."

I said, "That's the good news. Have you got any bad?"

Hartman regarded me for a moment without a great deal of liking. He took an envelope from the pocket of his white coat.

"With respect to the questions you asked," he said, "I can see no easy way in which the quinine reaction could have been induced, under the circumstances. However, there are certain compounds which could have brought on the original symptoms of tachycardia, and I have listed them for you with notes as to their availability and the methods by which they could have been introduced into the patient's system. I must say that I felt as if I were writing a mystery novel, and I hope you find it gripping; but let me advise you not to build too much on it. All our tests and analyses are consistent with a natural attack triggered by . . . Well, we simply don't know what triggers these episodes naturally, Mr. Helm." He looked past me. "Yes, Nurse?"

"Is this Mr. Helm? There's a call for you in three-fifty-seven, Mr. Helm. From Washington."

Unexpected calls from Washington are always hard on the nerves. I tried to tell myself that they'd just misplaced all the keys to the second-floor john and wanted mine so they could make duplicates, fully urgent.

41

"Thank you, Nurse," I said. I took the envelope Dr. Hartman gave me, and said, "Thank you very much, Doctor."

"You're welcome," he said, but I had a hunch that I wasn't, very. He didn't like my thinking that he could have overlooked a murder attempt, even if I were wrong; and I didn't think he was as certain of that as he pretended.

I went back into the room, where Astrid Watrous held out the phone to me. I took it, and said, "Helm."

The voice in the phone belonged to Doug Barnett. It said only three words. "Scramble. Repeat, scramble."

"Scramble received," I said and hung up. I looked at the woman in the bed. "Get your clothes on. The man says we've got to get out of here fast before the roof falls in."

## CHAPTER 5

I'D hoped she'd just hauled on a pair of old jeans and a T-shirt when it hit her in the middle of the night and she dressed in a panicky hurry and stumbled off to the hospital with her heart going crazy in her chest. Not that I really approve of girls in jeans unless there's a horse in the picture; but here I didn't know how long it would be before we could find her a change of clothes. In a good pair of slacks, or a skirt, one day on the run and maybe a slight accident along the way with some Coca Cola or hamburger juice generally qualifies a lady for membership in the slob club; but nobody gives a damn how long she's worn a pair of jeans, or how carelessly. In some quarters they aren't even considered respectable until they're thoroughly seasoned: what every well-dressed fugitive should wear.

However, even on such short acquaintance I should have known her better; she was not a dirty-denim girl. In the closet I found a pair of handsome brown flannel slacks, a brown blazer with brass buttons, a tan—well, call it beige—silk blouse, and a pair of brown sandals with heels high enough to be interesting. There was also a pair of short nylon stockings with elastic tops, and a pair of white nylon panties discreetly embroidered with little flowers. No brassiere. When I turned with the stuff in my hands, she was still sitting in the bed.

"Well, come on!" I snapped. "Let's see some action, Watrous!"

The idea was to rush her into it. I was taking for granted that, given time to think she'd delay us with a lot of stupid questions and pitiful protests: why was I doing this to her, didn't I know she was a poor invalid who couldn't possibly be expected to leave her sickbed, it would kill her quite dead, and how could I even think of suggesting such an outrageous thing! But I'd misjudged her badly. There were no interrogations or objections. There was only a small practical obstacle about which she felt obliged to remind me.

"Somebody must pull it out," she said calmly. "I am a bit of a sissy, Mr. Helm. I would rather it was you."

"Oh."

I laid her clothes on the bed and studied the needle in her arm. Having put in some hospital time myself, in the line of duty, I had a pretty good idea of how the withdrawal operation was performed. The supplies were readily available. I found a Band-Aid and laid it handy. I got some cotton ready. Steadying the needle, I yanked off the tape holding it in place. I held a wad of cotton at the point where the needle disappeared into the skin, slipped it out,

43

wiped off the small amount of blood that appeared, and stuck on the Band-Aid.

"Well, what are you waiting for now?"

She was still sitting there. "Aren't you going to turn your back like a gentleman?"

"After you sent a gun moll to visit me, what makes you think I trust you enough to turn my back on you?"

She studied me for a moment longer. I saw a faintly malicious smile touch her lips. She got out of the high bed. The modest next step, of course, was to pull on the panties under the hospital gown before removing the gown; but I'd challenged her and to hell with modesty. She caught the hem and made a slow and graceful production of pulling the gown off over her head. Clearly, she was confident that while her face displayed the haggardness of illness, there was nothing wrong with her body. She was quite right. It was a very nice, taut female body, moderately tall, adult but slender, lightly tanned except for very skimpy bikini-marks. Watching her unveil and dress it was a disturbing experience, just as she meant it to be.

"What did they tell you over the phone?" she asked as she zipped and buttoned herself up.

"Scramble. In our language, that means get the hell out of wherever you are, with whoever you care to preserve alive, because they're coming for you with homicidal intentions *now*."

"Who is coming?"

I shrugged. "How the hell would I know? I've had a little Japanese car tailing me, and a pretty blonde girl waving a pistol at me, and a handsome brown-eyed lady doing a reverse striptease for me. Things are tough all over. I'll worry about who when I'm clear; right now all I want is out of here."

"Well, you'd better fasten my shoes, then," she said. "If I try to bend over that far, I'll fall on my face."

I knelt at her feet, where she obviously enjoyed having

44

me. "Your heart pills," I said. "Have you got any spares?"

"No, they just bring me one four times a day."

"When's the next one due?"

"Two hours from now, at ten o'clock. Then I take it at four, ten, four—that's the ghastly early-morning one they've been waking me for—and ten again. They say it does no damage if I am a little over the time, or under, but I am not supposed to miss it by too much."

"We'll have to head for a drugstore I know where we can stock up, no questions asked. We should be there in time to keep you on schedule. You know the stuff you want?"

"Procan SR, five hundred milligrams."

"Smart girl."

She laughed rather grimly. "Would a smart girl let a strange man drag her out of the hospital half-dead on her feet?"

But she marched out of the room bravely enough, holding herself very straight, her high heels tapping crisply on the vinyl flooring; and nobody stopped us. I hated to make her take any detours, but it seemed inadvisable to use the front door. By the time we'd found our way to the rear of the hospital and used the stairs there and found an exit, she was sagging noticeably.

"Can you make a block and a half?" I asked. "I could leave you here and bring the car around, but—"

"I do not want to be left anywhere, please," she said. "Not if you think people are planning to kill us."

I had to steady her for the last half block. A stout lady who passed us thought it was disgusting, a nice-looking, nicely dressed young woman like that stumbling around drunk so early in the day. As we approached the place where I'd left the jazzy little Ford, I couldn't spot it at once. I had a moment of panic, wondering whether I'd remembered the street and block incorrectly, or whether the police tow truck had been around. There was no way my rubber-legged companion was going to make it clear to the Holiday Inn, where her Buick was parked, under her own power. I preferred the mini-Ford anyway. It was smaller and peppier and less conspicuous; and I was used to the way it handled.

Then I saw it, hidden behind a blocky green van, exactly where I'd left it, without even a parking ticket on the windshield. I got the door open and helped Astrid inside after reclining the seat to make her more comfortable. She lay back against the headrest and closed her eyes, looking very pale and vulnerable. I made her a silent apology. For all her glamour-accent and femme-fatale manner, she seemed to be a brave, tough woman, fighting hard to meet my unreasonable demands in spite of her weakness. I was beginning to get quite attached to her in a protective way; but I warned myself it was just a normal attack of the broken-wing syndrome. This was no time to get mushy about a pretty, crippled birdie that wasn't necessarily a harmless domestic pigeon.

We picked up I-70 just south of town and ran it as far as Frederick, Maryland, and let it continue east to Baltimore without us, while we turned southeast on I-270, the Washington Pike. Ceiling unlimited. Visibility unlimited. Passenger mostly asleep beside me. Escort: none. Apparently the hideout car had thrown them off, at least for the moment. Sloppy work. They should have known I'd arrived in something that had to be somewhere if it wasn't at the motel. They should have found it. But maybe the Honda had belonged to Karin Segerby and she'd decided she had no more gun-business, or other business, to transact with me.

Traffic density increased as we approached the District of Columbia. At last I cut out of formation at the proper exit, and drove for a while through residential districts that varied from luxury homes with green lawns and shade trees

46

to shabby old apartment buildings right on the sidewalk. My own domicile fell into the latter category, but if people were laying for us, that was one of the places they could be waiting, although you won't find my phone number, or address, in the white pages. Self-preservation. I chose a route that would pass a few blocks away.

Astrid Watrous sat up at last, and raised her seat back a bit. She tucked in her shirt and patted her hair into place, healthy feminine reactions.

"Feeling better?" I asked.

She shrugged. "After spending so many days in bed, my legs were starting to atrophy, I think. Where are we?"

"Washington, D.C. Tell me more about Lysaniemi."

"I do not know any more."

"Where did you get the name?"

"I am not able to tell you that."

I glanced at her irritably. "Nor where it is?"

"That I do not know. Truly. I am sorry."

I said, "A Finnish name. North of the Arctic Circle, you said. It probably wouldn't be in Alaska or northern Canada; I don't think many Finns settled up there. It could be in western Russia, near the Finnish border—languages particularly place names, have a habit of slopping across national boundaries—but that would make access pretty awkward for our conspirators unless it's all a sinister Russky plot, and I haven't been getting that impression. That leaves Norway, Sweden, and, of course, Finland. I guess we'll have to check them out."

She said, "You are very crazy if you are thinking what I think. I cannot possibly travel. . . ." She paused and frowned at me. "Is this what you really had in mind when you asked about my passport?"

I shrugged. "Maybe, but I wouldn't have dragged you out of bed so soon if there had been a choice. But since we're running anyway, why not there? All you have to do is sit. The Scandinavian Airlines System, or whatever, will

47

do all the work." I glanced her way. "Think about it. It's as good a way of keeping out of people's way as any. People who apparently want to kill us, motives as yet undetermined. But you're a strong girl. You can do it. We'll find a place to rest you up once we're across the big water, before we get into any strenuous Arctic exploration."

She was silent for a little; then she said, unsmiling, "Well, you could get another man to carry the feet."

I said, "With a skinny wench like you, who needs another man? I'll just toss you over my shoulder and walk off with you."

"Now you are boasting," she said. "All right, Mr. Helm. I will go along on your crazy expedition, just to see what you really do when I faint in your arms."

"Good girl."

She shook her head irritably. "Will you please to refrain from that smart-girl, strong-girl, good-girl nonsense? I do not need any pats on the head, thank you very much. I am not that sick, and my morale is very tremendous. Where is this pharmacy for which we are looking, anyway?"

## CHAPTER 6

FROM the pay phone at the corner of the lot, I could see the station attendant filling the tank of the little Ford. He was a young fellow in reasonably clean brown coveralls sporting the Chevron insignia. Waiting for the fuel to run in, he attacked the windshield with a squeegee, and then proceeded to clean the other glass surfaces including the mirrors, something that happens all too seldom these days even if you pick the lane marked "Full Service." But the miracle didn't end there. With the windows clean, he actually went so far as to open the hood and check the oil, using a rag to hold the hot dipstick after burning himself on his first try. Somebody ought to warn the kid to straighten up and fly right, or he'd be kicked out of the Service Station Attendants' Society for coddling his customers, instead of treating them like the dirt they were.

It had been quite a drive. After picking up Astrid's medicine, and a bottle of 7Up with which to wash down her ten-o'clock dose only half an hour later, I'd had her bring her seat back upright and pull her safety harness tight. We'd picked up a leech at last. Losing us in Hagerstown, somebody must have got right on the ball and determined that we'd need medicine, even on the run, and that it was medicine that required a prescription, which we didn't have. Somehow they'd known where I lived and which nearby drugstore would bend the rules for me a bit. . . . They'd known too much, too soon, for a bunch of kidnappers who might be interested in Mac but weren't likely to have dossiers on everyone working for him. However, that was something I could worry about later. At the moment, the significant fact was that they were right behind us in their white Honda. Two large men. No small blonde girls.

I'd expected, with my sporty little car and my knowledge of the city, that I could easily shake the even smaller car behind; but it had turned out to have more power than I'd thought, and a good wheelman. I'd had to use all the boost of the EXP's crazy little turbocharger, and all my driving skill, to get clear, perhaps because I came to front-wheel drive cars late. I'm still not used to the idea of having the same tires doing both the steering and the pulling, since you never know—at least I don't—if applying a lot of power in a corner is really going to drag you through it the way the 4WD advocates claim, or just break the front end loose and let you go sliding off into the boonies. Back

49

in the days when the power went to the rear wheels, you could kick them loose or not as you pleased, while the front tires kept right on steering the heap unless you got unreasonably violent.

Anyway, it had been a bit hairy while it lasted. However, in the end we'd managed to lose them, at least for the moment, and without picking up any cops in the process. Now I was standing at the open-air phone feeling exposed and vulnerable, and wondering whatever happened to those nice sheltering booths the phone company used to pamper us with. It seemed to be my day for nostalgia.

I listened to the instrument ringing in my ear and presumably also down in Florida. None of the cars or people on the street seemed to be interested in me. I'd already triggered the emergency-communication routine by an aborted call to Doug Barnett's St. Petersburg number from the drugstore where I'd picked up Astrid's pills. Five rings and hang up. That had let Amy Barnett, covering the number for her absent dad, know that she should await my next call at a safe phone we'd arranged to use a long time ago when we were setting up our crisis system.

Standing there, I watched Astrid emerge from the restroom and open her purse to get out some money. Smart girl. Credit cards have names on them; but a twenty is anonymous. I was counting rings. The suspense was considerable; but on the tenth ring, as prearranged, the instrument was picked up at the other end.

"Me," I said.

It was no time for a lot of secret-agent nonsense. If there was someone at the other end who didn't recognize my voice, we had real trouble.

Amy Barnett's voice said, "Well, I'm glad *me* finally got around to calling this super-duper secret number. I've been waiting around here for practically hours; I thought maybe I'd misremembered the instructions Dad gave me. Matt, are you all right?"

I said, "I didn't know you still cared."

She spoke impatiently: "Don't be silly; I wasn't asking for myself. But Daddy seems to have run into big problems in Washington."

"What problems?"

"You know he flew up there to form . . . well, I guess you'd call it a caretaker government in the absence of the man you all call Mac, who'd suddenly gone missing."

I said, "Yes, we knew that was coming; that's why I alerted Doug."

"It didn't work."

I frowned. "What do you mean, it didn't work?"

"Daddy said to tell you that the king has departed as expected, but the scheduled royal succession has hit a snag. If that makes sense to you."

"Did he name the snag?"

"Yes. He said it was somebody you knew better than he did; somebody with reason not to like your and Daddy's organization in general, and you in particular. That was why he was especially worried about you. He said that if you remembered a man named Bennett you could probably figure it out for yourself."

"Oh, Jesus!" I said. "Just goes to show what being soft-hearted gets you. Bennett? I should have shot the pompous, scheming, big-nosed bastard while I had the chance."

"You mean there's one bastard you didn't shoot when you had the chance? I thought you were the clean-sweep man." Her voice was expressionless, but it was of course the rock upon which our relationship had crashed, her uneasy suspicion that I was basically a homicidal maniac. She went on: "Anyway, I'm supposed to help you set up a rendezvous with an agent called Joel. I suppose that's a code name, like your Eric. Joel will brief you in detail."

Bennett's name explained a lot of things, of course. If he'd managed a political coup and taken over Mac's desk

51

in Mac's absence, shunting aside Doug Barnett, who was a good agent but no politician, he'd have the agency dossiers at his disposal; it was no wonder the white Honda had picked me up so fast. So now we had two hostile forces to deal with, the kidnappers who'd taken Mac, and Bennett, who'd usurped Mac's position in the agency and was apparently using it to settle old scores. With me, and presumably others.

Which left one big question mark: Joel. Now that Mac had vanished, as expected, Joel was supposed to track him directly to the lair of the vanishers while I sneaked up on them by another route, the Watrous route, independently.

I said, "First things first. Have you got something for me? I left a name with Mac at the special number, reporting from Hagerstown. I asked to have it checked out. Did he or your pop manage to get a report on it from Research before things went haywire? It would be close timing, but. . ."

"You're in luck," Amy said. "Daddy said it was just about his first and last act as prince regent. He signed for a communication for you, a quick preliminary survey of the problem; they're still working on it. Unless Bennett has stopped them now, of course. Daddy read it to me over the phone and I took some notes. Just a minute . . ." I heard paper rustle a thousand miles away. "Oh, here it is. How do you pronounce that name, anyway?"

"Leesanyaymee, more or less."

"Well, you called it Finnish, and you were right. *Lysa* doesn't mean anything in Finnish, apparently; but *niemi* means 'cape' or 'point.' Like Rovaniemi, a sizable city in northern Finland, on a point where two rivers meet. There's a query here: how reliable is your informant?"

"Totally unreliable, but with a charming Finnish-Swedish accent."

"I suppose she's blonde." Amy's voice was tart.

"What else?"

"Young and pretty, too, I bet."

"An old hag of thirty-two."

"An old bag of thirty-two, did you say?" Amy laughed shortly. "Well, to proceed, the name is Finnish, but the town is on the Swedish side of the border."

"So it does exist. I wasn't quite sure somebody wasn't kidding me."

"You'd better apologize to your blonde. It's a small village up in the wilderness well north of the main road through the area, Highway E4. That's the one that runs around the Gulf of Bothnia from Stockholm, the capital of Sweden, up to Haparanda at the very top of the gulf, and then down to Helsinki, the capital of Finland. If you've come up through Sweden, you turn off E4 before you come to Haparanda, which is on the border, at the little town of Porkkala, spelled with two *k*s. You take an unpaved road inland a hundred and twenty miles in the general direction of the North Pole, which isn't actually so awfully far away. You'll hit Lysaniemi, a metropolis of a hundred and fifty inhabitants, it says here, shortly after you cross the Arctic Circle."

I frowned at the phone. "Miles? Last time I was in Scandinavia, they worked their distances in kilometers."

"Just a minute, let me check my notes." There was a pause; then Amy's voice said ruefully, "So sorry. You're perfectly right. A hundred and twenty kilometers it is. Point six two miles per kilometer, right? Roughly seventy-five miles."

"And this is the only Lysaniemi they were able to find?"

"How many do you need?" Then she said quickly, "I'm sorry, Matt. Smart aleck me."

I said, "The trouble is, the damn' name came to me too easily. I don't trust anything I'm handed on a platter like that. Here I was expecting to have to work like hell for it, and it was whispered in my ear before I was well started on the operation. I have a sneaky feeling that people are being very cute at my expense or think they are: *Let's have some fun with the stupid government mercenary who carries his brains, the few he's got, in his trigger finger.* Not an entirely original estimate of my character, is it, Miss Barnett?''

She laughed softly, way down in Florida. "I never called you stupid, Matt." She hesitated, and changed the subject: "What about that Joel person? What should I report to Daddy when he calls back?"

"Tell Doug that Joel will have to catch me at Dulles Airport. National Flight three-oh-seven to Kennedy, departing two fifty-five. Say I'll see him at the gate; it's too late to set up anything more complicated. And I'd better put it on the road right now if I'm going to get there in time to talk at all before we board."

"Matt, be careful."

"Aren't I always?"

I heard her laugh disbelievingly as I hung up, but I don't know what she found so funny. When a man in my line of work lasts to my age, he's got to have been very, very careful. Astrid was waiting in the car. I got in and drove directly to the nearest freeway. Turning my back on Dulles Field, southwest of the city, where I was expected, I headed for the Washington/Baltimore International Airport, northeast of it, where I wasn't. The New York connection there was by way of Frontier Flight 74 to LaGuardia. Not quite as convenient for catching a transatlantic flight, but safer.

Like I said, careful.

## CHAPTER 7

FLYING SAS first class across the Atlantic is about as good as it can get, which still isn't very good. I mean, no matter how much they pamper you, it's a long, long flight; and comfortable or not, you're still six or seven miles up in the air with several thousand miles of ocean, several thousand feet deep, beneath you, and not a damn' thing you can do if things go wrong.

When the stewardess—excuse me, the female flight attendant—offered me a drink, I took two of her toy bottles of Scotch, J&B, if it matters, and poured them over the ice she provided, and drank gratefully. Cashews on the side. Back in the cheapo cabin, they probably had to settle for lower-class peanuts.

"Why, you are frightened!"

I glanced at the woman beside me, who'd gone to sleep, exhausted, immediately after having been led to her seat and helped with her seat belt. She'd slept through the inevitable preflight delays, and the taxiing, and the further waiting, and the takeoff, and the circling to the right course, and the climb to cruising altitude; but now her eyes were open. She'd obviously been watching me for a while.

"Welcome back," I said. "Would you care to have something to drink, too, or is that medically contraindicated?"

She smiled. "I do not think it is contraindicated; at least the doctors said nothing about it. If that is Scotch, I will have some. Unless you have already drunk up all on board in your terrible panic.''

''Oooh, what a sharp tongue it has when it's conscious,'' I said. ''Whatever happened to sweet, supportive little girls who encourage their men in moments of weakness?''

''But I am not very sweet, and you are not my man, are you, Mr. Helm?''

I grinned, and got her table down for her, and wig-wagged the attendant, who brought the drink promptly. Astrid raised her glass to me.

*''Skål,''* she said, smiling at me. ''I mean, we had better practice our Scandinavian customs, don't you think?''

''And our Scandinavian,'' I said, ''How are you on Norwegian?''

She shook her head. ''They have deliberately made their language impossible for other Scandinavians to understand. I do not think they understand it very well themselves. Years ago if one knew Swedish, one could communicate with the Norwegians, and even the crazy Danes a little, but no longer.''

''Yes, I have heard that linguistic purification is the order of the day up there. But you do speak Swedish?''

''And Finnish. Yes.''

''You are hereby appointed official interpreter for the expedition, Mrs. Watrous.''

She inclined her head in gracious acceptance. She'd been very close to collapse when I'd helped her aboard the plane, but the nap seemed to have revived her. I realized again that she was quite a striking woman. There's always something offbeat and intriguing about a brown-eyed blonde—genuine or phony, I still hadn't decided which I was dealing with here.

In a small department store in the same shopping center that housed the friendly druggist who did me medical favors from time to time, I'd managed to pick up a couple of inexpensive suitcases and a very basic travel wardrobe for each of us, not because I'd been seriously concerned about how we looked, but because I'd wanted to have some luggage in which to check the guns through, hoping that airlines hadn't got around to X-raying checked luggage yet, and that Scandinavian customs officers were still as relaxed as I remembered them. Since I hadn't wanted Astrid to waste her limited strength on shopping, I didn't even know that the clothes I'd bought her would fit, let alone that she'd consider them acceptable. However, her present costume was holding up well enough to get us across the ocean respectably, so my taste in ladies' wear wouldn't be put to the test at once, which was probably a good thing.

She was regarding me curiously. "I should think a man like you, who risks his life in a job like yours, would not be disturbed by merely flying in an commercial airplane."

"That's just the point," I said. "I like to pick my risks; that's how I stay alive. Here I've got no choice. I have to sit in this seat and take whatever dangers the flyboys up front choose to expose me to. Probably none, but how do I know? A Korean airliner got itself shot down a while ago, flying in the wrong place, remember?"

"Yes, that was a terrible thing. They are dreadful people, those Russians."

I grinned. "There's a good Finnish reaction. Has any Finn said anything nice about a Russian since the receding glaciers of the Ice Age uncovered their respective countries?"

"But it was cold-blooded murder!"

"Sure. Surprise, surprise. What did you think—what did anybody think—those paranoid bastards would do when a strange aircraft blundered into their airspace in a fairly sensitive area? Jesus, all the corny, outraged noises that were made because Russians behaved in a perfectly normal Russian manner! What I want to know is what the plane was doing so far off the course. Nobody seems to be a bit concerned about that. But if that's normal airlines navigation, I feel I'm entitled to a few consoling Scotches when I put myself into their hands. One airliner ran into a bunch of ruthless Muscovites; how do I know this one won't run into a bunch of rugged mountains, or mistake the North Pole for the Oslo airport?''

"Now you are being very silly. SAS has an excellent safety record. There is really no reason for you to be frightened.''

"Yes, Mama, I'll be brave if it makes you feel better.''

The oversized plane, some kind of monster Lockheed, rumbled on through the sky that was clear and blue at this altitude; but cottony white clouds obscured the world below us. The great circle course shown in the airlines magazine in the seat pocket before me indicated that we'd actually spend considerable time over land before venturing out across the big water; but if one of the eastern provinces of Canada was down there, it was well hidden.

"I do not really understand what has happened in Washington that we must flee like this," Astrid said at last. "Just because your chief has disappeared, and the person you expected to take charge in his place, temporarily, has been pushed aside by this man called Bennett . . . Why does that mean that we have to leave the country, Matt?''

I'd told her as much about the situation as seemed advisable on our flight from Washington to New York; now I said, "Washington is a funny place, Mrs. W. Discreet thievery is perfectly all right, of course—let's not be unreasonable—but if you're found with your hand in the till and the news gets out, they'll clobber you self-righteously to show how they really hate dishonesty, being so honest themselves. Even sleeping in the wrong bed can ruin you if there's any kind of a scandal; and Heaven help you if you're found smoking a little pot or—God forbid—sniffing a little coke, at least if your dreadful crime becomes public. The guardians of public morality will bury you. But if all you're caught doing is betraying your country, no sweat. Don't give it another thought.''

Astrid studied my face to see if I was kidding. ''Aren't you exaggerating a little?''

I shrugged. ''Oh, sometimes they don't quite have the gall to take you back into the government afterwards, and you'll have to make it on the celebrity circuit; there seems to be a good market there for traitors. I'm using the term loosely, to refer to individuals who betrayed either the laws they'd sworn to uphold or the country they'd sworn to serve, or both. It seems to be a very safe thing to do. I've now been involved in two different cases where a high-ranking bureaucrat allowed himself to become a patsy for folks who, let's say, were not exactly working for the good of the United States of America or the preservation of its constitution. In each case, even though we'd exposed him thoroughly, the man went on to more prestigious posts in Washington.''

''The Mr. Bennett we are discussing?''

I nodded. ''He's the most recent specimen, yes. We came up against him twice while he was head of a certain undercover agency—you might call it a rival agency—that wasn't being operated entirely in the public interest. The second time, a couple of years ago, we had him cold on various charges of conspiring and betraying; we could even have made him trouble about his involvement in other kinds of professional behavior including a spot of homicide and attempted homicide unauthorized by Washington. Not exactly the kind of public servant we should cherish, right? Well, his dubious organization was abolished; the FBI took up the slack. However, Bennett didn't appear to be a very bright guy, and it seemed that he'd merely acted as figurehead while the smart boys did the dirty work. We took care of them; but we decided that Bennett wasn't dangerous and it was safe to make a deal with him. We agreed to let him tell us some things we needed to know in order to wind up the dirty business, in return for immunity.''

"So he went free?"

I nodded. "The decision was mine, and I'm afraid I was wrong. Apparently the guy wasn't as dumb and harmless as he acted. Somehow, after we turned him loose, he got himself welcomed back to that screwball city on the Potomac we just left. He even promoted himself a new position with a bit of salary and influence from which, it seems, he's been keeping an eye on us, the agency that smashed his beautiful government career. Well, his first beautiful government career. Now, with my chief missing, he seems to have embarked upon a second, bossing our outfit. . . ."

I stopped, as our dinners were placed before us, steak for me, fish for her. Having been brought up on fresh-caught mountain trout as a boy in New Mexico, I avoid the tired, mushy stuff that masquerades under the name of fish these days in most parts of the U.S.A. I reminded myself that they do it much better in the European lands towards which we were heading; and I'd better start giving my prejudice a rest. I glanced at the handsome woman beside me.

"What about a spot of champagne, or would that be overdoing it?"

"What else is there to do here but overdo it?" Astrid asked, laughing; but after I'd got us the bubble-stuff, she grew serious again. She said, "So what it amounts to is, you have a new boss, at least until your old one returns. But even if you do not like or respect this Mr. Bennett, is that sufficient reason for us to flee out of the country?"

"I'm not fleeing out of the U.S., I'm fleeing into Sweden," I said, "By way of Norway, because that's the way the plane flies. But I'm afraid you don't quite understand the kind of people you've managed to get yourself mixed up with, looking for help with your private problem. Well, by this time you must have some idea of what our outfit really does. Counter-assassination is the polite description; we're the guys, and gals, who're sent out to kill the killers when nobody else is tough enough to deal with them. Naturally, with our special talents, we're also used for other work like visiting pretty ladies in the hospital—pretty ladies with mysterious illnesses."

I saluted her with my champagne glass. After a moment she smiled and returned the gesture, but her eyes were troubled.

I went on: "Now consider Mr. Bennett. After receiving a serious setback to his career through no fault of his own, as he sees it, he's managed to fight his way back to the kind of powerful position for which he is, he feels, superbly qualified by talent and experience. In this position he has at his disposal the services of a gang of rabid wolves like me, who don't much care whose throats they mangle as long as they get to taste a little blood. . . . What's the matter?"

"You are not like that, Matt."

I grimaced. "It's sweet of you to say so, but you don't know what I'm like, Mrs. W. You've only seen me on my best behavior. Anyway, Bennett's right where he wants to be now, in full control of a government agency pretty much like the one I helped smash for him a few years back. The appointment's only temporary, in Mac's absence, but do you think for a moment that Bennett's going to let it be taken away from him if there's any possible way he can prevent it? If Mac fails to return, he's got it made."

"But how *can* he prevent—" Astrid fell silent, and looked at me in a startled way. "You *can't* mean—"

I said, "Bennett knows that he probably doesn't need to take direct action against my chief. All he has to do is prevent help from finding and reaching him wherever he's being held. Okay, maybe he can break out on his own. Maybe. But he's not young, and he's had no active field

61

experience for a long time. He's counting on outside assistance. If Bennett has his way, it won't be forthcoming.''

Astrid was watching me warily. "So you think Mr. Bennett is going to order you off the . . . the rescue mission?"

I shook my head. "No. Because he knows me reasonably well after our previous disagreements. He knows I wouldn't obey any such order he gave me. He's got to have me taken out if he wants to leave my chief stranded without help. And as I think I told you, there's also another agent involved, a guy we call Joel, who's got to be dealt with somehow."

Astrid licked her lips. " 'Taken out.' That means killed, does it not?" She studied my face. "You are serious, Matt? You truly believe that this government official who has assumed temporary control of your organization will actually give orders to have an agent—his agent for the moment—murdered just so he can keep his new job? You think that somebody in your agency, somebody with whom you have worked perhaps, will accept those instructions and come to kill you?"

I said, "You just don't understand the kind of homicidal creeps you've got yourself mixed up with. Sure I believe it. When the man points the finger and says make the touch, we make the touch. Of course it depends a bit on who gives the order. I wouldn't kill just because a jerk like Bennett told me to, no matter what authority he claimed. I wouldn't trust his motives or his good sense; but there are younger agents around who'll go on the word, without question, like killer Dobermans. That's the way they've been trained."

Astrid shook her head. "That is what is wrong with an agency like yours. Perhaps it serves a useful purpose in the right hands, but in the wrong hands it becomes a terrible weapon; so would it not be better for it not to exist at all?"

I shrugged. "I'll let the political scientists field that one. In the meantime, my job is to get my outfit out of the wrong hands and back into the right ones. That means, for a start, following the orders I've been given and hoping the guy who gave them knew what he was doing. Well, he usually does."

"It is good to see a little faith in this mistrustful world."

"Don't think Bennett's driven only by ambition," I said. "He's got a full charge of hate working on him, too. Hate for Mac, who gave the orders, and hate for me, who carried them out. It wasn't just a matter of losing a lot of prestige and status; there was physical humiliation, too. Our interrogation teams play rough. I'm the man who had him put through that, on Mac's instructions. I'm the man who saw him sitting unshaved in his grubby underwear afterwards, with his head in his hands, broken and cooperative. He wouldn't settle for just calling me off the assignment even if he could. Joel, maybe, but he wants me dead. Along with Mac."

"I see. That is why you try so hard to . . . to shake anyone who follows us."

I laughed. "Mrs. W, you are really a very naive lady."

"What did I say that was funny?"

"You're dreaming pretty dreams," I said. "We can't shake them, not really. Not permanently. They've got us covered all the way. We lost them in Hagerstown because I had a car handy they'd overlooked; but they picked us up in Washington right away. Bennett may not be the greatest spymaster who ever lived, but he knows how to utilize an organization like ours. His boys moved fast, remember? The minute we picked up your pills, there was the Honda riding our tail again."

"But you shook them off by your crazy driving, ugh!" She shuddered reminiscently.

"Sure, and we probably got to New York unescorted, but there were only two planes heading for Scandinavia tonight, this one and a Pan Am flight about an hour later. Maybe we don't have company here on board—we were

63

lucky to get these seats at the last minute—but there'll be a reception committee waiting in Oslo, I'll bet on it. And even if we'd gone by way of London or Copenhagen or, hell, Berlin or Rome or Paris, we'd still have had to wind up in a known place eventually. I gave Lysaniemi to our Research section before I knew how badly things were going to be screwed up. Even if we should manage to shake off Bennett's boys and girls temporarily along the way, all they have to do is head north and park their little asses on the Arctic Circle north of Haparanda—well, Porkkala—and wait for us to drive by.''

She studied my face, frowning. "But then why are you making such big efforts to escape their surveillance?"

I said, "There are two ways of going here, dumb or smart. Dumb, I'd pretend I don't have any idea we're being followed. I'd have us moseying along happily as if we were quite unconscious of all the folks trailing along astern. But that would make everybody very nervous. I mean, I've been around for a while, and I didn't make it by being totally stupid, and Bennett knows it. So he'd be asking himself uneasily what I was planning to pull when I thought I'd conned him into getting careless; and he'd throw double teams into the action, backups behind backups, just to make sure nobody relaxed because I was making it look so easy. . . . Hey, look, we've got water down there."

"What did you expect, the Sahara Desert?"

"In one of these contraptions, I never know what to expect," I said.

"Tell me about the smart way."

"What? Oh, sure. I'm building up Bennett's confidence. Here I am, Superagent Helm who played all kinds of hell with him a few years back, doing my best to shake his people and failing. Ha, they're one step ahead of me the whole way; maybe I'm not as bright as I was cracked up to be. Every time I lose them, they pick me up again and, haha, they still have their ace in the hole, the fact that they know where I'm going, where I have to go eventually. Lysaniemi. Except that we're not going there, at least not now."

"Matt, I don't understand—"

"First things first," I said. "You're doing fine, you're a brave little heroine, but I can't see dragging you across the Arctic tundra in your present condition. I happen to have a large assortment of relatives all over Sweden. With one of the phone calls I made from Washington while we were in the clear, I arranged for us to move into a nice old country place that's been in a certain branch of the family for generations. . . . What's the matter?"

She'd made a small movement, as if what I'd said had surprised her. She shook her head quickly. "Nothing. I guess I had simply resigned myself to being dragged around the world until I collapsed completely. A rest would be very nice, thank you."

I said, "The villa happens to be standing empty at the moment. I won't guarantee the plumbing, it's apt to be a bit old-fashioned, and I doubt there'll be freezers and microwave ovens in the kitchen; but it shouldn't be too bad. We'll feed you up and take you for walks in the Swedish spring woods; and in the meantime, we hope, Bennett's boys and girls will be freezing their tails off up in Lapland, where it's still winter, waiting for the great undercover genius to walk into the deadfall they've prepared for him." I grinned. "We can't shake them; let's see if we can't outshuffle them. Bennett thinks he knows me. He forgets that I know him, too. I know that he's not a very patient man."

CHAPTER 8

THE night didn't last very long, since we were traveling eastwards to meet the sun at a speed approaching the speed of sound. It seemed very soon that the drawn shades went back up to show that there was once more blue sky outside the cabin windows instead of the brief blackness into which we'd flown. Well, traveling the other direction, the way they usually time it, you get no night at all, just a king-sized day.

We pulled ourselves together groggily and made the pilgrimage to the john—earlier, they'd passed out tricky little one-shot toothbrushes complete with toothpaste—and were served our breakfasts. Presently, land appeared far below us, a rugged landscape that still, this late in the spring, displayed quite a bit of snow. At last the plane let down gradually to deposit us at the Oslo airport, after which it went on to Stockholm. At least it was supposed to. I didn't watch it go. It had served its purpose; it had got us safely across the big water. Now I was checking for renewed surveillance. I was also worrying about the guns.

Bringing them had been a gamble, but under the circumstances I'd figured that it would be a bigger risk to go unarmed. Under normal conditions, of course, I'd have left my artillery at home and arranged to have somebody standing by in Oslo to slip me replacements after I'd landed. However, with Bennett holding down the boss desk in Washington, conditions were far from normal; I would get no cooperation from that quarter. I told myself optimistically that Norway wasn't like certain truly paranoid Third World countries, where a smuggled firearm would earn you a firing squad, or at least a very dark cell in a very unpleasant dungeon. Norwegian prisons, I recalled, had a pretty good reputation.

Like most worries, this one was wasted. Obviously there had been no X-rays; we picked up the luggage without even being asked to open our bargain his-and-hers suitcases, going through customs and immigration; they simply stamped our passports and waved us through. I felt a little guilty about taking advantage of such nice people, but not guilty enough for it to spoil my day.

The man at the Avis counter spoke excellent English, and, although I'd made no reservation, he had a car available: a Ford Golf. This turned out to be a red Volkswagen Rabbit mildly disguised by the addition of a couple of small Ford emblems—they hadn't even bothered to remove the original VW insignia. The schizophrenic vehicle had two peculiarities. Somebody'd forgotten to equip it with a motor, and the lights went on whenever you switched on the ignition.

I assumed that the feebleness of the powerplant—I've exaggerated slightly, there actually was one, but it seemed to be running on two rubber bands instead of the usual four—was due to some kind of Scandinavian government regulations; the ever-burning headlights certainly were. As we made our way into the city of Oslo through the dense traffic, I saw that all the cars on the road were burning their headlights even though the morning was well advanced. Well, maybe it made sense in a region where fog and mist were commonplace and where, at certain times of the year, daylight was limited to a few hours. Still, I found myself wanting to signal all those other drivers and call to them helpfully: *Hey, Mac, ya got yer lights on!*

"We've got company behind," I said, glancing at the

rearview mirrors. "I told you they'd be waiting here to pick us up."

But Astrid was asleep in her well-reclined seat. She was, I realized, very near the end of her strength. I knew it from the fact that she'd let herself doze off with wisps of blonde hair straggling down her shiny face, and a crumpled shirt-tail escaping from the waistband of her rumpled slacks. She'd put up a very good fight against her own weakness, she'd made it clear to Europe, but it had caught up with her now. I would have liked to keep going, but I didn't want a basket case on my hands.

I spotted a large motel on the other side of the six-lane boulevard. A concrete barrier stifled at birth any wild notion of making a left turn in the face of that flood of illuminated Nordic traffic. I had to drive several blocks before I found an off ramp that led me to an underpass that let me cross beneath the road and reenter it on the other side, going the other way. Then I fought my way back to the hostelry and went inside. Yes, they spoke English a little. Yes, they had a double room available. Would *Herren* be so good as to fill out the registration form, placing his passport number where indicated. No, *Damen*'s passport number would not be required.

So I registered us as Mr. and Mrs. Matthew Helm, Washington, D.C., U.S.A. I didn't think a Scandinavian motel would be stuffy about renting to an unmarried couple, but why flaunt it? When I got back out to the car, Astrid was awake and wondering where she was and where I'd got to. She had to steady herself against the car for a moment after I'd helped her out, but she made it to the room under her own power. As I was making sure the door was locked, after setting down the suitcases, I heard her gasp. She was regarding herself in the full-length mirror in the entranceway.

"Heavens, I look like something dumped out of a wastebasket!"

68

The sight of her reflection seemed to dispel her weariness. She started to reconstruct her disintegrating image in a systematic way.

"Did you take your early-morning pill?" I asked.

"Is it due? I've lost track, with all the time zones we've been through."

"I think we're supposed to set our watches ahead five hours, which makes it pill time again," I said. "I'll get you some water."

When I returned, she was sitting on the nearest bed, jacket off, hair tidy, blouse tucked in. I was glad to see that the beds were of normal twin dimensions. Years ago when I was there, the Norwegians often went in for strange, kiddie-sized sleeping furniture, although they're not small people. Astrid took her medicine and handed me back the glass.

"Well, what is next on the secret-agent agenda, Mr. Secret Agent?"

I showed her a pint of Dewar's White Label that I'd picked up in the course of my Washington shopping spree and wrapped in my not-yet-worn pajamas as emergency rations, since we were heading for a part of the world where the liquor regulations are almost as tough as, and even more complicated than, the firearms regulations.

I said, "Normally, I'm not a morning drinker, but this day's all loused up anyway. I'd like for us to share a little Scotch and exchange a few more confidences, if you're up to it. But if you're too tired, we can catch up on our sleeping first, and do our drinking and talking afterwards."

Astrid said, "I am all right. I simply cannot endure any more airplanes and automobiles at the moment; but I think I would very much like a drink before I sleep. But first of all I would like to get out of these grubby clothes and take a hot bath. Do I have a nightgown or a pair of pajamas in that bag?"

I said, "I hate pajama girls. But you have a nightie and

69

a negligee. K Mart's best or was it J. C. Penney, with lace that won't quit."

"Oh, my God. Save me from a man's taste in lingerie!" She laughed. "But if you would get them out for me, please? And give me ten minutes?"

"Don't take too long, or there may not be anything left for you to drink."

I dug out the garments in question, and the basic toilet kit I'd bought her, and passed them into the bathroom without peeking. Then I broke out the firearms. I checked Karin Segerby's .22 Magnum derringer and slipped it into my sock, one of the stretchy wool-and-nylon numbers. One size fits everybody from Bigfoot down. It did a pretty good job of holding the diminutive weapon in place. There was a simple up-the-sleeve rig for my own little backup .25 automatic, which I hadn't been wearing back home because the situation hadn't seemed to call for it. I strapped that on. I gave my short-barreled .38 a quick once-over and stuck it back into my bag. Then I poured myself a therapeutic dose of White Label. A doctor once told me that, medically speaking, two ounces were just about right, although he didn't say just right for what.

I sipped the stuff unchilled and undiluted, since I'd forgotten to check on the ice situation; and I didn't want to barge into the bathroom for water because the lady would be sure that all I really wanted was to steal another glimpse of the glorious unclothed body that she'd already displayed to me once, dressing in the hospital. She had some rather corny reactions—the proud-beauty syndrome, we'd have called it when I was in college—but I reminded myself that, although I'd hauled her rudely out of her hospital bed, and dragged her almost a quarter of the way around the world, she'd demanded no sympathy and burdened me with no complaints.

When she came out, brushing at the loose blonde hair that reached her shoulders, she said, "Thank you for the toilet things. That was thoughtful. But I must say I feel a little like a bargain-basement courtesan."

The negligee I'd bought her, like the gown underneath, was constructed of some kind of creamy, shiny, clingy material. It was trimmed with large amounts of lace, or what passes for lace in the lower income brackets these plastic days. Actually, it was a pretty good imitation of the real stuff if you didn't look too closely. It cascaded enticingly over her bosom, and dripped intriguingly from her wrists. Inexpensive though it was, it didn't leave me totally unaffected. She was a very attractive woman dressed in a seductive and becoming manner—never mind the price—and it was hard to overlook the fact that there were beds handy.

I cleared my throat and said, "Where else could you get that nice tarty feeling on sale for thirty-seven fifty plus tax? Best deal of the week."

She studied me gravely with the brown eyes that went so strangely and intriguingly with the shining hair. "Matt?"

I said, "Yes, Astrid. I guess I just like lacy ladies, and it did look pretty on the rack. You're under no obligation to live up to it. If that's what you're wondering."

"It did come to mind, sir."

"Let's clarify the situation," I said. "I'm a reasonably normal male, and you're a good-looking female, and it looks as if we'll be sharing accommodations for a while, for reasons of security. At the moment, our main concern is to get your strength back. Once we've got you reasonably healthy, well, let's just say that I'll take anything that's offered. I won't take anything that isn't offered. Satisfactory?"

She regarded me for a moment longer. "I'm beginning to think you may be a very nice man," she said at last.

I said dryly, "You think too many men are nice men. My boss. Me. No discrimination whatever. Here, grab your

71

drink and sit down and let's talk things over. Unless you'd really rather rest."

"No, I am fine." She seated herself and took a sip of her Scotch, setting it aside on the small table between our chairs. "What do we talk about?"

"First, this."

Reaching down for the revolver in my open suitcase, I tossed it in the general direction of her lap. Throwing firearms around is not recommended practice; but I'd discovered that you can learn a lot about somebody by their reaction to a flying pistol. Astrid's eyes widened with shock; but she managed to field the weapon at the last possible moment. Instinctively, she switched it around so the muzzle was pointing in a safe direction, and hit the latch to let the cylinder swing out.

"Oh, it's empty." Then she looked at me angrily. "That was a foolish thing to do. You almost frightened me to death."

"Yes, I noticed," I said dryly. "You've handled one before."

She shrugged. "I had a college friend who became a policewoman. We thought it a very strange profession for an intelligent and educated person to choose." She gave me a sharp glance. "Almost as strange as your vocation."

"It takes all kinds," I said.

She made a face at the cliche and went on: "Mary Alice—that was her name, Mary Alice Linderman—kept saying that she never could understand how women could be against guns, particularly women who were for equality. She said that it seemed obvious that the only thing that could make the average woman equal to the average man, physically speaking, was a good big revolver or automatic pistol. Or even a little one. That was what guns were for, to give a small, weak person a chance against a big, strong one. She insisted on showing me how her service revolver worked, although I wasn't really enthusiastic. She even made me go out with her and shoot it a little, enough so I'd know what it was like. She said that someday it might save my life, just knowing that much about it."

I said, "Swell, that saves me a lot of talking. Please snap it a few times to get the feel of it. . . . Good. Here are the cartridges. Load it and keep it handy. We'll be staying here until tomorrow morning; but I'd like to slip out after it gets dark, to see who's hanging around. While I'm gone, don't open the door for anybody, and if somebody tries to force his way in here, shoot him dead."

She licked her lips. "That could create . . . difficulties, couldn't it?"

I said, "Sweetheart, what would you rather have, some Norwegian officials hassling you alive, or the same Norwegian officials saying what a nice, law-abiding, humanitarian person you were, as they bury your cold, dead body? Keep your eye on the ball. Survival is first on the priority list, always. As your friend Mary Alice indicated, that gun can keep you safe if you use it properly."

She frowned, watching me. "You told me in Hagerstown you do not trust me even well enough to turn your back on me." She glanced down at the gun she was still holding, after filling the chambers expertly and snapping the cylinder into place. "Now you trust me with a loaded pistol. That does not seem very consistent."

"Maybe I've decided to take a chance on you. Or maybe I'm just testing you, all set to blow you away if you try to use that weapon against me." I grinned. "You can have a lot of fun deciding which. Meanwhile, do you have people keeping an eye on us? Two men in a small black Mercedes, for instance?"

"No."

I stared at her hard. "If you're lying, you're apt to lose some friends, Mrs. Watrous. One slim, dark, intense-looking, one of the long-haired pretty-boys, clean-shaven. The other huskier and whiskerier and not so dark. You're sure they're not yours? It wouldn't bother you if I dealt with them a bit, let us say, drastically?''

She swallowed. ''I do not understand what you suspect me of, Matt. If there is somebody following us, it is none of my doing, nobody I know; I swear it. But if you really mean to *kill* . . . Of course it would bother me if you killed them. It would bother me if you killed anybody. What do you think I am?''

I watched the hand that held the pistol. I said, ''I'm very glad you asked that question, Astrid. And I'm happy to answer it. That's why I organized this discussion session, to let a little honesty into our relationship. If you really want to know, I think you're a lady who's leading me on a wild-goose chase into darkest Scandinavia, for reasons yet undetermined. A lady who, in order to con my chief into assigning me to protect her, fed herself some pulse-accelerator pills to put herself into the hospital. That's who I think you are, sweetheart. Since you asked.''

There was a lengthy silence. Astrid's face was shocked and white. She whispered at last, ''You must be joking!''

''Sure, sure,'' I said. ''Just a great big kidder, that's Helm.''

She licked her lips. ''But . . . but you can't believe I deliberately brought on that attack of . . . Why, I almost died!''

''Yes, that must have been a nasty surprise,'' I said. ''And things had been going so well, too! There you were in the hospital with everything under control, ready to smile at me courageously from your sickbed, pale but lovely. Of course it was easy for you to be brave then. You knew your tachycardia was phony, induced by a careful dose of stimulant, self-administered; probably one of the compounds on the list the heart specialist gave me. You knew that even without treatment you'd soon be back to normal. It wasn't hard to play the poor martyred lady bearing her cross heroically. But you were unlucky; they picked quinine to treat you with. Nobody knew you were sensitive to the stuff, including you. Suddenly that night it went all grim and real on you, didn't it? It wasn't a charade any longer. The gent with the skull face was right there by your bed rattling his bones and breathing his graveyard breath on you. . . ."

She shook her head impatiently. "Please spare me the picturesque imagery!"

I said, "Sweetie, I've been there. I know that guy very well. One of my best friends, or enemies. Sometimes it's hard to tell the difference. Anyway, you hadn't expected anything like that; you weren't prepared for it at all."

She started to say something, and stopped. We listened to a man and woman entering a room across the hall. The woman was laughing at something the man had said as if he was the sweetest, funniest man in the world, and maybe he was.

I went on: "So when I arrived, there you were, still not quite sure you were even going to live, and not knowing, if you did live, if you'd be permanently damaged in some way. And the thing you couldn't bear to think about was that you'd done it to yourself: the clever, clever girl who'd outsmarted herself so ridiculously, and wound up lying there helpless, hooked up to a lot of medical plumbing, looking like something that had been pulled through a knothole backwards. Instead of the brave, bright, charming, convalescent glamour girl I'd been supposed to find there, and fall for, hard."

Astrid regarded me for a long moment. At last she took a deep swallow from her glass that left it empty, and gave a defiant little shrug that admitted everything.

"You can't prove it!"

I rose and refilled her glass, and replenished my own drink. Standing there, I studied her thoughtfully, until she looked down in a flustered way and did something feminine

to the lacy ruffles at her breast. I grinned and raised my
glass to her, seating myself again.

"For a beautiful lady, you're a damn' good man, Watrous," I said. "But you have some very corny reactions.
Why the hell should I want to prove anything? You know
the gag you tried to pull. I know. I can't see that it's anybody else's business, can you?"

She frowned quickly. "I don't understand." When I
didn't say anything, she asked, "How did you guess?"

"Well, you were much too bitter about that quinine reaction, as if you'd been double-crossed by somebody you
trusted; and I guess you had been. By yourself, your own
body. And you were working so hard."

"What do you mean?"

"The Bible covers it very neatly: *The guilty flee where
none pursue.* If I've got it right, and it is the Bible. Anyway, you were like a dame with an inconspicuous little run
in her stocking, horribly self-conscious, feeling that everybody must be staring at her. Pulling at her skirt, crossing
her legs awkwardly, anything to keep the dreadful blemish
out of sight, actually calling attention to what she's trying
to hide. Only you were trying to cover up the fact, which
seemed guiltily obvious to you now that everything had
gone wrong, that you'd put yourself into that hospital deliberately."

Astrid licked her lips. "For an undercover operator, you
are a very great mind reader."

"Thanks, but it didn't take telepathy. You're a lousy
actress, or maybe just a lousy criminal. At least what you'd
done to yourself seemed like a crime to you, didn't it? And
of course you were in bad shape and not thinking very
clearly, so you let yourself go off in all directions at once.
Practically charging the medical staff with malpractice at
the same time as you accused Karin Segerby of attempted
murder, to her face as well as to me. You even threw me
the name, Lysaniemi, just to keep my mind occupied, so

76

I wouldn't think too hard about you and your medical situation and how you might have got that way. Of course, the following morning you realized that you'd overreacted, and backed off from a lot of the wild stuff you'd said."

Astrid grimaced. "It still seems very clairvoyant to me."

I said, "There were other inconsistencies. The way you'd been beating at the gates of bureaucracy to help you find the missing husband you were supposedly mad about; but then it turned out you really weren't too crazy about him after all, or too jealous of the lady he'd run off with. You even asked me to give the lovebirds a helping hand. And finally, so weak you could hardly stand, you let me carry you off to Europe without any significant protests. Ordinarily, a lady as ill as you were would have screamed rape and murder at being asked to travel even across the street; you accompanied me stoically across an ocean, and didn't even complain about leaving behind your good suitcase and all your nice clothes except those you'd worn to the hospital. Why? Could it be that the original plan had been to decoy me over here, using the name Lysaniemi; and since I was being so beautifully cooperative, you felt you had no choice but to play along, regardless of the risks and sacrifices involved? Very admirable, ma'am, very brave considering your condition, but just a little suspicious under the circumstances."

She smiled slowly. "It is a very good thing you are not married. What woman would want a husband who could see through all her little deceits and subterfuges?"

"As a matter of fact I had a wife once; but that wasn't why she left me." I looked at the handsome lady in the elaborate, inexpensive negligee. "It's motive time," I said. "What's this all about, Astrid?"

She shook her head minutely. "I cannot tell you that, yet. Soon, perhaps, but not yet."

I said, "Your husband disappears, with feminine company. A lady named Beilstein disappears, with masculine company. Various other people disappear in equally plausible ways, at least so I'm told. You come to us for help in finding your missing hubby. Not satisfied with what's being done for you, you stage a phony heart episode—never mind that it backfired—to hint at a possible murder attempt and get a private bodyguard assigned to you by my chief, who then up and vanishes in his turn. Meanwhile, courageously overcoming your own weakness, you're leading the tame agent you've acquired, me, out of the U.S. and up into the Scandinavian Arctic to find a village with a funny name where the greatest excitement ever is probably the arrival of the reindeer with the weekly mail. Tell me something that makes sense of all this, sweetheart." I stared at her grimly; but she shook her head and remained silent. At last I shrugged. "Well, okay, for the time being. Let's see how it breaks. But please remember that the resemblance between me and a nice guy is fairly superficial. Next time I ask, I'll get an answer. One way or another."

She studied my face for a moment; then she smiled slowly. "You are very tough, are you not? Will you please show me what you hold in your right hand?"

I brought the hand into sight with the palm-sized .25 automatic I'd released from its clip earlier in the conversation. I said, "I don't like to be the only character in a room not holding a gun."

She glanced down quickly at the Smith and Wesson that still reposed in her lap, and seemed surprised to see it. "Oh."

"'I was trying to learn something," I said. "I thought it would be useful to see your reaction when I threw some nasty accusations at you, and you had a firearm handy."

"Did I pass the test?"

"Your hand never twitched," I said. "Your knuckles never even whitened. Obviously Mr. Smith and Mr. Wesson were wasting their time inventing that thing, as far as you're concerned. Even when pushed into a corner you don't think in gunpowder terms.''

She smiled. ''Maybe it was not so much of a corner you pushed me into, my dear. Or maybe I just knew I could not win doing battle on your terms. An amateur against a professional.''

''And maybe you're just a nice lady playing a crazy game of some kind that you don't feel is worth killing for. . . . No, keep the piece. You've earned it and you may need it before we're through, or I may. In the street gangs, I understand, the moll always carries the heater so if her man is frisked he comes up clean. I don't think my terminology is up to date, but who can keep track of the jargon nowadays?'' I looked at her. ''Tired?''

She nodded. ''I think I could sleep for a week.''

''Well, after that SAS breakfast, I guess we don't have to worry about lunch, so you've got until tonight sometime. I won't make any predictions beyond that. I could use some rest myself; I'll take a little snooze on the other bed. I'll try not to disturb you when I go out, unless you want to be waked for dinner.''

''No, please just let me sleep if I'm still asleep.''

She was.

CHAPTER 9

EVEN well after dark, the traffic on the big boulevard didn't seem to have diminished much. The cars zipping by were smaller on the average than you'd find in the U.S., even these economical days. The trucks were smaller, too, but the steady rumble was just about the same as you'd hear along a busy route leading into any large American city. It was hard to remember that I was in a foreign land where I didn't even speak the language.

I'd had a leisurely, lonely dinner in the flossier of the motel's two restaurants. It had plushy chairs and linen tablecloths. It even served cocktails if you hit them between four and ten pee em. Afterwards, I'd read for a while, sitting in the lobby so as not to disturb my roommate. Although we were in the Land of the Midnight Sun, that's a summer phenomenon and this was only spring, so I didn't have to wait much past eight for darkness. Now, having slipped out of one of the rear doors of the motel, I stood for a moment listening to the murmur of traffic from the highway in front of the building. It was still loud enough, back here, that it would have made a good cover for sneaking up on somebody, since even if you were careless and snapped all the twigs and kicked all the pebbles, nobody would have heard. However, I didn't have anybody to sneak up on. Yet.

I moved cautiously around the corner into the shelter of some decorative planting at the side of the motel, and studied the situation further. The parking lot was L-shaped. Most of it, including the space occupied by the Mercedes, was at the front, where I couldn't see it from my present position, but an arm of it extended down the side of the building towards me. It was there that I'd parked the little Volksie-Ford. Although I'd picked the spot simply because it was open, I could hardly have done better. There were only a couple of places from which the car could be kept under observation inconspicuously.

Not that I'd sneaked out of my room to watch my own car. I'd come out to see if I could spot somebody else watching it. I was operating on the theory that there were only two of them, so they couldn't cover all the exits of the sprawling motel. I'd taken the precaution of paying for the night in advance, not knowing how things would break, so there was no point in their watching the lobby to see if I checked out, since I could leave quite legitimately without doing so. For one of them to spend the night lurking in the corridor outside our room, keeping an eye on the door, would have been fairly conspicuous. They were pretty well forced to gamble that we had no alternative transportation available; that if we decided to slip away we'd do it in the rental Golf.

The evening was misty, and there were no stars. Dressed in stiff new jeans, a navy-blue turtleneck, and fancy-looking blue-and-white jogging shoes, courtesy of the same cutrate emporium that had supplied Astrid's sexy lingerie, I made a study of the terrain and decided that, since he wasn't hiding in the ornamental shrubbery with me, the watcher had to be located in the bushes at the foot of one of the steeply sloping yards of one of the small houses on the hillside behind and above the parked cars. The angle was considerable, but the Norwegians have had plenty of practice at making their dwellings stick to precipitous mountainsides. Considering their geography, they should be almost as good at it as the Swiss.

I was tempted to go hunting; but that was the restlessness of inactivity working in me. Well, relative inactivity. I'd spent too many days recently sitting in cars and planes, clear from Mexico to Norway by way of a large part of the U.S.A. and the Atlantic Ocean. I'd had it with sitting. I cringed at the thought of spending further hours in these prickly damn' bushes making like an evergreen. Action, action. Track the young bastards to their lairs, smoke them out. . . . But that was not the way to go here.

I had to remember who I was and who I was up against. I was an experienced older agent dealing with, if my guess was correct, a couple of possibly well trained but probably inexperienced young men sent after me by my own agency. Always assuming that Astrid had been telling the truth when she'd disowned them; and that I hadn't overlooked some-body else with a motive for keeping track of our movements. But whoever they were working for, they hadn't been around as long as I had. They hadn't been in the business as long as I had. Impatience might be their problem; I couldn't let it be mine.

Resignedly I made myself comfortable—well, more or less—where I could watch the steep, dark hillside. There was some illumination from the streetlights and the lights of the motel, but I wished I had one of those fancy image-intensifying gadgets they've been passing around lately; or just a pair of good $7 \times 50$ binoculars. However, when they did relieve the watch, I had no trouble seeing them. By that time I was very damp and cold, and wishing for a heavy coat; but the hint of movement against the vague patches of snow below the small yellow clapboard house on the hillside made me forget my discomfort instantly.

It was the right-hand of the three houses up there. The other two were barn-red with white trim; but the colors were almost indistinguishable in the night. I saw a dim figure disappear into the brush at the foot of the lot to my right. Presently another dim figure appeared, heading back in the direction the first one had come from; it moved in a less-agile fashion. I felt a certain sympathy: he'd be as cold and stiff as I was after his long stakeout. Well, maybe not quite as stiff, since he was younger. Anyway, my hunch had paid off.

Moving cautiously, keeping low, I slipped out of my evergreen nest and through the decorative shrubbery to the fence that bounded the motel property on this side. It was wooden and solidly built in good Scandinavian fashion, painted white, and about five feet high. Still crouching, I followed the fence to the right behind the rear parking lot that seemed to be earmarked for utility and delivery vehi-cles, along with some cars that probably belonged to the motel and restaurant staff. It was well lighted, a little too well for my liking. The fence ended at a small road that passed along that side of the motel and continued up the slope behind it, serving the houses up there. Some junk was piled inside the end of the fence, empty crates and discarded cartons too big for the trash bins, awaiting pickup. I found shelter among them and waited.

He'd done a good job up on the hill, sitting commendably motionless so I'd been unable to spot his location in four hours of watching. But now he made the mistake the inexperienced ones often make: he relaxed before he was actually home free. Well, he was safely out of the danger zone, wasn't he? His partner had taken over, and he was off-duty without a care in the world, heading back to his room to catch up on his sleep. When they're hunting you, particularly if there are more of them than there are of you, it so seldom occurs to them that you might have the temerity to turn around and come hunting them.

Through a crack in the fence I watched him march openly down the small paved road towards me, swinging his arms vigorously to warm himself after his long vigil. Suspecting nothing, he was taken completely by surprise when, as he passed the end of the fence, I rose up and threw the lock on him from behind. He was too big for me to mess with. The other, smaller one I might have tried to take alive; not this husky character. I gave it maximum effort instantly, therefore, and felt certain important items break in certain important places. I held him like that until there were no more kicks or quivers or spasmodic tremors left in him; and even a little longer. Too many good men have died— well, they thought they were good—because they were too sensitive, spelled queasy, to make absolutely certain.

Even now, after midnight, the boulevard made a satisfactory background rumble. There had been a little noise: the scuffle of feet, some heavy breathing—mostly mine, since my grip hadn't let him have much air—and a small, scraping, splintering sound as our straining bodies lurched against a wooden crate and rammed it back into the trash pile. However, with the covering noise of the traffic, nobody seemed to have noticed.

Releasing him at last, I stood over him for a moment catching my breath. Then I dragged him out of sight behind the sheltering junk and checked his pockets quickly. Wallet. Passport. Room key. And what I had hoped to find, confirmation: the familiar agency assassination piece with its built-in silencer—excuse me; I forgot, we're supposed to call them sound suppressors these double-talk days. I'll admit I drew a breath of relief at learning that I hadn't killed an innocent stranger.

To be sure, he was a stranger to me, but I never know all the new, young ones, and the weapon in my hand made it certain that I'd estimated the situation correctly. Bennett had sent this character after me with takeout orders; and an official takeout weapon with which to execute them. Execute being the operative word. That gun is not issued for defensive purposes.

As I straightened up with my loot, I thought I caught a glimpse of movement at the lighted rear door out of which I'd sneaked several hours earlier. I stood quite still, waiting, but nothing further happened over there, if anything had. I hesitated, and said to hell with it. If somebody was calling the Oslo constabulary, I'd know soon enough. There was an ugly smell from the man at my feet. The sphincters had let go as they often do. Carting dead bodies around isn't quite the nice clean fun they make it seem in certain jolly murder mysteries, literary and cinematic. However, I was going to have to move this one; but first I had to find out where.

I was fairly sure they hadn't been using the same rear door that I'd employed. Hiding just around the corner, I'd have heard something. I headed for the street side of the building, therefore. The first opening I found there was locked, and there was a small sign behind the glass that I translated, roughly: *Between Hours of 1000 and 0600 Be So Good as to Employ Front Entrance.*

But my homicidal young friends would have made provision for re-entering the building without passing the front desk. I made my way to the next side door. It bore the same sign; however, it hadn't latched properly due to a Norwegian paperback novel—a Scandinavian-Gothic romance by the cover—jammed between the threshold and the bottom of the door. I slipped inside, reflecting that it was no way to treat a good book, or even a bad one. I checked the room key I'd confiscated. Number 137 was just down the corridor, left-hand side, very convenient. I entered the room, hauled the coverlet off one of the beds, and went back out to the dead man and rolled him up in it. Traffic still ran busily on the big main drag, but the side street was empty, and everything was quiet around the motel. I caught no further uneasy hints of movement anywhere.

I drew a long breath and went into my Hercules act, hoisting the long bedspread-wrapped bundle to my shoulder and staggering off with it. By the time I got him to the room, he weighed at least four hundred pounds. Panting, I dumped him onto the bed I'd stripped, and straightened up painfully, rubbing my back. I yearned for a drink, but there seemed to be no liquor on the premises. The idea of being stalked by a pair of earnest, dedicated, young teetotalers was a little frightening. You like to think that, like you, the opposition, whatever it may be at a given time, has a few human weaknesses. I consoled myself with the thought that maybe, being of the younger generation, they took their comfort from drugs instead of booze.

James Aloysius Harley was the name on the passport. Unmarried. Occupation, newspaper reporter—at least for this assignment. Credit cards. Membership cards. Press cards. American money. Norwegian money. Swedish money. So they had apparently learned from Research about my interest in a certain village up in Swedish Lapland, as I'd anticipated. Preparing to follow me there, they had supplied themselves with suitable currency, which was more than I had done.

I studied the gun. It was the short-barreled High Standard .22 automatic that looks like the Colt Woodsman, although the lines aren't as graceful; but the old Woodsman, like many fine old things, is no longer in production. Not that the High Standard isn't a good enough gun; and it has one big advantage. The barrel is removable, meaning that you can pull off and ditch the silenced barrel, highly illegal just about anywhere, and stick on a plain barrel, and have a gun that's only moderately lawless in most jurisdictions and doesn't convict you on sight of being a professional hit man. The clip held a full complement of ten rounds, but there was nothing in the chamber; he hadn't anticipated any emergencies requiring instant artillery. Searching the room more thoroughly, I found no spare pistol barrels; but each man had a box of match grade ammunition in his suitcase, each box with ten cartridges missing out of the fifty.

It looked as if Bennett had been passing out silenced agency automatics to everybody in sight. I knew that the boys were not employing the target stuff for super precision; they were using it simply because it was slower than the .22 ammo you buy off the shelf. The speed of sound is 1,088 feet per second. It was discovered long ago that for maximum accuracy an ordinary .22 bullet must not be driven faster than that. So farm kids shoot rabbits and squirrels with .22 caliber projectiles that scream along at around 1,200 feet per second, but expert smallbore target shooters settle for something like 1,050.

This has another advantage of more importance than championship accuracy to the sinister folk in our line of work. A silencer—to hell with the latter-day jargon—can muffle the noise of the powder exploding inside the gun, but it can't do anything about the crack of the bullet, outside the gun, passing through the sound barrier. Keeping the bullet velocity subsonic is, therefore, essential to silencing a gun effectively, which was why my pursuers had chosen the relatively slow target ammo to kill me with.

Presumably they'd been waiting to deal with me in a more private place than the capital city of Norway. I had no doubt they had people standing by to dispose of the body or bodies discreetly after the silent execution. In his precarious position as temporary director of the agency, Bennett couldn't afford to leave corpses around. It might be noticed in Washington that some U.S. agents were busily killing off others at his orders.

I stuck the weapon inside my waistband and approached the figure on the bed reluctantly. By the time I got through, Mr. James Aloysius Harley looked as if he were nicely tucked in and sleeping peacefully; but it hadn't been the most pleasant task I'd ever performed. I made a bundle of the soiled stuff, hauled it into the bathroom, dumped it into the tub, and closed the door on it. Then I turned out the light and sat down to wait some more. This time I had a warm room and a comfortable chair, so it wasn't too bad, even if the company left something to be desired.

I figured dawn would be the time. Mr. Harley's partner wouldn't be likely to hang around in somebody's backyard after daylight. Unfortunately, I had no almanac to tell me when the sun was supposed to rise in this part of the world at this time of year. All I could do was peek through the window curtains occasionally. They were the heavy light-proof draperies provided in that part of the world to let you sleep at those times of the year when the day lasts most of the night. We weren't in that season yet, but some time after four the luminous misty sky out there seemed suddenly to be a little grayer than it had been. Then I heard his footsteps in the carpeted hall outside, and his key in

87

the lock. I slipped into the dressing alcove just before the door opened and the room light went on.

"Jesus Christ, Jim!" said the young man in the doorway angrily, after surveying the peaceful scene. "What the hell do you think you're doing; you're supposed to be dressed and ready to go in case they make an early start. . . . Come on, Sleeping Beauty, rise and shine!" He was over by the bed now, shaking the figure under the cover. It rolled over onto its back, displaying the slack gaping mouth and the staring blind eyes. "Oh, my God!"

"Just hold that pose, amigo," I said.

Standing in the doorway behind him, I held the silenced automatic on him, cartridge in chamber, safety off. There was a tense moment while he thought of various things he'd been taught to do in such a situation. He decided not to do them.

"Helm?"

"It ain't Santa, Sonny. Okay, you can turn around now, very slowly."

Holding his hands safely clear of his sides, he swung around to face me. His face was contorted with shock and anger.

"You killed Jim, you damn' traitor!"

"Unbuckle your belt and drop your pants," I said. "And I want to hear a good, solid thump when they hit the floor. Like there was something in them, a gun perhaps." When he didn't move, I said, "What's your name? The one on your current passport will do."

He was watching the automatic in my hand and thinking hard, planning hard perhaps. We were both aware that the .22 is not a manstopper like the .38; even that is marginal. He might make it. He'd have some little holes in him, but he might manage. He might get his own pistol out. He might even put a bullet into me; but it would also be a .22 and the chances of its being instantly fatal weren't overwhelming. It would be a brave sacrifice play, but it prob-

88

ably wouldn't bring in the winning run. To hell with it, there'd be better chances later. That's what we always tell ourselves when we don't feel like dying today.

"Lindner," he said. "Marshall Lindner."

"The pants," I said. "Strip right down, please. . . . Now the sweater and shirt and undershirt. And the shorts and shoes and socks. Turn around slowly. Nothing taped to the body beautiful, swell. Okay, you can pull the shorts back on if you're feeling modest. Sit in that chair by the window, please."

He did as he was told. Sitting there, looking scrawny and vulnerable in his knitted jockey shorts—he was one of the dark, wiry ones; and I judged he'd be fast but not dangerously strong—he regarded me bleakly.

"They said you were very polite and always said excuse me when you shot a man to death. Or a woman."

"Or a baby, like you?" I grimaced. "What kind of dumb-dumb games were you boys playing on that hillside, anyway? Four-hour watches, for God's sake! The way you were milling around up there at midnight, it was like watching the changing of the guard at Buckingham Palace. What's the matter, can't you little fellows sit still a whole night? You've got to go peepee, maybe? They must be slipping, out at the Ranch, to turn loose a couple of incompetent infants like you." I looked at him, frowning. "What's this traitor crap, anyway?"

"Are you denying it?"

"I don't have to deny anything, friend. I'm holding the gun. Are you denying that you and your friend were sent here to kill me with your cute little noiseless peashooters?"

I kicked at the clothes on the floor, felt a solid object, and reached down for it left-handed; but it was the Nordic paperback romance that had been keeping the outside door from latching. I tossed it aside and tried again. This time I got a silenced High Standard just like the one I was holding.

I said, "One for me and one for my female companion, right? Did you flip coins to see which of you comic hitmen would get the great sexy thrill of shooting a woman?" He flushed, and I saw how it was and said, "Or did you feel sentimental and flip to see which of you wouldn't have to. The ladies will hate you, Lindner. That's sexual discrimination. What did they ever do to you, that you won't treat them as equal to men, even with a pistol? Who won me?"

"Won? Oh, well, I did." He licked his lips and went on quickly: "Big funny talk for a defector!"

"Who am I supposed to be defecting to, the local chapter of Vikings Incorporated? Do I get to ride in a dragon ship, with my own battle-axe and horned helmet, just like a real Norseman?" I grimaced at the young man who'd won the right to kill me, and wondered if I'd been heads or tails. "Incidentally, I read somewhere that they didn't really wear those horns, that's movie stuff. Some people take all the romance out of life, dammit."

Lindner glared at me. "A lot of words saying nothing! We know all about you, Helm. The hotshot secret agent; the chief's right-hand man. Only the great Mister Mac thought he wasn't being given the recognition he deserved, so he sulked and sold out; and now you're on your way to join him. He's got it all arranged for you, hasn't he?"

"Tell me about it."

"Oh, we know where you plan to contact your Russian friends. It's a little village called Lysaniemi, population one-fifty, up in northern Sweden. You slipped there, Helm, trying to get information about the place out of Research; but of course that was while you thought you'd still have people high up in the organization to cover for you. Like Barnett, who was slated for the top spot, reporting daily to Mac in Moscow no doubt; only he had to duck for cover very fast, didn't he? And your slippery friend Joel. Well, your fancy little subversion scheme didn't turn out so well, and we'll catch your accomplices eventually. In the meantime we've done some work on Lysaniemi for you. In case you didn't know, it's on a small lake called Porkkajärvi—*järvi* means lake in Finnish, and there seem to be a lot of Finnish names in that part of Sweden. It's still frozen at this time of year, solid enough for a helicopter to land; and the Russian border is only . . .'' He stopped. ''What do you find so humorous now, Mr. Helm?''

I stopped laughing and said, ''You've been smoking that dreamy-stuff again. You ought to watch that.'' He started to speak angrily, and checked himself. I went on: ''The Swedish space program is centered at Kiruna, about a hundred and twenty miles northwest of Lysaniemi. I think they're planning a launch soon; it seems unlikely they'd welcome gate-crashers. And the biggest military installation in Sweden, as far as I know—it was the biggest last time I was in the country—is at Boden, a real fortress of a place, only some sixty miles southwest of Lysaniemi. Do you really think a Russky whirlybird is going to try to make it first across a couple of hundred miles of Finland where the radars can see it coming, and then across this sensitive frontier and into this sensitive security zone of northern Sweden? Do you think even the dumbest Russian is stupid enough to think he can make an air pickup there without attracting attention? After the continuing scares about Russian subs down along the Baltic coast, the Swedes are paranoid as hell about anything approaching their country from the east. Anything larger than a Commie mosquito will set the sirens wailing and the red lights flashing. Even if I wanted to go to Russia, there isn't the remotest chance of my doing it that way. You're hallucinating, or somebody is.''

''Then why were you so interested in Lysaniemi?'' When I didn't answer, Lindner shook his head abruptly. ''Shit, what difference does it make where you're planning to cross? Maybe we've got that wrong, but the fact that you're going over is obvious. Now.''

"How do you figure that?"

"You're here, aren't you? Why else would you slip off to Europe without clearing with anybody?" He waved his hand at the bed. "And if you aren't guilty, if you're not a defector, why would you kill Jim Harley, a man from your own agency?"

I stared at him incredulously. "My God, who've they got teaching you kids now out in the Arizona desert, Elsie Dinsmore and the Little Colonel? Look at me, Sonny. I'm twice your age; and if you have any ambition to make it as long as I have, listen closely. This is the basic principle you've got to remember: if something comes after you with a gun, if *anything* comes after you with a gun, it isn't human and it belongs to no agency and you owe it nothing. Stomp it quick before it stomps you. I earned that knowledge with a lot of hospital time, Buster; it could have been grave time if I hadn't been lucky. I'm handing it to you free of charge."

"That's no justification—"

"Bullshit. The fact that I'm breathing and he isn't, and he intended to have it the other way around, is all the justification I need. I'm not going to take a quiet little forty-grain bullet in the back of my skull, I'm not going to run the slightest risk of taking a quiet little forty-grain bullet in the back of my skull, just because a dumb young agent bought a lot of crappy misinformation about me from a gent in Washington who happens to be an expert at shoveling that kind of manure. Your partner was armed and stalking me. Or Mrs. Watrous, who's under my protection, but that's the same thing. It wasn't my job to have a heart-to-heart talk with him and tell him what a big mistake he was making, and maybe get my head blown off trying to persuade him that he should lay off because I'm really a very patriotic guy. No, it was his job to get his facts straight before he set out to kill people. He didn't do it, so now he's dead. And you'd be dead, too, if I didn't need you to bury him and take a message back to Mr. Bennett.''

''If you think I'm going to—''

''You're going to,'' I said. ''If you give it a little thought, you'll see you have no choice. Mr. Bennett can't afford to have any dead agents lying around, whether or not their names are Helm. You've got the machinery all set up for making a body disappear, haven't you? My body. And maybe Mrs. Watrous' body. Well, put your dead pal into that hopper and push the button and disappear him instead of us. And then deliver a message to that guy in Washington?''

''What message?''

I said, ''Tell your Mr. Bennett that I said that obviously I made a mistake out in Santa Fe, New Mexico, a couple of years back. I didn't shoot him then, when I had a great opportunity; but I'm not too proud to admit my errors and correct them. Tell him that if he keeps looking down the street, sooner or later he'll see me coming for him. He'll have to wait till I clear up this business; then I'll take care of him. This time permanently.''

''My God, you're an arrogant bastard!'' Lindner stared at me for a moment, and frowned. ''You're bluffing, aren't you?''

I said, ''You don't know me, but Bennett does. I don't think he'll kid himself that I'm bluffing. And since you've got another chance to live, why don't you spend a little time asking yourself why he picked a couple of puppies like you and Harley to run down a battle-scarred wolf like me, instead of selecting a brace of seasoned old hounds that might have been able to handle me. Could it be that he couldn't sell his subversion-defection scenario to the old-timers in the outfit, so he had to use a couple of gullible kids?''

''He didn't know how far the corruption had spread in

93

the agency. He didn't know how many of the older men . . ."

"Sure, sure," I said. "He's a very persuasive guy. Handsome and impressive, too, with that big Roman nose, the kind of man you enjoy taking orders from, right? A commanding presence, I believe it's called. Makes you feel all warm inside to know that a man like that trusts you and has confidence in your ability to carry out his instructions even though you're a bit short of experience. Well, no hard feelings, I hope."

I'd already pocketed one of the silenced automatics. Now I rammed the other under my belt and held out my hand in a friendly fashion. Kid stuff: kiss and make up. He hesitated, almost falling for it, but he wasn't quite dumb enough. I saw the sudden hope in his eyes as he realized what a beautiful opening I was giving him. He took my hand and made the obvious move. He was as fast as I'd expected, but I was ready for him. I countered with an instant wrist lock that immobilized him and left him twisted around to ease the pressure, gasping with pain. Holding him right-handed, freeing my left hand, I found the little spring-loaded hypo that was ready in my pocket, and fired it into his bare thigh.

"Relax, you're not dying," I said when he struggled against the agonizing grip, wide-eyed with sudden panic. "You'll wake up in four hours as good as new. Sleep well."

When I returned to the room I shared with Astrid Watrous, she was asleep; but she wasn't wearing the lacy nightie in which I'd last seen her. She was lying on top of the covers, facedown, dressed like me, in jeans and jersey and rubber-soled shoes. She stirred when I closed the door behind me. After a moment she rolled over and sat up abruptly to stare at me. I saw that her face was streaked with old tears.

"I saw you!" she breathed. "I woke up in the middle

of the night and you were still gone, so I dressed and slipped out to see if maybe I could help you in some way. Help, my God! I saw you, I tell you! I saw you kill him and carry him inside. The poor boy never had a chance. You caught him from behind and murdered him in cold blood.''

The old directional fetish. I have never figured out why clobbering a northbound victim when you're standing south of him is so much worse than annihilating one heading south, but they've all got this thing about front and back, as if it matters to a corpse which side it was killed from. But at least I knew I hadn't been hallucinating when I thought I saw something move by the motel's back door.

"You never listen," I said. "I told you any resemblance between me and a nice guy was strictly accidental. Now stop talking sentimental nonsense and pack your things. Washing your face wouldn't hurt, but it isn't mandatory. We're getting out of here.''

CHAPTER 10

WE left Oslo by the harbor road that continues south down the coast for a little, after which it forks and you have to decide whether you're going to keep on along the water—the eighty-mile-wide sound between Norway and Denmark called Skagerrak—or turn inland. Either way you'll hit Sweden.

Driving, I spoke without looking at my companion: "In case you're wondering, the second guy is resting peacefully in the same room as his defunct partner. No, I didn't kill him, I just used some sleepy-stuff on him that'll give us roughly a four-hour start on them, unless somebody doesn't believe the *Forstyrre Icke* sign I hung on the doorknob. It does mean 'Do Not Disturb,' doesn't it?''

''Yes.''

She wasn't speaking to me, except for monosyllables like that. We were driving along the four-lane highway in sparse morning traffic and weak misty daylight. She sat silent and pale beside me, still in her jeans and turtleneck, but she had taken time to wash her face, put on a touch of lipstick, and do up her hair. But she'd done nothing about her air of horrified disapproval.

I said, ''Reach into my right-hand jacket pocket, please. Take out what you find there.''

She hesitated, and put her hand where I'd asked her to. She glanced at me sharply, startled, and drew out one of the silenced automatics. Holding it very gingerly, keeping the muzzle away from both of us, she drew back the slide just far enough to expose the chamber and released it again.

''Good girl,'' I said. ''Your lady-cop friend did a swell gun-safety job on you. No cartridge in the breech, right? Now take a good look at that gun, because it's what that poor boy you were weeping for was going to use to kill you with.''

There was a lengthy silence. Astrid licked her lips and spoke at last: ''Matt, I do not understand.''

''What's so hard to understand?'' I asked. ''We agreed that Bennett likes the job he usurped when my chief went missing, and wants Mac to stay right where he is, disappeared, vanished. In the end, killed; at least I'm sure Bennett hopes so and will take steps to see that it happens. In the meantime, any potential rescuers have to be wiped out, along with any potential assistants who may know too much. Which means you. The late James Aloysius Harley, whatever his real name may have been, was issued that neat little pistol for the job. Which job he will unfortunately be unable to perform because I just wrang his neck for him. Wrung? Wringed?''

"Don't, Matt!'' She swallowed hard. "I'm sorry. I didn't realize. . . . But how could you be *sure*?''

"Sure that they meant to kill us?'' I shrugged. "If I'd wound up murdering an innocent bystander, I'd have been sorry as hell; but not half as sorry as if he'd murdered me. In this racket, if you wait until you're absolutely, for-sure certain, you generally wind up dead.''

She said stiffly, "I don't think I could ever take such a casual attitude towards human life.''

"And it makes you feel very virtuous,'' I said. "But you wind up owing your life to a wicked, careless, homicidal creep like me.''

After a moment, she shrugged, dismissing the subject, and turned to look at the passing Norwegian scenery of small, hilly farms—I'd have hated to plow some of those fields without a surefooted mountain horse, to hell with tractors.

"Where do we drive now?'' Astrid asked at last.

I said, "That's what Bennett will want to know, when he learns that his boys have lost contact. Among other things they've lost, like lives and guns.''

"What do you think he'll order them to do next, Matt?''

"Let's look at it from the point of view of the guys behind us. By the time they dispose of the body and call in a suitable replacement and get back into the action, they'll know we have a considerable head start. Say we can average fifty MPH on these highways, four hours lead time will put us a couple of hundred miles away, roughly three hundred kilometers using the local unit of measurement. What direction? Well, they'll also know that we'll be heading north eventually, since we seem to have a thing about a certain Arctic community. They could just relax and set up shop there and wait for us to come to them. However, they won't be very happy doing that.''

"Why not?"

"That's their backup, their last line of defense. If they miss me there, I'm gone for good. And I've threatened their leader; they can't afford to let me slip through to carry out my . . . What did you say?"

"You didn't tell me that."

"I didn't sense a great deal of sympathetic interest in my homicidal activities."

"Please do not rub it in. What did you say you would do to Mr. Bennett, kill him?"

I grinned. "I'm going to have to switch girls. This one's learning too much about me. Sure I said I'd massacre him. I said, what did he expect when he sent people out to assassinate me, a bouquet of roses? I said that his termination will be my next job, self-assigned, after I've finished the one assigned me by Mac."

She hesitated. "I don't want to criticize, Matt, but what do you gain by making wild threats like that."

"Bennett isn't the bravest man in the world, and he has good reason to know, if other people don't, that I don't generally make threats I have no intention of carrying out. If I say I'll go hunting, sooner or later I'll go hunting. Him." I gave her another cheerful grin. "I'm putting pressure on him, sweetheart, turning on the heat. He may have felt calm and uninvolved, sitting there in Washington sending out the guns; now I've made it personal, him or me. And he's not forgetting that I came after him once before and got him. Unfortunately I let him go, but with his life definitely on the line this time, and that old grudge gnawing at him, there's a good chance he'll fly over here to handle the troops personally. Which will be fine for us since, while he's a good enough administrator and a hell of a politician, he's not all that great a field man; he'll have them all running around in panicky circles trying to intercept us everywhere. Meanwhile, we'll be sitting tight and let them wear themselves out trying to figure where we've got to."

"Sitting tight?" she said. "Where? And why did we get off the plane in Norway instead of continuing on to Sweden, if that is where we are going anyway?"

I said, "We stopped in Oslo because the place where I want us to hole up temporarily is near Stockholm. I didn't want us to draw attention that way by disembarking there. This way we've got running room enough to make sure we arrive with no fleas or ticks or chiggers stuck to us. . . . Ah, here's our junction ahead."

The highway sign by the roadside gave us a choice between driving straight ahead to Gothenburg, or turning left to Stockholm. I turned left, and we found ourselves on a narrow, winding, little two-lane road through the mountains. Presently I pulled out at an area marked with a large P, white on blue. P for *Parkering*.

"What's the matter?" Astrid asked. "Why have we stopped?"

"Give me that .38 I lent you, please," I said, gathering up the rest of my arsenal. "My God, I can't seem to take a step these days that somebody doesn't present me with another firearm."

The hiding places I found around the car weren't very original, and any good drug sniffer could have located them in two seconds flat; but if we were subjected to that much of a search, it meant we were in trouble anyway.

"Okay, here we go," I said, getting back behind the wheel. "Swedish customs may not even make us open our suitcases, but there's no sense in taking chances. Keep your fingers crossed and hope that the Sleeping Beauty I left back in Oslo hasn't awakened prematurely and sent some friends to intercept us at the border."

Actually, we still had well over an hour of driving on that slow little twisty road before Sweden appeared ahead. Then we came to a frozen lake on the right, surrounded by snow and evergreens. Across the highway from this pretty scene was a mass of restaurants, filling stations, and souvenir shops. Just over the hill was the frontier, which consisted of no gate or barrier, just several uniformed gents standing by the roadside in front of a building that sported the blue-and-yellow Swedish flag. They waved us over. One officer came up to my window and asked for our passports, glanced at them, and handed them back.

"You have rented this car in Oslo?" He spoke in English. "Where in Sweden do you travel?"

"We're heading for Stockholm," I said.

"Be so good as to open the trunk." When I'd got out and done so, he said, "And that suitcase, please . . . Very good. That is all, thank you so much."

I took my time closing the suitcase properly, and the trunk lid, and getting back into the car beside Astrid. It didn't seem like a good time to display any haste, or show any relief. After the border installation had disappeared from sight behind us, Astrid drew a long, shaky breath.

"I will never, ever make a successful criminal," she said. "I am certain my expression was very guilty. I kept thinking of all those pistols."

"You did fine," I said. "Watching the handsome officer trustingly with your big brown eyes, obviously quite certain that such a nice young man would never do anything to distress pretty little innocent you." I grinned. "Well, we've made it into Sweden. Now all we have to do is find our hidey-hole and pull it in after us."

Perhaps because we were soon out of the mountains, the main highway across this part of Scandinavia was considerably bigger and better in Sweden than it had been back in Norway. While it was still only two lanes wide, they were larger lanes, with generous paved shoulders.

I wondered idly, as I drove, why anybody would waste so much asphalt out there on the edge of the road. Then I saw two cars roaring at me side by side, one passing the other in spite of the fact that I was right there in plain sight in the other lane, coming the other way. I noted that the driver who was being passed had swung out onto his shoulder of the road to give the other guy some room. In self-defense I eased over to put the right-hand wheels of my car onto the paved extension on my side of the road, and the passing car shot through the space we'd opened up between us. I hadn't finished swearing at the driver for being such a reckless jackass when the same thing happened again.

Okay, I could take a hint. Obviously the Swedes didn't believe in the docile, follow-the-leader driving technique favored in the U.S., where it's considered pushy and immoral to pass another car on anything but a multilane freeway. (Hey, Mister, where's the fire?) Coming up on a slower vehicle, I tried it myself. Sure enough, when he spotted my ever-burning headlights moving up in his mirror—I still felt uncomfortable at having all those lumens expending themselves in broad daylight—the driver ahead pulled over politely to let me by, and an approaching car took to the shoulder to give me room.

I decided that, although it would send the safety-minded folks back home into screaming fits, it was really a nice, sensible, cooperative way of utilizing a two-lane road to the fullest. I waved my thanks to everybody, as seemed to be expected of me, and settled down to some interesting driving. Beside me, Astrid had reclined her seat fully and fallen asleep. The pavement remained clear and mostly dry, although there was still snow in the fields we passed. They were less precipitous than those of Norway, but they'd never make you think nostalgically of the endless cornfields of Kansas. More like New England. There were numerous lakes with ice on them.

We stopped for an early lunch in Karlstad, on the largest lake in Sweden, called Vänern, an inland sea by local standards, also icebound. The snack bar served a delicious, spicy sausage that would make a bland Yankee hot dog crawl into a corner and hide its head in shame; and there

101

was a little marzipan cake for dessert that far outclassed the soggy bakery goods served in U.S. roadside eateries. Obviously we'd arrived in a backward land that had not yet mastered the modern culinary art of rendering all food tasteless. Afterwards, I took evasive action northwards, just in case Bennett, or whoever was running the local operation for him, decided to gamble on assigning a man or two to watching this main highway east in the hope that, having disabled the pursuit temporarily, we'd be overconfident enough to stay with the easy route clear across the country.

The day remained gray and misty. We ran through a single snow flurry that lasted just long enough to powder the pavement lightly without slowing us down. Dodging from one winding little road to another, we got quite a distance northeast, and then angled back to the southeast. We reached the picturesque university town of Uppsala late in the afternoon, still with no company trailing along behind. I checked this out with a brief scenic tour—well, detour—through the city. There was a massive old brick castle on a hill and a fine cathedral. There was no shadow in the mirror. Beyond Uppsala, we picked up the four-lane highway that, if you wanted to go there, would take you to Stockholm some seventy kilometers away. Forty-three miles to you.

We didn't want to go there; but I almost missed our exit. I'd been told what to look for, but Uppsala had spread southward since my last visit, so the distance was shorter than I remembered it. The sign appeared before I expected it: Krokvik, translating to Crooked Bay. It seemed an odd name for a community well inland. Actually it was a reminder that geography is not a constant in those parts. The land is rising steadily out of the sea. Nowadays the Baltic coast is many miles to the east, but within historical times it had been much closer, and the small stream we soon crossed, running between high banks, had been a river inlet large enough to be used by the Viking longships. But I found it a bit claustrophobic to be in a country I could drive across in a day, after coming from one where it had taken me the best part of a week to traverse barely half of it.

Astrid stirred beside me, opened her eyes, and jacked up the back of her seat so she could sit up and look around.

"Where are we now? What was that stream we just crossed?"

"It's called Ulvan, however you pronounce it."

"Ulvan, please. Uhlv-own. Meaning the Wolf River. *Ulv,* wolf, also called *varg. An,* the river."

"Yes, ma'am," I said.

She laughed. "I apologize. I just woke up. I did not mean to sound like a schoolteacher. . . . Then we must be near Uppsala."

"Correct. We left it about ten kilometers back up the valley while you were still asleep. And here we go, if that's the right turn ahead. The right left turn. It's a long time since I was here."

"Do you find many changes, Matt?"

I shrugged. "There weren't any four-lane highways back then, to amount to anything, and Uppsala has grown a lot, of course. But things don't look very different out here among the fields and farms."

"How far is it now?"

I'd made the turn, and we were on a very narrow unpaved farm road that was muddy in spots. However, drainage ditches on both sides carried away the water from the melting snow, so the track remained reasonably firm. A wide place was marked by a blue sign sporting a white M to indicate a meeting place—*Mötesplats* to you—where you could turn out to let opposing traffic go by, or vice versa. I waved my hand at the snowy field to the right.

"Look way over there in the trees. The place is called Torsäter. You can see the smaller white villa below the main house. Old Baron Stjernhjelm was living in the big house when I visited him, at the time of the yearly *älg*

103

hunt—as you probably know, it's a moose, not an elk as the sound of the name might make you think. But I understand that when his son got married, the old man moved into the guesthouse and let the young couple take over the mansion, if you want to call it that. It's not enormous, but it's a very handsome old place. I gathered over the phone that the old man has had to move to a sanitarium, and the little villa has reverted to its original function of a guesthouse. There's nobody in it at the moment, so we're welcome to it.''

Astrid glanced at me sharply. "Stjernhjelm?"

"I told you my dad chopped it down to something Yankees could pronounce, when he got to America."

"And Swedish titles go to all the children, not just the oldest son; so you're a baron, really?" She sounded impressed.

"Not really. My folks renounced all foreign titles when they became American citizens. It's required. You can call me Mister Helm if you wish to be formal. Even over here, they don't take that stuff too seriously these days. Old Baron Stjernhjelm always preferred to be called by the military rank he'd earned rather than the aristocratic one inherited. *Överste* Stjernhjelm. Colonel Stjernhjelm."

Astrid hesitated. "While I'm being inquisitive, I might as well ask if you got one."

"Got one what? Oh, an *älg*?" I shook my head. "I did have a good shot at one, but . . . Well, normally I enjoy hunting, but I'd just been up north shooting at people who were shooting at me. Somebody'd died whom I . . . Well, let's just say I'd seen enough death for the moment. I wasn't in the mood to inflict it upon a poor old beast that intended me no harm. Softhearted Helm. It didn't do the moose a bit of good. The gent in the next stand knocked it over with one shot."

"You're kind of a strange man, aren't you?"

"Why, because I'm always ready and willing to kill a

104

two-legged animal that's trying to kill me, but occasionally I pass up a shot at a four-legged one that isn't? Seems quite logical to me, ma'am.''

She smiled faintly. ''Perhaps, but it casts some doubt upon the validity of the bloodthirsty image you keep trying to project for me.''

I said, ''You're reading a lot into the fact that I once refrained from shooting a moose on a day when I wasn't very hungry for moose meat. Not that I'd have got any even if I'd fired. It's a community hunt. The meat is sold, and the proceeds are distributed among the landowners forming the local hunting association. All the successful hunter gets is the antlers. Well, you probably know the Scandinavian customs better than I do.'' I glanced at her. ''And now you'd better do something about your hair. We'll have to get the key from my distant female cousin at the big house; and I don't think you want to meet the local aristocracy looking like a sheepdog.''

A glance at the mirror on the back of the sun visor showed her that she was coming down rather badly after her nap. Hastily, she got to work on the job of reconstruction. Although she was naturally a tidy lady, I had the impression that she was working harder at her appearance than she normally would because she might be meeting a baroness. It disturbed me. Such respect for an outmoded title was out of character for the sensible and self-confident person she'd seemed to be.

When we pulled up at the house, in the graveled circular drive that had once accommodated handsome horses and shining carriages, the door was opened by the Swedish aristocracy in the form of a sturdy, brown-haired young woman with a pleasant face. She had a baby on her hip, sex indeterminate. The mother's complexion, like that of many Swedish girls—I remembered one called Karin Segerby—was miraculous. Behind her stood a toddler I guessed to be male, and a somewhat older child I judged

105

to be female by the long blonde hair. Except for the infant in diapers, blue jeans seemed to be the uniform of the day.

"You are Cousin Matthias . . . Matthew?" she asked. "We have been expecting you. I am Margareta." She held out her hand for me to take, and looked at Astrid. "And you must be Mrs. Vaahtruse . . . Watrous. Welcome to Torsäter."

Five minutes later, having received the key and an invitation to tea the following afternoon, when the husband, Torsten, would be home, we were letting ourselves into the villa. It had been warmed up in anticipation of our arrival, but we'd been given instructions on how to jack up the performance of the ancient heating plant in the basement in the event that we did not find the temperature high enough for our American tastes.

"Disillusioned?" I asked as I set down the bags inside.

"What do you mean?"

"A husky young baroness in jeans and sneakers with a brat on her hip? Well, it's tough to face, I know, but these days we aristocrats look just like ordinary folks. . . . Astrid."

"Yes?"

"A confession. Since they'll probably let it slip during the tea party tomorrow—Torsten Stjernhjelm was a boy when I saw him last, but he'll probably remember—I might as well confess that I do know a little Swedish, enough to get by on. Well, you're probably aware of that already."

"What makes you think so?"

"The pompous way you've been lecturing me on the language. You're not a pompous lady. I figure you've been kidding me in your sly way, right?"

She laughed. "You overdid it a little, Matt. It seemed unlikely that anybody who'd grown up in a Swedish household—even a transplanted Swedish household—would pronounce the Scandinavian words quite so badly. But what was the point?"

"Hell, we secret agents get in the habit of keeping our secrets secret," I said. "It's a simple knee-jerk reaction: *Don't never give nothing away to nobody for nothing.*" I went back to close the front door I'd left ajar. "Now let's see if we can find the baronial liquor cabinet. It's been a long, dry day."

CHAPTER 11

ALTHOUGH small by the standards of the grandiose age in which it had been built, when even the main house at Torsäter had been considered rather modest, the guest villa was a good-sized two-story dwelling in its own right. I already knew, from my previous visit, that it had a living room, dining room, and kitchen downstairs, plus a room and bath off the kitchen for the kind of live-in servant that no longer existed in this socialistic society. There were three reasonable bedrooms and a bath upstairs. Presumably it had been designed to accommodate a whole brood of younger Stjernhjelms when they came to spend the summer, or Christmas, on the old folks' estate generations ago.

It was a pleasant house with high ceilings. The walls were all papered, and the fading patterns were pleasantly old-fashioned. No Kem-tone here. The two-part upstairs bathroom was apparently an afterthought that had been inserted into a couple of preexisting closets. One small chamber was devoted to ablution, the other to excretion. The john had an overhead cistern discharged by means of a pull-chain. The bathtub was enormous, standing on feet above a drain in the tiled floor.

"My God," Astrid said. "Six fast laps up and down that tub should take care of your exercise for the day."

After the long journey that had commenced in the hospital in Hagerstown, Maryland, U.S.A., some three days ago more or less—what with the time changes I'd kind of lost track—my attractive companion had kind of folded at last, once we were safely inside the house with the door closed. That is, she'd been about to fold when I returned from locking up; and I'd steadied her and led her into the kitchen and parked her on a straight wooden chair and put a loaded glass into her hand.

Sipping my own drink, I'd figured out the elderly and feeble electric stove that had been inserted beside an even older coal-fired range. I'd heated the contents of a couple of cans I found in the pantry, peas and meatballs, if you must know. She'd discovered that her weakness was at least partly due to hunger. A cup of coffee in the rather elegant living room had finished off the meal pleasantly and given us both the strength to fight our way up the steep, curving stairway. I'd placed Astrid's suitcase in the room she selected, and mine in the one on the other side of the upstairs hall. I guess I'd picked the doorway farthest from hers to reassure her that no togetherness was expected. Now we were studying the ancient plumbing, to see if it presented any serious problems.

"I hope you do not plan to sneak back down and wash the dishes," Astrid said.

"Seems like an odd thing for you to hope," I said. "If I don't do them, you'll have to. As a matter of fact I was toying with the idea, cautiously. My mom brung me up real good."

"You frighten me, darling," she said. "Such a nicely housebroken man, he can even open a can and heat some meatballs, he is not too proud to wield a dishtowel, and yet . . ."

"It's all an act I put on to keep people guessing," I said. "Have you got everything you need?"

She smiled faintly. "Everything I need? That could be construed as a leading question. Just what unfulfilled needs did you think I might have, my dear? No, don't answer. I am teasing you, and it is very naughty of me. We are both very tired, and I do have everything I need. I will take a quick bath and sleep very soundly. . . . Matt?"

"Yes?"

"Was it a girl?"

"Was what a girl?"

"The . . . person you mentioned who died up north all those years ago?"

I said without expression, "Of course. Next question, was she pretty? Answer: of course. Was I mad about her? Answer: naturally. So she wound up taking two or three slugs from a 9 mm pistol, which is what usually happens to pretty girls unfortunate enough to become objects of my affection, although the weapons and calibers vary. Let it be a warning to you, Mrs. Watrous."

"What was her name?"

I said irritably, "It was long ago and the wench is dead, to misquote somebody, I forget who. Why this interest in my ancient love-life? Actually, we never got as far as . . . All right, if you must know, her name was Elin von Hoffman, and she was a very, very distant relative of mine. As you probably know, practically all the old Swedish families are connected in some way if you look hard enough, and far enough back. Now you'd better take your bath and go to bed before you fall on your face. You look as if you'd just about had it for the day."

I went back downstairs and washed the dishes, leaving them in the rack to dry. After pouring myself a drink, I wandered into the living room and looked around for a book that's as standard in aristocratic Swedish houses as the Bible is in religious American homes. I found it on a fragile-looking little table that looked as if an antique-dealer would pay well for it; but I know more about Colt and Remington and Smith & Wesson than I do about Louis XIV and Chippendale and Queen Anne. Or whatever. I turned on a tall lamp at the end of the well-worn, brocade-covered sofa with the funny carved legs—another old piece that would have to remain unidentified—and sat down to do a bit of genealogical research.

The rather small, very fat book was the *Adelskalender*, the Swedish equivalent of the German *Almanach de Gotha*, the English *Burke's Peerage*, and Sir J. B. Peel's *Scots Peerage*. My own family, being prolific, had a sizeble section. I glanced at it briefly and saw that the *huvudman*, the headman of the family, was still a gent named Axel, who, I reflected, must be a fairly old party by this time. Then I realized that this must be the son of the Baron Axel Stjern-hjelm who'd been *huvudman* when I was a boy. I passed up the rest of the Stjernhjelms and went on to the tail of the alphabet. Watrous might not sound like a Swedish name—neither do Kennedy or von Rosen, both of which were listed—but I found Astrid's husband among the off-spring of a certain Greve *Erik* Gustav Adolf Watrous. The italics indicated the given name by which he was customarily addressed.

*Alan* August, *1950 23/11, oceanographer vid Oceanic Institute (Gloucester, Mass., USA). G 1979 m *Astrid* Sofia Land (Landhammar), *1954 15/2.

That didn't tell me anything I didn't know, except that Astrid's maiden name had been Land (originally Landham-mar), that her middle name was Sofia, and that her husband was four years older than she was, hardly earthshaking news; and that the guy outranked me socially, since he'd had a count (greve) for a daddy instead of a baron, some-

110

thing I wasn't going to brood about. But the kicker was higher up in the same column. At the time this edition of the *Adelskalender* had gone to press, Count Erik Watrous, Alan's papa, had still been alive, whatever his present state of existence might be. However, his mother had not. The paragraph referring to them gave considerable space to Count Erik's career and achievements, but ended on a rather sad note: G 1947 m friherinnan Charlotte Viveka Stjernhjelm, +1959. The asterisk, I'd already determined, marked a birth date; but here was a cross indicating a death date.

Hi, Cousin Alan, sorry you lost your mom so young.

For some reason I wasn't entirely comfortable about learning that Astrid's husband was a relative of mine; perhaps my thoughts about his wife hadn't always been as pure as they should have been. Even as this went through my mind, I heard movement on the second floor. I rose and went to the foot of the stairs.

"Are you okay?" I called.

Her head appeared above me, looking over the railing of the elaborate staircase, with a towel working on the wet blonde hair. Her shoulders were bare; maybe the invisible rest of her was, also. I found it an intriguing idea, but dismissed it firmly. She looked rosy and young and pretty.

"Yes, I am fine," she said, "but I almost fell asleep in that great wonderful tub. Now I am really going to bed. Good night again, Matt."

Returning to my drink, I gulped down what was left of it, and headed for the front door. Hanging on a hook in the nearby closet, I found a well-worn and grimy old tweed overcoat that had obviously been used for chores around the yard. Putting it on, I discovered to my surprise that it was large enough for me. Apparently we Stjernhjelms came in tall sizes on two continents. I slipped outside cautiously. It was a dark and misty night. The patchy snow around the house showed up vaguely in the blackness as blotches of dirty gray. After giving my eyes a little time to get accommodated, I made my way around the corner of the house and waited.

Presently a shadow moved among the nearby trees, and a voice spoke softly: "McGillivray?"

Only the more senior operatives in the outfit know Mac's true name, in particular the middle name from which the nickname is derived. I had therefore, when I called a special number from Oslo, specified it as the contact code for this occasion.

I answered with the full name. "Arthur McGillivray Borden," I said. "Hi, Joel."

"You took your ever-loving time getting out here," he said. "I'm damn' near frozen solid. What a lousy climate!"

He was a husky character in what seemed to be tan slacks and a quilted brown ski jacket, although the exact colors were hard to determine in the dark. His head was bare. He had all his hair—thick and black—and he'd grown a bushy black moustache since I'd last seen him. Maybe it was a disguise. Tough-looking, with a pug nose, a square jaw, and heavy shoulders, he was about five years younger than I was, and he thought he could take me. Which was just one of the things I didn't like about him; but affection between agents is not mandatory.

"Let's get around to the other side of the house," I said. "There's a window I want to keep an eye on. Keep it quiet."

"Aw, shucks, I was thinking of firing off a gun and singing 'The Star-Spangled Banner.'"

"Back behind those berry bushes or whatever they are," I said. When we were established in the proper vantage spot, not too badly scratched, I said softly, "So you lost Mac."

"Hell, I was supposed to lose him," Joel said defensively. "My instructions were to lose him."

"And find him again."

"Yeah, but how? How do you track down a man who vanishes off a busy Washington sidewalk in front of a big department store?"

I considered this for a moment. "No leads at all?"

"Sure. Valuable clues. Subject purchased one tie, blue with white. Subject purchased six pairs of gray socks, size ten. I can give you the prices if you think they'll help. Maybe it's a code. Shit. After chasing around for a day or so and getting nowhere, I was tipped off by old Douggie Barnett that that bastard Bennett had outshuffled him for the top spot in spite of the contingency plans Mac had set up; watch out. A neat political coup, Washington style: if a vacancy comes up you want, fill it now, and dispose of any staff loyal to the previous incumbent fast. Only usually the disposal isn't so permanent. The sonofabitch actually put a couple of juvenile bloodhounds on my trail with take-out orders."

"Join the club," I said.

Joel glanced at me in the dark. "You, too? Well, it figures. Bennett's got things made the way it is; he doesn't want Mac found by anybody. And this cutthroat agency of ours is real great for a spot of private extermination, but he didn't pick his exterminators so good: a couple of young punks still wet behind the ears. After taking care of them, I used an escape identity I keep in reserve and headed this way to give you a hand, since you couldn't be doing worse than I was. When I checked in with the old-boy network in Denmark, I found you'd called from Oslo telling me to get in touch if I was available, and where."

I said, "I figured you'd come after me if you lost the trail, or never found it. If you were still alive."

"Well, here I am, Mr. Paul Haraldsen taking a nostalgic vacation in the land of his Norse forebears." His big white teeth flashed in the darkness as he grinned at me. "Actually, I'm a good Polack named Valdemar Konowski—

113

you didn't know that, did you?—and to hell with all these mad Scandihoovians, present company included. Why are we freezing our balls off out here?"

"Because I don't want the pretty lady, or anybody else, to know I've got you in reserve. And because I have a hunch she's up to something. . . . *Shhh!*"

We were silent, listening to footsteps approaching from the direction of the road: an occasional squelching sound as a shoe found some mud still unfrozen, an occasional crunching noise as it mashed down some crusty snow. A dark figure appeared, a shadow among the dark trees. It stole forward and bent down and rose again to toss something at a dark window above, a pebble by the sound of it. The window opened and something dropped out of it to be caught by the man below. They have mostly swing-out windows over there, not the slide-up variety favored at home that are harder to manage quietly. The man stole away, not as unobtrusively as he'd have liked: I heard him swear softly in Swedish as more crusted snow crackled under his feet.

I said sadly, "I keep talking to her, telling her what a mean sonofabitch I am, but I don't seem to make any impression."

Val Konowski, alias Joel, said, "You'd better know there's something going on up at the big house. Several cars have pulled in and out while I was waiting for you. Seems like a hell of a lot of traffic for a farm in the country, even an aristocratic farm in the country. You'd better watch yourself. Remember, you ain't no Swede; you're a goddam foreigner here. Your fancy Svenska family could be cooking up something cute for the poor American relation. Like selling him to somebody who wants to nail his hide to the barn, and mine, too."

"It's a thought," I said. "Keep your eyes open. Cover me, but don't be too damn' quick to move in for the rescue, if anything should happen. Whoever makes a move, let them commit themselves all the way."

"Sure. I won't interfere until they've got the coffin buried and the gravestone in place."

"Keep an eye out for Bennett's hopeful hotshots, particularly. Try to spot them and find out what they'll be up to next. We'll use the regular contact routines."

"Yes, sir, Mr. Helm, sir!"

I grinned. "Good to have you on board, mister. It was getting kind of lonely, up here in the frozen north, with nothing but a beautiful woman for company."

"I should be so lonely." Joel hesitated. "Hey, do you really come from a bunch of barons? Far out!"

"Yeah, with that and twenty cents I can make a phone call, except where it costs a quarter. And talking about phones, there are a couple of things I'd like you to check out for me when you get a chance. I shouldn't be needing you here until I've had tea at the baronial hall tomorrow afternoon, so in the meantime . . ."

I gave him his instructions, and waited while he slipped away into the dark. Being friendly with people I don't like but have to work with always makes me feel slightly fraudulent. But I had to hand it to him, even though he was a husky specimen, he made less noise than Astrid's midnight visitor. Well, people will keep sending amateurs to do the work of pros.

I stood there leaning against a tree trunk in the misty darkness, comfortable in my borrowed coat, telling myself that this ancestral-homeland routine was a lot of bull. My folks had left this country for reasons that seemed good to them, and there was really nothing pulling me back. I had a home, three thousand miles away. At least I had a perfectly good apartment in Washington, D.C. And if I wasn't really a big-city man at heart—and I wasn't—my spiritual home, if you wanted to get fancy, was out in the wide, arid, sunny American Southwest, where I'd lived both as

115

a boy and a married man. Not in this cold and wet and gloomy little northern land where I could manage the language only clumsily.

Still, I'd been brought up on the old Norse names and legends. King Olaf Tryggvason sailing to his doom among the islands, at a place called Föret, where a great coalition of rival sea-kings lay in wait for him and his ship, *Ormen Lange*, the *Long Serpent*. Styrbjörn Starke landing his invading army not too far from where I stood, and burning his ships before marching on Uppsala, to let his men know that, one way or another, they were there to stay. And they were; they died right there, all of them, driven back to the beach and the smoking embers of the ships that had brought them. I could visualize the final stand: the shield wall shrinking as men fell and those still standing closed ranks above the bodies, the long bloody swords and great gory axes cleaving and smashing under the dull sky while the flights of arrows searched for the weak points in the heavy chain mail that got even heavier as the deadly day wore on. . . .

"Matt?"

The metallic din of the ancient battle faded. I saw that the side door of the house was opening.

I said, "You're supposed to be asleep."

Astrid stepped out onto the little stoop, an incongruous figure in the chilly night in the flimsy lingerie I'd bought her. I went up the steps and reached for her wrists and raised them until the lace fell back to show that her hands were empty.

I said, "I told you to keep that Smith & Wesson handy."

"You've been watching out here? I was afraid you might be."

"I've been watching."

"Don't be angry, please. It's not what you think. I mean, it's not a dark plot against you. Please believe that."

"We'll see," I said. "But when I'm responsible for

116

somebody, friend or enemy, I like them to follow my instructions at least a little.''

She hesitated. ''I know, but it just didn't seem . . . advisable.''

''Advisable?''

''You weren't in the house; I couldn't find you. I was afraid that if you were actually out here, if you'd seen . . . Well, if you were angry with me, suspicious of me, I didn't want to run into you with a pistol in my hand and maybe have you misunderstand and do something . . . something hasty.''

''You mean, like Wild Bill Hickok shot his best friend because, according to the version I heard, the stupid bastard came blundering into the alley behind him with a drawn revolver when Hickok had just fought his way out of an ambush and didn't know who else might be gunning for him?''

''Something like that.'' She laughed softly. ''It's really rather like playing house with a saber-toothed tiger. You have to be so careful not to startle the beast.''

''Flattery, flattery,'' I said. ''What man minds being called a tiger?''

''What are you doing out here, anyway, Matt? Now that you've seen me pass the secret message.''

''What secret message?'' I shook my head quickly. ''Never mind. I won't put you to the trouble of making up a lot of lies. I presume it will all become clear in time. And if you must know, I was just fighting the battle of Uppsala. It must have taken place somewhere around here.''

''Actually, I believe this was seabottom back in those days. The beach on which they fought must have been farther inland. Styrbjörn the Strong burned his ships within sight of the church at Old Uppsala, remember? The famous one that's still standing.''

"That's right. I'd forgotten that detail. But how do you know it?"

"My father was enthusiastic about all Scandinavian history, not just the Finnish part. He used to tell me the old sagas, even though they were not very suitable entertainment for a small female child, all that torture and bloodshed."

I said, "Well, we'd better get you back inside, or find you some long wool underwear. Inside is more practical." I guided her through the door and locked it behind us. I found a light switch, and studied her for a moment in the sudden illumination, and said, "It would really be very nice to know what the hell is going on here, Astrid. I suppose I could beat it out of you."

"I suppose you could," she said without expression. "I am not very brave. But it is not my secret, and you will know all about it tomorrow afternoon."

"When we go to the big house for tea?" I asked, still watching her. She nodded. I said, "It looks as if that could turn out to be quite a tea party the young baron and his wife are throwing for us."

She said quietly, "Please, you must do nothing drastic. Nothing violent. I promise there is no threat to you. Or your country, our country. Quite the contrary. Remember that your chief assigned you to help me, after I had told him what would be required of you and why."

"And after you'd made yourself sick as a dog. Well, bitch."

She hesitated. "All right. That, too."

I said, "I have only your word for how much you told him, and how much of that was the truth. And not much of a word, at that. I never saw such a close-mouthed wench."

"Yes." She smiled at me, and reached up to touch my cheek. "Of course, I could try to distract you from all these questions with that ancient Mata Hari nonsense, but you

118

are much too experienced and cynical to fall for that, are you not, darling?"

The brown eyes, which contrasted so strikingly with the fair hair, were laughing at me.

I said, "Oh, God, the old seduction routine. You seem to forget that you're supposed to be a sick lady."

"You could try to make me well." She grimaced. "That is pretty terrible dialogue, is it not? I always wondered how those fascinating females worked up to . . . to the subject. You do not trust me, of course; but have you ever made love to someone you did not trust? I think, after these days together, we are both curious. You have been wondering what it would be like, what I would be like. I certainly hope you have. And maybe I have been wondering what you would be like. This may be our last chance to find out. If you lock the door carefully and keep your pistols handy . . . I am certain you have managed love before under somewhat risky circumstances, a man like you. And actually there is no risk. You say we have thrown off the ones who were following us, and you are not wanted hurt or dead by anyone here, quite the contrary." She studied me for a moment longer. There was a challenge in her eyes. "Well, what is it to be, my dear? Shall we proceed upstairs?"

She was playing femme-fatale games with me, and I was tired of her games. I was tired of acting the grim menace to her playful mystery; the moth-eaten saber-toothed tiger she kept poking with a stick because she liked to hear it growl, but not too loudly. I'd been a very good boy as long as she'd indicated her desire to remain a very good girl; but now that she'd decided that we must indulge in a little genteel sex to sidetrack my curiosity, I didn't feel obliged to follow her carefully written script. In fact I was damned if I was going to act it all out with her: the laughing hand-in-hand romp up the stairs, the breathless disrobing scene, and the final, slightly embarrassed—at least at first—nude encounter between the sheets. Cutie pie stuff.

I reached for her instead. I'd promised I wouldn't take anything that wasn't offered; but now the offer had been made, and I hadn't promised to be a gentleman when the time came. My crude intentions were obvious, and she stepped back quickly, but not quickly enough.

"No, Matt!" she protested as I pulled her to me. "Matt, not like that, please don't—"

She got no further, because I'd already swept her up all entangled in her bedroom finery; and I was carrying her across the living room. I was trying to make it look easy, of course: the masterful male to whom a hundred-and-thirty-pound female was a mere feather. But I must admit I was glad to deposit her, not very gently, upon the antique sofa, which, I suspected, had over the centuries had other ladies in long, flowing gowns planted on it for purposes strictly immoral. I didn't think it accidental that some ancestral baron had picked it long enough even for us tall Stjernhjelms; and I didn't think the old living room was seeing anything new as I skipped the cutie-nudie scene and merely displaced enough clothing, male and female, to expose what needed exposing. Then I did what needed doing, rather competently if I do say so myself. I hadn't realized how much tension had built up in me during the days I'd spent in her company pretending to be a gentleman.

There was some token early resistance; but it quickly turned into willing cooperation—so much willing cooperation, in fact, that afterwards, when pulse and respiration had had time to return more or less to normal, I sat up to look at her warily. I was beginning to realize that this rude exercise in passion had not, after all, been entirely my idea. She'd been playing a game, all right; but it had not been quite the polite bedroom game I'd thought she was playing.

Astrid sat up beside me and pushed the tangled hair back from her face and patted it into some kind of order. She tugged and hauled her lingerie back to where it would again meet the basic demands of modesty. Well, if the light wasn't behind her and you didn't look too hard.

"I thought you were ripping me to shreds," she said after making a thorough inspection. "But I guess it's more durable than it looks; there doesn't seem to be any damage. Except, of course, to my dignity." She looked at me at last. She giggled abruptly, a rather girlish sound to come from a mature and experienced married lady. "You were being much too good to be true, darling. I had to see how far you would let yourself be teased. I am happy to know that you are human, after all."

"And that you can still drive a man slightly haywire," I said dryly.

"That, of course," she said. "I was beginning to feel like an old, untouched hag." Then she leaned over to kiss me lightly on the cheek. "But we must not spoil it by analyzing it, darling. It was really rather . . . nice, wasn't it? Primitive but nice."

CHAPTER 12

THE following day the clouds broke up and the snow melted rapidly in the sunshine—rather cool and pale sunshine by the standards of my native New Mexico, but I could imagine what it meant to the local people after their endless dark winter. There was some activity up at the big house, but it could be perfectly normal. I had no idea what their day-to-day routines were up there, or how many visitors they usually had. Down in our guest villa there was considerable awkwardness. Our old relationship, all of three days old, had been shattered, and we were fumbling around to get comfortable in our new one.

"I wish you'd got me at least one attractive dress," Astrid said irritably after lunch. "That skirt you bought is much too big—you must have been thinking of the fat lady in the circus—and I can hardly have tea at the mansion house in jeans. I guess I'll have to press my good slacks and wear those; but I just know our hostess will be all done up in a dress and nylons and high heels, even just for afternoon tea."

There was that uncharacteristic hint of insecurity again. I'd judged her as a woman who could attend a formal ball in shipwrecked rags without turning a hair, but obviously I'd been wrong. Even though the *Adelskalender* had told me she'd married a Swedish aristocrat, it seemed that afternoon tea at an obscure baronial mansion house had her badly worried.

I said, "Hell, I might as well be married again. She hasn't got a *thing* to wear, she says. Where have I heard that one before?"

Astrid made a face at me and scurried off to find an electric iron. When I helped her out of the car in front of the big house a couple of hours later—we could have walked up, of course, but we'd have had to wade through a lot of melted snow—she looked very good to me, in her neat slacks and jacket and tailored silk blouse; but her nervousness was still apparent. She stood there for a moment uncertainly, looking at the other cars: two sizable Volvos and a Mercedes, not the economy-model Mercedes that had shadowed us for a while but a large luxury job.

I said, "I don't have anything to worry about, you said. They aren't laying for me behind the door with tommy guns, right? You're not leading me to my execution, so what's bugging you?"

She said, "It's not that; it is merely . . . I think I am

just an Indiana country girl at heart, Matt. All these barons and baronesses . . ." She squared her shoulders. "That is stupid; why should I care what they think of me? To hell with all of them, right?"

"That's my girl," I said, guiding her up the front steps of the house.

Margareta Stjernhjelm opened the door for us herself. As Astrid had predicted, she'd dressed for the occasion, in a smart blue dress; and she had the slightly awkward, coltish look of any modern young outdoors woman who doesn't find herself in a silk dress and high-heeled pumps very often. Behind her was a tall man who was too old to be her husband—anyway, I thought I would recognize Torsten, since I'd met him the last time I was here. However, this man had to be related to me also. He was almost as tall and bony and ugly as I was.

He didn't like me. We'd never seen each other before, but he made it quite clear that he wasn't ever going to be a bosom pal of mine. For a start, he let me know by his contemptuous scrutiny that he thought I looked pretty damned ridiculous in this northern climate in the light slacks and seersucker jacket I'd worn for the Mexico job. Of course he was perfectly right, but it seemed unnecessary to make a point of it. While the strange Stjernhjelm was giving me the evil eye, our hostess was greeting Astrid; then she shook hands with me.

"It is a great pleasure to have you visiting us, Matthew," she said. "Torsten has told me much of you. You do not mind that I call you by your first name? We are very informal within the family. Anyway, we are delighted that you have come to Torsäter again; and we are only sorry that we must take advantage of your visit like this. Mrs. Watrous will have told you?"

I noted that Astrid was not yet included in the informality of the family; and I could see that she realized it, too. Then I understood that it was a matter of protocol. By the rules, it was okay for Margareta, a lady, to suggest to me, a gentleman, that first names were acceptable here; however, between two ladies, the initiative had to come from the older.

I said, "Mrs. Watrous doesn't tell much. I do get the impression that it's not entirely a social gathering."

"I am afraid not. But let me introduce Baron Olaf Stjernhjelm. . . . I believe you are already acquainted with Countess Watrous, Olaf. And this is our relative Matthew, from America."

The tall man bowed formally to Astrid and turned to me. I can spot a knuckle-grinder a mile away on a dusty New Mexico day; but while there are responses that will preserve your finger joints and even make the other guy a little unhappy, I saw no reason to give anything away to this hostile character, not even how strong my grip really was, or wasn't. I let him knead away painfully, telling myself that I shouldn't judge my family, or the land of my forebears, by one macho creep; we've got them on the western shore of the Atlantic, too.

"I, too, have heard much of you," Cousin Olaf said, releasing me at last. His eyes were very blue, I noticed; a china-blue shade that was disconcerting. There was something familiar about them, but I couldn't place it at once. He went on: "The black sheep of the family. The sinister American expert who calls himself Helm. Some people await you in the living room, Mister Helm. If the ladies will excuse us . . . Come this way."

"There will be tea, as promised, when you have finished, Matthew," Margareta said. "Or something stronger if you prefer."

When I glanced towards Astrid, she said, "Do not worry about me, Matt. I am certain Margareta will take very good care of me. . . . You do not mind if I call you Margareta, do you, my dear; and I hope you will call me Astrid."

She winked at me as I turned away to let me know that

she could play this game as well as anybody. Obviously, now that the initial suspense was over, she was no longer taking this noble gathering so seriously.

Cousin Olaf managed to bump me slightly or, rather, brush me with his arm as he made the gesture of showing me the way. It told him I was carrying a gun in my waistband—one of the silenced .22 automatics—but it told me something about him, too. He'd been just a bit too slick about checking out the local artillery. He was not a gentleman farmer, nor had he gone into one of the other peaceful occupations adopted by most of my Swedish relatives when the baron business became unprofitable. The army, maybe, since the family history showed a lot of military Stjernhjelms including the previous master of this house; but if so, I would have bet on one of the darker branches of military intelligence.

But I thought it quite possible that, with some early military training perhaps—they all have to put in some army time in that country—Cousin Olaf had been a roving mercenary fighting any way that was handy. These days there are plenty to choose from. At least I'd identified what it was I'd recognized in his eyes. They were killer eyes. As they say, it takes one to know one. But I hadn't expected to find one in these fine surroundings.

Under the circumstances, it was no fun turning my back on him; but I let him be polite and usher me into the living room ahead of him. I was a little startled to find six men waiting for us there, dressed in sober business suits complete with vests and ties. They were standing to greet us, all except old Colonel Stjernhjelm, who was in a wheelchair, with his son pushing him towards me. He'd been a tall, straight old gentleman when I'd seen him last, but he was bowed and shrunken now—he had to be well up in his eighties. His eyes were still clear, however, although his hand felt very fragile in my grasp.

"It is good to see you again, Matthew," he said. "I am

125

pleased that you remembered us when you needed a place to stay here in Sweden. That is what the family is for. I trust you are finding the little villa comfortable."

"Thank you, sir, we couldn't be more comfortable," I said. "And we certainly appreciate the hospitality."

"You remember my son Torsten," the colonel said.

I shook hands with the tall young man behind the chair, blond and blue-eyed; but no killer eyes here.

"And here is someone who wishes much to make your acquaintance, Matthew," said the old man. "The original plan was that you should be invited to his estate down in Skåne for this meeting; but before those arrangements could be made, you made things easy for us by asking to be allowed to come here. So the plan was changed, and we are all meeting here at Torsäter instead. . . . Axel, this is Matthew, from America."

The man who had come forward was in his fifties. He did not have my height, or the blond hair of Olaf and Torsten; but there was no mistaking the family features. I was glad I'd done my homework last night. This was the man whose name appeared in capital letters at the beginning of the Stjernhjelm section of the fat little book I'd studied. This was the chief of the clan, as my mother's Scottish ancestors would have put it. In Swedish: the *huvudman*.

I told myself what the hell, it was just another Swede in a good dark suit of European cut. Okay, a relative; but I'd lived most of my life without much contact with my relatives, and I could have made it the rest of the way alone quite comfortably. This guy meant nothing to me, although he was a competent-looking character I wouldn't have minded doing business with, if I'd had any business to transact. Brown hair. Gray eyes. No Stjernhjelm beanpole, he was actually a little on the stocky side.

Still, we shared something; we all shared something in this room, something old and once considered very important. Something in the blood or, if you wanted to be scientific, the genes. I couldn't even disown Cousin Olaf, behind me. Often, looking in the mirror, I'd seen the same eyes there. Not quite the same porcelain-blue color, of course, but the same. I took the hand the headman offered me.

"A pleasure, sir," I said.

"Perhaps," he said with a faint smile. "That remains to be seen, does it not? But we are very glad to welcome you here, Matthew. We have gone to considerable trouble to bring you to Sweden. It was young Torsten's suggestion, as a matter of fact. He remembered you from your visit here when he was a boy; he seems to have been impressed by you. He suggested to his father that, since there was a specialist of sorts in the family, it might be well to make use of him in this crisis, if he was willing."

I thought it over for a moment. Apparently I'd been correct when I accused Astrid of leading me on a wild-goose chase into darkest Sweden, except that the goose to which she'd led me wasn't very wild and the region wasn't very dark. Somehow she'd talked Mac into dispensing with my services temporarily, or had she? Was he? Or had he taken advantage of the family's request for my help, and used it, and me, for purposes of his own—purposes involving a place called Lysaniemi?

"Crisis?" I said. "May I ask what kind of a crisis?"

"I will answer that question in a moment," Axel said. "But first let me introduce some more of your *släktingar*, your relations. . . ."

I shook hands with Jan, Gunnar, and another, older, Torsten—I remembered that it was a very common name in the family. These were, apparently, solid middle-aged Swedish citizens like the headman. Having taken care of the formalities, we sat down on the stiff-looking, brocade-covered chairs that reminded me of an antique sofa I'd recently employed for purposes much less respectable.

127

Axel said, "Very well. I am told that you do not do so well with the Swedish, so we will continue in English. I think everyone here understands it although our accents may leave something to be desired. You have never been to one of the family gatherings we have every few years?"

"It's a long way across the ocean," I said. "No, I haven't."

"Well, those are mainly social functions. But we do try to keep track of the members of the family everywhere. For instance, we know that you were in Sweden some years ago under rather mysterious circumstances. You were involved in trouble up north. At the time, it was known in official circles that you were working for the United States government, although the fact was never made public. Later during the same visit to Europe, you came here to Torsäter and participated in our yearly *älg* hunt."

"Without much success," I said.

"Yes, as you will see, that is important. Very important. We have trouble, Matthew. It could be serious trouble. A certain younger member of the family has become involved in an unpleasant conspiracy. . . . Well, you know how some young people are these days. They must forever be proving, and sometimes proving violently, that they are for the peace and against the atom. This particular plot could have serious consequences internationally which, I understand, is why Mrs. Watrous was able to persuade the head of your agency to let us make use of your services. With your consent, of course."

I said, "Mrs. Watrous seems to have done a good job as your emissary, but I don't understand the necessity for all the elaborate mystification in which she has involved us."

Axel said, a little embarrassed, "I do not know the details. I do know that your chief asked certain things of us in return for his cooperation. . . ."

Okay. Mac was up to his old tricks. Apparently he'd taken advantage of Astrid's request to get me to Sweden with a convincing cover story. Now all I had to do, while solving my family's problems, was figure out what I'd really been sent here for with the name Lysaniemi so carefully planted in my brain, and how it related to Mac's disappearance and that of all those other missing people, an ocean away.

Axel was speaking again: "Of course, while we do consider the national and international danger, our motives are not altogether unselfish. Whether the conspiracy succeeds or fails, the family name will inevitably be involved in much unfavorable publicity, unless drastic measures are taken soon."

"Drastic? How drastic?" The thought that came to me was fairly incredible in these polite surroundings, but I put the question anyway: "Do I gather that you had me brought all this way because you want some shooting done?"

Axel Stjernhjelm watched me thoughtfully for a moment; then he said, "Some years ago, as we mentioned, you were here on a hunt. You had a very good shot at a trophy moose, but for reasons of your own you did not take it. More recently, we know—we received a complete evaluation last night from Mrs. Watrous; I hope you will not blame her for keeping us informed—a certain young woman aimed a loaded pistol at you. Although, with your skill and experience, you could undoubtedly have created an opportunity to use your own weapon in self-defense, and would certainly have been justified in doing so, you did not. Instead you disarmed her at some risk to yourself." The headman's glance touched Olaf Stjernhjelm, and returned to me. "If shooting were all that was required, well, you are not the only expert marksman in the family. For that, we did not need to bring you here over such a distance; we already had a . . . a suitable candidate available. But for the young person involved to suffer violence

129

would create exactly the publicity we are trying to avoid, besides being distasteful to almost all of us. What we need is a man who knows when *not* to shoot; a specialist capable of solving our problem discreetly. We hope you are the man.''

I could feel Cousin Olaf seething a couple of chairs away. It was clear now why he hated me. He'd obviously proposed himself for the job of saving the family from shame, but he'd been turned down in my favor presumably because, with his killer eyes, he'd never been known to pass up a shot at anything, animal or human. I found it ironical that, after a lifetime in a savage business, I should be receiving so much credit for a couple of triggers I hadn't pulled.

I said, "I see, sir. And what exactly is the problem? Or should I say, who is the problem?"

"You have already met her. She was just mentioned: the young lady who threatened you with a pistol. Karin Segerby, née Stjernhjelm."

I hadn't been aware that the little blonde girl with the gun was a relation of mine, but I wasn't surprised. It seemed to be that kind of family.

CHAPTER 13

THE drinking habits of the Swedes are very odd, at least by the American boozing standards to which I subscribe. I've heard that public drunkenness is a big problem in the country, but I don't see how it can be, since nobody ever offers you a real drink when you need one. That afternoon, after all the surprises that had been sprung on me, and all the strangers I'd had to meet, I still had to make it on a cup of tea and a glass of sherry.

Later, after we'd parked the red Golf in front of the guest villa once more, and gone inside, Astrid said, "If you are heading where I think you are heading, please make mine a double. How can one be expected to be sociable to a group of important new relations on *sherry*, for Heaven's sake?"

I grinned. "I thought you were the little girl brought up to consider Scandinavia the Promised Land. You sound more like a hard-drinking Yankee wench to me." In the kitchen, I paused by the refrigerator. "Ice? I think this thing makes all of eight cubes. I'll split them with you."

"You are all heart, my dear. What do we do now?"

I glanced at her sharply as I put a glass into her hand. "We? You've done your duty, ma'am. You've delivered the warm body, complete with a psychological analysis I'd love to read some time."

A little color came into her face. She busied herself testing the contents of her glass. "I just said that you were a dreadful man; what else could I say?"

"Sure." I studied her for a moment longer. "Well, Cousin Olaf is coming over to give me a detailed briefing. In the meantime a few questions come to mind."

"Yes?"

"The original story I heard was that you approached my chief in Washington on behalf of your missing husband. Now I learn that's not true; you went there on a recruiting mission on behalf of his family, which happens to be my family, too. You went there to arrange for the loan of my services, right?" When she nodded, I asked, "Where does that leave your lost husband, Astrid?"

She hesitated. When she spoke, her voice was hard: "Why should I care about him and his Hannah Gray? Wherever they are, they have each other, do they not?"

131

"So you're not really the forgiving woman you wanted me to think you?"

She laughed shortly. "If you believed that, you are really a very gullible man. Any other questions?"

"Always, but let's go sit in the living room where it's comfortable," I said. When we were there, I asked, "Those heart palpitations. They were my chief's idea, weren't they? It's just what he would do, to give himself a plausible reason for assigning me to protect you, in your weakened condition."

"Yes, of course. He gave me the pills to take. I don't even know what they were. He said I'd be uncomfortable for a while, but there was no real risk; I guess he was not aware of the possibility of a quinine reaction." She shrugged. "Or perhaps he did not care. He is really a very ruthless person, is he not?"

"And you've been telling me what a nice man he was!"

"Yes, I have told you many things." Her voice was subdued and her eyes wouldn't meet mine. "You should not believe anything I tell you, ever."

"I'll keep it in mind, Countess."

She laughed shortly. "I am no more a countess than you are a baron, Matt. Alan was naturalized well before I married him. They just like to hang on to the old traditions around here, and I admit it is rather nice and being a countess would be fun; but actually we are both just good democratic American citizens visiting a foreign land."

I said, "Whether or not you acquired a title by marriage, you've got a pretty classy family of your own, don't you? No titles, but aristocratic enough to rate the book, here." I reached for the *Adelskalender* on the nearby table. "Landhammar, Landhammar . . . I checked on your husband last night and learned that was the original form of your maiden name. Yes, here it is. Apparently an old Swedish-Finnish family, one branch of which returned to Sweden . . . But you're not in here."

132

"No. That was our name, certainly, but my parents shortened it to Land when they came to America, just as your parents changed Stjernhjelm to Helm. But we would not be in the Swedish book, since we came from the Finnish Landhammars. Does it matter?"

"No, I'm just being nosy." I went on quickly: "Tell me about Karin Segerby. How well do you know her, really?"

"Well, it was just a social acquaintanceship at first," Astrid said. "Alan started spending much time in Washington trying to get money for the Institute; he turned out to be very good at it. Usually, I went with him to help him entertain the important people. We heard of the Segerbys and looked them up, since they were relations. We started seeing them fairly often when we were in Washington. He was assigned there by his company, of course."

"What company?"

She looked surprised. "You do not know the name Segerby? Segerby Vapenfabriks Aktiebolag?"

I said, "My God, you mean SVAB? I always thought that stood for Svenska Vapenfabriks AB."

"No, it is a Segerby family concern. The Segerby Weapons Factory Company, if you wish a literal translation. Frederik was their Washington representative. When he was murdered, of course, the popular theory was that some pacifists killed him because he was a merchant of death, so-called."

"But you think she did it. Karin?"

"The two theories are not mutually exclusive, Matt. Karin was engaged in many pacifist and antinuclear activities. I think she was protesting Frederik's work; they had arguments about it, I know. I think she was madly, blindly in love with him when she married him—such a handsome and considerate and sexy man, somewhat older, with a great deal of money. What girl could resist? But after a

133

while I think she found his business more and more intolerable.''

"So you think she just hauled off and clobbered him because she couldn't stand his warlike activities.'' I shrugged. ''Well, it's a motive, I suppose. How and where did it happen?''

Astrid said, ''I do not really know much more about the crime than what was in the Washington newspapers. Apparently Frederik was shot to death in the parking garage in which they kept their two cars. Karin had come home an hour earlier in her little Saab. The attendant remembered seeing her drive in. She is a type that is noticed by young male parking-lot attendants.'' Astrid's voice was dry. ''He did not see her leave the garage on foot. The walking exit she would normally have employed was not visible from his station. So she could have hidden among the parked automobiles until Frederik arrived in his Mercedes. She could have shot him and run home to wait for someone to bring her the tragic news. The shooting was done by a woman.''

"How did they figure that?''

"The pistol was found on the garage floor near the body. They said it showed signs of having been carried in a woman's purse. Among other things, there were traces of face powder in the checkering of the handle.''

"Grips, please. Except for the old broom-handle Mauser, you hold a handgun by the butt or the grips, not the handle.''

"It must be nice to be an expert,'' Astrid said.

"What was the police reaction?''

"Karin was investigated very thoroughly. However, while nobody had seen her returning to the apartment when she said she did—they lived two blocks from the garage— nobody had seen her sneaking home after her husband was killed, either. The face powder on the gun turned out to be a shade only a brunette would normally wear; and Karin is quite blonde, you will remember. But apparently the deciding factor was that the police ran some kind of tests that showed she had not discharged a firearm recently, if that makes sense.''

I nodded. "The test is for nitrates produced by the burning of gunpowder. They're very persistent on the skin; if you've done any recent shooting, they won't wash off." I grimaced. "I suppose it's possible to wear long rubber gloves; but if she'd made that kind of preparations for committing murder, wouldn't she also have arranged an alibi? And I'm not sold on that motive. How many people shoot their spouses for ideological reasons? If she didn't like his work, if it really turned her off him, she could just move out, couldn't she?"

"Perhaps not." Astrid smiled thinly. "Suppose she shot Frederik, or had him shot, because he had discovered evidence of her involvement in certain sinister plans. Maybe one of those protest organizations she joined, apparently a very noble and worthy cause, was actually a cover, if that is what you call it, for something more dangerous. Frederik's suspicions, and the necessity for silencing him, delayed the scheduled incident, whatever it might be. Karin was forced to behave very properly until the murder investigation was over—which could be the reason she reacted so strongly when I gave her the idea that you might be reopening it. But now that Frederik Segerby is safely buried and forgotten, the plans for violence have been revived, and she is returning to Sweden to help execute them.''

I grinned. "You're bound to make a real she-devil of this cute little bouncing blonde.''

"I am apparently not the only one. From what you have told me of the conference you just attended, certain important members of your family—my family by marriage—consider her a serious menace, also." Astrid laughed. "Someone must keep all the possibilities in mind, darling.

Someone who is not too impressed by a pair of wide blue eyes.''

''Nevertheless, you don't seem to have crossed her off your social list.''

''Of course not. There was no proof; and the family sticks together. As a matter of fact we were very kind to the poor young widow, if only to demonstrate that we took no stock in those nasty official suspicions. It was rather a strain, and I was happy when Alan was no longer needed at the current hearings and we could go home; although Karin acted as if we were very cruel to desert her. However, when we came again, this year, she had pulled herself together, I was glad to see; but she was still not a relaxing person with whom to associate, under the circumstances. We tried to avoid her without giving offense; but when Alan vanished like that, Karin decided that it was her turn to comfort me. She got on my nerves quite badly. I suppose that is why I lost my temper with her at our last luncheon in Washington.''

''But in spite of your fight she turned up in Hagerstown to see you in the hospital.''

''Because of our fight, actually,'' Astrid said. ''She had been brooding about the quarrel, she told me; she wanted to fix things up between us. So she called my parents to ask them to have me telephone her as soon as I arrived; but she found them much distressed. The hospital, unable to reach Alan, listed as next of kin on the cards I carry, had somehow managed to get hold of them instead. I guess I must have been in a truly critical condition for a few hours; they felt obliged to notify someone. My parents were desperate. They are too old to travel; they did not know what to do. Karin told them she would take care of everything, and drove to Hagerstown, which was really very nice of her.''

There was a little silence. We had pretty well taken care of Karin Segerby as a subject of conversation.

I asked casually, "How did a Finnish girl from Indiana manage to meet a Swedish count working as oceanographer in Gloucester, Mass? Was it your Scandinavian backgrounds that drew you together, or do you know something about oceanography?"

Astrid laughed. "My dear man, I have one degree in the subject and I am working towards another, although I may be an old lady before I get it, at the rate I seem to be progressing these days." She moved her shoulders resignedly. "Education and matrimony don't seem to mix very well."

"I see. Is that how you met, professionally?"

Astrid nodded. "I was Alan's laboratory assistant, one of his laboratory assistants. It was a considerable honor, I will have you know, to work with Dr. Watrous. I was very proud of it. After a while I lost my student awe of him and we became good friends. The fact that we came from similar backgrounds, as you said, didn't hurt. Finally we decided to . . . No!" She shook her head quickly. "Why not the truth for a change? That is what we let people believe, but it is not the way it really was. We were certainly friends, Alan and I, as well as professional associates; but for me there was someone else. Someone I considered even more wonderful than the eminent Dr. Watrous; and I was careless; I became pregnant. A tawdry and common little story. Learning that he had . . . had knocked me up, to use that revolting phrase, my great love—my great lover—disappeared over the horizon very rapidly." She glanced at me quickly as I stirred. "Are the true confessions boring you?"

"No, but I think we can use a small refill apiece."

"I will do it." Before I could rise, Astrid was on her feet, taking my glass. "I only want a very little. You would be too generous, so I had better do it."

"Go easy on mine, too," I said; and when she had returned with my drink, I said, "Carry on, Scheherazade."

She settled down beside me and took a sip from her glass. "Well, if you wish. Alan soon realized that there was something wrong. My work was suddenly very bad and my temper was atrocious. Finally, as a friend, he got the sordid truth from the shamed tearful lady. He helped her make arrangements for terminating her embarrassing condition. . . . It was the logical escape from my predicament; but I found to my surprise that I could not be so logical. When the time came, I found that I simply could not do it. I was incapable of . . . of having it killed. Stupid sentimentalism!"

I shrugged. "We all have things we can't do."

"But not many things, in your case." Her voice was sharp. Then she said quickly, "Sorry, I am just being nasty because I hate to confess that I am such an irrational person. But I said I would rather struggle along comically as a supposedly intelligent professional woman who had made a ridiculous mistake and become a mother, although it was hard to imagine anyone less fitted for motherhood. However, nowadays there are many unwed mothers, and I could hope that my life would not be totally ruined; that I would not become the complete social outcast I would have been a generation or two ago. But it would certainly be no help towards the academic career I had hoped to attain."

There was a little pause. At last I said, "I gather that your good friend came up with another helpful idea. Since abortion was unacceptable, he generously married the pregnant lady to save her reputation and her career, right?"

Astrid turned on me sharply. "You must not sneer! It was a very fine thing; do not be sarcastic! Yes, Alan suggested that if I could not bear to terminate the situation, perhaps I would be willing to legitimize it. He was very stiff and funny, and very . . . beautiful. He said, we were not madly in love, but we did get along well together, and since he had at the moment no other candidate for this great honor . . . Making a joke of it to put me at ease and save

138

my pride. A very nice man. I should have refused to let him do such a generous thing; but I was feeling so cheap and ill and humiliated! I told myself that divorces were readily available; and it would be such a great relief to have my problem solved so . . . so respectably. I told myself I would make it up to him in every way possible."

"What about the child?"

She drew a long breath. "After all that, after all the misery and generosity, I had a miscarriage six weeks after we were married! But it makes no difference to what I owe Alan. It was still a very wonderful thing for him to do."

I spoke without expression: "For a lady who got married merely to give a name to her unborn child, and then lost the child, you seem to have stuck with matrimony much longer than one would have expected."

She gave me a crooked smile. "Please, do not be so tactful, my dear. I think you have guessed that I would continue to stick with it, if the decision were mine. Forever, if Alan were willing; in which case I would not have let us behave as we did last night."

"Misbehave, you mean." I grinned briefly. "So propinquity did its dirty work?"

"Yes, I would happily have settled down to be Mrs. Watrous for the rest of my life. But I had made my bargain. It had always been understood between us that our marriage was only a temporary expedient to insure that the lady's good name would remain untarnished. Even though we had stayed together longer than originally planned, I could not possibly object when he asked for his freedom at last. So as soon as all this is settled, there will be a divorce, and the eminent Dr. Alan Watrous will discard that dull blonde wife of his, and marry the lovely dark girl of his dreams. If we can rescue them in time."

"Yes," I said. "Rescue them. In Lysaniemi?" I was watching her carefully.

Astrid hesitated. "I do not really know what we will find in Lysaniemi, Matt."

I said, "As a matter of fact, that's just a name you were supposed to feed me, isn't it? As part of the deal you made with my chief that made my services available to the family." I took another pull of the fresh drink in my hand, a short one as I'd requested. "He gave you that name, didn't he? With instructions to whisper it to me at the earliest plausible opportunity. Did he tell you anything about it?"

She shook her head. "No, Matt."

"Lysaniemi, Lysaniemi?" I frowned at my glass. "That's all? No hint of what it means or what I'm supposed to do about . . . Oh, hell, there's Awful Olaf now!"

Somebody was knocking at the front door. I drained the last of the Scotch and set the glass aside. I rose and started for the front hall, and bumped into an antique chair that seemed to have moved into my path of its own accord. The whole room had suddenly become shifty and unstable.

I was aware that Astrid was watching me with the wary but slightly pitying look that always means the same thing. Then her eyes widened and she pushed herself out of her chair in an attempt to flee, staring at me with shock and fear; but what did the stupid broad expect? She knew what I did for a living, and whom I did it for; did she think we wouldn't have an answer for the tired old knockout-drops routine? It was too damn' bad; she was an attractive wench and good company, in or out of bed—well, sofa—but you don't go around feeding Mickeys to people like me if longevity is your ambition. The standing orders are very specific on that point.

The little .22 High Standard automatic was comfortable in my hand. It was the only thing in the world, in my shut marksman's world; and the fact that my knees were weak and I was beginning to have trouble with my breathing didn't matter a bit. When I squeezed off the first round I found that the agency silencer was really very good these days, with that low-powered target ammo. The early ones weren't so hot, and sometimes you'd blow some kind of sound-absorbent packing out of them and have all kinds of trouble. But this one worked fine; and I'd have made more noise pulling a wine cork.

Well, three wine corks. I quit shooting when the pistol started becoming oddly unsteady in my hand, or maybe it was my hand that was becoming unsteady. There was no sense in just making stray holes in the premises.

Three should be enough to get the job done.

## CHAPTER 14

ı awoke folded into a small dark space that jiggled uncomfortably and smelled of exhaust fumes and rubber, or whatever passes for rubber these synthetic days. Analyzing the received data, slowly and painfully, the sluggish mental computer arrived at the conclusion that I was sharing the trunk of a moving automobile with the spare tire. My wrists and ankles were bound, tightly enough to induce considerable discomfort and some numbness. My position was very cramped since few cars these days, particularly European cars, have trunks large enough for convenient transportation of gents my height. I had a throbbing headache, and my stomach didn't like something that had been put into it. I had to fight to control a panicky attack of claustrophobia. I felt fine, just fine.

I mean, as they say, halitosis is better than no breath at all. Whatever it was that Astrid had slipped into my last drink, the one she'd insisted on making for me, it hadn't proved fatal yet, so it wasn't likely to. To be sure, I was a prisoner, in not too great physical condition, but what the hell, somebody besides Bennett had made a real move at last. Sooner or later the assignment might actually take some kind of comprehensible shape, and I'd know what was expected of me. Assuming that I survived, of course.

There was a gradual change in the motion of the vehicle. We'd apparently been cruising at a fairly good clip on an open road—their normal highway speed limits range from ninety to a hundred and ten kilometers per hour, very roughly fifty-five to sixty-five MPH; but they've been known to bend the law a bit just like at home. Now there was braking and gear-shifting and lane-changing as the traffic became heavier. I decided that we were coming into a city, maybe Uppsala, maybe Stockholm. But that was guesswork. I could have been unconscious for hours. It didn't seem likely that we'd crossed any international borders, but we could be entering any one of a number of other Swedish towns. However, those two were the largest, closest, and most likely.

There was a considerable amount of stop-and-go business; and finally a complete halt, motor off. I heard the doors open and footsteps come along both sides of the car towards the rear where I lay. Two people, or maybe three, I wasn't certain. Call it three. One made shorter, crisper sounds with the heels than the others. A woman? The key went into the lock, and the trunk lid went up, admitting some light, but not glaring sunshine. I saw no reason to try to roll myself over so I could face my kidnappers and greet them with cries of joy. While I wasn't exactly comfortable jammed into that car trunk, I had a hunch the situation wouldn't improve much wherever they were taking me.

*"Kanske han kvävats."*

A youthful male voice I didn't recognize was suggesting that maybe I'd smothered in there. The owner of the voice wasn't gloating about it, but he wasn't greatly concerned about it, either.

*"Nej, han är för elak att dö."*

This was an older male voice saying that, no, I was too mean to die. It was a voice I'd heard before. Well, I'd been anticipating a discussion with Baron Olaf Stjernhjelm, but I hadn't expected it to take quite this form. He gave an order, sending somebody named Greta off to watch an alley, lane, or driveway. The word was *gränd*, pronounced "grend." I wasn't certain of the exact translation. The female footsteps moved away at a crisp trot.

Olaf's voice spoke in English: "Helm, it is of no use for you to play o'possum, if I have the correct slang phrase. I am instructing Karl to cut you free. Please do not try to take advantage. I have a pistol, your very convenient silenced pistol, with a cartridge in the chamber; and I have refilled the magazine from one of the boxes of ammunition found in your luggage. You have no chance whatever of disarming or overpowering me. . . . All right, Karl."

Something, presumably a knife, tugged at the ropes that bound my ankles first, and then the ones about my wrists.

I said without moving, "Okay to sit up?"

"What? Yes, it is okay. If you are careful. . . . Stand back, Karl; allow him room. Do not get between us." The last two sentences were in Swedish.

I disentangled myself painfully and pushed myself up and around with numb hands so I could swing my almost inoperative legs over the rear lip of the trunk. Olaf was facing me, still in his dark business suit, with one of my automatics in his hand. Well, on second thought, I don't suppose the agency weapons were exactly mine, considering how I had obtained them; I'd merely had custody of them for a few days. Now this pistol had entered Olaf's service, for the time being.

Off to my left stood Karl. He was as young as he'd

sounded; but it wasn't really a question of age. There are street-smart, street-tough kids in their teens who're effectively older than I am—older in wickedness, let's say—but this wasn't one of them. This was just a nice, slim, blond, young fellow in his early twenties, wearing jeans and a big ski sweater and a matching knitted cap, who undoubtedly considered himself a fully adult male who'd been with girls and everything; but the question of sexual maturity was not relevant here. What counted was the way he held his knife, a medium lock blade, letting everybody know that he could whittle real good and would never, ever cut himself; but that he didn't know much about cutting other people. . . .

Then he lifted his head and looked at me; and I changed my mind about him abruptly. He had those nice, clear, blue, Scandinavian eyes; but they didn't really see me. They didn't see anybody. They were fanatic's eyes that saw only a shining cause, a glorious goal in the remote distance towards which this boy was marching; and if he had to kill you and wade through your blood to get there, that was your problem. I don't think I scare more easily than the average guy, but true believers always give me chills, regardless of what they happen to believe in at the moment. There is no reason or mercy, and more important, there is no humor, in them.

He looked away, and he was just a nice-looking Swedish boy once more; one to whom you'd entrust your young daughter without hesitation. I glanced around. It was night, I realized belatedly, and we were in a well-lighted courtyard surrounded by brick buildings that seemed to be apartment houses, three and four stories high. Not new. It was apparently a service court. Our corner was sheltered by some trash bins—I seemed to be spending a lot of time associating with Nordic garbage. Olaf spoke in Swedish, instructing Karl to take the car and pick up Greta; they should put Olaf's vehicle away in the parking garage across Torsvägen and join him in the apartment.

"Torsvägen, that is Thor's Way," Olaf translated for my benefit. "But you know some Swedish, I believe. Parking is very difficult here in Stockholm. The police are very strict. . . . What is it, Karl?"

The boy spoke in English too rapid for me to follow. However, I caught the general drift: he wanted to come with us and let Greta park the car. His attitude hinted that he might not have complete faith in his older colleague, probably because Olaf, whatever his reason for being here might be, was not so emotionally involved in the cause that had earned Karl's fierce loyalty, whatever that movement might be.

Cousin Olaf made a gesture of annoyance, and said sharply, "I can manage him alone, I do not need an assistant. The lift only accommodates two in any case. Now put away that knife and do as you were told." He watched Karl get into the car. After the door had slammed shut, he glanced at me and laughed shortly. "What are you thinking, Helm?"

I said, "It must be fun, running a Children's Crusade."

"They are running it. I am merely an adviser."

"Sure. There are nations down in Central America that are full of advisers like you, loaded down with weapons till they walk bowlegged."

He shook his head. "Do not underestimate these young people, Helm. They do not have the training or the experience, but they have the attitude. They are not only willing to die for this thing they believe in. They are willing to kill for it; and that is rare among the idealistic youth of today, brought up to think that inflicting death upon anything, for any reason, is unforgivable. Considering that death will be inflicted upon us all eventually, it is an odd philosophy; and these young men and women have rejected

145

it. They realize that some must always die a little earlier in order that others may live a little later."

I asked, "What is this thing they believe in?"

He shrugged. "Peace, what else? They all seek it now, just as other generations have searched for Eldorado or the Holy Grail."

I sensed that I'd extracted all the benefit I could from his chatty mood. It was no time to get greedy and ask, for instance, what young Karl's ruthless peace organization was called. Patience, patience.

I merely grinned, therefore. "That's a hell of a thing for you to be helping them with. If they ever manage to achieve their peaceful world, you'll be out of business."

"And you," he said curtly. For a moment we'd been seasoned veterans together, considering the vagaries of youth; but now he realized that he'd been talking too freely and brought the meeting to order: "This way, Helm. That door over there. No tricks, please."

I found that I was capable of walking in a shuffling manner; but it was a good thing the courtyard was well sheltered, since a gust of wind would have blown me down. Behind me, I heard the car drive away—the Mercedes I'd seen at Torsäter. I opened the door to which I'd been directed. There were half a dozen steps inside, leading up to another door, which I also opened, on command, finding myself in a small hallway, actually a stairwell. The stairs wound upwards around an elevator shaft protected by grillwork that let you see the greasy cables inside. The elevator was awaiting us, the kind of tiny two-man job you often find over there. There was a swing-out metal door and, inside, a folding metal gate operating on the principle of a baby's folding playpen. The whole contraption looked ancient and insubstantial; it scared me more than the gun in Olaf's hand. I've always been allergic to heights and depths.

Olaf spoke behind me: "Enter, please. . . . Now push the button for Number Four."

At my signal, the little cage began to rattle upwards uncertainly. It was a cosy fit even for two people; I could see why Karl's offer of help had been rejected. There was no room for reinforcements here. In theory, in such close quarters, a break might have been possible; but my captor was, for the moment at least, in much better shape for combat than I. With half-paralyzed hands and feet, I couldn't match him for strength; and I didn't really want to.

I mean, there were more things to be learned here; and I'd come a long way to learn them. If these people had wanted me dead, they'd have given me real poison instead of the sleepy-stuff they'd used. They could have hauled away my cold body as easily as my warm one. It would have been taken for granted, up at the big house, that I'd simply slipped off to embark upon the job I'd let myself be talked into, with my attractive female companion—at least I assumed Cousin Olaf hadn't left her bleeding there to upset the folks. Since they hadn't killed me there, it wasn't likely they'd brought me all this way just to kill me here. At least not right away.

The rattletrap elevator came to a shaky halt, missing the fourth-floor landing by a couple of inches. Having entered last, Olaf backed out first.

"Very well, you may come out," he said. "Now close the doors and send the lift back down; that is the custom. The lower button. NED means down, but you know that. Now knock on the door to the right, if you please."

There were two apartments off this landing. I knocked on the door Olaf had indicated. It was opened by a rather small, intriguingly well-shaped female figure with blue eyes, and blonde hair that was cut boyishly short but didn't make the wearer look a bit boyish—an observation I remembered making once before. She was wearing snug

147

black pants and a big white turtleneck sweater that was not really designed to keep her neck warm; the collar was much too dramatic, large and loose.

"Come inside," she said. "I am Karin Segerby. I hope you remember me."

"How could I forget?" I said.

"I thought, in your work, you must meet so many awkward little girls with guns that one more might not make any impression. But I understand that our family has brought you here to deal with me, to prevent me from besmirching the sacred name of Stjernhjelm." Then her voice changed, losing its playful tone. "You were considerate the day we met in Hagerstown. Why could you not have been equally considerate today? It was not necessary, what you did to Astrid!"

"We'll see," I said. "In a day or two, I'll know how necessary it was. If I'm still around."

"We did not drug you and bring you here to kill you, Mr. Helm."

It was nice to have my optimistic theories confirmed; but I said, "So let's get on with what you did bring me here for, Cousin Karin. Or is Cousin Olaf going to do the honors? I assume an interrogation is next on the agenda."

She frowned quickly. "What makes you think—"

"Oh, for Christ's sake!" I said. "Do you know how long I've been in this racket? What else would you want me for? And when they say they're not going to *kill* you, with that emphasis, it always means just one thing: you're going to get your face rearranged or your feet toasted. Well, I don't know what the hell I know that you want to know, but I'm sure I'll find out shortly. Just do me one favor, Cousin Karin."

"What is that?"

"Don't tell me how it hurts you more than it hurts me, please. I wouldn't want to think of your suffering so."

She stared at me for a moment with wide, shiny, blue eyes; then she turned and hurried away through one of the doors opening onto the entrance hall. I heard Olaf chuckle behind me.

"You were not very kind to the sentimental little girl."

"If that's a terrorist," I said, "I'll eat it."

"Maybe not," Olaf said. "Maybe she is just a pretty girl with a social conscience. But aside from being decorative, she has one quite valuable attribute."

"What's that, money?"

"Well, that, too; but more valuable is her name. With that name, not the one with which she was born but the one she acquired by marriage, she will be happily received by any organization interested in weapons and explosives. Who'll reject a member, an impressionable and cooperative member, with connections at SVAB?"

"Makes sense," I said. "I guess a Mrs. Krupp, or a Mrs. Remington, would be just as welcome."

Waiting for instructions, I looked around the little hallway, and saw two familiar, inexpensive suitcases. One was open, mine. Above it, on a rather handsome little veneer table, lay the guns I'd collected along the way. There was also, I noted, the snub-nosed .38 Special revolver I'd lent to Astrid. Well, at least they were tidy; they'd apparently removed all our belongings from the guest villa at Torsäter including the firearms.

Olaf came forward and regarded the display for a moment. "You travel well armed, Helm. One would think you were planning a revolution."

"People keep giving them to me," I said.

"It would be interesting to know how you smuggled all these weapons into the country."

"No sweat," I said. "Nobody really looked."

"So typically American, this obsession with firearms!"

I glanced at the pistol in his hand. "You're not exactly walking around naked," I said. "A gun is a useful tool. I

149

wouldn't leave a good hammer or saw lying around to rust either. I might need to drive a nail or cut some wood. Same principle."

"Well, you do not hold one of your pretty guns now, you trigger-happy Yankee assassin!"

He was quick, but it had been easy to see he was working himself up to something, and I managed to duck a little as he slammed the High Standard against the side of my head, so the blow was a glancing one. Nevertheless, it made things go bright red for a moment. I let myself stagger back against the wall and slide down to a graceless sitting position, legs apart. It's always best to let them have the fun of knocking you down a few times and making you look foolish. It relaxes them and makes them feel more tolerant than if you insist on being brave and stubborn and staying on your feet no matter what. I'm referring to a simple intimidation-beating now, of course, not a fight to the death in which the boots may be a factor.

Olaf stood over me, glaring down at me. "There was no need for you to shoot Astrid over a little harmless sedative," he said harshly. "You murdering swine!"

That was a nice old-fashioned word. I hadn't been called a swine in years. I touched my head gingerly and found that the safety catch or slide release of his weapon, or maybe the front sight, although it's pretty low on those silenced jobs, had gouged my scalp, causing considerable bleeding. Fine. I could spare a little gore. The more helpless and bloody and terrified I looked, the shorter the coming ordeal would be, I hoped.

## CHAPTER 15

THE kitchen was big and old-fashioned, like that of the guest villa at Torsäter. It had a well-worn gas range and an ancient refrigerator, manufactured back in the days when, to paraphrase Henry Ford, you could get a kitchen appliance in any color you wanted as long as it was white. The Swedes, at least the ones with whom I was associating, had apparently not yet joined the disposable society; they believed in hanging on to stuff as long as it was working, whether or not it had long since gone out of style.

There was a wooden table against the wall and three wooden chairs. Although everything was old and showed evidence of hard use, it was quite clean; and the thin white curtains on the single window were crisp and immaculate. I found myself attributing this to Olaf's bachelor fussiness, although I had no really good reason to think he didn't have a wife somewhere around. They marry the damnedest guys, I reminded myself; one even married me, once. I'm not counting the times, including a recent night in Oslo, when I've faked the man-and-wife routine in the line of duty.

Olaf called through the door in Swedish, telling Karin to blow her nose and haul her ass in here. Well, that's a loose translation. She came in reluctantly and, on instructions, turned on the lights and pulled down the heavy roller-blind.

"In that chair," Olaf said to me. "Sit down, please."

I sat down. Karin came over; and shortly I found myself attached to the sturdy wooden chair by two-inch duct tape, the immensely strong, silvery stuff that has largely transformed the prisoner industry, rendering obsolete the old-fashioned methods of restraint employing ropes, wires, chains, or manacles. Then the small blonde girl disappeared silently, closing the kitchen door behind her. I wondered how many people there were in the apartment; I sensed the presence of some I hadn't seen. Certainly two more would be coming as soon as Karl and Greta got the Mercedes tucked away in its garage. Well, they had the troops. I could only hope it would make them overconfident.

Olaf stared at me for a moment after we were alone. He turned abruptly and walked over to the stove and lit one of the burners. The equipment was old-fashioned enough that he had to use a match. A sharpening steel hung beside a knife-rack on the nearby wall. It had a black plastic handle and a cross hilt to prevent you from slicing your fingers off when you were whipping the knife back and forth against the steel like a show-off chef. The business end was a tapering length of round stock about a foot long and almost half an inch in cross-section at its thickest point. Of the visible props, it was the one I'd have chosen if I'd been planning on staging the ordeal by fire. Olaf was of the same mind: he took down the steel and arranged it carefully on the stove top, with the end in the burner flame.

"The heat will do it no good, I suppose, but I have another," he said. "While we wait for it to warm, let us discuss our problem." He stood looking down at me. "You are an unfortunate complication, Helm. Even though the family does not like me very much—I, too, am a Stjernhjelm black sheep—they were forced to consult me because Sweden is such a peaceful country, and there was no one else available with experience in these violent matters. Unfortunately, I misjudged them; they were even more timid than I had anticipated. They took me too seriously when I suggested that we might resort to homicide, those fine gentlemen with their white manicured hands! I was only trying to prove that I had no interest in what happened to that troublesome little Karin Segerby; that I was even willing to arrange for her death if they wished to authorize such a drastic solution to their problem. However, it shocked them terribly; it made them afraid of me to the extent that they were no longer willing to leave the matter in my hands. Instead they listened to that stupid boy Torsten when he suggested your name, because you were so peaceful and reasonable that you had once refused to shoot a moose!" His voice turned accusing: "But there was no hesitation about shooting a woman this afternoon!"

"No moose ever fed me a Mickey Finn. And if you'd done your homework, you'd know what our standing orders are in that situation." I stared back at him. "What the hell is this all about? Just how do I complicate things for you?"

He walked over to the stove and picked up the sharpening steel. He put on a show of testing it and deciding that it wasn't as hot as it should be. He laid it back in the flame, a nice little menace bit that was designed to make me sweat and was reasonably successful. I don't enjoy being burned any more than the next guy. Or waiting for it. Olaf returned to stand over me.

"What is this Lysaniemi business?" he asked.

I was surprised by the question, and saw no harm in letting it show. "Lysaniemi? Why would you be interested in that? As far as I know, it's got nothing to do with you, or Astrid, or Karin Segerby, whatever it is you've all been up to. At least I get the distinct impression that you've been working together: Astrid knocks me out for you, Karin tapes me up for you, and you question me. Cooperation." I shrugged. "But I really can't see how Lysaniemi concerns any of you. To be honest, I can't even figure out how it concerns me."

Olaf regarded me bleakly. "Since Astrid called me from your Oslo motel room, I have done some research, but I have learned very little. That Lysaniemi is a village of a hundred and fifty persons in the country of Norbotten, the northernmost county in Sweden. That it lies just above the Arctic Circle, a hundred and twenty kilometers north of Highway E4, the main road to Haparanda on the nearby Finnish border. That it is not too far from our Swedish space facility at Kiruna, not to mention our big military installation at Boden, and our new communications center at Laxfors." He had been watching me closely to see if I reacted to any item on his list. Now his eyes widened slightly with satisfaction. "Ah, you are interested in Laxfors!"

"I'd like to know what it is," I said. "This is the first I've heard of it."

"*Lax* means 'salmon,' ", he said, still studying my face. It seemed as if every Stjernhjelm relative I met felt compelled to teach Swedish to the stupid American cousin. He went on: "A *fors* is a 'rapid,' or 'torrent.' A loose translation would be Salmon Falls; but in fact it is too far to the east, too far from the mountains, for a true waterfall. It is simply a minor cataract on a minor stream, not even large enough or steep enough to be harnessed for electric power. . . . You have not heard of Laxfors? It has been the subject of some controversy in the Swedish press. There have been suggestions that it is not exactly what it pretends to be; that the government is keeping secrets from the people, American secrets." He regarded me bleakly, and threw me a question in Swedish: *"Har du faktiskt aldrig hört om Mörkrummet?"*

It didn't seem necessary to pretend not to understand. "I said, "I know, I know; don't tell me. *Mörk* means 'dark';

154

*rummet* means 'the room.' So *Mörkrummet* means 'the darkroom.' How'm I doing?'' I gave him a grin. ''And to answer your question, no, I've truly never heard of the Darkroom, whatever the hell it may be. At Laxfors?'' When he nodded, I said, ''I presume the name doesn't refer to a simple photographic facility. You started out by saying that Laxfors is a communications center.''

Olaf shrugged. ''There is a windowless building, there at Laxfors, with an elaborate ventilation system. An imaginative Stockholm journalist called it the Darkroom, and the name has persisted. I understand the Russians are as curious about it as anybody else. After all, it was apparently built in response to all the numerous violations of Swedish territorial waters by Soviet submarines during the past few years. As I said, there have been suggestions to the effect that it was built with American advice and cooperation, which has upset a great many people in this country, who associate America primarily with the atom bomb and nuclear warheads. Any such cooperation has, of course, been firmly denied by our government, which insists Laxfors was built strictly for purposes of military communication.''

''A communications center should have antennas,'' I said, making it a question.

''To be sure,'' Olaf said. ''Large and conspicuous fields of tall antennas, out there on the tundra. But what transmissions are really involved? It is not as if Sweden had a global defense system. Our military forces are concentrated in a limited area, easily covered by ordinary radio. However, the American military might find good use for elaborate electronic equipment close to the Russian border. . . . But you say that Laxfors and its Darkroom do not concern you?''

I said, ''How do I know what concerns me, at this point? How close is Laxfors to Lysaniemi?''

"The distance is about eighty-five kilometers, roughly fifty-five of your English miles."

"You'd think if my boss was interested in this mysterious Darkroom of yours, he'd have given me an aiming point that was a little closer, and spelled out his wishes a little more clearly."

Olaf made a sharp gesture of annoyance. "Still this pretense of ignorance! You have never heard of Laxfors. You know nothing of the Darkroom. And you have no idea why you have been presented with the name Lysaniemi. You are completely mystified by the fact that your superior, now apparently *försvunnen*—vanished—considered this lonely Arctic village so important that he had the name passed to you indirectly by a courier of sorts rather than risk compromising it by giving it to you directly over the telephone. About all these things, you are totally in the dark! I am supposed to believe this?"

I said, "If my possible interference bothers you so much, why the hell did you get in touch with Astrid and ask her to help decoy me to Sweden?" A thought came to me, and I looked at him sharply. "Come to that, how did you make her acquaintance in the first place. . . . Acquaintance, hell! You're the demon lover who took off when she got pregnant, according to her story, leaving it up to nice Cousin Alan Watrous to pick up the pieces, and redeem the family honor by marrying her."

He hesitated, and shrugged. "Very well. I . . . knew her in America. I have never said I did not. But it was not the way you suggest. When she became *enceinte*, to use that old term, I offered to do whatever she wished. What she wished was for me to leave, and let it be thought I had deserted her. She preferred Alan, and the position and security I could not provide; she was certain she could persuade him to look after her and her unborn child, and she did. But we have remained friendly enough

156

that I was not embarrassed to ask a favor of her when one was needed."

I studied him for a moment. Some odd relationships were involved here; but then, these were odd people, my Swedish relatives. Well, I've been told I'm a little odd myself.

I said, dismissing the subject, "Which brings us back to the question: why did you ask her to approach my boss and request my help, when the last thing you really wanted was my interference?"

"You are being very obtuse," Olaf said irritably. "I had to go through the motions of doing what those important family members required, in order to retain a little of their uncertain confidence. I could not have them thinking I resented too much being bypassed in your favor. They would have summoned you anyway, even if I had refused to help. Better to remain in a position to know if you were becoming dangerously suspicious; in a position, also, to discover that your chief in Washington had not, apparently, released you from your government service to assist your aristocratic Swedish relatives entirely out of the kindness of his heart. He had another axe to grind, to use your American slang; he had another fish to fry. Lysaniemi."

"Okay, say he's using me to kill two birds with one stone, to keep the cliches coming; suppose he's sent me here to solve the Segerby problem for my family and at the same time solve the Lysaniemi problem, whatever it may be, for himself; what difference does it make to you?"

Olaf shook his head grimly. "We cannot afford to have his problems conflict with our problems. We have serious plans. They will be implemented soon. We must know that nothing will interfere with them. You seem to be a dangerous man in your clumsy, blundering way. Years ago, for instance, you came to this country and managed, somehow, to smash an important Soviet espionage operation, you and your foolish guns. Although we are not dealing with Russians or espionage now, we cannot afford to have you stumbling around in the wrong places shooting everything in sight while you try to prevent Karin Segerby from bringing disgrace to the family. What an old-fashioned idea; some people still live in the Middle Ages, here in Sweden! As if the tired old Swedish nobility means anything these days!''

I said, ''That ought to be my speech, Baron Stjernhjelm. I'm the democratic character who calls himself Mr. Helm.''

''And who, nevertheless, like all Americans, is tremendously respectful of any title.'' He laughed shortly. ''Astrid is even worse; I think she even allowed me to make love to her, at first, simply because I was a baron. She is very impressed and somewhat intimidated by us obsolete aristocrats, even though her own Finnish family is as good as any. Barons frighten her, counts positively terrify her— it was a great shock to her, working with him, when she discovered that Alan had a title, even one he had put aside to become an American—and Heaven help her if she should ever meet a prince. I suppose it is the result of being brought up in Indiana.'' Olaf shook his head quickly. ''But enough of that. We have more important things to discuss. Like Lysaniemi.''

''I keep telling you—''

Olaf didn't let me finish. He interrupted: ''We have you now, and we will keep you until it is too late for you to interfere personally; but we must also leave no loose ends to trip ourselves up. We must know that this other problem you have been sent here to deal with is not going to backfire without you—is that the proper word, backfire?—and damage our plans. We must know the significance of Lysaniemi.'' He glanced towards the stove. ''We do not like to employ such methods, but an answer we must have!''

Since the beginning of time and torture, they've always announced that they were too good, too pure, to use the rack and thumbscrew, or the knout, or the hot irons, and gone right ahead and used them anyway, for the simple reason that they work.

I put some desperation into my voice when I answered. It wasn't hard to do under the circumstances, and I managed a nice scared quaver: "For Christ's sake, can't you get it through your head that I don't know what it means? Lysaniemi, Lysaniemi. *Lysa* means 'light' or 'shine' in Swedish, doesn't it. Or it could be a girl's name, perhaps derived from Elizabeth. Elise. Elyse. Lysa. *Niemi* means 'point' or 'cape' or 'promontory' in Finnish. Or 'naze' or 'ness,' like in Inverness, if you want to be old-fashioned. Derived from the Scandinavian *näsa*, meaning 'nose,' in case you're interested. Shining Nose, Lapland. Lizzie's Point. If that means anything to you, you're welcome to it."

He backhanded me alongside the head. I was grateful that, once I'd been securely taped, he'd laid aside the pistol.

"You are playing games with me!"

I said, "Damn it, you're the one who's been making with the languages; I thought you liked the semantic stuff. I don't know what the hell Lysaniemi means. If it's a code word, I don't have the code. As for why it was passed to me like that, by way of the lady instead of through normal channels, I have absolutely no idea except that, as she'll have told you, our channels aren't very normal at the moment."

"You will talk," he said, stepping forward. "You will talk, I guarantee it."

He was very systematic about it. He carefully untied my necktie and unbuttoned my shirt. Then he took out a small penknife, opened the larger of the two blades, and slit my undershirt down the front from throat to waist. He pulled it open to bare my chest, and frowned.

"Those old scars. You have been burned before."

I said bravely, "Sure, the last guy used an electric soldering iron plugged into the wall, very modern. The hot ends of lighted cigars and cigarettes are also very popular for the purpose, as I've discovered the hard way. But don't be bashful, carry on with your old-fashioned branding-iron technique."

"You are trying to tell me that you are so hardened to this type of interrogation that you cannot be made to talk?"

I said, "Oh, for Christ's sake, Stjernhjelm! I'm a pro, not a fucking hero. It's only the lousy amateurs who're supposed to be superhuman. And the armed forces: if captured tell only your name, rank, and serial number, that bullshit! Who're they trying to kid? Our outfit is operated on the principle that people are practically all human, even our people. When the pressure really comes on, they'll wiggle and scream and wet their pants, and cough up every last bit of information they own. Oh, there may be a few stoical supermen around, but I guarantee I'm not one of them. What do you want, the agency roster? You want some secret passwords? You want the boss's middle name, highly classified information? You want our in-house cipher? Ask and it shall be yours as far as I can supply it from memory—I might have a little trouble with the cipher—with the blessings of Washington. If I were carrying critical information, I'd have had a kill-me capsule handy, and choked it down when I realized what that bitch had put into my drink, rather than wind up in a cook-in like this. Otherwise, we're allowed to spill our guts to save ourselves; except that in this case I have no guts to spill. I don't know what the hell Lysaniemi is all about. I haven't any idea."

"You'll forgive me if I don't believe you."

That was stupid. I hadn't the slightest intention of forgiving him if he carried out his painful intentions; but there's never any sense in blowing off about all the terrible things you're going to do to the sadistic creep by way of retaliation—the old *you'll-be-sorry* routine the loudmouthed heroes are always pulling in the movies to show the audience what brave fellows they are. In real life, you don't want to antagonize the guy unnecessarily, or give him the idea that, since you're such a fanatic vengeance hound, maybe the only safe thing for him to do, when he's through with you, is kill you.

I watched Olaf turn and pick up the smoking steel and come back to me. Well, I guess it was the plastic handle that was smoking a bit, with that acrid petrochemical stink, as the heat traveled up the metal to it. I told myself that I was a very stoical character, practically impervious to pain, and it was just another toast-fest like I'd endured before; but I quickly discovered that the nerve endings get no less sensitive with practice. . . .

Only one thing helps. You don't have to bluster about it, but you can think about it; and I concentrated on visualizing the scene when it was my turn. First I worked it out with a gun: smash the knee and elbow joints, shoot the fingers off one by one, blast the eardrums with the muzzle held close, and blow away the testicles. One thing you don't want to do is blind the bastard. You want him to be able to watch you enjoying yourself. You want him to see and appreciate what's happening to him. You want him to know he played his scorching tic-tac-toe on the wrong guy's chest and got himself totally ruined; and then maybe you can afford to be nice and put one between the eyes to end it. Or maybe not. Okay. So what about a knife, let's figure it with a knife. A knife is always good, and you can perform more delicately painful operations with a blade than you can with a bullet. . . .
Oh, Jesus, how long is the sonofabitch going to keep this

161

up, anyway? How long does it take to convince the bastard I don't *know*?

Or do I?

It came to me quite suddenly. After all, I'd worked with Mac a long time; I should by now have a pretty good idea of how his mind operated. I should have realized what he was trying to accomplish here. I should have understood that I hadn't been told what Lysaniemi meant for the very simple reason that it didn't mean anything. At least not yet. Not until the fish took the bait, the meaningless bait, and got itself hooked and netted and gutted, up there in the lonely wilderness above the Arctic Circle. But that was no help at the moment. . . .

"Stop it, Olaf!" It was a woman's voice. The kitchen door had opened. It was Astrid Watrous' voice. All kinds of stray females were turning up here, live and dead, I reflected hazily; but I couldn't deny the powerful sense of relief that hit me, and not merely because somebody was trying to put an end to the blister bash. She cried, "Please stop it now! I told you he doesn't know. Haven't you done enough to prove it? Can't you *see* he doesn't know?"

## CHAPTER 16

HOLLYWOOD has the right idea. A movie hero is allowed to have it tough, sartorially speaking. In an action drama he's always losing the knees out of his pants, the elbows out of his jacket, and the buttons off his shirt, not to mention winding up covered with dirt and gore. A screen heroine, on the other hand, is seldom permitted to suffer anything more damaging to her appearance than some mildly mussed hair and a smudge alongside the nose, even in the most violent disaster epic. That's as it should be. I mean, you want *somebody* in the cast looking reasonably attractive even through all the rough stuff, right?

But this was not a movie. The hero, if I qualified for the title, was in a normally heroic and bedraggled cinematic state, to be sure, bloody and burned; but no Hollywood heroine would ever have allowed herself to be filmed in Astrid's condition. When she came around to where, still taped to my chair, I could get a good look at her, the first gory impression was shocking even to a gent, like me, who's seen a reasonable number of casualties.

Two of my bullets seemed to have taken effect, one nicking her left ear and the other drilling through her left arm at the lower biceps, presumably missing the bone, since I doubted she was tough enough to be walking around with a shattered humerus, not even properly immobilized yet—she just had the hand tucked into her waistband for support. She was doing well to be upright at all. A gutsy lady.

But a distressingly beatup-looking one, like something off a battlefield. Both wounds had bled copiously, soaking the shoulder and sleeve of her jacket, and the collar and shoulder of her blouse, one sleeve of which had been ripped away to bare her wounded arm, and used to make a crude bandage knotted a few inches above the elbow. She was wearing the stained blazer over her shoulders for warmth; she was undoubtedly feeling chilly and shivery from reaction. The nicked ear had been patched with a Band-Aid, and blood was drying down the side of her neck, and on her exposed arm, as well as on her clothes; even her slacks were badly spattered.

We faced each other for a moment without speaking. I saw her note my damaged scalp and seared chest.

I made myself speak harshly: "Jeez, what lousy marksmanship! One miss. One graze. One flesh wound. The instructors back at the Ranch would have my hide. That must have been very sudden and potent stuff you dropped into my Scotch.''

She studied my face for a moment. She smiled faintly. ''What, no remorse or apologies, darling?''

''I don't see you weeping any big tears of sympathy for me,'' I said. ''Sure, I always regret fouling up a shooting chore. I'm supposed to be a specialist, remember?'' I glanced at Olaf, who was watching us with interest. I said accusingly, ''You let me think she was dead. Murdering swine, you called me. Yankee assassin.''

''Well, you are a Yankee assassin and a murdering swine, are you not? Even though you failed to kill in this instance.'' Olaf smiled thinly. ''The torture scene is always more effective if the torturer establishes a personal reason for hating his subject. It seemed advisable to let you believe that your bullets had been accurate, and that I was terribly distressed by the lady's demise, relishing every minute of your suffering, and willing to prolong it indefinitely. Actually, I do not like these interrogations very much. But you are not the only professional in the game, Helm.''

I said, ''It was a great performance, but all it got you was what I told you in the first place. I don't have the slightest idea what's awaiting me in Lysaniemi; I just assume I'm supposed to get up there and find out.''

He shook his head irritably. ''You will go nowhere until we have completed our operation!''

I shrugged. ''Okay, okay. You hold the cards, no need to get tough about it. I don't suppose it's any use asking you what this mysterious operation of yours is.''

''No use whatever. . . . Yes, what is it, Karl?''

The blond boy who'd been sent off with the Mercedes must have entered the apartment while the kitchen door was closed and my attention was distracted by the hot iron. I hadn't heard him arrive; but now he stood in the doorway. A little behind him I could see a wiry dark girl in jeans, attractive in an intense way, with good cheekbones and a generous mouth. That would be the so-far invisible Greta. She was wearing large glasses, but they did not hide the dedicated look in her otherwise fine brown eyes: another fanatic. No makeup, of course. Would Joan of Arc wear eye shadow to the bonfire?

I still couldn't really follow what Karl was saying, except that in this case it concerned a doctor. The Swedes often use the same word, but spelled with a *k* instead of a *c*; however, Karl employed the equivalent term, ''läkare,'' meaning healer.

Astrid said to me, ''The physician I have been waiting for, one we know who will not talk about bullet wounds, has just telephoned. He has been delayed by an emergency. He cannot come to me for some time. If I require immediate attention, I must go to him.'' She straightened up, and winced, and glanced down at the stained rag of silk around her arm. ''It has been neglected too long already, so I will go. Fortunately his office is not too far, I am told. You might show a little concern, my dear. I am hurting rather badly.''

''Join the club,'' I said unsympathetically. ''Do I get a doctor, too?''

Olaf said, ''All you require is a little lard and some aspirin, both available here.'' He turned to Astrid. ''Greta will drive you in the rental Golf in which you were brought here, Helm's car. . . . You watch this one, Karl, while I make the arrangements. Mr. Helm is supposed to be very tricky, although he has shown no evidence of it so far.''

''I watch,'' said Karl in English, the first time I'd heard him use the language.

Astrid hesitated for a moment, still standing over me. ''Good-bye for now, Matthew.''

''I'll try to be here when you get back. Unless something important comes up.''

"I am sorry it must be this way. I am sorry we must be enemies and hurt each other."

She hesitated, as if she wanted to say more; then she turned quickly and hurried out of the kitchen. Cousin Olaf turned off the stove and hung up the sharpening steel, discolored by flame and maybe, a little, by me. He gave a keep-your-eyes-open sign to Karl, and followed her, closing the door behind him. Waiting, we could hear sporadic activity and conversation out in the hall: I assumed that Greta was being sent to bring her car around so Astrid would not have so far to walk, not only to conserve her strength but because she wasn't really presentable enough to appear in public. At last the front door slammed a final time.

There was a lengthy period of silence. I wondered if Olaf was resting, or holding a council of war with Karin Segerby; but I hadn't got the impression that the girl was as important to this outfit as the family seemed to think. Perhaps it was prideful thinking: if a Stjernhjelm was involved in something wicked, she should at least be playing a starring role, not just a bit part. Or maybe Olaf was simply making love to her; I'd heard that inflicting pain was sexually stimulating to some people, as enduring it was to others. Well, it takes all kinds. I hate to admit it, but that hot iron had done nothing at all for me.

Karl apparently felt no need to talk. Neither did I. We waited in silence. At last the kitchen door opened and Olaf entered briskly, carrying an aspirin bottle and a tube of ointment.

"This is better than lard, I believe," he said cheerfully, approaching my chair. "Anesthetic and antibiotic, says the label. Hold still now."

"I've got a choice, the way I'm stuck to this chair?" I gritted my teeth as he smeared the stuff on my chest; but I had to give him credit, he was no rougher than he had to be. I said, "The time I got those other scars, I had a pretty girl to administer the first aid."

He grinned. "Yes, I asked Karin if she would do the honors, guessing that you would prefer it; but she said that pain, hers or anybody else's, made her sick. So you must endure my ministrations. A terrible hardship case, as I believe you Yankees call it." He paused to look down at me. "You are a big fraud, my friend."

"How so?"

"All that talk about screaming your head off; and the best—or worst—I could get out of you was a grunt." He smiled faintly. "Yes, you are a professional. They always talk about what big cowards they are. It is the amateurs who must make brave sounds to give themselves courage. . . . There, that should make it feel a little better. I will put the tube into your pocket; you can have more applied when the anesthetic effect wears off. Would you rather have your shirt buttoned or left open?"

"TV tells us that bare-chested men are all the rage these days. Let's not have any unnecessary friction in the critical area."

"To be sure. Here is the aspirin. . . ."

He stopped as Karin opened the door. Her glance touched me for a moment, and found the burns on my chest. She looked away quickly, swallowing hard. Obviously the girl was in the wrong line of work: she couldn't pull a trigger, and damaged people made her queasy.

"Yes?" Olaf said impatiently.

"There is another telephone call," she said in Swedish. "A man, I do not know the voice. He must speak with you."

Olaf said, "Swallow that, Helm. . . . I will be back in a minute."

"I can hardly wait," I said.

He followed the small blonde girl out of the room. He was gone considerably longer than a minute. They build

167

well over there, with solid walls and doors. At least they did when that old apartment house was constructed; and we could hear nothing of the phone conversation from the kitchen. At last the door opened again, and Olaf came in. The call he'd received seemed to have caused a drastic transformation in his personality: he was no longer the friendly, chatty jailer who'd treated my burns. His face was grim, and he carried the silenced pistol in his hand. He stood there for a moment, regarding me without expression; then he gestured with the gun.

"Cut him loose, Karl. . . . Just a moment. Button up his shirt and tie his cravat first."

I said, "We're going somewhere?"

He stared at me as if he'd never really seen me before. The High Standard was steady in his hand.

"I should have known that where you find one clever Yankee assassin you are likely to find more!"

Well, it was about time. I'd been wondering if Joel could have lost us completely; and if not, what the hell he was waiting for.

I said, "Would I attend a family reunion without having somebody covering me, a professional like me? You know how dangerous families are, particularly this family. What's the word from my colleague?"

"He has the women."

Well, it was the obvious move. I said, "The good old hostage gambit."

Olaf licked his lips, and spoke in a strained voice: "He has tortured Greta. He used her to force Astrid to speak."

"Greta is hurt?" This was young Karl, who'd been having trouble following the English conversation. "She is badly hurt?"

"I insisted on speaking with Astrid, to confirm the situation," Olaf said. "She says that Greta . . ." He hesitated.

"Tell me!"

"They are at Doktor Hasselman's office," Olaf said. "There was no emergency. That telephone call was a trick. The man, Helm's associate, must have followed us all the way from Torsäter here; then he stood watch outside this building. When he saw the doctor with his bag, he guessed that he had come here to attend Astrid. He made the doctor a prisoner, took him back to his office, tied him up, and forced him to make the call. When Astrid and Greta walked in, they were also captured. The man started to question Astrid. When she refused to tell him what he wanted, he took one of the doctor's scalpels and simply . . . Greta will live, she is not dangerously injured, but Astrid says there will probably be some disfigurement."

The boy made a choking sound in his throat. He turned on me sharply and slapped my face hard. "Animals!" he gasped. "Can you wonder that we must change a world that is run by people like you and your brutal accomplices?"

His English was improving by the minute; but I couldn't help staring at him in wonderment. As I said, they scare hell out of me. Anybody who can complain self-righteously about a little bladework, when he's just been a willing accomplice to a hot-poker session, is operating according to a logic beyond my comprehension. But I guess the world is full of folks who are serenely convinced that anything they do is right, and anything that's done to them is wrong.

"That is enough, Karl," Olaf snapped. "Now free him, please."

When the duct tape had been cut, I peeled it off my wrists and ankles, sitting there. I said, "I want my guns and my suitcase, please. And Karin Segerby."

"You want!" Olaf's voice was contemptuous. "What you want cuts no ice here, Helm. If I have the proper phrase."

I said, "Wake up and smell the coffee, friend. If I have

169

the proper phrase. The question now is simply, do Astrid and the girl mean more to you than I do to my pal Joel. I think they do, because Joel isn't really my pal. He's just a guy assigned to do a job with me; and the job comes first. He's a fairly cold-blooded character. If things go sour—if, for instance, you shoot me with that pistol you keep waving at me—Joel will simply put bullets into the two girls and the doctor, because they've seen his face and he doesn't want the Swedish cops, or you, on his trail too soon. He'll disappear into the night and try to do my job for me. *Scratch one Helm; Operation Lysaniemi still running; signed Joel.*" I looked hard at Olaf. "If that's the way you want it, pull the trigger. If you want it any other way, remember that Joel's training is exactly the same as mine. He doesn't bluff any more than I do; and he doesn't have a skinful of dope the way I did when I had Astrid under my gun, so his marksmanship should be considerably better. If he tells you he's going to shoot if you do something, and you do it, somebody'll wind up dead, you can count on it."

"If he does any more harm to the girls I will kill him!" Olaf's voice has harsh. "I will be waiting up there in *vildmarken* when he comes. I am very good in the wilderness."

"Joel's a pretty good *vildmark* boy himself. Not having seen you in action, Cousin, except with the other guy taped to a chair, I wouldn't bet on it either way. But suppose you do kill him; what's left for you except to blow your own brains out and make a clean sweep, dead bodies all over the lousy place. Just because you got trigger-happy here without thinking it through. Why not deal?"

"What deal do you suggest?"

"Two for two. You want your Astrid. Young Galahad here wants his Greta. I want my me. And I want Karin Segerby. I won't hurt her. I've been imported to keep her from being hurt, among other things, remember?"

170

"What will you do with her?"

"Hell, I don't know, yet. But I'm supposed to get her away from the bad company she's been keeping, for the family's sake; I might as well start doing my chores. . . ."

Watching him, I couldn't really believe it was happening. I mean, the man obviously considered himself a tough professional, one of us, yet from his expression I gathered that he was actually beginning to consider the bargain I'd offered him. He was contemplating giving up a dangerous prisoner, a serious threat to his plans, one he'd gone to considerable trouble to capture, for the sake of a pretty blonde lady with big brown eyes. How sentimental could you get? Well, maybe I was being too hard on him; maybe I was too strongly influenced by my own tough indoctrination. We are trained not to play the hostage game under any circumstances unless . . .

My thoughts stopped right there. I'd forgotten the kicker: *unless the hostage is of extreme value to the operation, essential, the very heart of the mission.* I looked at Olaf's long Norse face again, so like my own in many ways, although I hated to admit it. This was not the face of a man who, with a big assignment in the balance, would get mushy about a woman, even a woman who'd meant something to him once and perhaps still did. He'd know the world is full of women, and hearts don't break so easily, at least not the vulcanized organs that pump life through men like him, and me. If he was willing to make a deal for Astrid under these conditions, it meant that I was going to revise my estimate of her importance drastically. She was more than just a stray dame he'd called on for help because she happened to be on the proper side of the Atlantic and was willing to do him a favor for old times' sake.

"Very well," he said. "You have your deal. And you will get your belongings back when the two women are safe."

171

"And Karin?"

"I will speak with her. She is free to go with you if she wishes, but I will not force her."

"Fair enough," I said. "Let's put the show on the road. Another Yankeeism for you, Cousin."

## CHAPTER 17

KARL drove the Mercedes with Karin sitting up front beside him; Olaf and I occupied the rear seat. It was getting close to midnight, and there wasn't much traffic. For a big city, Stockholm pulls in its sidewalks early. Olaf's directions to our young chauffeur, who was apparently imported talent and didn't know the neighborhood, soon brought us to a newish two-story medical building called Vasakliniken, only half a dozen blocks from the apartment.

The Vasa Clinic—they do love to run two or more words together—was presumably named for Gustav Vasa, the ancient monarch who holds just about the same Father-of-His-Country spot in Sweden that George Washington does in the U.S., having earned it by creating a unified country out of a bunch of squabbling minor kingdoms.

I'd been cleaned up, more or less, and given another big Stjernhjelm overcoat to cover my stained seersucker jacket, so we aroused no interest as we marched through the lobby after parking in the lot outside that was almost empty at this late hour; but I'd noted my red rental VW-Ford standing there. Following orders, I led the way with Olaf close behind, hand in pocket. After him came Karin Segerby, with Karl walking beside her carrying my suitcase. I'd

172

noted when we left the apartment that Astrid's suitcase had no longer been in the hall; presumably she'd taken it with her so she could change into a less beat-up costume after treatment. An elevator took us to the second floor.

"To the right," Olaf directed me. "Now, the third door on the right. Open it. Remember, any tricks from you or your friend, and I will make certain of you, no matter who else dies for it."

I didn't really believe him. At least I thought that, with Astrid's important life probably at stake—and I'd better find out fast just what made her so important—he'd hesitate to start the shooting; but I reminded myself that he was no Karin Segerby, unaccustomed to guns and afraid of them. He was my brand of Stjernhjelm, the mean kind, and he might have in him enough of the old, suicidal, charge-to-a-glorious-death berserker blood to set off a massacre if directly challenged in this awkward situation.

In military terms I believe it's called a disengagement, and it's always a problem. You've met the enemy and fought him to a standstill, or vice versa. Now you don't want to fight him anymore under these no-win conditions, and he feels the same way; but how do you break contact without giving either side an advantage that can be exploited by a sudden sneak play?

"Just take it easy, Cousin," I said. "Let's not decimate our family tonight; think of all the generations of Stjernhjelms that fought and loved so hard to make us."

"And enjoyed every minute of it . . . Open the door."

I opened it. The tableau inside was intriguing. It was a shiny little medical waiting room that any American patient would have felt at home in; but Joel's three prisoners were seated stiffly, like the three monkeys, facing the door on three straight chairs set in front of the receptionist's counter. Joel wasn't visible.

I had a moment in which to note that Dr. Hasselman, a plump, balding man in a dark suit, seemed to be scared and angry but unhurt. Astrid, in the middle, looked as I'd last seen her, except that she had some kind of trench coat wrapped around her and her expression was a bit more haggard due, presumably, to the continuing pain of her wound. The dark girl, Greta, had joined the night's casualties, holding a large, bloody wad of gauze to her left cheek; there was blood on her clothes as well. Hemoglobin was the color of the day, or night. Greta's hair was wildly disordered, as if somebody had used it to yank her head around the way he wanted it. She'd lost her big spectacles, and her naked eyes were wide and shocked. It was not a good evening for attractive ladies. If my chest hadn't been giving me hell in spite of the anesthetic ointment, I might have been ashamed of Joel and myself for being so unchivalrous.

Joel's voice spoke from the corner to the left, out of our range of vision: "Come inside slowly."

Behind me, Olaf said, "Show yourself, first. I should mention that I have a weapon aimed at Mr. Helm's spine."

Joel's voice said, "Helm gives me my orders, not you. But you'd better keep in mind that, whatever happens, I'll have a bead on the pretty lady in the middle. You can blast me with a .458 Magnum elephant rifle, and I'll still get her as I go down."

Deadlock. There was a little silence. No traffic sounds reached us from outside the building; and nobody came down the corridor inside it. Up here on the second floor, we seemed to have Vasakliniken, all of Stockholm, to ourselves.

I said sharply, "To hell with this. Let's cut out this hair-trigger stuff before somebody else gets hurt, Cousin Olaf; we've shed enough blood for one night. What do you say?"

His voice was expressionless: "What do you suggest? That we trust each other? That would truly be a new departure. Tell me how you would like us to implement this revolutionary concept."

174

"First, young Karl," I said. "I'm willing to trust you up to a point, but I'm not willing to trust an untrained boy who thinks he has a grievance. Let's get him out front, where we can all keep an eye on him. Ask him to leave Karin and the suitcase in the hall and slide past us and walk over to stand by his girl. I'll accept your assurance that, if he's armed, he won't blow his stack in some stupid way if he sees a chance. Okay so far?"

"It is okay. Karl, you heard. Walk over there and behave yourself."

The boy made his way past the two of us. We watched him cross the waiting room to the seated girl. She reached up to take his hand and squeeze it hard with the hand that was not holding the stained gauze. I found myself wondering how badly her face was damaged underneath it. Undoubtedly Karl was wondering the same thing, and telling himself firmly that it didn't matter, since it was her beautiful soul that he loved, anyway.

"Thank you, Baron Stjernhjelm," I said. "I appreciate the token of faith. Now, in return, I'm going to instruct Joel to come out where you can see him, and put his gun away. That gives you a chance to wipe out both of us if you can shoot fast enough and feel so inclined. If not, I suggest you step well forward, turning to cover us if you wish, but giving us room to withdraw peacefully together, right out this door. Deal?"

I heard him laugh shortly. "If you can imitate an honorable gentleman, Mr. Helm, who am I to do less?" As Joel came into sight, hands empty, I felt a sudden weight in my right-hand overcoat pocket, and realized that Olaf had given me back my silenced pistol—well, the agency's silenced pistol. That didn't mean, of course, that he didn't have a weapon of his own; but it was still a respectable gesture of confidence. He said, "Now I will walk past you and out into the room where your man can kill me. . . . It is too bad that we are on opposite sides in this, Cousin. We seem to think along similar lines.''

I said, "Hell, I still don't even know what the sides are, let alone who's on which one. . . . Come on, Joel, let's blow the joint."

Leaving, I had a last glimpse of Astrid Watrous watching us go, her brown eyes grave in her pale face. Karin Segerby awaited us in the corridor.

"Olaf said you wished me to accompany you," she said.

"I think it's time for you to get out of this, don't you?"

She hesitated. "Very well. I come with you."

When I started to pick up the suitcase at her feet, Joel beat me to it. "I'll carry it; you look kind of rocky. Problems?"

"Only third-degree burns over ninety-five percent of the body," I said as we headed towards the elevators. "A slight exaggeration; but you took your sweet time moving in."

"Hell, you said to hold off long enough for them to commit themselves." After the elevator door had closed on us, he turned to the girl. "I'm Paul Haraldsen."

"I am Karin Segerby. Mrs. Karin Segerby. But my husband is dead." She seemed to be a little dazed by the events of the evening, although she hadn't played a very large part in them. But she wanted everything to be perfectly clear, including her exact marital status. Her wide blue eyes studied Joel's face. "Did you *have* to do that to Greta, Mr. Haraldsen?"

"Greta? Oh, the dark kid." Joel shrugged. "It's too bad, Mrs. Segerby. I don't know why people never seem to believe I mean what I say. I told the blonde one, the older one, Watrous, that I'd cut her young friend if she didn't cooperate. The choice was hers. If she doesn't want scar-faced friends, she can answer what she's asked and do what she's told."

The elevator doors opened, releasing us into the lobby.

176

Outside, we walked briskly across the driveway into the parking lot. Joel steered me past the red Golf to a black vintage Volvo. He tossed my suitcase in front and climbed in after it. I opened the rear door for the Karin and followed her in. Joel took us away.

"What's the name of your peace outfit?" I asked the girl beside me after we'd driven for a while.

"I don't think I want to tell you that," Karin said. "Or will you cut my face if I don't answer?"

"UFO," Joel said without turning his head.

"What?" I asked.

"That's what I was asking the Watrous woman," he said. "One of the things. They call themselves UFO, but they pronounce it differently. Not You-Foe, but something like Ooh-Foo. It stands for Ungdomen's Fredsorganization. You know how they run their words together. *Fred* means 'peace.' *Ungdom* means youth. Youth's Peace Organization."

I sighed. Now Joel was getting into the act and teaching me Swedish—a lousy Polack named Valdemar Konowski, for God's sake!

"Olaf Stjernhjelm hardly qualifies as a kid," I said. "Even Astrid Watrous can't be considered a dewy juvenile."

"A youth organization needs a little adult guidance," Joel said. "At least this one does; it was apparently set up with considerable assistance, financial and otherwise, from a well-heeled parent organization in America. Naturally, they wanted to protect their investment, so they arranged to have a grown-up adviser riding herd on the wild-eyed kids."

"Olaf?"

"Correct. They had him over in the States for a while for indoctrination; that's how he met Mrs. Watrous, visiting his relative, Alan Watrous, in Gloucester. Only she was still Astrid Land back then."

"And the name of the American peace group?"

"You know them. The People for Nuclear Peace, or PNP. You had some problems with them in the Bahamas recently, I understand."

I said irritably, "It's a screwy world when you've got to fight a bunch of folks whose basic motives you respect, just because their methods are so haywire. But I thought we'd pretty well put that outfit out of business."

Joel's voice was cold: "You thought you'd put Bennett out of business, too, but he's right in there plugging; he's even sitting in the boss chair now, for God's sake! Maybe you're getting soft in your old age. Next time you've got a trigger to pull, maybe you should think about pulling it. Hell, even when you did pull one, you missed the shot, just pinking the Watrous woman in the arm!"

There was something in what he said, but it wasn't his place to say it. On the other hand, it wasn't my place to get involved in a disciplinary hassle. Looking out the car windows, I realized that I didn't know where in Stockholm we'd got to.

"Where are you taking us?" I asked.

"Mrs. Watrous said something else; something I think we'd better check out. She gave me an address. I'm pretty sure that having been forced to betray it to me, she'll be heading there herself to pass a warning. Let's hope she won't want to use the doctor's phone in front of everybody there, not to mention talking through the clinic switchboard; and that she'll take time to get her arm fixed so we can beat her to it."

"Mystery?" I said.

"Bear with me, pal. Better for you to come to it cold. I want to see your reaction."

He was pushing hard, but he always had been a pushy guy to work with, forever testing to see how much tolerance he could expect from the man in charge of the operation; which could be the reason he'd never been put in charge, himself. But again, this wasn't the time or place for a showdown.

"Whatever you say," I said.

"Afterwards, I'll take you back to your car; I got the key off the Lagersten kid. You'll be heading north next, I suppose. Watrous said you had something going at a wide place in the road up near the Arctic Circle."

"North?" It was the small girl beside me. "You are traveling north, Mr. Helm? Will you drive anywhere near the government's so-called communication center at Laxfors?"

I started to ask a foolish question, like why did she want to know, and checked myself. "My destination is about eighty-five kilometers from there," I said. "Why, do you want to come along for the ride?"

"Yes, I would very much like to come along. If you do not mind."

I looked at her and grinned. After a little, she looked away. Even in the erratic lighting inside the moving car, I could see the color rising under that very fair, very smooth skin. I didn't say anything.

At last she gulped, and said, "All right. Before we left the apartment, Olaf told me that it was very good that you had asked for me, and that I am supposed to stay with you as long as I possibly can, since Astrid is no longer traveling with you as . . . as observer. I am to keep Olaf informed about where you are and what you are doing. . . ."

Before I could speak, the car stopped and Joel spoke from in front: "There's the address the Watrous woman gave me. That doorway just up the side street to the left. We'll wait right here and see what goes in. Or comes out . . . Whoa, hold everything, our timing is perfect, there's Mrs. Watrous going in now, all clean and bandaged. Somebody must have driven like hell to get her here so fast. I suppose that fancy Mercedes is waiting up the street while she runs inside with the warning."

179

Astrid was a slender, dark figure hurrying down the far sidewalk—well, dark except for the neat blond hair. As Joel had said, she was in much better shape than when last seen; she'd changed to the jeans and dark jersey I'd bought her on another continent. Her left arm was supported by somebody's blue silk scarf doing duty as a sling. At least I thought it was blue; at night, at the distance, it was hard to tell.

She vanished into the doorway Joel had pointed out. We waited. Somewhere nearby, undoubtedly, Olaf was also waiting to make the pickup, as Joel had suggested, probably with Karl as wheelman. It seemed likely that Greta had been left behind at the clinic, however. It would have taken longer than this to attend to her wound properly, under anesthesia. I wished I had a little anesthesia, and remembered that I did have the tube Olaf had given me, but it was hardly the time to be smearing goop on my chest.

"Back door?" I asked.

Joel said, "I suppose there's got to be one, but I didn't ask. I didn't want to seem too interested. Let's hope they'll figure that knowing the city better and driving faster, they've made it far enough ahead of us so they don't need to get tricky . . . There's our girl again, checking to see if the coast is clear. Come on, baby, tell them it's safe as houses; get them out where we can see them!"

Karin stirred beside me. "I do not understand. Whom do you expect, Mr. Haraldsen?"

Joel didn't answer. He was watching Astrid in the distant doorway. She turned briefly to beckon to someone inside; then she came down the two steps to the sidewalk and looked back once more to make sure she was followed. Two people had appeared behind her. The man was better than medium height for a man, blond, with a sizable blond moustache; he was wearing flannel slacks and a tweed jacket. The woman was about the same height in her high heels, which made her quite tall for a woman. She was wearing dark slacks that made her look incredibly slim, and a short fur jacket. There was something odd about her face. When she turned our way to speak to the man, I realized what it was. I was looking at a quite young and very handsome black woman.

Joel stirred in the seat in front of me. "If you don't recognize them, I do, from their file pictures. That's our girlfriend Astrid's supposedly missing husband, Alan Watrous, and his current passion flower, Hannah Gray. Gray! Some name for a nigger wench, hey?" He turned his head. "What the fuck is going on here, Helm? Those two were supposed to've been kidnapped in the U.S. and held prisoner over there with Mac and all the others who've vanished recently. What the hell kind of a game is Mac playing, anyway? What's the beat-up old wolf trying to pull, getting us all chasing over here after people who aren't missing at all, and a lousy little Arctic village called Lysaniemi nobody ever heard of. . . ."

Down the street on the far side, the three people on the sidewalk—the wife, the husband, and the husband's paramour, a cozy group—had stopped and moved to the curb. Presumably they'd seen the Mercedes coming, although it wasn't visible from our angle. I had a good look at the supposedly missing couple. She was certainly a striking young woman; and he was a good-looking man, but I wondered what his hangup was. Probably the Galahad complex. I mean, clearly he had a thing about rescuing ladies in distress, first a pregnant girl and then a female member of a minority race. Maybe he couldn't face the man-woman relationship if he didn't have the advantage of being such a generous and tolerant fellow, with the dame bound to him by gratitude. Not that Hannah Gray looked like a person who'd appreciate being patronized in this way, or rescued from her miserable black condition by a big-hearted whitey; but maybe she just hadn't caught on to his true motivation yet.

"It's a trap, it's a lousy trap, isn't it, Helm?" Joel's voice was indignant. "That's the bait over there. That old bastard in Washington, or wherever he is at the moment, has set us up, damn him! He's keeping Mr. Bennett and me and the boys all busy tracking you around Scandinavia, decoyed over here by a phony kidnapping and a crazy village name, while he and some of his other pet agents deal with the real business back in the States."

I said softly, "Mr. Bennett and you, amigo?"

He threw me a defiant glance over his shoulder. "What the hell does Mac expect, playing favorites the way he does?" he demanded bitterly. "Why shouldn't I switch over to a new top man who knows how to run an outfit like this, a *real* administrator who recognizes talent when he sees it instead of forever keeping younger men down and handing the plum missions to superannuated incompetents just because they've been with him since Bull Run, or was it Verdun? Or maybe Valley Forge?" He started to turn around, and I knew his gun was in his hand, although I couldn't see it; but he'd always been a talkative slob who had to make a speech before he could shoot. "Don't move, Matt. I'm sorry, but . . ."

I didn't tell him what I thought of him: how deeply hurt and disappointed I was at his dastardly treachery, not to mention his total incompetence—he apparently took for granted that, having been Olaf's prisoner, I had to be unarmed, which is the kind of assumption no professional should ever make. Just as every gun should always be assumed to be loaded until you check it out personally, so every agent should be assumed to be armed, no matter what the circumstances.

But I didn't make any speeches; I simply shot him, through the back of the seat. A .22 hasn't got all the penetration in the world, particularly with soft lead bullets and target loads, so I kept on firing until the clip was empty. The silenced automatic didn't make much noise even inside the car; but I was glad that he never managed to pull the trigger of his .38. With that short barrel, in that enclosed space, the muzzle blast would have left us deaf for a week.

## CHAPTER 18

AFTER a moment of stunned silence the girl beside me moved abruptly, hitting the door release and starting to throw herself out of the car. I managed to catch her wrist and haul her back inside. I exerted some leverage that made her gasp with pain.

"Relax, or they'll be fitting you for a sling, too," I said. "Where the hell do you think you're going? You're here on Olaf's orders to keep an eye on me, remember, not to go rushing around in the night. . . . No, don't slam that door; they'll hear you. Let it hang open until they're gone."

We sat like that, watching as the Mercedes drove up and made the pickup. I'd wondered why Astrid had always made a point, whenever Hannah Gray's name came up, of referring to her as dark—I suppose it had seemed like a bitter sort of secret joke to the blonde wife displaced by a beautiful black girl. A moment later the street was empty and silent except for the murmur of the city, gentle at this time of night.

I said, "Olaf trusted me, a little. I trusted him. I'll trust you a little if you give your word that you'll behave yourself. Otherwise I can tie you up with your belt . . . What's funny?"

"I'm not wearing a belt."

"My mistake. The way those jeans fit, I can see why

you wouldn't bother. Simple molecular attraction should do the job. You can close the car door now.''

She pulled it shut, and drew a long breath. "I am sorry. I lost my head. I . . . I have never seen anybody killed before, Mr. Helm. I thought that since I am a witness you must kill me next.''

"Who're you going to tell, the Stockholm police? Why? This guy was no friend of yours, was he? I don't really think you want to explain the whole situation to the cops any more than I do. If you did get involved with them, they'd want every last thing you know, and you wouldn't like that, would you? So just sit still while I pry the dear departed out from behind the wheel. What's the matter now?''

She licked her lips. "He's dead. You might show a little respect—''

I said, "I didn't think much of him alive; why should my opinion improve just because he's stopped breathing?'' I glanced at her. "You said you wanted to come along on this safari into deepest Lapland so you could spy on me for Olaf. Have you changed your mind?''

After a moment, she shook her head quickly. "No, I have not changed my mind.''

"All right, sit still while we switch drivers.''

It wasn't fun. I went around and opened the right front door of the ancient heap, and tossed my suitcase into the back seat to keep it away from the leaking bodily fluids, not all red. Then I hauled him over into the right-hand seat and arranged him gracefully against the door, just another passed-out drunk. Fortunately, I'd shot only for the body, so nothing showed on the head or face.

Coming back around to the left side of the car, I took off my borrowed overcoat and used it to cover the messy place behind the wheel. I was surprised to find that one of the feeble little .22-caliber slugs had actually penetrated both a car seat and a human torso and wound up smashing the speedometer. I wouldn't have expected that; but ballistics is not always an exact science. I got in and closed the door. To my relief, the overenergetic bullet didn't seem to have affected any essential systems; the motor started at the turn of the key.

I said over my shoulder, "You're welcome to join us up front here, but it might be a bit too cozy."

I heard her gag. "Do you have to make tasteless jokes?"

I put the car into gear. "Mrs. Segerby, cut it out," I said. "We've got a long way to travel together. We'll get along better if you dispense with that timid-little-girl routine of yours. I don't think you fainted when Astrid came in all shot up, and I know you didn't lose your lunch seeing Greta after her face had been remodeled with a scalpel; and those were friends of yours. Well, at least acquaintances. Don't try to kid me you're in deep shock over the death of a man you never even knew. I think you're a very determined young lady who's trying to fool people into underestimating her; but I've had the gag pulled on me before."

After a little silence, she said, "If you want to get back to your own car at Vasakliniken, as he said, you must turn left at the next corner."

"Thanks."

"He really smells quite dreadfully. Why did you not put him in the boot?"

"Boot? Oh, Limey for car trunk."

"I am sorry. I really learned to speak the language in England when I was a student; it comes back that way when I am under strain."

I said, "In answer to your question, if anybody was looking down from any of those apartments we were parked under, I didn't want them to see me dragging a corpse around the car. Open a window if you like."

"Thank you. Do they always . . . I mean, I didn't know they did *that* when they died violently."

185

I said, "You're a funny girl. What are you trying to pull, anyway, pretending to be a cream puff?"

She said softly, "Cream puff. That is a nice word. One day you will understand, Mr. Helm. One day they will all understand. You must take this big boulevard to the right now."

"Check."

Even with a dead body in the car, it seemed like a shorter drive; but then it almost always seems shorter going back, wherever you've been. When we reached the clinic, the red Golf was standing in the parking lot where I'd last seen it. There were no indications of a stakeout. After cruising past once to make reasonably sure, I drove into the lot, parked alongside, and robbed the dead man for change, since I was short. In a way, it made me feel more guilty than shooting him. I also retrieved the key of the rental car.

I walked over to a lighted structure that sheltered, more or less, two pay telephones that looked very deserted at this time of night. It took a while to get a call through to Washington. I could see Karin Segerby waiting patiently in the Volvo, but her patience was nothing to that of her companion, whose head was also visible, resting against the doorpost.

The phone was answered at last by a woman I did not know, which wasn't unusual, since we don't have much to do with the office help; but she was sticky about accepting a collect call, something that had never happened while Mac was in charge. She made me wait while she cleared me with someone higher up. That meant, of course, that my name was on the alert list, and my calls were to be traced if possible, and certain people were to be notified, while she stalled to hold me on the line.

"Sorry for the delay, sir. I'm trying to reach Mr. Bennett for you. Can you give me a number where he can call you?"

186

I said, "No. I'll call back in ten minutes. Have him on the line."

"But sir—"

"Exactly ten minutes from . . . mark!"

When Mac was in charge, he could practically always be reached; but the girls on the switchboard were just as apt as not to tell you to keep your pants on, Big Boy. Now they were nice and respectful and called you sir, and apologized for making you wait, but Bennett was unavailable. Typical.

I dug through the phone book, which wasn't as easy to find things in as the U.S. equivalent, at least for a foreigner, and finally managed to reach the proper airline at Stockholm's big international airport at Arlanda, where Astrid and I would have landed if we hadn't got off in Oslo. I made a late-morning reservation for two to Luleå, the city up north that had the closest large airport to Lysaniemi. To make it look good, I then got hold of Avis and asked them to have a car waiting for me up there when I arrived—a nice little red herring that would keep everybody happy for a while, I hoped. I made another local call, and one to Denmark for some information I'd been promised. Then time was up and I got Washington on the line again.

The same super-polite female answered: "I think I can reach Mr. Bennett for you now, sir. Please hold."

Waiting, I watched three tough-looking Swedish youths, all blond, all in black, denim and leather, stroll past the parking lot. They looked me over appraisingly, where I stood under the lights, wondering if I was worth hassling. I told them silently, come on, come on, boys, I've only killed one man since I got up this morning. Oh, and I shot a woman, but only in the arm, so it doesn't count. Let's make it a worthwhile day, fellows, let me make it four deads just for the record, please . . . But predators, human and otherwise, have very good survival instincts; these sensed danger, as I'd hoped they would when I laid the thought on them so hard, and they went on to easier prey. I released my grip on Joel's revolver in my pocket, and waited some more.

At last Bennett's voice came on the line. "Yes?"

"This is Helm," I said.

He spoke reprovingly: "We use the code names on official business, Eric."

He was slightly incredible; but then he always had been. "My business with you is always unofficial, Bennett," I said. "As far as I'm concerned, so are you."

"Eric, I order you to—"

"Cut that crap," I said. "I have one of your boys here. If nothing's done about him, come morning somebody'll discover, surprise, surprise, that he isn't really asleep and the stuff that's dripping under the car isn't really crankcase oil or hydraulic fluid. They'll notify the police, and the whole business will go public. If that's what you want, okay. If not, you'd better get a cleanup crew here, fast. I presume you do have some people in Stockholm waiting for the word from Joel. Well, here's your word from Joel."

There was a long silence. "Where in Stockholm?"

"It's an old black Volvo four-door sedan, if they don't know the car," I said. I gave him the license number. "The key will be under the floormat, left front. Parking lot, Vasakliniken, the Vasa Clinic, Stockholm. Repeat: parking lot, Vasakliniken, Stockholm. Somebody can look up the address for you, I'm sure. Do you want to know something funny? He acted kind of odd about all us barons, so I had him checked out. Turns out his family had a title, too, once. Prince Valdemar Konowski. Of course we Swedish aristocrats don't think too much of that titled Polish trash."

"Helm, I promise you'll regret—"

Bennett's voice was harsh, and he'd forgotten about the code names; but maybe it wasn't business anymore. Maybe it had become very personal indeed. I was certainly doing my best to make it so.

I cut him short: "Sure, and one good threat deserves another. I sent you a warning a while back. Just in case it went astray, let me repeat the gist of it for you. You should make a note of today, amigo. You may not know it, but this is a special day for you. The day you died."

"If you think you can frighten me—"

I grinned at the wall of the booth. They never say that unless you can frighten them.

I said, "We gave you a break once; and one is all you're entitled to. In case your boy Marshall Lindner didn't pass you the word from Oslo, I'm giving it to you now. As soon as I clean up this assignment, I'll be coming for you. Don't bother to try to hide. I'll find you. That's my specialty, remember, running them to earth and digging them out of the holes they try to hide in. I've never missed yet. As of now, you're a dead man walking. Good-bye, Bennett. *Hasta la vista.*"

I hung up the phone and drew a deep breath and headed back to the car. The Lone Avenger. Menace, Ltd. Annihilation, Inc. All I needed was a black cloak and a white horse. Or maybe a white cloak and a black horse. Death on the hoof, that was Helm, at least to hear him talk. But with corny people you've got to play corny games so they'll understand you.

Walking back to the cars, I played the conversation back in my mind, listening to the sounds of the phone and trying to guess where Bennett had been talking from. The fact that it had taken them so long to get him on the line was a hopeful sign. Of course, he could have been dining out in downtown Washington, or having drinks with a girl in her Georgetown apartment; but the delay suggested that he could be here in Sweden talking through a roundabout connection. They can make phones do the damndest things these days. And if he wasn't here already, I could hope

189

that my latest threats, delivered personally from beside Joel's dead body, would give him the final nudge needed to get him to come here and take personal charge of the manhunt. The Helm hunt.

"Out you come," I said to Karin as I reached the Volvo. "Crank up the window and bring the suitcase. We're switching transportation . . . Just a minute while I stash the Volvo key and cover him up a bit."

Rather than leave him sitting there in plain sight, I got him down on the floor and covered him with the overcoat so he just looked like some clothing piled there. Karin was waiting in a docile manner when, having shut the door on him and inspected the Volvo for obvious flaws, I turned away.

She spoke mildly: "You could have let me move over to the other car before you made your call. It wasn't a very nice place to wait so long."

"At least you weren't bored by his constant chatter," I said.

She winced. "Do you *have* to be so callous?"

"Do you *have* to pretend it bothers you?"

"I think you misjudge me, Mr. Helm."

"And I think you just wish I would, Mrs. Segerby. Hop in. You can toss that suitcase in back. We'll get you some stuff to wear along the road. I'm getting very good at selecting ladies' wardrobes." I walked around and got behind the wheel. The rental car started on the third try, and acted very reluctant for the first few blocks; I hoped it would last the course. As we drove, I said, "Tell me how we get to Liljehamn. There's a city map in all that junk on the floor, if you need it."

She made no move towards the maps and guidebooks at her feet. "Just turn left as you come out of this parking area. I will direct you. Why do we drive to the ferry terminal? It is not the right direction?"

"At the moment, any direction is the right direction as

long as it's away from here," I said. "What's going to happen up there at Laxfors?"

After a little pause for reflection, she said, "I see. That is why you wanted me with you, for information."

"Also, as you know, to keep you from giving the family a bad name. But I would like to know what we may be running into up there. Tell me about Laxfors."

"Another left turn at that traffic light ahead," she said. "It is to be a big demonstration. We have been moving people north for many days, singly and in small groups. Members of UFO, our Youth Peace Organization, and the other groups with similar goals we have persuaded to join us in this protest. You will try to stop it, I suppose?"

Even busy driving the car, I was aware of the sharply questioning glance she gave me. I said, "It's no concern of mine. Why should I stop it, a foreigner like me? Let the Swedish authorities handle their own riots and protect their own communication centers." I shrugged. "This ethnic and sentimental stuff is all very well, but I've got a country and it isn't this one. Without direct orders from Washington, I'm not about to interfere with anybody's hell-raising in a land that isn't mine. It's none of my damned business."

After a moment, she laughed. "You are a very interesting person, Mr. Helm. This should be a very interesting trip. Turn left up ahead, and we will be on the road to Liljehamn."

## CHAPTER 19

IT was, as she'd promised, an interesting trip. It started getting interesting in our cabin shortly after the ferry left Sweden headed for Finland. She was a vigorous, not to say frantic, young lady in bed; maybe she was making up for a year of widowhood. At last, after we'd lain together for a while, recovering from our exertions, she gave me a light kiss and a little squeeze, and sat up to turn on the light at the head of the berth.

When she spoke, there was some sharpness in her voice. "You do quite well for a man whose heart is elsewhere."

I didn't pretend not to understand. I said, "I didn't know it showed."

"You were being very skillful and mechanical. Clearly you have satisfied a great many yearning little girls in your time." She laughed shortly. "Never mind. It was what I needed, after all the months of being the pure and grieving Widow Segerby. One cannot order up love, or even true passion, on demand, can one?" She shook her head quickly. "No, please do not apologize. That is the only unforgivable thing."

Somewhere outside it was full daylight—my watch read ten-thirty A.M.—but making the reservations so late, I'd only been able to get us a cabin in the windowless interior of the ship. Still, it did have a john, and two beds where beds ought to be, sitting firmly on the floor or whatever it's called on shipboard. I hate clambering into those damned uppers, which are generally pretty cramped for a

192

gent my length. Ship designers seem to figure that only short people travel by sea.

I'd hoped to be able to sail clear to Helsinki, the capital of Finland, population almost half a million, located on the Gulf of Finland, the arm of the Baltic that penetrates east as far as Russia and Leningrad. It's easier to confuse the trail in a big city. However, I'd learned over the phone that the Stockholm-Helsinki ferries ran only at night, one each way, so I'd settled for the morning boat that, after a stop in the Åland Islands, would deposit us in Turku, on the Baltic at the southwest corner of Finland, about eight this evening. In a way it was a better port of disembarkation for us, being somewhat closer to our goal; and a little research in the tourist stuff we'd picked up on board had informed me that Turku was still a substantial metropolis of around a hundred and fifty thousand inhabitants, big enough that we could get lost in it if we needed to.

I hoped we wouldn't need to. So far there had been no indication that we'd picked up any fleas along the way. We'd apparently made a clean getaway from Stockholm; and when we didn't turn up at the Arlanda Airport, I hoped Bennett would assume I'd laid that false trail in order to give us a head start as we raced up through Sweden by road. There were several possible routes for him to cover, and it would probably take all the manpower he had in this part of the world, leaving none to waste on the remote possibility—if it even occured to him—that we'd leave Sweden altogether, make a big detour across the water, and come up the other side of the Gulf of Bothnia.

It wasn't as outlandish a maneuver as it might seem at first glance. We'd waste twelve hours on the ferry ride, of course, and have a little farther to drive even after we hit shore, but I'd been given no time limit for the mission. The road distance by way of Finland was still less than five hundred miles, and there were several roads from which to choose. We could easily be up north tomorrow, weather permitting, re-entering Sweden at Haparanda, only a few hours' drive from our destination.

To be sure, having failed to intercept us elsewhere, Bennett would have plenty of time to set an elaborate final trap for us in the neighborhood of our known destination, Lysaniemi; but I'd worry about that tomorrow . . .

Karin was standing at the little cabin's rudimentary dresser, uncapping the bottle I'd set out, and served us from in moderation, before the situation had turned amorous. I watched her turn towards me, unselfconsciously naked, not one of your standard long-stemmed northern beauties, but small and strong and compact. I took the drink she handed me, and moved aside to give her more room to sit on the side of the bed.

She spoke absently: "I was afraid I was going to be seasick on this voyage, the way the wind was blowing when we drove aboard. I am not a very good sailor. But it is really just like being in a hotel, except that the rooms are smaller."

There was hardly any motion to let us know we were afloat; just the pervasive, muted rumble of the ship's machinery.

"They must have pretty good stabilizers," I said. "We should be out in open water by this time."

She said ruefully, "It is sad. I wanted you to like me; but I have been such a pure widow for so long, I had no control . . . Now you are thinking that I am a wicked, insatiable nymphomaniac." She gave me a crooked little smile. "And I am sure that you are also thinking it is much nicer, at least for a man your age, with a dignified older woman than with an athletic and demanding child. You are in love with her, are you not? That is why you did not kill her with your gun that night at Torsäter."

I stared at her indignantly. "What do you mean?" I demanded. "Are you suggesting that I pulled my shots deliberately?"

194

Karin laughed softly. "It was a very good performance, Matthew. You sounded most convincing when you talked with her afterwards, pretending to be so distressed because you had shot so badly and failed to kill her."

It was hard to evaluate the girl's intelligence coldly, cute and blonde and nude as she was, but she did seem to see a lot she wasn't supposed to.

I shrugged resignedly. "Well, maybe I have let myself get a bit too fond of Astrid. She's a very attractive lady."

Karin shook her head abruptly. "No, you are not that susceptible; you would not miss your shots if killing were indicated . . . That is the answer, is it not? It was never your intention to kill! You talked with her very freely that evening, very carelessly. She told me. You said too much; you let her guess that you were beginning to mistrust her. Of course. You did it intentionally, hoping she would take some action; and she did. But you had to make it convincing, drinking that adulterated whiskey like a gullible boy instead of an experienced agent. So you pulled out your gun as you were supposed to according to your agency's rules, and you carefully shot her in the arm and drew a little blood from her ear, hurting her just enough so that she would feel she had missed death by a hair."

"Actually, she did," I said. "That damn' automatic threw left; the ear was an accident. Another inch or two over, and the shot would have killed her. Shows what can happen when you try to get tricky with firearms. Scared me all to hell."

"But it made your behavior very believable; no one suspected that you had taken that drugged drink willingly, as they might otherwise have done. Nobody guessed that you had *wanted* to be taken prisoner, so that you could learn all about them . . . us. What we were actually doing. Astrid and Olaf and I. How we were working together. What we were planning. The UFO Laxfors. Everything."

195

"Give Joel credit; he extracted most of the important information."

Karin shrugged. "You would have obtained it somehow without him, I am sure. But you are a brave man; you must have known that you might be questioned, painfully questioned, but you let yourself be captured anyway. Of course you knew that your associate would come to your rescue eventually; it was in his interest to do so for the information you held, although he might betray you later." She hesitated. "Did you know that he was a traitor?"

I said, "That's a big word, too big for use for a simple business accommodation such as Joel made. No, I didn't *know* that he had switched allegiance, but I did know that he was supposed to be following another lead back in America. When he gave it up so easily and came rushing over here to join me, so cooperative and helpful, I decided that he could be useful, but he'd better be watched."

"As I must be watched?" She was smiling faintly as she said it.

"Sure. At least until I figure out just why you're really here. And don't give me that stuff about keeping an eye on me for Olaf Stjernhjelm. I think you're here for reasons of your own." I grinned. "And please don't tell me how you've been yearning for me passionately ever since the first moment you saw me back there in Hagerstown, Maryland."

She laughed. "You mean, back where you almost spanked me?"

"Life is full of missed opportunities."

Her smiled faded. "All right. I will tell you. I wish to accompany you up into *Norden*—the North—as we planned; and then I wish you to do me a big favor."

"What favor?"

"When you have learned what you need in Lysaniemi, and done what you need to do—and if there is any way for me to help you I will be happy to do so—then I would like

196

you to help me. I think there will be time, even traveling
by this indirect route, if your business does not take too
long. I want to be at Laxfors to watch the protest demonstration, but I do not want to be part of it. Please do not
ask my reasons. I want to see, but I do not want to be
seen. A man like you should be able to find us a good,
concealed observation point.''

I would have loved to know what was going on inside
that tousled blonde head. "It depends on the terrain," I
said. "But I guess I'm kind of curious about this demonstration myself. I'm particularly curious about your contribution to it. In fact, let's say that's the price I'll charge for
seeing that you get where you want to go. Tell me about
it.''

"My contribution?''

"Don't play dumb; you're about as stupid as Einstein,"
I said. "You are also Karin Segerby, grieving widow of
Segerby Vapenfabriks AB, or a prominent member thereof.
SVAB for short. Obviously this UFO gang had that in mind
when they recruited you and flattered you and pampered
you—Olaf told me as much—even though you're not really
the grim-faced idealist type they seem to go for normally,
if Karl and Greta are typical specimens.''

"Well, they are not quite typical; they love each other,"
Karin said dryly. "Most of the others have no love at all,
not for people. They only love their cause, the cause of
peace.''

"Sounds harmless enough," I said. "In fact quite worthy. But Christianity was supposed to be a gentle, loving
religion; and how many have been killed for that?''

"It is never the cause or the religion itself, it is the
fanatics who adopt it who make it dangerous.'' She
hesitated. When she spoke again, it was in a totally different tone of voice. She said, "You wish to know my
contribution to the great cause? My contribution was
HG(E)Typ7F.''

197

Well, actually what she said was *Hoa Geh Eh Teep Sju Eff*, and it took me a moment or two to convert the Swedish pronunciation into comprehensible English symbols in my head. Then it took a little longer to translate them into militarese.

I said, "Let me guess. HG, that would be a hand grenade, *handgranat* in Swedish. Am I right?"

"Yes."

"What does E stand for?"

She licked her lips again. *"Eld."*

"Fire? An incendiary grenade, Type Seven. We're gaining on it. And F?"

*"Försvars."*

"Defensive? What's the difference between a defensive and an offensive grenade? I'm afraid I don't know as much about military weapons as I ought to."

"The offensive grenade is less powerful. You are running forward, attacking, and you do not want to run into the effective field of your own *granat*. With the defensive one, you are presumably fighting from a trench or other type of cover, and you can take shelter after you throw so the blast will not hurt you. So it can be designed to take effect over a larger area. But as a matter of fact, this is not primarily an antipersonnel grenade. It is made for use against armored vehicles, personnel carriers, tanks up to a certain size. It will burn—melt—its way through the armor and incinerate anybody inside."

"Must be quite a gadget."

"Yes, it is a new design. Grenades employing thermite have been made, and of course napalm; but this one employs a new incendiary ingredient that is particularly hot and unpleasant. There is also an ingenious adhesive cover that, before it burns away, makes the grenade stick to any object at which it is thrown long enough to take effect. SVAB is very proud of it." Her voice was dry.

"You seem to know a lot about it."

"I have spent the year since Frederik was killed learning about this and other weapons."

"I thought you were employed by an outfit called Nordic Textiles."

She laughed. "A Segerby company. The family was very pleased when the young widow began to take an interest in the other, less peaceful, branches of the business. They helped me keep busy to prevent me from dwelling on my grief. Of course I had been instructed by the UFO, once I had attained a trusted position, not to concentrate on one SVAB product in particular; it might have drawn attention that way. Do you wish the specifications of our new recoilless rifle? The cyclic rate of our improved SVAB submachine gun?" She shrugged her shoulders. "I do not disapprove, you understand. Not anymore. I have learned what some people are like. And if some people are like that, other people must have the means to shoot them."

This was a different girl from the one who'd been unable to watch me being burned. I said, "You're pretty tough for a little girl with a weak stomach."

"What makes you think . . . Oh, because I simply could not bear to see you in pain? That was the other Karin Segerby, the timid and obedient one. The one to whom nobody paid very much attention because she was so obviously harmless. Naturally I acted shocked and horrified; it would have been out of character not to. The character I had created for their benefit." She shook her head quickly. "I know you have questions, but please do not ask them. What I do, it does not concern you; it will not affect your business up north. It is a very private affair."

"Sure. May I ask about the Laxfors demonstration, or is that out of bounds, too?"

"Ask."

"Are these UFO people crazy? Are they expecting the Swedish Army complete with tanks to join the party; and, if so, are they going to try to fight back with these incendiary whizbangs of yours? How many did you get for them?''

"I have obtained for them secretly one case of twenty-five grenades."

"That won't last long in a real combat situation, and most of those pacifist kids don't know anything about combat except that they're agin it, do they? Any halfway respectable military force will walk right over them, grenades or no grenades; and I gather the Swedes are pretty good soldiers for all their love of neutrality. Staging a pitched battle is idiotic, anyway. How can even a bunch of screwballs think that's going to advance the cause of peace?''

Karin shook her head quickly. "You have jumped to the wrong conclusion. All I said was that the Type 7 grenade was designed for use, primarily, against tanks. I did not say that they planned to use it so. They do not expect the army to intervene. They will stage a big rally, with banners and angry slogans, with shouting and speeches, outside the fence of the LSA, the Laxfors Signalanstalt, literally the Laxfors Signal Institute. The so-called communications center. While the attention of the security guards is held by this disturbance, a small striking force will cut the wire on the far side of the installation and slip inside to attack the true objective. *Mörkrummet.*"

"The Darkroom? That mysterious concrete blockhouse, or whatever you want to call it?''

"Yes. It has no windows, but it does have ventilators leading underground to where the equipment is located. The ventilators are, of course, protected by grills; but a device that will penetrate armor will make short work of those flimsy grills as well as any other obstacles it may encounter as it drops down a ventilation shaft." She shrugged. "I have watched a demonstration. In addition to melting, practically vaporizing, anything with which it is in contact, even durable metal, the Type 7 also creates a fireball that consumes any organic material it envelops.

Outdoors, it is not a very big fireball for obvious tactical reasons; you do not want to burn up the soldier who threw the grenade. However, it will turn an enclosed space into a raging furnace.''

"What's supposed to be down there worth burning up? Do they think we sinister Yankees have smuggled a nuclear device into your country and persuaded you to build a camouflaged silo for it?'' I made a face. "If that's the case, setting fire to it doesn't seem like a very bright idea; and I'm not sure I want to help you find a spot from which to watch the radioactive pyrotechnics.''

She laughed shortly. "You have a point, but the idea that our government would permit the secret installation of a foreign missile with a nuclear warhead anywhere within our borders is not very plausible. However, the constant probing of our coastal defenses by the Soviets over the past few years, and the repeated invasion of our waters by their submarines, could have caused our military people to take a few unpublicized steps towards cooperation with America. There have been many rumors to the effect that American assistance, or at least American advice, was involved in the construction of the Laxfors facility. And with those fields of antennas . . . The thought that LSA may be a forward control station of some kind for missile guidance, American missile guidance, nuclear missile guidance, chills the blood of the ordinary Swedish citizen, who likes to feel secure in his country's neutrality. And of course our anti-war and anti-nuclear movements, like the UFO, are capitalizing, loudly and energetically, on this feeling.''

"What is there besides rumor to indicate that Laxfors serves our evil American interests?''

"The best evidence in the world. The Russians are trying to discredit and destroy it. Or have it destroyed by others.''

I said, "The Soviets are famous for their paranoia. Remember that Korean airliner. Any time a housewife in Cincinnati picks up a paring knife to peel a potato, it's actually a secret dagger aimed directly at the heart of Mother Russia. And how do we know how the Russians feel about it, anyway? Even if they talk indignant, that's just their normal way of conducting a conversation on practically any subject.''

Karin hesitated. ''They have done more than talk, with respect to Laxfors. They have sent people to make certain the place is put out of action. You do not think all this unfavorable publicity is accidental, do you? They are the world's greatest rumor-mongers. They are using UFO and other groups as unwitting tools with which to achieve their purpose.''

I studied her face for a moment. ''What people have they sent?''

''At least one person.'' Karin looked back at me without expression. ''I do not know about Olaf Stjernhjelm. I do not know if he is betraying his country deliberately or if he is merely a dupe for an attractive woman.'' Karin stared at me definatly. ''An attractive woman named Astrid Watrous. An attractive woman who is a Soviet agent!''

There was a short silence; then I grinned and said, ''This is a hell of a serious discussion for two people of opposite gender sitting on a bed without any clothes on.''

''You do not believe me!''

I shrugged. ''Sure I believe you. So what else is new?''

Karin frowned in a bewildered way. ''I do not understand. . . . You are not surprised?''

I laughed shortly. ''After all the years I've spent in this business, I'm supposed to be surprised because a pretty lady isn't what she pretends to be? Hell, you've been pretending, one way or another, ever since I met you waving that toy gun in that Maryland motel. Fine. Everybody tries to con dumb Helm. It's an international sport, and I'm hardened to it. So why should I flip my lid because of Mrs. Watrous' little deception?''

''But you knew?''

"Let's say I guessed." I hesitated. "What else do you know about her?"

"What else is there to know that is important? She is working for the Russians. She is a traitor to the country of her birth, your country, the United States of America."

"No," I said.

"What do you mean? You just admitted—"

"I admitted what she is. Sure. But let's consider what she isn't."

"I do not understand what you mean."

I said, "Astrid Wastrous is a Soviet agent. But she isn't Astrid Watrous."

CHAPTER 20

IT seemed too bad to land in Finland at night. You like to get your first view of a new country by daylight; but the sun was down by the time we got the word to return to our cars. Presently we felt the ferry settle into its slip at the eastern end of its voyage. Customs was as casual as it always seems to be in those Scandinavian lands, I suppose because they don't have our obsession with drugs, or the weapons-sensitivity of the newer and more insecure nations, forever concerned about arms and insurrection. I'd found my arsenal back in my suitcase, courtesy of Olaf Stjernhjelm, and I'd done my usual half-ass job of hiding it around the car, but they didn't even look.

Then we were driving through Turku, which even at night looked very new and clean like most cities in that part of the world, even those that were founded long before young Chris Columbus first got his feet wet; and most of them were. The odd thing was that, for the first time on this cockeyed overseas mission, I felt that I was really on foreign soil—more foreign than any I'd visited in a long time. I suppose this was due to the total incomprehensibility of the Finnish words on the lighted signs and billboards we passed. It's an orphan language spoken nowhere else in the world. It seems to employ an awful lot of *k's*, both singly and tandem. Even the Coca Cola signs looked weird.

"Can we talk now?" Karin asked.

She was mad at me; she'd wanted to spend the whole day on shipboard eagerly discussing Astrid Watrous and kindred subjects. A sleepless night, and a vigorous sex session, had apparently had no effect on her vitality; but I'd cut our morning conference short by telling her there would be plenty of time for further conversation after we got off the boat. Right at the moment, I'd said, with a bed handy and a five-hundred mile drive ahead of me, on foreign roads and mostly in the dark, I wanted to recharge the human batteries, good night, wake me in time for dinner.

"Think about Astrid, and you'll see that what I said makes sense of a lot of things," I'd said. "We'll talk about it in the car, later. Sleep tight."

One thing you learn in the business is to sleep anywhere, day or night, under any circumstances, even with a nude blonde flouncing around the stateroom and making a big thing of visiting the miniature bathroom and preparing her bed and thrashing around in it to make herself comfortable—and me uncomfortable, she hoped; but I was asleep before she stopped squirming over there. The next thing I knew, she was shaking me awake and saying that dinner was in half an hour; if I wanted to eat before we landed I'd better get dressed. I refused to discuss business of any kind over the meal. Now she was still pouting. For a bright girl, and one who'd proved herself to be fully adult in various important respects, she had some childish reactions.

The lights of Turku faded behind us. It was a relief to be on the road, headed in the right direction, even though I knew from the map that this fine dual highway wasn't going to last very long. Like the Norwegians and Swedes, the Finns aren't very generous with the four-lane stuff. Unfamiliar with local night-driving customs, I took it easy; and we rolled sedately through a country of dark evergreens, and frozen lakes that gleamed gray-white in the night. As a final precaution against being intercepted, I'd rejected the coast road as too obvious, and angled inland instead to pick up, eventually, the main thoroughfare north from Helsinki, Highway E4, the same road that I would have taken if I'd headed straight north through Sweden, although I was now catching it at the other end, the Finnish end, and running it backwards.

"Actually I gave you a slightly bum steer," I said after we'd driven for a while. "Astrid really is Mrs. Watrous; she did marry the guy. But she is not now, and was never, Astrid Sofia Land, of the Finnish family Landhammar."

"I do not understand. How could she deceive everybody . . ." Then Karin glanced at me sharply. "How did you find her out?"

I said, "She flunked two tests I tried on her."

"Tests?"

"Yes. First there's the artillery test. Very useful these days when most females—at least in the U.S., I don't know about other countries—pride themselves on fearing and hating guns and not knowing anything about them. In order to determine if you have a normally gun-phobic American girl on your hands, you simply toss her one of those fearful pistols unexpectedly and see if she panics properly. Astrid Watrous didn't."

Karin grimaced. "That is very ingenious, if rather cruel. I am afraid that, although I am not an American girl, I

205

would not have reacted calmly to your frightening test. I am glad you did not try it on me."

I said, "I didn't need to. I saw the way you handled that crazy derringer of yours, as if you were holding a live tarantula; so I knew that whatever you were, you were nobody's trained agent. Astrid, on the other hand . . . I didn't give her time to think, and she reacted instinctively, catching the weapon and flipping it open expertly to see if it was empty or if I was totally insane, playing catch with a loaded revolver. The first girl I tried that stunt on dropped the gun as if it were hot and practically wet herself. Not Mrs. Watrous."

"I see."

"Of course there are a few people around, both male and female, who are sensible about guns, even though they have no professional dealings with them. If she'd let it alone, I'd still be wondering a little; but she didn't. She knew she'd betrayed herself, and she quickly improvised a story about how she'd been given an instant course in gun-handling by a policewoman friend. She gambled on using the name of a real person, hoping that if I did check up, at this distance, I'd be satisfied when I learned that a certain Mary Alice Linderman did exist and had graduated in the same class. But my informant dug a little farther and learned that Linderman was never a policewoman. She's Mrs. Vincent Marchesi now, happily married to a chemistry instructor at the university from which they graduated, she has two babies, and she wouldn't dream of letting a filthy firearm in the house. Anyway, Astrid's story was phony from the start. You don't develop gun reactions like that in one outing with a friend; and a session with a police revolver wouldn't have told her how to check out an automatic expertly, as she did later. Obviously, she'd been subjected to some pretty stiff firearms training, and she was trying to cover up because she didn't want me asking where. Which was not the response of an innocent girl

206

who'd simply joined her college pistol team; and the real Astrid Land hadn't.''

"Yes, that is rather revealing," Karin said. "And the other test?"

"Let's call it the aristocracy test, although it wasn't exactly a test," I said. "I mean, it wasn't something I sprang on her deliberately, like that revolver. But I began to notice that she had some very odd reactions to our screwy family. Here's a girl whose own family, in America, stuck to the old Finnish ways closely enough that the American-born daughter still speaks with an accent; the daddy is hipped on Scandinavian history and the girl has the old sagas at her fingertips. Is it likely that she wouldn't have learned to be proud of her own aristocratic ancestors? Yet she didn't seem to know quite how to cope with us obsolete noblemen and our obsolete titles. Hell, she practically panicked at Torsäter when we were going in to meet all the barons.''

"But she was already acquainted with Olaf and me," Karin protested. "She had been given plenty of opportunity to see that we were . . ."

"Just ordinary folks?" I said when she hesitated. I shrugged. "Well, maybe; but that was back in the U.S. The idea of encountering aristocracy in the mass, in its native habitat, kind of threw her. It wasn't the gee-ain't-it-wonderful response of a naive American girl about to get to mingle with some real honest-to-Jesus sirs and Honorables. But it was a perfectly natural reaction for a young woman who'd been brought up in an altogether different way, under a totally different system."

Karin licked her lips. "Yes, I think I see what you are driving at."

I said, "Astrid was apprehensive and wary the way somebody's wary who's been taught since babyhood about the evil aristocrats drinking the blood of the slaughered hero-workers and laughing fit to kill. It wasn't the reaction of a girl, even one born in America, who'd been brought up to remember a family tree full of high-class Landhammar ancestors. But it was a good Communist attitude; and while they'd undoubtedly run her through that tough Americanization process they use over there on agents they're hoping to plant on us, it hadn't covered dealing with the nobility, since that's not a common problem in the U.S. of A. She'd retained the proletarian instincts hammered into her as a child, when she'd learned all about the innate wickedness of the upper classes, particularly the titled upper classes.''

Karin thought for a little. I was aware of her shaking her head beside me. ''But her parents . . . She was on her way to visit them when she got sick in Hagerstown. Well, she had planned that, up to a point; she knew she would not complete that journey; but she had visited them many times before. It is not possible that they would not know their own daughter!''

''That's just the point. They do know their daughter. They know where she is; they knew where she was. And she was not in Washington, D.C., or Hagerstown, Maryland.''

Karin said, ''You mean that the real Astrid is a . . . a hostage somewhere? All this time?''

I said, ''A few years back, Mr. and Mrs. Land moved from the town in which they'd lived all their later lives to the town where you called them. A town where they knew nobody, and nobody knew them—or their daughter. This happened shortly after Astrid Land had visited northern Europe. She'd toured Scandinavia, with particular emphasis on Finland, the land from which her parents had emigrated. She'd also made a side trip that's pretty standard for American visitors to Helsinki who want to catch a short, safe glimpse of Communist Russia: she'd taken the package tour overnight to Leningrad. I have a hunch that if somebody checks up on that particular group of tourists, they'll find that one particular young lady missed the return trip, perhaps hospitalized due to a sudden illness. She came back with a later group—a group that, not having seen her before, didn't realize that the Astrid Land who'd gone into Russia wasn't the Astrid Land who came out.''

''And the real Astrid . . . That is why her parents moved, because they were told to move? I see. They were needed to support her identity, so they were ordered to make a new home where no one would realize that their 'daughter' was now an impostor, a Soviet agent. And they obeyed because the real Astrid was a prisoner in Russia and would suffer if they did not cooperate fully.'' Karin drew a long breath. ''Yes, that is understandable. And when I spoke to them on the telephone and found them so upset because the false Astrid was so sick in Hagerstown—of course I did not know she was an impostor at the time—it was not because they loved her so much, they probably hated her; but if she died, what would happen to their true daughter, languishing in Soviet hands, when she was no longer needed to insure their cooperation?''

''Something like that,'' I said, watching the road unrolling in the headlights. The forest was black on either side, and there was no traffic in sight for the moment. ''If you're so smart, can you figure out what her target was? Who her target was?''

''Target? Oh, you mean the person in whom she and her Russian superiors were interested?'' Karin hesitated, and glanced at me sharply. She spoke in tentative way: ''Astrid married Alan, did she not? She must have been sent to spy upon his work.''

''I have no doubt the Russians are interested in oceanography, but there's no evidence that Dr. Watrous was engaged upon any project important enough for them to go to great lengths to put a beautiful lady agent in a position to spy upon his research.''

''Beautiful?'' Karin made a little face. ''I have never thought her terribly attractive, Matt.''

209

"You're not a man, honey," I said. "And you're stalling. You know damn' well who Astrid's target was. You."

Karin didn't seem to find the idea outlandish. She said thoughtfully, "Yes, I have wondered. Although he spent considerable time in Washington, and was related to me, Alan Watrous never showed much interest in Frederik and me until he became married; then they gave us a big rush, if that is what you call it. Obviously, it was she who wanted very much to make friends with us. I wondered why at the time, but I dismissed it as just a general interest in her new husband's aristocratic family."

"I'd say her interest was focused very specifically on you."

Karin shook her head dubiously. "If the people behind her really wanted to . . . to seduce me, would they not have sent a handsome man?"

"Maybe they felt that was too obvious," I said. "Or maybe, having studied the situation, they came to the conclusion that although you fought with your husband about his work, you really loved him too much to be a good prospect for the gigolo approach."

There was a little silence; then Karin said quietly, "Yes. But I did not realize quite how much I had loved him until he was lost to me." Then she spoke more briskly: "But with Astrid, it is such a complicated thing! She could simply have come to Washington and arranged to meet us socially, could she not? She did not have to obtain for herself a position at the Oceanic Institute and scheme to marry the man in command because he was my relative. And do you not mean that her target was really Frederik and his company, through me? And how does Laxfors come into this conspiracy? I thought that was supposed to be the Russians' true objective; but Laxfors was not even built when Astrid first took employment at the institute."

The little girl was smarter than she let herself look; she asked some good questions. I said reprovingly, "You've been thinking. You've got to watch that; it can be habit-forming." After a moment I went on: "I'm beginning to realize that we've been looking at this thing backwards. In the Russky master plan, Laxfors was an afterthought. I think their original objective was, and still is to a great extent, Segerby Vapenfabriks Aktiebolag. SVAB."

Karin frowned. "But why? It is by no means the biggest . . ."

"That's just the point. SVAB is a respected family concern, not a great soulless corporation. If you're a Swede, even if you're firmly opposed to war and munitions of war, you can't help being just a little proud of this solid Swedish company competing successfully with the multinational giants."

Karin sighed. "Yes, I have felt that myself, even when I disapproved. You mean that a scandal touching SVAB would be more disturbing to the country and the industry?"

I nodded. "I'm theorizing now, but I think I'm close. The Russians are obviously exerting deliberate pressure on Sweden. There have even been suggestions here, I'm told, that they're studying the feasibility of an Afghanistan-style takeover. That may just be Swedish paranoia talking, caused by living in the shadow of the bear so to speak; but there's got to be a motive behind the submarine probes and other unsettling Soviet actions. It's a testing and softening-up process of some kind; and strikes and scandals have always been weapons in their arsenal. So they give a female agent impeccable Scandinavian credentials: a fine Finnish family, marriage to a titled Swede. Then they have her move in on the rebellious young wife of one of the directors of SVAB, establishing a friendly and understanding relationship with the younger woman. Finally they look around for some way to use the idealistic girl's distaste for her husband's business to decoy her to her destruction, and his."

"Laxfors?"

"Yes, at just the right moment, the Laxfors question arises. A totally different problem for the Russians, presumably being handled by a totally different undercover team—until somebody in Moscow sees how the Laxfors Project can be combined with the SVAB Project to produce a double whammy: the LSA installation sabotaged by fanatics employing Segerby weapons; and the Segerbys discredited by the terrorist involvement of the girl who'd married one of them, who'd supplied the weapons." I grimaced. "My family was concerned enough about the bad publicity you might give us to put me on the job; but it's the Segerbys who should be doing the real worrying." I glanced at the girl riding beside me. "Maybe they are. Maybe they've taken action to stop you, too?" I made it a question.

She shook her head. "Not that I am aware," she said.

We rode in silence for a while. I held the car steady on the lonely forest road—they're practically all forest roads up there. There had been some stars earlier, but they were gone; and the night seemed to have become darker. I should probably have tried to get a weather report somewhere, in a language I could understand, but it would have made no difference, really, since we had to make the drive regardless.

"You know that she killed Frederik," Karin said at last. "Astrid. She shot him down in that parking garage, and only a few hours later came to the apartment to hug me so affectionately and express her deep sympathy for my terrible bereavement!"

I was a little startled by the revelation. Not the revelation about Astrid. I'd been fairly certain that she'd been responsible for Frederik Segerby's death, since no other answer made sense, the people involved being who and what they were. But I hadn't been quite prepared to learn that this small blonde girl had been aware of the identity of her husband's murderer—well, murderess—and had still man-

212

aged to play along with Astrid and her associates without revealing her knowledge.

"I think you're probably right," I said, "but what brought you to that conclusion?"

Karin shrugged. "How can I know? The way she looked at me that morning, perhaps. I simply knew that she had done it the moment she walked into our Washington apartment the day after the murder. There was no doubt in my mind from the moment I saw the false look on her face: she was the one who had killed him!"

The legal geniuses would have sneered at that answer, but I don't discount female intuition; I've even encountered some interesting examples of male intuition.

Karin said, "I came very close to . . . to attacking her. I wanted to scream accusations at her, but I had no proof. Who would believe that the respectable wife of the director of the Oceanic Institute was a Communist spy, maybe even a trained Communist assassin? And the terrible thing was that Frederik had warned me, but I had laughed at his warning. He was always seeing reds under the beds, I told him; and he could put his company sneaks to investigating the UFO and Astrid if he wanted to, but they would find nothing, absolutely nothing. But clearly he had been right." Karin drew a long breath. "So I swallowed my anger and accepted her condolences. I made myself cling to her helplessly, weeping. I forced myself to make tearful sounds of gratitude and treat her as my very dearest friend from that moment on. Ugh."

There was a brief silence as the roadway changed and our four lanes shrank to two, but the pavement remained reasonably wide and smooth; however, the Finns don't let you play that stimulating passing game employing the shoulders of a two-lane road allowed by the Swedes, so it was pretty dull, straightforward driving. I could have used more power getting around a few slowpokes; but there really wasn't enough traffic to slow us down. I could employ the high beams most of the time, and the headlights were good.

I steered around a beat-up Saab without slacking speed. I said, "Let's see how they worked it from the start. You weren't good seduction material, but you were a member of a very large family that took itself seriously as a family. Okay, find another Stjernhjelm relative in America to work through. There were actually several, they discover, but Alan Watrous looks best; he lives on the East Coast and often has business in Washington. He is single and should be vulnerable. Probably they considered a straight meet-cute pickup of some kind, but in studying the situation they learned about a nice Finnish-American girl from the distant Midwest who'd applied for a job as laboratory assistant, ideal, particularly since she was spending the summer in Europe before coming in for an interview on her way home. So they picked a very bright girl of their own and put her through a massive cram course and either gave her brown contact lenses or bleached her hair, since the chance of their having on tap a smart brown-eyed blonde of approximately the right dimensions aren't very great."

"I am certain that Astrid uses a strong rinse, at the very least."

"I'm glad to get a woman's opinion. I looked and couldn't tell," I said. "Anyway, one Astrid Land went to Leningrad. Another Astrid Land appeared for the interview in Gloucester, Mass., smiled prettily, and got the job. But apparently Dr. Watrous had some inconvenient principles about playing around with the female help; she couldn't get beyond a nice platonic friendship. Along came Olaf Stjernhjelm visiting his scientific seventy-second cousin, or whatever the relationship is. Astrid made a play for him, caught him, and even, apparently, recruited him for Moscow; but mainly she used him to make Alan Watrous very jealous. Dr. Alan probably cringed every time he thought of her dainty loveliness in the clutches of his crude soldier-of-fortune relative. Then Astrid staged a break with Olaf and let Alan see that she was in terrible trouble. She knew her man; he couldn't resist being magnanimous; he offered his help; in the end he even married the girl, who then managed a convenient miscarriage. Pretty soon Dr. Watrous had to make one of his trips to Washington; and of course the attractive new Mrs. Watrous went along and made certain they looked up those nice relations of her husband's, the Segerbys. Contact accomplished, mission running. Only the male Segerby had a suspicious nature and did some snooping so in the end he had to be killed; but it all worked out for the best, since the stupid little female Segerby, his wife, in her shock grabbed at the nearest warm body for sympathy and support and was, as they say, mere clay in the hands of the older and more experienced woman. At least so the older woman thought." I glanced at the still profile of the girl beside me. "Just what the hell are you trying to pull here, Karin?"

"What do you mean?"

"Why are you playing along with these people, even supplying them with incendiary whizbangs from your late husband's company . . . Oh, Christ, here comes the snow!" I reached down to switch on the defroster. I said, "You're not really sold on this fiery protest they're planning with those grenades, are you?"

When Karin spoke, her voice was reluctant: "No . . . no, but I do not want it stopped until they have committed themselves fully."

"I see." I didn't really, except that I'd certainly made a mistake in taking this girl at face value; and apparently Astrid and Olaf and their wild-eyed young associates had made the same mistake. I said, "You've got something up your sleeve?"

"Up my . . . Oh, yes, that is one of your American phrases. Yes, I have something up my sleeve, Matt." She hesitated. "I should not tell you this, but certain arrangements have been made, by me and others. It is all taken care of. Please do not get patriotic at the last moment and spoil everything.'' Before I could speak, she said quickly, "And do not ask questions, please. I have already told you more than I should. I have trusted you more than I should, much more . . . I would not worry about this snow if I were you. At this time of year it should not be very troublesome."

She knew her northern climate better than I did. Throughout the night the thin snow flurries never managed to coat the pavement to amount to anything; not enough to worry about. What did worry me was the car. Feeble to start with, the little four-banger up front seemed to be losing more power as we drove, and there was an occasional miss that had me holding my breath waiting for total failure. It was a strange ride northwards through a foreign land, with the snow tires hissing and the windshield wipers clacking steadily. In that empty country, with an uncertain power plant, I stopped for gas whenever I saw an open station, but they weren't numerous, and none had a mechanic on night duty. With the price in Finnish marks—I'd exchanged some money on the ferry—and the quantity in liters, I had no idea what I was paying for the stuff at the pumps; but I had a hunch it wasn't cheap.

A gray dawn found us well up in northern Finland. They picked us up after we'd had a breakfast of herring and hard-boiled eggs just south of the sizable town of Oulu.

## CHAPTER 21

BELOW Oulu the road we'd been following, Highway E4, came slanting up out of the interior of Finland to join the coast road I'd shunned earlier. The map showed that from the junction both ran together around the upper end of the Gulf of Bothnia into Sweden. Except for some unpaved wilderness tracks much farther north, there was no other road that would take us there, so it was a logical spot for an early intercept; and there were the interceptors in my mirrors, coming right along a discreet distance behind us.

There were two of them, in a sizable maroon sedan— well, sizable for Europe—that obviously had enough under the hood to cope with any speed our sick little power plant could have produced even if it had been well. The driver was trying to vary the interval between us so as not to be too conspicuous. Once in a while the maroon car would even disappear for a while, only to pop up in my mirrors again. After all, we didn't have to be kept in sight constantly, now that we'd been sighted approaching the target area. Our destination was known: Lysaniemi. However, there is really no way for one car to tail another for any length of time without being spotted. That takes several vehicles, good communications, and plenty of teamwork.

It shook me badly. I'd never had much respect for Bennett. I was the experienced field man, dammit; he was just a lousy, desk-bound bureaucrat who'd managed, by political trickery, to achieve a shaky position of power in the undercover services. He wasn't supposed to outguess me like this, catch me like this. It was like the brave lion hunter getting himself bitten by an overfed housecat. It was embarrassing.

"What is shit?" Karin asked, hearing me swear. "You are angry because there is suddenly a car following us?"

I glanced at her. "Don't get too smart, or I'll draft you into our agency. Fate worse than death."

She showed me the little mirror in the palm of her hand. "I have been watching," she said. "It is an Audi Quattro. A very fine car. Expensive. With four-wheel drive, so that you do not get your evening clothes wet and dirty digging your way out of a snowdrift on your way home from the opera. It is driven by a man, and there is a woman beside him."

"A woman?" I frowned. I would have bet that Bennett was a male chauvinist who'd never employ a female operative in a critical spot that did not involve sex; but maybe I'd better stop betting on my judgment of Bennett. "You're sure? I've been too busy driving to get a good look at them."

"Yes, I am sure." I was aware that Karin was smiling faintly, perhaps a little smugly. "She has a bandage on her left cheek, and her name is Greta Lagertsen. The name of the driver is Karl Johanson. You have met them. Astrid must have sent them . . . You thought the car had been dispatched by somebody else?"

I drew a long breath. I guess it was relief. I wasn't losing my grip. I hadn't let myself be outsmarted by a lightweight like Bennett after all; I hadn't been wrong about him. He was still looking for me over in Sweden, where I wasn't. Having Astrid read my mind didn't disturb me greatly; I was willing to admit, reluctantly, that she was at least as smart as I was.

"Yes, I thought it had been sent by somebody else," I said. "So Greta is back in the game, all patched up? She

218

must be a determined chick, to be running around the countryside after the shock of getting slashed like that.''

"Perhaps she is angry. Fearing that she is horribly scarred for life, she is hating very much, I suspect.''

"Well, let's hope so," I said. "And let's hope her boyfriend, Karl, is hating right along with her. They're amateurs at this work; and with a good hate working on them, they've probably parked the few brains they've got, for the duration. They shouldn't be hard to handle, if and when we decide to handle them.''

Karin hesitated. "Matt?"

"Yes?"

"Those people behind. That car. It is a very nice automobile, that Audi. And the four-wheel drive, well, we do not know how the roads are around that village you wish to visit. After all this rain and snow, they could be impassable to an ordinary vehicle. And I think you are worried about this car; I think it does not function so well any longer. Do you understand what I say?''

I looked at her with respect. "We'd really better get you under contract, fast. You have some very nice larcenous notions. But what happened to the idea that you were working for Olaf?''

"That obedient little Karin Segerby has served her purpose. She has been retired.''

"And you're not saying what purpose she served?'' When there was no answer, I shrugged and went on: "Any ideas about how to hijack them?''

We worked it out together, and the first step was to do a little shopping in Oulu, partly to show that we were totally unaware of being followed, but partly because we did need some equipment, if we were going to tackle the Arctic boondocks. Mostly, I was after sturdy boots and warm clothes; but Karin needed a costume to fit a certain role, and I also saw her buying something pale blue and brief and lacy that was not specified in the script. Apparently she planned to give me a treat tonight, if we wound up in an appropriate place, still together.

Although the border crossings we'd had to date had all been easy, I made sure once more that the lethal contraband was hidden as well as I could manage before we reached the Swedish line at Haparanda. No sense in lousing up the mission at the last minute by relaxing prematurely. However, getting back into Sweden from Finland turned out to be even easier than entering from Norway had been in the first place. The officials here didn't even make me open the car trunk. We pulled away, next waypoint Porkkala, where we could pick up the minor forest road north to Lysaniemi—if we chose to drive that far before switching to a more cautious approach mode and a more competent vehicle. However, I had a hunch that would deliver us into Bennett's waiting hands for sure. It was time to start getting sneaky after all the hard, straightforward driving.

I said, "Hang on, we're about to have our infuriating breakdown; wouldn't you think, the prices they charge, they'd rent you cars that run properly? Play up to me . . . But first, here's something for you." I reached up under the dashboard and got one of the silenced agency automatics I'd confiscated way back in Oslo. It seemed a long time ago. Guiding the car with my elbow, I jacked a cartridge into the chamber and set the safety catch. I said, "Now it's ready to go. You push down this gizmo here with your thumb. It's called a safety. Then you pull this gizmo here with your finger. It's called a trigger. The magazine holds ten cartridges. But we want these people alive and talking, preferably, so try not to blow their heads off unnecessarily. Okay? Now this feeble crock of a car had better conk out on us before we have too far to walk back to town."

I reached down and turned the ignition off. The little sedan lost momentum abruptly. I turned the key the other way; and the engine fired again, sending us forward jerkily. I made a show of fighting it, pumping the accelerator to throw, I hoped, some nice puffs of unburned gas out the exhaust; then I cut the switch once more. As we slowed again, there was a blare from a rather musical horn. The couple in the maroon Audi had let themselves come a little too near us. Perhaps they'd closed in to determine whether we'd continue down the highway or make the turn into Haparanda. Now they swerved out to avoid us and roared past, since they could hardly do anything else except hit us or come to a halt behind us. I guided the Golf to the side of the road and out onto the shoulder, nice and wide now since we were back in Sweden.

I tried the starter a couple of times, as would be expected of me, killing the engine when it caught, hoping the vibrations would not be noticed from a distance if Karl and his bandaged girlfriend had pulled up around the curve ahead and sneaked back to watch from hiding. I got out angrily and kicked one of the front tires dramatically and jerked the hood open. Karin came around the car to join me, indicating disapproval.

"Why be angry at a piece of machinery?" she said. "It is inconvenient, to be sure, but we are fortunate it happened here and not out in the forest. We just passed the intersection. The town cannot be far down that side road."

She was very convincing as the reasonable member of our twosome. I stuck to my flashy temper tantrum: "Oh, God, save me from the eternal optimist! If there's anything I can't stand, it's a goddam Pollyanna!"

She stiffened resentfully. "I do not know what that is, one of your odd Americanisms, but I am sure it is rude. You are behaving very badly. I do not think that motor intends to function any longer; it has been trembling on the verge of collapse for several hundred kilometers. I will take my things and walk into Haparanda and find a hotel. There cannot be so many that you will have trouble finding me, when you decide to behave reasonably."

"What makes you think this wide place in the road has

even one hotel? But suit yourself; you will anyway. Good-bye!"

I busied myself poking around the hot engine, doing nothing in particular, while Karin collected the little ruck-sack—locally known as a *ryggsäck*—that she'd picked up in Oulu to hold her purchases; then she marched off briskly, back straight, chin high, obviously an insulted lady leaving an impossible gentleman to his own ill-tempered devices. I made a show of looking under the car for the cause of the engine failure; mechanically a stupid idea, but it let me collect some hidden armaments. I retrieved the others from the interior, tucked some away in my clothes, and slipped the remainder into the suitcase I'd bought in another coun-try while traveling with another lady. Then I marched back up the road the way Karin had gone, after kicking the car door shut in a final display of irritability. Mad Matt Helm, the short-fuse specialist.

I didn't see her ahead of me. Well, I'd given her a good start. I turned at the marked intersection and soon emerged from the woods to find Haparanda right there, rather old and shabby, looking like a town that had been bypassed by progress. A short hike brought me to the town square, the most prominent structure on which was a massive old red brick building with a sign saying *Stadshotellet*, the City Hotel. Since I'd passed no other hostelries, it seemed likely that Karin had taken refuge there; but in order to give her, and other people, plenty of time, I hiked over to some gas pumps across the square—*plaza*, we call it in the American Southwest where I grew up. The establishment was kind of a grocery as well as a filling station; but they had a reasonable shelf of automobile stuff. I found what I wanted and stood in line to pay.

Then I was out in the damp gray day once more, lugging my suitcase and my paper bag back across the square. The big hotel had obviously once been the pride of Haparanda, back when travel was slower and this made a logical overnight stop at the top of the world for folks journeying between the larger towns down in Sweden and Finland. Now it was decaying slowly; but the doors were still impressive. Inside, the elderly man behind the desk told me, in awkward English, that Fru Helm had, indeed, checked in. Room 217. It was clear from his tolerant expression that he had no faith whatever in our declared marital status, particularly now that he saw the difference in our ages; but the hotel business wasn't so good in Haparanda that he could afford to disapprove even if he wanted to.

I marched up the fine old staircase and down the hall to the left. It was a long hike, down a corridor with a frayed carpet, past endless doors that, I was sure, hid only empty rooms. There wasn't a human being in sight. A ghost hotel. I found the right door and knocked. After a little, the lock rattled and the door swung back.

I said breathlessly, "Hey, baby, I think I've got it! The car. You know how those Volkswagens are. The old bugs could go swimming without turning a hair, but the new bunnies stop in a heavy dew. But I got some bottles of fuel desiccant, you know, that alcohol stuff that takes water out of the gas; hell, I bought out the store, and I have a hunch that if I dope up the fuel tank real good . . . Hey, what's the matter with you? Are you still mad at me or something?"

Karin's face was pale. She licked her lips and said, "Matt, I am terribly sorry to trick you like this. I hoped so much I wouldn't have to."

"What—"

Somebody stepped out from behind the door and shoved a gun into my back, kicking the door closed. A voice I'd heard before, the voice of the boy called Karl, said, "Put your hands up, Mr. Helm. I know you are a dangerous man, so I intend to take no chances with you. Please do not force me to shoot!"

## CHAPTER 22

A man who says he isn't going to take any chances, as he jabs a gun amateurishly into the back of a trained agent, makes it very hard for said agent to take him seriously. It's one of the situations for which we're taught several responses, mostly lethal, even though no sensible person with a firearm is going to move in that close. After all, the whole point of guns is that they can hurt at a distance.

However, I managed to control my hysterical laughter and ignore the various opportunities he gave me to take away his silly pistol and toss him across the room—which, I noticed belatedly, was a rather fine, big, old hotel room with good-sized twin beds; but the coverlets were frayed and the wallpaper was faded and badly stained. Still, with its high ceiling, it had an air of space and grace lacking in the cramped efficiency cubicles found in more modern hostelries.

I saw Karin's little backpack on the farther bed, alongside some clothes that had been dumped out of it. The girl herself, after letting me in, had backed away to a safe distance. She was still in her snug black jeans and big white sweater, rather grubby by this time; but she'd discarded her shoes. Having got my feet stomped painfully upon occasion, I'm not sold on the barefoot routine, or even the stocking-foot routine, but you can hardly keep an American girl in her shoes, and apparently Swedish girls shared the same woodsprite impulses.

As she watched me steadily, Karin's face had a convincingly pale and troubled look; the look of an obedient little girl who'd followed the orders of her associates but couldn't help feeling guilty about the betrayal to which they'd led her. We'd agreed that some ambivalence was in order here; it wouldn't do for her to hate me even to impress her UFO colleagues. The character she'd established with them, that we'd revived for this occasion, was not that of a hating girl. However, I couldn't help thinking, as one does, that this was also the way she'd look at me if she were actually betraying me. A double-double-cross was not of the question here. I was putting my life into the hands of a young woman I didn't really understand, and had no very good reason to trust except that instinct told me it was a reasonable gamble. But instinct had been wrong before.

Karl poked me in the back again. "*Händerna mot väggen*. . . . Hands against the wall, feet out," he snapped, just as he'd heard it in the movies. I assumed the position in docile fashion. He managed to find the .38 I'd once lent Astrid, which had been returned to me in Stockholm with the rest of my arsenal. He got it out of the belt holster, having some difficulty with the catch. "So. Now you can straighten up. . . . Yes, yes, what is it, Karin?"

"He has another gun, one he took from me. I think it is in his sock."

Okay so far. This was part of the script we'd sketched out while driving: we'd agreed to use the derringer as a sacrifice piece to make her phony betrayal more convincing—but even if she'd rewritten the script she'd want me disarmed. Well, I told myself firmly, there's only one thing worse than trusting everybody, and that is trusting nobody. Karl was momentarily disconcerted by his mistake; his voice had lost authority when he spoke again:

"Oh. Do not move, Helm!"

"Move! Don't move! Make up your cotton-picking mind!"

I was aware of him bending down behind me, checking my ankles, and extracting the little two-barreled monster of a weapon from its place of concealment. He straightened up. I got a sharp rap on the side of the skull that made bright lights flash across my vision.

"So! That is for your tricks! Now you can turn around."

I turned to look at him. He wasn't a bad-looking boy, I suppose, if you like them lean and soulful; but at the moment he had the overbearing, triumphant look that comes to some people holding guns who don't know anything about guns. They feel they've grabbed hold of the key to the universe, instead of merely an ingenious mechanical device designed to propel a small hunk of metal a certain, rather limited, distance at a certain, rather limited, velocity. His weapon, I noted, was the Browning 9mm automatic with the thirteen-round magazine. Plenty of firepower. He was in the same jeans and sweatshirt he'd worn in Stockholm, and he could have used a shave, but he didn't grow it very fast.

Normally, I wouldn't have chosen this moment for conversation. Recriminations are a waste of time, and making threatening speeches at a man with a gun, just to show how mad you are and how brave you are, is stupid. Even if you plan to convert him into dogmeat eventually, why announce your intentions? Let it come as a big surprise when it comes. But we weren't doing real life here, we were doing a movie; and in the movies they're always shooting off their big mouths to impress the customers.

"You treacherous bitch!" I snapped at Karin; then I turned and gave Karl the tough-guy speech beloved by every two-bit scriptwriter: "You can't get away with this!"

"I am doing just that, am I not?" He gestured with the gun. "Sit down in that chair and be quiet!"

Seating myself grudgingly where indicated, I came up with another scintillating line: "When I get my hands on you . . . You'll be sorry!"

226

It made Karl feel fine; it made him feel right at home. This was exactly the blowhard behavior he'd seen in every bang-bang American film he'd watched since he'd been old enough. Not as a youngster, of course, because there in Sweden such movies are all *barnförbjuden*—officially child-forbidden, due to all that violence, all those guns, to which no young Swede must be exposed. They grow up very sheltered in that country. The odd thing is that after being protected since infancy from the slightest hint of movie or TV violence, particularly violence involving firearms, each one is then grabbed as he approaches maturity, handed a gun, and run through a year of tough military service. You'd think, if it's going to teach them real killing when they grow up, their government wouldn't make quite such a production of saving them from celluloid homicide while they're kids. Well, hell, governments aren't noted for consistency.

"Tie him up while I keep him covered; there is some cord in my hip pocket," Karl said to Karin. "Make him very secure. I will check your knots."

She glanced up with some irritation, kneeling before my chair as she fastened my ankles to it with tough white twine, having already lashed my arms behind me. "Check what you please! I have traveled with him as instructed and . . . and allowed him to make love to me as instructed. I have showed you how to trap him, and helped you. I have even told you about that extra hidden pistol which you overlooked. But check, check, check if you wish. Maybe I tie him with slipping knots so he can free himself and kill me for my trickery, as he undoubtedly wishes. Of course you must check!"

Karl looked slightly embarrassed. "You misunderstand; it is not that I do not trust you. But women often do not tie knots very well. That is all I meant."

She shrugged at this piece of male arrogance, and rose. *"Se om du kan göra bättre!"*

Having told him to see if he could do better, she marched across the room, picked up her ryggsäck, and started to repack the stuff she'd dumped out on the farther bed. Then she looked up quickly, as somebody knocked on the door in code. Three shorts. One long. Repeated. Beethoven's Fifth Symphony. V for Victory, for God's sake!

Karl said, "It is Greta. Let her in."

"Yes, of course. I am sorry; I did not mean to be rude, but you made me angry."

Karin put down the pack and went to the door. The dark-haired girl who came in seemed to have lost weight overnight; she looked more thin and intense then I remembered her. She'd changed from the bloodstained clothes in which I'd last seen her, in the doctor's office in Stockholm; now she was wearing red wool slacks, a white mannish shirt, and a thick maroon sweater. The right side of her face looked pale and drawn; the left side was pretty well masked by the big dressing. The eyes were sunken in the bandaged face; they looked hot and bloodshot. They acknowledged the presence of Karl, and of Karin, and focused on me.

"So you have him captive. Good!" She continued to stare at me as she spoke to Karl. "I watched him walk into the town. He obtained something in the store, something for the car that does not function, but he telephoned to no one, and no one follows him. I waited outside to make certain. There is no one."

"Astrid should be told that we have him," Karl said. "She was concerned that he might interfere tomorrow."

The bandaged girl made an impatient gesture, dismissing Astrid. "She will be told. She will not leave her command post in Lulea until later this evening; there is time. She will be told after we have finished with him. After he has answered my questions."

Karl said dubiously, "It is not authorized. Astrid will not like it."

"All Astrid wants is for him to be immobilized for the

228

next few hours, until it is all over tomorrow morning. Well, he is going nowhere and doing nothing. We are insuring that he makes no trouble, as ordered, are we not? If he suffers a little damage, that is too bad and does not affect the work at Laxfors at all.'' She stared at me. ''But perhaps he will be cooperative. Perhaps coercion will not be necessary. Perhaps he will tell us where to find the other, the one who . . . who hurt me.''

Karin stirred. ''He cannot tell you that.''

Greta turned to look at the smaller girl. ''What do you mean?'' she demanded sharply.

''The man you want is dead, killed by this one.''

''That cannot be true! They work together!''

''I was there; I saw it. There is a conflict in the American spy organization that employed them both. There are two factions. One fights the other. Just like gangsters; just what one would expect of such people!'' Karin licked her lips. ''But there is no need for you to . . . to question this one; he can tell you nothing. Actually, you should be grateful to him; he executed the man you wanted; he did your work for you.''

''Grateful!'' Greta's voice was scornful. She didn't take her eyes from me. ''You! You killed your friend?''

''No friend of mine,'' I said. ''A man I worked with. We had a slight disagreement about which of two gentlemen we were working for.''

''But while he was working with you—actually for you— he did this!''

She made a dramatic gesture towards her bandaged cheek and glared at me, challenging me to deny the accusation, or my responsibility for what had been done to her.

I said casually, ''Tough, but what's your gripe?''

''Gripe?''

Karin said smoothly, ''He means, Greta, what complaint have you?''

The dark girl stared at me, shocked. She started to speak

angrily, but changed her mind. Instead she turned sharply away and took a couple of steps that brought her to the dresser opposite the twin beds. She bent forward to get closer to the mirror. I couldn't make out what she was doing; then I heard Karin gasp, as Greta turned with the bandage in her hand and the injured side of her face uncovered. She marched back to stand over me, leaning close for my inspection.

"Look!" she said harshly. "Look at me! Look what your man did to me! You can ask what complaint I have? Look!"

Karl was staring at her, aghast. I guess he hadn't had an opportunity to view the damage before, or at least not when it wasn't masked by blood. And I have to admit that I found it disturbing, myself; the world isn't so full of even moderately attractive girls that you like to see one chopped up. Still, it wasn't the first knife-slash I'd ever viewed; and it was a nice clean incision that had been neatly closed by someone who knew his business.

Of course it wasn't very pretty at the moment. There were the sutures, there was some crusty dried stuff, and there was a normal amount of swelling and inflammation; but with a little luck in the healing she wasn't going to be too badly marked.

She snapped, "Well, what say you to *that*, Herr Helm?"

"I still say, what's your beef?" I shrugged elaborately. "*Vad har du at beklaga dej om?* If you'll excuse my bastard Swedish. Hell, you joined a violent organization. You're planning a violent demonstration of some kind up here in Lapland, in which people may quite possibly get hurt, right? And in the meantime you've been accessory to kidnapping a man and burning him with a hot iron. Me. And you're complaining because somebody sliced you up a bit? As a great American once said, if you can't stand the heat, baby, stay out of the kitchen."

It worked almost too well. She seemed to have trouble

catching her breath; she tried to speak angrily, but only a wild sound of protest came out; an irate howl. She was clawing for something under her sweater, at the waist; and her hand emerged with one of the souvenir sheath knives they sell in that part of the country—actually in most parts of the country. The blade was about four inches long and probably of pretty good steel, since steel is something they do well over there. The hilt was of figured birch; and there were silver decorations. She held it like an icepick rather than a fighting knife.

*"Se hur du tycker om det!"* she gasped, raising her hand into a position from which she could stab downward at my face. "See how you like it!"

There was a momentary pause; there always is. They don't ever just do it, no matter how angry they are. They've got to have their kicks first; they've got to see you cringe and, if possible, hear you beg. That's part of the fun and they never want to miss it.

"Now you're mad," I said solicitously. "That's very bad for you, Greta. You must keep your face calm or it won't heal properly."

"Greta!" That was Karl. "Greta, you must not do this ugly thing; you will never forgive yourself!"

"Forgive myself? He is the one I cannot forgive!"

I said, "Well, come on, come on, start carving; I can't stand the suspense!"

"Why do you taunt her, she is not herself; she has had too much to bear. . . ."

That was Karl again. Everything was fine, everything was great, I had the full attention of both of them as planned; but where the hell was the Seventh Cavalry that was supposed to come riding to the rescue. . . . I could see the girl above me making up her mind, and I watched the knife, very nice and shiny and new and probably not very sharp, since they wouldn't want a lot of tourists cutting themselves right there in the shop. But plenty sharp enough to rip open my face or, if I managed to lean my head to the side fast enough to avoid it, drive down into my shoulder or chest.

As Greta tensed herself to strike, there was a soft plopping sound behind her, and the gleaming blade wavered oddly. An expression of shocked surprise came to the disfigured face above me. Greta started to turn, to discover what it was that had struck her so painfully. The silenced automatic spoke again, in its quiet way, and her body jerked once more to the impact of a little .22-caliber bullet. She dropped the knife and went to her knees before me.

Karl had whirled, reaching for the Browning he'd tucked away into his waistband. There was total incredulity in his voice: *"Karin! Karin, vad gör du?"*

Three bullets drove into him, answering his question as to what Karin was doing. He collapsed on top of his gun. Little Mrs. Segerby came forward, clutching the automatic I'd lent her, in both hands. She took careful aim downwards and put a final forty-grain slug into the back of Karl's head. Then she moved to Greta, who'd slumped across my knees where I sat tied to my chair. Karin reached out and grasped the other girl by the hair, pulled her off me, and let her sprawl on her back on the rug. Moving like a mechanical doll, Karin then took deliberate two-handed aim once more and gave Greta the coup de grace. The bullet had probably been intended for a spot between the eyes, but it punched out the left one instead; not that it mattered, since Greta was already dead. Karin stood there clutching the automatic, swaying slightly, her face quite white, her throat working.

You don't want to startle a beginner who's worked himself—or herself—up to the killing frenzy. When they're in that state, everybody's the enemy; and the one thing they fear is that having started it, they won't finish it properly; that they'll leave somebody unshot who should have been shot and have it all to do over again. They'll fire at any movement, any sound. . . .

I waited, therefore, until some of the wild tension had left her. Then I spoke very gently: "Watch it. That's a ten-shot clip, and you've still got three rounds left. If you're going to puke, please put the safety on first and lay the piece on the bed. No sense blowing a hole in yourself by mistake. Or me. Then, when you get back from the john, you might consider cutting me loose with that pretty knife down there on the carpet."

<br>

## CHAPTER 23

THERE were no telephones in the rooms of the ancient hotel; in fact the only available phone was at the desk downstairs. That made things awkward, since I'd have to use it in front of the old gent in the office, and I didn't know how much English he really understood. It was going to have to be an exercise in double-talk.

*"Min herre."* The elderly clerk, having fought the battle of the Swedish telephone system to get the number for me, held out the phone. *"Var sa god."*

*"Tack."* I took the instrument and said, "Helm here."

"Helm?"

The voice at the other end was painfully familiar. It brought her back very clearly: a lady considered a murderess by some, but in our business we do what we have to, and I've terminated a few lives myself in the line of duty. What I remembered was the courage she'd demonstrated in her illness, even if that illness had been self-inflicted, and the adult passion—very different from the insatiable, youthful frenzy of my present companion—with which she'd responded to my own passion, and the simple pleasure of her company.

I found myself visualizing her in another hotel some eighty miles away in the city of Luleå, the largest in northern Sweden. She'd undoubtedly chosen it as her headquarters, although it was some distance from Laxfors, because strangers would be less conspicuous in a city that size. Apparently her hotel was more modern than ours; there were phones in the rooms.

"How's your arm?" I asked, as a matter of identification as well as courtesy.

"My arm is not too bad," Astrid Watrous said. "How did you learn this telephone number?"

"Well, I figured you must have instructed Karin to keep an eye on me as we traveled together, and report when she could. Or Olaf had. That meant you must have told her how to get in touch. I persuaded her to share the information with me."

"Persuaded? Yes, that little girl would not be hard to persuade. She is really a rather dull and docile little thing; or have you found her otherwise?"

Astrid was a clever woman where men were concerned; apparently she wasn't quite so smart in evaluating other women.

"Docile, maybe," I said, straight-faced, "but I wouldn't say I've found her dull. Are you jealous?"

Astrid laughed softly, some eighty miles away. "Of course. To forget me so soon for another woman, and a mere child at that!" Her voice changed. "But you did not ring me up to boast of your love life."

"Right. I just met a couple of young friends of yours. They've been very obliging and let me have their car, since mine isn't working right."

There was a little pause. She spoke carefully: "That

little one we rented in Oslo, you and I? It never did operate correctly."

"No."

"How did you convince Karl and Greta . . . or perhaps I should not ask."

"Not unless you want me to tell you. The reason I called is that, being without wheels, they're going to need a lift out of here. A discreet lift out of here, if you know what I mean. They're waiting for you in our hotel room. Haparanda. Stadshotellet. Room 217. Got it?"

She repeated it mechanically: "Haparanda. Stadshotellet. Room 217."

I said, "There will be a Do Not Disturb sign on the door, however, that reads in Swedish. I mean, they are very tired and need their rest."

In the office the old man was shuffling papers on his desk. Astrid was again silent for several seconds. "Both of them, Matt? Was that necessary?" There was anger in the question. When I didn't answer, she said, "I was afraid you would decide to interfere with our plans. After all, there is some American involvement that could give you an interest. That is just the point of our demonstration. Peaceful Sweden does not wish to be dragged into America's warlike troubles."

"Save the oratory for the suckers," I said. "I don't think peaceful Sweden is something you brood about during the long northern nights, sweetheart."

"Perhaps not, but I thought, under the circumstances, you might receive orders to intervene, in your usual brutal fashion. Karl and Greta were merely instructed to stop you and hold you until it is over."

I said, "That wasn't very bright, a couple of untrained kids like that. And didn't it occur to you that Greta, after what had been done to her face, might have some notions of retaliating involving, say, an edged implement and my face. You should see the shiv she was packing, just for

235

me. Well, actually for Joel, but she was happy to settle for a substitute, just so she got to whittle on somebody."

"I did not know. She . . . they were available, so I used them."

"Anyway, they're here, and they won't be leaving under their own power. You'd better have somebody fetch them away inconspicuously."

"And if I don't?"

"Then they'll eventually go out of here publicly, if you know what I mean, and I'm afraid there'll be something of a fuss that could interfere with your plans."

"Your plans could also be interfered with if the matter becomes public."

"Sure. But you can probably scrounge up the manpower locally to cover things up and I can't, which puts it up to you."

After a pause, she said, "I suppose you are right. Very well, I will see to it . . . Matt, I am sorry. Sending them was a miscalculation on my part. What about the little blonde girl?"

"Aside from being sicky to her tummy, she contributed nothing to the fracas either way. But I'm still supposed to be looking after her for the sake of the family, so she goes with me."

"Is that the only reason you take her with you?" I heard a soft laugh in the phone. "I am still jealous, darling."

"You say such nice things," I said. "I wish there were something practical we could do about your jealousy. But I don't suppose we'd better meet again. Even if it could be managed, it wouldn't be a very good idea, for a lot of reasons—reasons that you know as well as I do. Good-bye, Astrid."

"It is too bad; but you are right, of course. Good-bye, my dear."

You hit them every now and then in the business, the man-woman relationships that might have worked out if the world were a different place and the two of you were different people with different loyalties, but it isn't and you aren't. So you stick some more adhesive tape on your poor fractured heart, which is pretty well plastered already, and carry on bravely. Love, who needs it?

I gave the phone back to the old gent behind the desk and thanked him, seeing nothing in his expression to indicate that he'd heard anything unusual. I told him that my wife and I were going out and probably wouldn't be back until quite late, but first we were retrieving our car, which no longer operated, and, if he did not mind, putting it into the hotel parking area. We had made arrangements to use another; we'd have the crippled vehicle picked up in the morning. How much of this got through, what with my lousy Swedish and his lousy English, I didn't know; but a certain amount of money, over and above the telephone charges, changed hands, the universal language, and he seemed satisfied.

It took us half an hour to fetch the Golf from the side of the highway where we'd left it and park it where it would cause no official comment, at least for the time being. We spent a little more time having the tank of our commandeered vehicle filled with *soppa*, as the Swedes refer to gasoline when they're being informal. Soup, to you. Finally we were on the road once more, in the maroon 4WD Audi, which, according to the manual in the glove compartment, had power to all the wheels all the time; but if you had some particularly large stumps to pull, there were a couple of differentials you could lock for additional traction. The upholstery was very plushy, and practically everything was either electric or hydraulic, including the windows, the sunroof, the brakes, and the steering. A real luxury heap, in spite of the go-anywhere drive train.

Karin spoke at last: "You have said nothing, Matt."

"About what?"

"You know. About what . . . what I did back there in Haparanda."

"What's to say?" I shrugged. "If you want, I'll ask what happened to the idea that we were just going to lure those two kids into the room and have you get the drop of them while they were concentrating on me, and maybe put a few questions to them, before we tied them up and gagged them and drove off in their car."

I heard her swallow hard, sitting beside me in the silent and comfortable sedan rolling smoothly through the northern forest along Sweden's Highway E4.

"I . . . She took me by surprise with that knife; I had to shoot, or she would have stabbed you. Then I just . . . went a little crazy, I think."

"Sure. Gun-happy, we call it." I shrugged. "It's one of the two normal beginner reactions."

Karin licked her lips. "And the other?"

"Just when he's needed most, when people are counting on him, the tender-hearted novice drops the gun and bursts into tears saying he can't possibly be expected to *shoot* a fellow human being, can he? Or she?"

"You are very callous."

I said, "For obvious reasons, I prefer your response. You did fine. Maybe you overdid it a bit, but you hit them, and you didn't hit me. Don't sweat it."

After a moment, she said, "One of these days I really *must* learn all these Americanisms. 'Don't sweat it.' I will try to remember that. . . . What did she say?"

"Who, Astrid?" When Karin nodded, I said, "She was upset but not very. She's a pro like me, remember? Losses are expected in our line of work."

"Did you do as I asked?"

"I took all the credit, if that's what you mean," I said. "It wasn't hard. She took for granted that I'd been the one who'd dealt with them. I said that your only contributions to the struggle were a few whimpers and a little vomit."

Karin said resentfully, "You did not have to make me sound quite so . . . so disgusting!" Then she laughed. "I am sorry. You did just right. We do not want to change what you would probably call her image of me. Her contemptuous image of me. I told you, there are plans; but if she should begin to suspect that I am not quite as useless, quite as ineffectual, as I have made myself seem, she might look too closely at . . . at certain things with which I was involved before I drove away with you. Do you understand?"

"More or less," I said. I left it there, and there was silence between us for a while.

At last she said, "You know what I have to ask you. You heard what they said."

"H-Hour is tomorrow morning. That's sooner than you expected, isn't it?"

"Yes, they must have advanced the demonstration date. I thought there was still plenty of time; but if I am to be there, I must go tonight."

"And you'd like me to pass up my own mission and give you a hand with yours?"

"I will still help you as we planned, afterwards. I promise! And there is no specific time for you to do what you do at Lysaniemi; another day or two will not hurt; am I not correct? But I must be there at Laxfors early tomorrow when they made their protest, I *must*!"

I hesitated, but she was prefectly right. Lysaniemi could wait; Laxfors couldn't. And although I had no directive on the subject, if a certain lady with Soviet interests at heart was afraid I might interfere because American interests were involved, I'd better at least take a look to determine what the hell was going on up there at Salmon Falls on the Salmon River.

"You've got yourself a bodyguard, or whatever the hell my function is supposed to be," I said. "But maybe you'd

239

better let me handle the shooting end from now on; we don't want to depopulate the entire north of Sweden.''

## CHAPTER 24

THEY were starting to move in on Laxfors a day early. Apparently they'd decided to make a pilgrimage of it: *Fredsmarschen*, some of the signs read, the Peace March. There weren't many signs, however; it was a long way to hike carrying a big placard, although I saw a couple being lugged that weren't very favorable to the U.S.A. They were heading north in scattered groups with an occasional independent character striding along purposefully alone. These were the rugged ones who were willing to spend a chilly night in the open. Presumably the more delicate idealists would come up the road by car in the morning to join the demonstration.

Although the march could hardly be a secret to the government, we saw no policemen. Presumably the authorities were playing it smart, knowing that there's nothing like a bunch of tough, armed, glowering cops to plant thoughts of riot where none grew before. The marchers were mostly young people, the males and females mostly indistinguishable in boots, durable dark pants, and sturdy coats or sweaters; but the weather had cleared, and Scandinavians tend to strip at the first rare gleam of sunshine, so there were quite a few in hiking shorts and lederhosen. It wasn't really that warm, and their bare knees looked red and chapped.

There was almost always, of course, a *ryggsäck*. I

240

couldn't help wondering which of these little backpacks contained only the marcher's food, and a spare pair of socks and some raingear, and perhaps a tarp and blanket; and which also held an incendiary grenade or two. SVAB HG (E) Typ7F, twenty-five to the case, one case missing from stock, somewhere. I wondered also how many of these pacifist pilgrims were aware that violence was intended. Mostly they looked like nice enough kids, without the cruel fanatic gleam in their eyes that had characterized Karl and Greta.

We made our way past the straggling protest parade; at last the pavement was empty ahead. Presently the scraggly northern forest died away and we found ourselves in a different kind of country. This was the open Arctic landscape I remembered from my last visit: large vistas of low brushy vegetation broken by scattered islands of gnarled trees clinging to the areas of higher and drier ground, like palmy atolls in a tropical sea, except that they weren't palms and this wasn't the tropics. The sodden earth was drained by many little brown brooks and rivulets and, of course, by the Laxfors itself, the Salmon River. It was a rocky stream of moderate size. The road ran along the west bank.

We drove a considerable distance; at last a bridge took us over to the east bank, warning us that we were getting close to the Laxfors installation. I parked so we could study Karin's map. The Swedes go in for a lot of cross-country hiking; in fact, the schools teach a course, mandatory I believe, in orientation, where the students have to learn to find their way on foot over some pretty wild terrain, not a bad idea. To go with this obsession with the boonies, Sweden produces a lot of good topographical maps, readily available.

Karin's was an old one, printed before the Laxfors facility had been thought of. I didn't know whether she was using an obsolete map to save money, or whether an updated version of this particular sheet was unavailable now for reasons of security. The age didn't really matter, because the basic geography indicated by the contours wasn't likely to have changed much, and she'd drawn in the new roads, and the boundaries of the fenced area, very neatly, in pencil. Inside this perimeter, shaded blocks represented the buildings. There were three rectangles, perhaps machine shops, storage sheds, or living quarters. They were not labeled, but the largest structure was; a carefully drawn octagon of considerable size marked, in block printing: MÖRKRUM. I wondered what scientific reason there could be for the odd shape of the so-called Darkroom, but science is not my specialty.

The building was located not too far from the western fence of the headquarters area, which was not very big. To the north was a much larger fenced area, blank on the map, marked only: ANTENN. Karin had made no attempt to sketch in the individual antenna masts or towers. I wondered where she'd obtained her information and how accurate it was; but I had a hunch it could be trusted.

"Well, where do you think we should make our stakeout, Matt? That is the proper term, is it not, stakeout?" Karin frowned at the map. "How about that ridge to the west, if it has not too many trees? It is a distance from the fence, but it seems to be the only place from which we will be able to get a satisfactory view."

I said, "That's what I'm afraid of. If it's the only place from which to watch the show, who else are we going to find up there, watching the show?"

"There is really not much choice. Do you have an alternative to suggest?"

"No, but we can be careful making our approach, and make it early. It's easy from the south; so let's not go that way. I think we can hike clear around that spread of antennas to the north before dark. We'll spend a cold damn' night up on that ridge, but we'll be in the right position in the morning, ready to spot anybody else who decides to sneak up there to see the fun.''

She sighed. "You are the expert. We will do it your way, no matter how uncomfortable it is." She put her finger on the map. "I think this little road, here, would be a good place to leave the auto. . . ."

At dusk, I was sitting on the ridge watching the lights come on all over the Laxfors installation, which was laid out before me. Behind me, Karin slept wrapped in a couple of blankets we'd picked up in the course of our shopping spree in Oulu, back in Finland. The fenced area below me was shaped like a pear, a geometrical pear. I was looking at the small end, and could see all the way across it from fence to chain-link fence. This area was well lighted, unlike the large antenna field that extended off to my left, the fat end of the pear. It displayed few lights except high up on the tall antenna masts and at the tops of the seven peculiar-looking black towers, chunky and rather low, that we'd got a good look at on our way in. Not that it had helped much, since neither of us knew enough electronics to guess what function they might serve.

The place seemed to have no defenses except for the fence itself and the distant gatehouse where the road entered the premises from the east. There was a lighted window in the little shack, but I couldn't make out the watchman inside without binoculars; however, we'd seen him step out, earlier, to admit a couple of cars. We'd made a careful survey with the glasses that we'd also picked up in Oulu, while we still had daylight, and determined that he was the only visible security personnel—which didn't mean there weren't concealed batteries of electronic eyes watching every square inch of the area; and a room full of TV-type monitors somewhere; and a hidden, armed protective force ready to spring into action the instant something that shouldn't be there showed on one of the screens.

But to look at, it was a very peaceful scene. The three

rectangular buildings I'd seen on Karin's topo map formed an open square, not uncommon in the snowy north, where farmhouses, barns, and sheds are often grouped around a courtyard for shelter and convenience when the white stuff gets ass-high to a tall giraffe, to quote an old hunting guide of my acquaintance. This court faced south, and I could look into it at an angle. There had been some foot traffic over there earlier, both male and female, but I hadn't seen any movement recently. However, the windows of the nearest of the three buildings, apparently a residence or dormitory, were one hundred percent lighted on the first floor and fifty percent on the second.

That could all have been part of any government facility. It was the *Mörkrum* that made the place unique. The great octagon had looked curious enough on Karin's map; it looked even weirder in the flesh, so to speak. It was quite obviously a roof—the roof and part of the topmost story of a tall building sunk into the ground. It looked as if somebody had taken one of those Holiday Inn towers and dug a hole and buried it, all except the upper ten feet. I don't know how it managed to convey the iceberg impression that there was a hell of a lot more below the surface than showed on top; but I found myself visualizing elevator shafts and emergency stairs leading down into the bowels of the earth. I couldn't help wondering why, if they were going to make an underground facility, they hadn't sunk it completely below the surface.

The fact that what showed aboveground was painted dead black didn't help to explain it, but suggested that there might have been a simple and non-photographic reason for the structure to be called the Darkroom. It was surrounded by what seemed to be a wide safety zone of neatly raked gravel that, in summer, would make an interesting contrast with the green grass, still winter-brown at this time of year, around the other buildings. There was a connecting concrete walk bordered by flower beds, which seemed kind of like putting window boxes on a Sherman tank, but the Scandinavians do insist on having their flowers during the short season that anything grows up there. I couldn't see the doorway from where I sat; it was on the far side of the structure that faced the other buildings.

Some hint of its function—at least it might have been a hint to someone with a better scientific background than mine—was given by the fact that a sizable rectangular shaft ran up each of the four sides I could see, and three of the ones I couldn't see now but had glimpsed as we made our approach earlier; all except the wall of the octagon through which people entered the place.

These shafts emerged from the ground alongside the building and terminated a couple of feet above the roof, like large chimneys. I wondered if the Swedes played basketball; it was going to take an accurate throw to put a grenade into one of those things. Why they had to be so big was not clear, since a simple four-inch pipe would have carried the heavy electrical cable that came out of each one, with room to spare. Apparently the seven cables, in addition to needing plenty of room in the conduits that brought them up from their mysterious sources underground, also had to be well separated from each other, presumably for electronic reasons. Each one, therefore, was carried on tall poles straight out from its wall of the building; it then swung around the building at an even distance—some fifteen feet—from its neighbors. I noted that no cable was allowed to cross the walk employed by people. A couple were brought the long way around the building instead, suggesting that there might be energy fields involved that were not entirely harmless. Finally, all seven cables, neatly parallel, marched off together on their poles in a northerly direction to be distributed among the seven peculiar towers in the antenna field.

I was debating awakening my relief, towards midnight, when she roused of her own accord. I heard her putting herself together behind me; then she came up and touched me on the shoulder.

"My turn, I think," she whispered. "Is anything happening?"

"Nothing has moved for the past hour." I yawned. "Well, wake me if you see or hear anything you don't understand."

"Ha, I do not understand anything I see over there. That strange, buried building! All those tall masts and thick wires and fat little towers with strange saucers on them!" She laughed ruefully. "Good night, Matt."

It wasn't the most comfortable night I ever spent out; but it was by no means the worst, either. The ground was damp, of course, but we had no rain or snow to contend with, and not much wind. I was running pretty far behind on my sleep, so I managed to doze off all right; but towards morning I found myself awake and reaching for my gun, although I wasn't aware of having heard anything disturbing. I lay listening for a while. Nothing moved along the ridge or, if it did, it was very good at moving silently.

Karin started when I touched her. "Oh, you are awake. Good, I hated to disturb you, you were sleeping so well, but I am having much trouble keeping my eyes open."

"Anything to report?"

"I have seen and heard nothing. Except that they changed people in the *Mörkrum* at midnight, right after you went to sleep. Eight men and two women went in; four women and six men came out. They were all dressed in white overalls. Overalls? Coveralls?" She shrugged. "And another man in uniform relieved the one at the gate."

"Nothing else?"

"No."

I said, watching her shadowy face, "It's your show, but I wonder if it might not be a good idea for me to make a little scouting expedition along the ridge just to see if anybody's managed to sneak up on us."

Karin was silent for a little, then she spoke carefully: "No, Matt, it would not be a good idea." After a little pause, she went on: "You are a very clever man, and very good at what you do, but I do not want you to be so good and clever tonight. Just sit here and be a good boy while I take a nap, please."

"You're asking a lot. I haven't had much practice being a good boy. But I'll give it a try."

After she'd settled down in the blankets in the small hollow above and behind me, I sat there listening, but there was really nothing to hear. I just knew they were out there, and so did Karin. She'd practically admitted it, and ordered me to leave them alone. I wondered who they were, and how many, and what the little girl thought she was up to. . . .

Well, it would probably all become clear in time. I let my mind drift through memories unpleasant and pleasant, mostly of a sexual nature, as a man will. The girl sleeping nearby, who'd found me lacking in warmth if not in experience. The somewhat older woman in whose arms I'd performed quite passionately, perhaps even overdoing the virility bit; but she hadn't seemed to mind. There was really no use in thinking about her, however, because we obviously had no future together. She had her country and I had mine and never the twain could meet, although it might be better for the world—certainly for us—if they did.

Then they were there. I was aware of distant shadows drifting along the outside of the Laxfors fence, approaching from the south, from my right, the easy way we hadn't come. There were a good many of them, half a dozen or more. That was the main force. A smaller group, by the sound, was already in among the trees of the ridge. They were still well off to my right but angling towards me, moving more stealthily than the others; but it was difficult terrain for the silent sneak, with plenty of rustling brush and loose rattling rock. I stole back up to where Karin slept.

"Company coming," I whispered.

She sat up, shoving back her blankets. "How much company, Matt?"

"The hostiles are infiltrating the area in two waves," I whispered. "Or are they friendlies? Whose sides are we on, anyway? I can't tell the players without a scorecard. Anyway, six or seven or eight—it's hard to count shadows—are approaching along the fence. I assume they're heading for the place closest to the Darkroom, with penetration in mind. Two or three or four, more than one anyway, are coming up the ridge at a slant, presumably for purposes of observation. They could even be aiming for this lookout spot of ours."

"Well, why should they not?" Karin asked. "We decided that it was the best place from which to watch; preliminary scouting could have brought them to the same conclusion."

"We'd better pull back to the crest," I said. "Let me have those blankets. . . . You haven't left any monogrammed compacts, or signet rings with the family crest? Okay, let's go. Take it very easy." I'd already, like a good commander, selected a vantage point to which we could retreat if dislodged from our first position. "Okay, now keep your face down. . . . What the hell is *that*?"

A sudden blare of sound had broken the stillness of the morning. It was distant, but it was obviously choral music and we could even make out the words: *Vårt land, vårt land, vårt fosterland, ljud högt o dyra ord.* . . . Somebody had obviously set up a PA system over by the gate; but the record or tape being played was reinforced by the singing of flesh-and-blood people, quite a large number of them. They were belting out the Swedish national anthem at full volume: "Our land, our land, our native land, sound high, oh, precious words. . . ." Okay, so anthems don't trans-

248

late very well. Try "The Star-Spangled Banner" in Swedish sometime. Or those amber waves of grain.

The weird thing was that they'd sing it at all. American protesters don't go in for patriotic songs much, regardless of what they're protesting against. Or for. These Swedish kids were proclaiming, I guess, that what they were doing was not only for peace but for their country; they were putting the fatherland, or motherland, back on the right track, and to hell with the sneaky *Amerikanare* and their vicious toys.

CHAPTER 25

THE boys and girls put on quite a show. There were a lot of them around the gate, and they all had blazing torches, which they waved as they sang; quite spectacular even at the distance, like a rippling lake of fire. But the time for torches was slipping away: the eastern horizon beyond them was lightening noticeably.

Karin touched my arm warningly. I lowered my face and lay very still; but it was only a shadowy figure that had taken a few steps up the hill from the little group of three that had usurped our lookout spot some fifty feet down the slope. With his back to his friends, he relieved himself— obviously a man, since he had the equipment to do it standing up. As he zipped himself up, I could see, vaguely, that he was a tallish gent with a lot of light yellow hair, which he displayed briefly, taking off his dark cap and patting his golden coiffure into place. He spent a moment setting the cap back on his head at the proper angle. So presumably

there was a woman along. Unless he was of that persuasion, he wouldn't be fixing his hair so nicely to impress a
bunch of the boys.

Then I heard her voice, very soft: "Ragnar?"

*"Jag kommer."*

The blond one turned away from us, and moved back
down the slope to rejoin the woman who had spoken. There
had been no mistaking that feminine voice, even speaking
just the single name. I suppose I should have known that
there would have to be a final meeting.

"Yes, it is Astrid." Karin's lips were close to my ear.

"So that's why we're here," I breathed.

"Yes, I knew she would come here!" Karin's voice was
triumphant. "She is too important, of course, to demonstrate in company with the peace-loving mob she has gathered for her Communist purposes, and perhaps be arrested;
but I knew that she would not leave without seeing her
plans executed. I knew she would have to come to this spot
or somewhere close by. I knew that if I could come here
this morning, with your help, I would find her here. Now
you must remember, deal with the men how you wish, but
keep them from interfering. That is why you are here,
please. But do not touch Astrid, no matter what happens.
I know what I am doing. Please leave her to me no matter
what she attempts to do. She is mine!"

"Shhh, not so loud, they'll hear you. . . ."

We lay there for a moment, quite still; but the silence
below us did not indicate that we had been detected. The
music protected us. They'd switched to an old Swedish
folk song now, one my mother used to sing. Astrid and her
companions were waiting for something. A bright metal
wand gleamed down there: the antenna of a walkie-talkie.
Astrid was holding it. The man called Ragnar had his left
arm in front of his face; I realized that he was peering at
his wristwatch. He spoke one word to Astrid, and she spoke
one word into her radio. Then all three of them turned to

250

look in the direction of the fence, where it made its closest approach to the low, black, geometrical structure known as the Darkroom. Shadowy figures were now slipping through a hole that had been made in the wire, and running to distribute themselves around the building in a very organized fashion, splitting up systematically left and right. I counted seven of them, one person for each face of the octagon except the front. Or to put it differently, one grenade for each ventilator shaft.

"I don't think much of the Laxfors alarm system," I whispered.

"They have taken care of it," Karin breathed. "That is, they think they have taken care of it."

"What about those fat cables on poles the kids are running under?" I asked. "The way they've got them isolated, there must be some kind of radiation. . . ."

"It is not good with long or repeated exposure, but a few minutes will not harm." Karin drew a long breath. "Now it is our turn. Remember, you are to take care of the men as necessary; but you must leave her to me!" She put her hand on my arm. "Please trust me. I am on the right side, I promise you. There will be no sabotage here if you help me. It has all been arranged. I give you my word that it is acceptable for you, as an American agent, to help me."

I'd been wondering what an honest, straight-shooting Yankee boy was doing with a gun in a spot like this, not knowing what the legitimate targets were, if any. But I did know what side Astrid was on, and presumably that went for her two male associates. It wasn't mine. Which put me on Karin's side, if only by default; and her intensity carried conviction.

"Okay, I'm with you," I said. "Cut loose your wolf."

" 'Cut loose my . . . ' I really *must* learn that language!" Karin drew a long breath and raised her head. *Astrid!*"

There was a moment of frozen silence; then the two men started to move simultaneously.

"Look behind you, Astrid!" Karin called. "That was Frederik's mistake; he turned his back on the wrong person. You should have learned from that experience, Astrid!"

Blond Ragnar was faster; he got halfway turned around. I could see the gleam of his gun. There's nothing like a firearm swinging your way to resolve all humanitarian doubts: I put one into the middle of him and turned my attention to the other, also armed; but he was slow or just hesitant. He hadn't fired at my muzzle flash, so I took a chance and put one past his head. He turned and ran, blundering away through the trees that were just becoming faintly visible as the east grew brighter. I looked at Ragnar; but he was down, facedown, and his pistol gleamed faintly a few feet beyond his outstretched hand.

I saw that, strangely, Astrid had not stirred. She was standing perfectly still where she had been, her back to us. Now, moving very deliberately, she laid the walkie-talkie down on my old sitting-rock. She turned at last, steadying the shoulder strap bag she carried. Unable to see us in the weak dawn light, hidden as we still were in the brush of the crest, she took a step up towards us. When she spoke, it wasn't to Karin.

"Matthew?"

"Right here."

I stood up, keeping an eye on the darker shadow on the ground down there; but Ragnar of the Golden Locks, although I thought he was breathing, made no move to reclaim his lost firearm.

"Yes," Astrid said quietly. "It would be you. I knew we would come to this in the end. I am sorry." She drew a long breath. "Where does that noisy little Segerby girl hide?"

Karin rose to stand beside me. "Here I am, Astrid. I have come to kill you. Do I have to tell you why?"

Astrid laughed scornfully. "You are a stupid child, and your Frederik was an interfering fool!"

Karin took two steps down the slope towards the shadowy figure that was becoming clearer by the minute as the sky became lighter in the east. The smaller girl had her derringer out, I saw. She'd reclaimed it earlier, giving back the silenced High Standard with the depleted magazine. She'd said she preferred the little two-barreled job because it was her own. Where she'd stopped was still long range for the snub-nosed piece, and I remembered the overheavy triggerpull; but this business was between the two of them and I knew that Karin would have accepted no coaching from me even if I'd been inclined to give it.

Astrid looked up at the younger girl. She spoke quite calmly: "You will never hit me with that toy, my dear."

There was a momentary pause as Karin struggled with the gun; then the sharp crack of the .22 Magnum shattered the morning stillness. Untouched, Astrid laughed and brought her hand out of her big purse. She was holding, not a firearm, but a dull metal cylinder about the size of a can of beer, but there was gadgetry at one end not to be found on any beer can. I checked the impulse to throw myself backwards, putting the crest of the ridge between me and the *handgranat*. Curiosity kept me motionless. *I know what I'm doing*, Karin had said, confidently. She was taking a long time with her second shot. Astrid laughed again at the threat of the little pistol. Her hands came together; I saw her pull the pin. Starting to raise the grenade for the throw, she let the firing lever flip upwards. . . .

There should, of course, have been a delay, perhaps as short as three seconds, perhaps as long as five or six. The instant crack of the incendiary's bursting charge came as a shocking surprise. I thought I caught a glimpse of Astrid as the thing blew up in her grasp; but perhaps I just imagined her torn face staring incredulously at her mangled hands, in the moment before the fireball enveloped her, sending a wave of heat our way. I did see her clearly as the first incendiary blast faded. I told myself I was a tough guy and wasn't going to look away, dammit; and I saw her still standing there with her hair on fire and her clothes melting into flaming driblets of petrochemical material that no longer bore any resemblance to cloth, just as she had already ceased to look like flesh and blood. . . .

Then there was nothing but a blackened, smoking stick figure lying stiffly on its side in an area of scorched and smoking brush, like something wild left behind among the charred stumps of the forest fire that had caught and killed it. Karin was the first to stir. She ran down past the body and picked up the walkie-talkie and spoke into it. Somebody asked a scratchy question in Swedish, presumably about the fireworks up here.

*"Ja, vi maste skynda,"* Karin said. *"Gör det nu!"*

Yes, we must hurry; do it now, she'd said; and a whistle blew, down by the fence. Immediately, there were sharp cracking sounds all around the octagonal building down there, followed by horrified screams of agony. I could see four of the fireballs from where I stood; three were outside my field of view. Karin watched coldly as the incendiaries burned out; then she put down the radio and came back up the slope to the inhuman figure lying there. I moved down to her. When she raised her head to look at me, her face was bleak and much older than it had been. She started to speak, but there were suddenly figures in the woods all around us. Karin put her hand quickly on my arm.

"No. Do not resist. It is all right."

They were mostly in Swedish Army uniforms, mostly armed with the SVAB machine pistols. The Segerby Weapons Company was doing a land-office business in the north-land today. These were, I knew, the men I'd heard moving

254

in during the night; the ones Karin hadn't let me investigate.

Another voice spoke: "Please put your gun away, Helm; it makes my soldier friends very nervous."

It was Olaf Stjernhjelm's voice. He came out of the trees and strode up to me. He as not in uniform. Except for his hiking boots, he looked as if he were about to do a bit of cross-country skiing. We faced each other for a moment, before he spoke again, choosing his words very carefully.

"You have reason not to like me. I regret what happened in Stockholm. It was necessary to impress my fanatic young accomplices with my utter ruthlessness and complete devotion to their cause. Will you accept my apology?"

I'd had pleasant dreams of dismembering this man joint by joint; but if you're a pro, you can't waste your time getting even with everybody.

I said, "Be my guest. Hell, it only hurts when I breathe. Do I gather that you actually work for the Swedish government? And Karin, too?"

He nodded. "Yes, she offered her services after her husband was murdered. She has been very useful."

I looked around. A couple of men were bending over the one I'd shot, Ragnar, who was apparently alive enough to receive first aid. Off to one side, another pair of uniformed characters watched over a prisoner, presumably the man who'd run. Down around the *Mörkrum*, various people were doing various useless things around the remains left by the incendiaries, and a man with a fire extinguisher was operating on the smoldering brush around Astrid's body, although the chances of starting a forest fire, or tundra fire, in that sodden country, were not very great.

I drew a long breath. "You kids play rough."

Olaf looked me straight in the eye. "I do not understand what you mean, Cousin Matthew. By infiltrating a dubious activist group with suitable agents, we learned of a forthcoming attempt at sabotage employing a certain type of infantry weapon, a case of which had been reported missing. We took certain obvious precautions. For instance, we had ceramic plates installed in the vulnerable ventilator shafts of the target laboratory. As it turned out, this was unnecessary, since the grenades stolen by the saboteurs proved to be defective. We have no idea how it could have happened, and we are shocked at the resulting loss of life. Our plan, of course, was simply to surround the area quietly, allow them to incriminate themselves fully, and then take them into custody without injury to anybody. But then, these terrorist types are always blowing themselves up with their own toys, are they not?" His eyes touched the unrecognizable body surrounded by fire-blackened bushes. "It is too bad that some must always die. And there is really no pretty way of doing it, is there, Helm?"

His voice was not quite steady; he wasn't as tough as he wanted to appear. But tough enough.

## CHAPTER 26

ı watched Karin emerging from behind the granite boulder she'd selected for a dressing room, with more modesty than I'd have expected of her, considering her behavior on the Turku ferry. But then I'd never found her very predictable. She came back to the car, picking her way carefully to keep from getting her smart new boots wet. She tossed the backpack with her old clothes into the open trunk of the Audi, slammed the lid, and turned to present herself for my inspection.

"How do I appear?"

Leaving Laxfors, we'd driven back to the main highway and turned north the way we'd come the day before. Now we were costuming ourselves—or Karin was—for the next phase of the northland operation, my phase. To make these preparations, we'd driven up a little woods road a dozen miles short of the town of Porkkala and the turnoff to Lysaniemi. I found it a relief to be back dealing with my own business and that of the U.S.A. Watch out, Bennett, here comes Helm. At last. Well, the waiting would have affected his nerve and disposition adversely from his point of view, favorably from mine.

"You appear very well," I said.

However, looking at her, I knew a pang of regret for the careless boyish companion in the creased Levi's—or whatever the Swedish equivalent may be—and well-worn sweater to whom I'd become accustomed. But that girl, and that relationship, was gone anyway, consumed by the intense heat of the *handgranat* (E) that had taken the life of Astrid Watrous.

Karin's transformation was actually quite startling. Now she was a fashionable young lady wearing a tailored pantsuit that, fitting nicely in all the right places, emphasized the rounded femininity of her small body. It was a spring outfit, constructed of some pale-blue stuff that resembled linen, except that real linen would have been a mass of wrinkles after being crammed into that ryggsäck; this looked as crisp as if it had just been pressed. For us hero-agents, and particularly our heroine-associates, the synthetics have certain advantages. Her low little boots had soft uppers and moderately high heels. There was a white silk blouse with a round collar and a small white bow at the throat. Working behind that rock, without a mirror, she hadn't got the bow quite right. I retied it for her.

I said, "There. Now you're beautiful."

But I couldn't get the right playful note into my voice, and she was as aware of it as I was.

She said quietly, "I am sorry. I did not realize that you loved her, or I would not have asked you to help. That is why I did not trust Olaf to deal with her; he loved her also, in his way."

I said, "Love, schmove. This isn't *True Romances,* small-fry."

She said, "I had to do it. She killed my husband. That . . . that is not permitted! They were all responsible. So when they became interested in the incendiary grenades, I had this idea of how to deal with them. His company. His grenades. He would be striking back at them from the grave, the ones who had caused his death." She smiled faintly. "I suppose that is what you would call a corny idea. Corny?"

"I wouldn't call it exactly corny," I said. I hesitated. "One thing I don't get. If you were working with Olaf, why did you need me?"

"I told you. He had known her too well. I did not trust him to deal with her properly. I did not want her arrested, I wanted her dead. But he would not even let me be present; it was no place for me, he said. So I came anyway, with your help; and he did not dare to attempt to remove us because he knew we were armed. A misunderstanding in the dark, a shot, and his whole trap would have been ruined."

I said, "So you teased her into going for a grenade with that popgun of yours. You took a chance. I told you she'd probably had firearms training. If she'd come up with a gun instead, at that range, you'd have been dead while you were still trying to squeeze the second round out of your idiot derringer."

She laughed shortly. "It is a rather impossible weapon, is it not? I thought I would never get it to shoot, even using both hands."

"Well, you'll have a chance to get in a little practice with it shortly. If you're still of a mind to help."

"Of course. I owe—"

"Never mind owe," I said.

She licked her lips. "I want to help. Perhaps you will think better of me then. . . . No, no, do not say polite things. I know that when you look at me now, you will always see her dying like that, horribly. But at least I can show you that I pay my debts. Shall we go?"

"Just one more question, Karin."

"Yes?"

"In Haparanda. You didn't really lose your head in that hotel room, did you?"

"No. I hated them, all of them. I wanted to kill them all. There I had a gun and a chance at two of them; and I took it quite deliberately. I told you, I am not really the sweet little girl I sometimes pretend to be." She laughed shortly. "But be not concerned, I do not intend to spend my life at this vendetta. It was over when she died. Those remaining are now safe from me. Get into the car and I will cover you up."

I squeezed my six-four frame into the space between the front and rear seats of the Audi, adequate for a starving midget. She covered me, more or less, with the blue military-style raincoat we'd picked up in Oulu with the rest of her fashionable spring costume. I had a *ruggsäck* of my own for a pillow, containing the contents of my inexpensive suitcase and an intriguing assortment of my own and other people's firearms and ammunition. I'd been afraid Olaf might get stuffy about them, but he hadn't. The suitcase itself was being left behind here so that, when I bailed out, later, there would be nothing in the car to indicate, if anyone should look, that Karin wasn't traveling alone. Crammed into my crack, I found the ride painfully bouncy as far as the paved highway. Even after that, as we picked up speed, it could hardly be called restful.

"There is the Porkkala signpost," Karin reported at last from her position behind the wheel. "Five kilometers more

. . . Now we enter Porkkala. There is the village store we saw yesterday, when we were driving the other direction, that also sells petrol.'' After a little pause, her voice came again: "I hope you can hear me. I do not wish to move my lips too much if somebody watches. But there are not many automobiles among the houses, and I see no sharp-eyed gentleman in American clothes observing the highway conscientiously.''

"I'm betting there is one, though, even if he's keeping out of sight," I said. "With a special little two-way radio tuned to a special frequency; we've got one that can't be picked up by anybody who doesn't know just what he's tuning for and has special equipment to do it. Wherever he's actually laying for me up there, Bennett's bound to have the approaches to Lysaniemi covered. There are only two, this one from the south, and one from the north that involves a hell of a lot of roundabout driving on little forest roads, all unpaved. He'll have men posted well out on both of them, to give him advance warning of my approach.''

Karin said, "Now I make the turn, just beyond the store. The signpost says Lysaniemi one hundred and twenty-three kilometers. I still see nobody watching. It is not so bad a road as the little one to the place where I changed my costume, but it is not paved. . . .''

"I can tell," I said dryly.

"I am sorry; are you much uncomfortable? Should I slow down more?''

"No, just do what comes naturally.''

'Nobody follows. I see no one in the mirror.''

"They wouldn't follow closely enough to be seen, even if they knew I was in the car. They'd just report me on my way; then they might get instructions to come on up towards Lysaniemi well behind us, cautiously, kind of herding us along. But let's hope you fooled them. Now you'd better find a place for me to ditch, fast, before we get clear out of earshot of the town. Then pick a spot for your picnic as soon as possible. Do your stuff and don't look over your shoulder. I'll be somewhere around."

There was a brief pause before Karin said, "Prepare yourself. I think over this little hill you will not be seen. . . . Yes, *now*!"

I went out of the car fast and low with my *ryggsäck*, hit the gravel shoulder of the road, and rolled into the bushes, almost continuing down into a roadside creek or ditch; but I managed to catch myself. I heard the Audi's rear door slam as Karin closed it after me; I heard the car rumble over what sounded like a wooden bridge, picking up speed again. The noise of its progress faded as it topped the next low ridge.

I waited there for several minutes, well hidden in the brush, to make sure that I'd been right and nobody was tailing us. Satisfied, I stood up and checked the road, but it was well graveled, and old buckskin-clad Hawkeye himself wouldn't have noticed the spot where I'd unloaded. Or did he wear homespun or linsey-woolsey? It had been a long time since I'd read my Fenimore Cooper. I shouldered my pack and slid on down to the roadside stream and waded it, thankful, as I'd been last night, that I'd operated in this part of Sweden once before.

A good many years had passed since that mission, which had been concluded farther north and west, up near the great iron mine at Kiruna, but I hadn't forgotten one lesson it had taught me: except when it's frozen solid, which it wasn't now or then, the Scandinavian northland is one of the wettest, soggiest places on earth, and knee-high rubber boots are an essential part of the uniform of the day. Minutes later I had a larger stream to cross, the one that rushed cheerfully under the road bridge; but by jumping from rock to rock I managed to keep my socks dry there, too.

I took a course paralleling the road. When I heard a vehicle approaching from the north, I crouched behind a tree to study it as it went rattling by; but it was an ancient and very muddy Volvo truck and the face of the driver was elderly and Nordic. I marched on and almost immediately spotted the Audi in a clearing that had once been a lonely farm. The weathered remains of the house still stood in the middle of the open area, silvery gray, with the roof falling in. There was a collapsed gray ruin of a barn nearby. The Swedish hinterland is full of these derelict homesteads, empty since the kids took off for the cities and the old folks passed on.

Karin had turned out onto the dim old driveway leading across the field to the house. It was apparently quite soft, and she'd made only some forty yards, plowing twin tracks through the mud. At first glance, the maroon sedan seemed to be badly stuck; but she'd been careful to come off the main road uphill, smart girl. With four-wheel drive, and the Audi's tricky differentials locked, and gravity to help, there should be no trouble backing out when leaving time came.

The girl was waiting behind the wheel. She was supposed to give me long enough to find a good position before she went into her act—we'd decided on half an hour from the moment we separated. I glanced at my watch: seventeen minutes to go. Checking the terrain, I picked up a clump of brush at the edge of the clearing fifty yards from the car, made my way down there cautiously, and settled down to my vigil. Presently, Karin got out holding a paper bag, and set it on the hood of the Audi. She extracted from it a bottle of beer, which she opened—they use the screw-type bottle cap over there; you don't have to pry it off with an opener. She took several deep gulps, set the bottle aside, and brought out a plastic-wrapped sandwich and started to unwrap it, but changed her mind after a glance at her wrist.

The half hour was up. Karin found a small paper bag in the car and set it on the hood. From it she took the little derringer and the box of cartridges. She looked around for something to use as a target. Aha, the beer bottle. She polished off the contents and wiped her mouth with the back of her hand, very unladylike. She was getting into the spirit of it; she was a gun-girl now, full of determination to learn her new trade. She was doing her very best for me, in return for my help this morning. She marched up to the wrecked old house carrying the pistol and ammo; and the empty bottle, which she put on the front step, after peering in one of the windows to make certain the building was empty. She backed off a short distance, loaded up, dropped the cartridge box into her jacket pocket, took careful two-handed aim, and fired. And missed, as she had this morning.

The .22 Magnum cartridge made an impressive noise under that low gray sky; somehow they always sound louder on a damp day. Karin stepped a little closer and tried again, and missed again. She reloaded both barrels and tried once more, standing even closer. The beer bottle exploded. I heard her laugh triumphantly. She stepped forward and found the bottom of the bottle still intact, and set it up for a final target. She reloaded the discharged chamber and fired twice, as fast as she could manage the heavy trigger pull. On the second shot the thick disc of glass disintegrated in a very satisfactory manner.

Returning to the car, Karin dumped the last two empties out of the gun, wiped off the weapon with a Kleenex, and put it back into its paper bag, along with the ammunition. She was, I reflected, doing extremely well for an amateur: acting it all out meticulously as we'd agreed, even though there was no reason to think she had any audience besides me at the moment. I wondered if she planned to keep on working for Olaf and his undercover outfit, whatever it was; with a little training, she'd be an asset to any agency. She found another bottle of beer and leaned against the car drinking it. After a while she unwrapped her sandwich and took a bite of it, eating and drinking very slowly. . . .

At last we heard a car approaching from the south, the direction of Porkkala. You can use a sexy call to bring in an elk or turkey. Where man is the quarry, under circumstances like this, a few mysterious gunshots will do as well.

## CHAPTER 27

CROUCHING in the brush watching over my decoy car and my decoy girl, I had the fine breathless feeling you get out in the marsh at dawn when that first flock of mallards turns towards the blind, setting their wings and slanting down through the morning mist towards the phony ducks on the water. . . . Well, it had been inevitable that the sound of shooting would bring us somebody. The Porkkala man, hearing it, would be bound to report it to the Lysaniemi man by radio. Bennett would be consulted. He'd figure that one of his people must have run into me even if none of them was supposed to be wandering around in this particular neighborhood. He'd try to check them all out to identify the agent involved, but when you set up an intricate ambush such as he'd undoubtedly organized here—the fewer the brains, the greater the complexity of the field operation—there's always some agent who loses contact; it's one of the laws of nature.

So unless the approaching vehicle was local, say a game warden or forester who'd heard the shots and was checking for poachers, or the elderly Viking in the Volvo truck returning from a quick trip to his Arctic corner grocery, it meant that Bennett's man down on Highway E4, patiently watching the Lysaniemi turnoff, had been ordered to investigate the gunfire he'd reported. The question now was whether he'd use the direct approach, just driving up the road looking innocent and rubbernecking all the way, or whether he'd park at a distance and make a thorough scout on foot.

Soon the vehicle was close enough to establish that the driver had no intention of stopping to play Hiawatha in this soggy Arctic terrain. I heard it top the low rise behind me, but I couldn't see it yet for the brush in which I hid. Suddenly it came into view. It was slowing down. The driver had spotted the Audi apparently stuck out on the muddy little side road; and the chic feminine figure, very much out of place here, beside it. Chivalry had lifted his foot from the accelerator; then self-preservation took over, and the car picked up speed once more and continued out of sight. It was a Golf sedan like the rental job I'd left in the parking lot of Stadshotellet in Haparanda; but instead of being red and sick it was blue and sounded quite healthy. . . .

*Porkkala reporting: reconnaissance of gunfire area reveals no obvious hostile activity; however, questionable vehicle present, apparently in difficulties, driver female. Is further investigation authorized?*

Well, something like that would have passed over the air. After an interval—actually only eight minutes by the clock, but it felt longer—I heard the Golf returning. Authorization had apparently been granted immediately. Okay. My next move was obvious: cut Bennett off and leave him guessing, up there in Lysaniemi. No more communications from the southern front. No more information. Nothing coming up the road. Nothing coming over the air. No word from the man he'd sent to investigate. If I knew my Bennett, he couldn't take too much of that kind of silence, following a breathless report of mysterious and unexplained shooting. He'd start seeing the bleak woods full of hostile, armed forces sneaking up on him. His imagination

265

would turn the trap he'd set for me into a trap closing in on him. Sooner or later, probably sooner, he'd scrap his fancy ambush and come charging down here in force to find his missing operative and learn what the hell was going on.

At that point, if I figured it right and put myself in the right place with the right weapon—by now I had a large collection to choose from—I could do the job I'd been sent here for, if I'd deciphered my murky orders correctly.

As I read it, Mac had been fully aware of Bennett's bureaucratic maneuvers to replace him as head of our outfit, in retaliation for humiliations suffered at our hands. Mac had known that the other man was just waiting for an opening that would let him move in—a serious professional slip on Mac's part, say, or an illness, or an accident that might not even be accidental. Then the multiple kidnapping case had come up, and one of the missing people was somebody who meant something to Mac. I was guessing now, but I still didn't think he'd chosen to describe Mrs. Beilstein's case by accident; he does very little by accident. He was letting me know his motive for acting foolishly. He was, by God, going to pick up the warped old lance he'd set aside years ago, and the battered shield, and the rusty sword, and ride out to rescue his ladylove personally—and at the same time, of course, solve the case of the vanishing citizens. And if he failed and met disaster, he wanted me to know about his lady and do something for her if there was still something that could be done.

But in the meantime I had a more important task. Mac had presumably been quite aware that when he deserted his office to handle the kidnapping case personally—which involved letting himself be kidnapped as bait—Bennett would make a flying leap into his vacated chair. Then Bennett would obviously work as fast as he could to consolidate his position, using violence as necessary, since he was now acting head of an organization that dealt in violence. It was easy to predict that he'd do his best to make certain that neither Mac nor the loyal operatives who'd disappeared with him ever returned.

It was highly possible, I reflected, that Mac had hoped and planned for all this to happen. Tired of waiting for Bennett's move, Mac had deliberately teased the man into action. Mac had also, anticipating Bennett's campaign of extermination, laid a broad trail for the other man to follow in the wrong direction, using Dr. Watrous and his girl-friend and me as bait. If I wanted to kid myself, I could say that Mac had chosen me because I was the best he had, or simply because Bennett was unlikely to use good judg-ment where I was concerned, since he hated me. But I knew it was really a punishment of sorts: I'd been left off the important kidnapping case and sent chasing across the ocean on this unrelated mission because I was the naive jerk who'd turned Bennett loose once, thinking him harm-less; and it was up to me to rectify my error person-ally. . . .

The blue Golf was coming into sight now where the road appeared at the end of the neglected fields; and it was time to stop daydreaming. From my place of concealment, I watched the vehicle come to a stop at the point where Karin had turned off the graveled road onto the muddy farm track. The driver got out and took a couple of steps towards the stalled Audi.

"Are you stuck, ma'am?" he called; and then with a Swedish accent even worse than mine: "*Har fröken svå-righeter*? Do you have difficulties, miss?"

Karin called back, "No, it is all right. I am all right." After a moment's hesitation, she went on: "Did I not see you driving northwards a few minutes ago? Did you come back just to see if I was in trouble? That was kind of you. Can I give you a beer, perhaps, by way of thanks? I have some extra."

I saw the young man fighting it out with himself. On the

one hand it was a fairly obvious sucker trap: a pretty girl handing out drinks in the middle of the wilderness. Yet, on the other hand, he was supposed to investigate, wasn't he? After a moment, his decision made, he walked up the track to the maroon sedan and took the opened bottle Karin offered him. He was nobody I knew. Well, there are a lot of those in the outfit; we do not have cozy get-acquainted office parties, quite the contrary. Mac operates on the principle that the fewer of your colleagues you've met, the fewer you can betray if somebody starts asking the tough way. This one was fairly young, still in his early twenties, with his indoctrination course at the Ranch not too far behind him. He was dark, moderately tall, clean-shaven, hatless, in jeans and a heavy black wool jacket, like a pea jacket, that came almost to his knees.

He was not a bad-looking young fellow. I felt a bit sorry for him. I mean, you don't wander into an outfit like ours by accident. He'd wanted it, and he'd worked hard for it—the Ranch training course is no picnic—and when he'd got it at last, suddenly he'd found the agency he'd struggled so hard to join falling apart around him and himself forced to choose between the former administration, run by a character who'd gone missing—an older gentleman who was, they'd probably told him, getting a bit senile anyway—and the new regime, represented by a handsome and confidence-inspiring administrator in the prime of life with a profile that belonged on a Roman coin, obviously a man who'd make undercover work as glamorous as our youthful postulant had always hoped it would be.

They were talking by the car now. "Perhaps I am happy that you did come back," I heard Karin saying. "I did not realize how muddy this road was. My auto does have the four-wheel driving, if that is what you call it, but perhaps if you will stay until I have extricated myself, to be absolutely certain . . ."

"I'll be happy to, ma'am. But if I may ask, what are you doing here, anyway?"

"I was driving up to the old house when I realized that I had better not proceed any farther. It seemed like a good place for . . . well, for a picnic. . . ."

She did it very well: the guilty attempt to conceal the little paper bag on the hood of the Audi, not the one that had held the beer and sandwiches, the other one. In her effort to hide it from view behind her without, of course, ever looking that way, she managed to hit it with her elbow instead, and knock it to the ground. There was a heavy thump when it hit. The young man beat her to it, straightened up with it, and hefted it appraisingly. He drew out the small black pistol, sniffed the muzzle, and looked sharply at Karin.

"Some picnic!" he said. "So it was you I heard shooting."

She nodded, showing embarrassment. "Yes," she said. "Yes, that is why I drove to this desolate place. It makes me feel very . . . very melodramatic, but I really must learn how to use it. It is very important."

"Why would a lady like you need a gun, ma'am?"

"You do not recognize me?" she asked. "You have not read the newspapers and seen the photographs?"

"I don't know enough Swedish to read the papers over here. Just enough to find the beer and the bathroom."

Karin said, "Well, I am Baroness Karin Segerby, and my lover's wife tried to kill me; it was a big excitement. . . . Now I have shocked you. Is it because I am a baroness, or because I was involved in a notorious love affair? But you can see why I obtained the little pistol to protect myself, since the woman is quite mad and the stupid police will do nothing. However, I do not know how to use it very well; I even had great trouble putting the bullets into it."

She had him now. I hated to think that the title had

269

impressed him that much; whatever happened to the good old Yankee proposition that all men—and women—are created equal? But of course we all love to teach pretty girls how to shoot; I'm not immune to the impulse myself. Whatever the reason, he was clearly captivated by this nicely dressed young woman with a glamorous title and intriguing past who obviously needed the expert help of a trained, knowledgeable young man like . . . well, just like him.

"You don't call them bullets, ma'am; they're cartridges, unless you're using a shotgun, when you call them shells. But let me show you. . . ." He demonstrated the mechanism for her. "Just break the piece and stick two rounds into the chambers, like this. Then close it again, like this. Why don't you try a couple more shots, and maybe I can give you some pointers? I know a bit about guns. Here, see how close you can come to hitting that white rock."

He gave the pistol back to her. There was a pause while she got her hands wrapped around the small curved butt and started to take aim. Then he cleared his throat, rather loudly. She glanced aside, annoyed by the distraction.

"Yes?"

He was a little embarrassed. "You always check a gun after it's handed to you, ma'am, even if you think you know it's loaded. Or unloaded." He held out his hand, palm up. "Here. Better use these; it'll shoot better."

She studied his face for a moment, and laughed shortly, and took the two cartridges he was holding out to her. "You slipped them out of the gun when I wasn't looking? Anybody would think you mistrusted me, Mr. . . ."

"Crown, ma'am. Hank Crown. It used to be something like Kronfeld, but my granddad made it simple when he got to America. . . . It's a standard trick of range instructors, ma'am, to teach the beginner never to assume that he knows what's in a gun until he's looked for himself."

"Well, I'm glad you educate me properly, Mr. Crown."

She busied herself loading the derringer. She spoke casually. "I believe there is another rule: One must never point a firearm at anything one does not intend to shoot, am I correct? But then . . ." Suddenly the pistol came up and steadied. "But then, it is perfectly okay, because I have every intention of shooting you if you move a muscle. . . . Matt!"

I spoke quickly, from the brush behind him, "Don't try anything, Crown. You're covered two ways."

There was a little pause while, like the one I'd dealt with in Oslo, he thought over all the pretty tricks they'd taught him at the Ranch, and decided not to use them.

"Helm?"

"That's who."

"Take it easy, Helm. I'm peaceful."

"Sure you are. But even so, how about taking out your gun and laying it on top of the car and backing away from it. . . . Okay."

I crossed over and got the weapon, a short-barreled .38 like my own and the one I'd got from Joel, not the silent midnight killer the boys in Oslo had been carrying. I had him put his hands on top of the car for the frisk. He laughed shortly.

"Who do you think I am, Two-Gun Hank, the Terror of the North?"

I found no more firearms; but there was a throwing knife in a neat little sheath at the nape of his neck. "Nice try," I said, confiscating it. I studied him for a moment. "What, no recriminations? Aren't you going to tell the lady what a treacherous bitch she is?"

He laughed again, without bitterness. "She sure did a good job on me. That scared-baroness routine was a dilly."

I said, "The wronged and murderous wife was a figment of her imagination, I'm afraid, but Mrs. Segerby was born a perfectly genuine baroness, although I believe that here in Sweden a lady baron actually calls herself a *friherrinna*,

271

meaning 'free lady.' I guess she just didn't want to complicate the situation with aristocratic technicalities."

He glanced at the girl, ruefully. "I suppose I knew I was being suckered, which is why I tried her with an empty gun. . . . How did you know I'd slipped the loads out, ma'am?"

Karin smiled. "You looked so very guilty when you gave me the pistol that I knew there had to be a trick."

I frowned at him thoughtfully. Although it hadn't worked, he'd been smart enough to try it; he wasn't quite the impressionable patsy I'd thought him. He was doing okay under the gun, too. No threats or accusations. No loud-mouthed *I'll-get-you-for-this* routines. Maybe I'd hit a good one for a change.

I said, "Aren't you going to give me that dirty-traitor line I heard from one of your pals in Oslo?" When he didn't answer but just watched me warily, I went on: "For the record, Crown, there's no treason involved here, on either side. I could tell you some stuff about Bennett's previous history, but it's irrelevant at the moment. All we have here, to be perfectly objective about it, is a power struggle between two high-ranking bureaucrats which has got to the shooting stage because that's the kind of bureaucracy that's involved. I happen to be Old Guard; you happen to be New Guard. I'd like you to consider making a switch. I'd like you on my side in the showdown that's coming up very shortly. Or at least right after the showdown. This outfit has spent time and money training you and your contemporaries. I'd hate to see it wasted."

He licked his lips. "What are you offering?"

I grinned. "You're hoping I'll try to buy you for a million dollars so you can spit in my eye. To hell with you, Crown. The man I'm working for has just put his life on the line to solve a problem that may threaten the welfare of our entire country." It was the truth; and I saw no need to complicate it by mentioning that a private motive might

272

also be involved. "Meanwhile, what's your man doing? He's deserted his desk and his duty and he's wasting the resources of the agency chasing around the world after a guy he happens to be afraid of; in other words, to save his own lousy skin."

Crown said quickly, "Mr. Bennett isn't scared of . . ."

I held up my hand. "Never mind it. There's no point arguing about it. All I'm really trying to say is that there's going to be a confrontation here. Maybe I'll lose out, in which case you have no problem until Mac sends another man to take my place and he puts the choice to you again. But if I win, I'm hoping you'll reconsider your loyalties and pull your friends off my back so we can all stop fucking around like this and get on with the real work we're supposed to be paid for. There will be no recriminations, no reprisals. We need trained people who can take orders, and you boys took them. From the wrong man, but he's a very persuasive character, and he was sitting in the right chair, so how could you know? I'm not expecting you to make up your mind immediately—I wouldn't believe you if you did—so I'll tie you up for a while and give you time to think things over while you watch the show. Now let's see how long it takes your hero-leader to come to your rescue."

Over an hour passed before I caught the first glimpse of them filtering into the trees around the clearing. I only spotted two, but there were probably more. Then I heard them coming down the road from Lysaniemi. A gray van of some kind appeared—I have a hard enough time sorting out all the look-alike passenger cars these days; I don't even try to keep track of the various vans—and came to a halt by Crown's little blue sedan. Several armed young men jumped out, four to be exact, followed by Bennett himself. So far, so good. We were face-to-face, or would be in a moment, and nobody'd gone off half-cocked and started shooting up the premises.

273

I saw that Bennett hadn't changed much in the years since I'd seen him last: a moderately tall, middle-aged gent with graying hair that was clipped quite short where it grew at all, but his barber really didn't have much to work with. There's always something tough-looking about a skinhead, particularly a tanned skinhead, like one of the meaner Caesars. That's probably why he had it cut so close. The shorn stubble of hair was, perhaps, a little grayer than when I'd last seen him, and the figure was perhaps a little thicker than I remembered it; but not much.

He was wearing natty cord pants, a tan wool shirt, and a tan ski jacket. There was also a neat brown necktie, not as silly as it sounds, since in those formal European countries the gentlemen often put on ties even to go hunting. He was merely following local custom. The outfit looked a little like a military uniform, and the resemblance was probably not accidental. Bennett gestured, and his squad spread out in a skirmish line and moved toward us. I noted that he let them get a few steps ahead before he followed along. Despite his tough haircut, he'd never been what you'd call an overeager leader of men when there was danger involved.

While all this was going on, I'd been leaning against the Audi in plain sight, an interested spectator. At the moment, I was sharing the last beer with Karin, who stood beside me. Our well-secured prisoner sat in the back seat of the Audi. Karin looked a bit concerned, watching us being surrounded.

"There are so many!" she said.

"I make it eight, but I could have missed a couple out in the brush. Ten minimum, counting our tied-up friend and Bennett himself. Flattering that he thinks he needs those odds to deal with me, don't you think?"

"But what are you going to *do*?"

"You'll see. Just stay behind the car, here, and get your head down if things start getting noisy. . . ."

But Bennett was approaching now, and the time for idle chatter was past. He came up warily while his youthful centurions formed an armed ring around the car, covering us. Bennett looked at me for a moment, and then at the hood of the car. Except for my personal .38 in its clip-on holster, and Karin's little derringer, I had our entire arsenal piled there. I reflected that it was amazing the number of guns a man could collect just traveling through foreign lands minding his own business. Of course, it depended a little on the business.

I said, "Sorry, we're all out of beer. You boys will have to keep on down the road if you're thirsty."

"Put your hands on top of your head, Helm!"

I ignored him and went on, "Karin, this is the Mr. Bennett I've been telling you about. Bennett, this is Mrs. Karin Segerby, born Stjernhjelm, a distant relation of mine. She's also the widow of the late Frederik Segerby, one of the directors of Segerby Vapenfabriks AB, otherwise known as SVAB. You may have heard of it."

"Are you trying to hide behind a woman's skirts?"

I said, "No. Just pointing out that molesting her could cause you trouble. She's only here as a favor to me, paying me back for something I did for her. She's not involved. You'll be smart to leave her that way."

He bowed towards Karin. "I have no quarrel with the lady. As for you . . ." Bennett glanced at the pile of weapons on the Audi's hood. "Do I gather that you are turning over those guns as a preliminary to surrendering? That shows more sense than I thought you had."

I said, "No, no, you've got me all wrong, amigo. Although I'm usually a very modest guy, today I thought I'd do a little boasting to the boys. Showing off my trophies, so to speak. That .25 sleeve gun doesn't count; it's mine. I didn't want you worrying about a hideout weapon. What you see is what you get. But those two automatics with the hush-tubes, which you'll recognize, I took off your two characters in Oslo, Lindner and Harley. One of the .38s I took off your sneaky pal Joel after I'd shot him. The other, and the knife, I just got from your boy Crown, who you see in the rear seat of the car unharmed. And that big Browning HiPower I took off a couple of folks you don't know, but you should; you have things in common. They don't like me, either. Or didn't. Unfortunately, they're no longer with us.''

Bennett frowned. "I don't understand what you're driving at. Are you trying to frighten . . ."

I said, "The boys have probably been wondering why you had to use ten men to chase down one lonely little me. I'm just showing them that you were perfectly justified in taking every precaution. I'm clearly a very dangerous fellow. How many people have I killed and disarmed in the past week? Just count the guns. Move over, John Wayne, Wild Bill Hickok, here comes Helm. Obviously, you need to have a lot of manpower along when you go after a lethal character like me. Hell, I might hurt you if you tried to track me down all by yourself. Better to lose a few expendable agents, right? Like Harley and Joel, both dead trying to rid you of that nasty character called Helm . . .''

"Disarm him!" Bennett snapped.

He was realizing, belatedly, that he'd let me talk too long. The boys were listening too carefully. In any organization like ours, legends grow about the senior operatives who manage to survive, passed along in whispers to the new boys: *Hey, that's Barnett, who had to blow up his own boat on that Bahamas operation and almost went up with it.* Or Fedder, or Rasmussen, or Helm. They weren't going to switch sides because they'd heard a few interesting things about me; but they weren't going to pass up a chance to study me in action, at least for a little, like young wolves learning from one of the old lobos they hope to replace eventually.

Bennett snapped. "Well, Bradford? I told you to take his gun!"

The dark young man addressed didn't move. Nobody moved. I went on talking. I was in a rut, of course, employing the same needling tactics I'd used on the girl called Greta—just about the same that Karin had used to prod Astrid into disastrous action—but why change a winning, we hoped, game?

I said, "You're right here in front of me, Bennett. Why don't you take my gun? Come on, come on, all that's required is a couple of long steps and a short reach. If you live long enough to reach." I grimaced. "Isn't it about time we settled this for good, amigo? You aren't after me because I'm a defector; nobody believes that dumb story. You're after me because you once had to make me a humiliating official apology after you'd made a particular damned fool of yourself. You also want me dead because later, when you were trying to hunt me down just like this, I trapped you neatly on a mountain road and threw you to an interrogation team that made you spill every last thing you knew about the folks with whom you were working at the time—rather unpatriotic people, as it happened, but they were your associates and you sold them very cheaply. And you particularly want to kill me because I saw you after the I-team was through with you, sitting on a little stool in your grubby skivvies with tears running down your face, pleading with me to let you live; and I was a damn' fool; I did, one of the worst mistakes I ever . . . Ah, that's better! Go for it, amigo! Reach for it. Shoot me down like a dog—if you think you can make it!"

I hadn't been sure I could give him the idea; but his hand did move. Then it hesitated, and failed to complete the angry arc it had started that would sweep aside the ski jacket and bring out the gun that rested in a forward-slanting holster on his right hip, FBI fashion. It's a good enough draw, if you're sure your right hand will always be available to do the work. I prefer the gun in front of my left hip, where it can be reached with either hand, although it's kind of a tricky, twisty maneuver with the left. Bennett drew a long breath and straightened up.

"Pretty obvious, Helm! A desperate last minute stratagem, trying to goad me into a ridiculous gun battle now that you're caught . . ." As he said it, I saw him start to consider it seriously. I hadn't believed it could be that easy. I mean, I'd thought I would have to spit on him or urinate on him to get him mad enough to accept the idea; but there it was in his head, full-grown. He cleared his throat. "On the other hand, as you say, it *is* about time we settled this for good."

"What's on your mind, amigo?"

I knew exactly the melodramatic plan, born of hatred, that had come into his mind, but I wanted him to be the one to say it.

He spoke contemptuously: "You seem to think that pile of firearms proves what a dangerous man you are! But how many of the owners of those guns did you meet honestly, face to face, Helm? If I know you, most of them were taken from behind or from ambush."

I said, "Christ, this is real life, not a TV show! What am I supposed to do, stage a Wild West facedown every time some chair-bound moron like you sends a trigger-happy idiot after me?"

"Maybe you wouldn't be so brave if you had to stand and face a pistol in the hand of a man who knew how to use it!"

He was full of it now, eager for it. It was his brainstorm, and he couldn't wait to translate it into action. He was beginning to disturb me. This headlong rush towards a life-or-death confrontation was out of character. Well, perhaps he was good with that thing on his right hip, and, having read my dossier in Washington, knew that I was no split-second *pistolero*. The long-range rifle is what I do best.

278

But there's more to it than skill; and I'd faced a lot more guns than he had.

"A man like you?" I sneered. "Hell, there'll never be a day when a desk-jockey in ice-cream pants could worry me! Face to face or back to back or any damn' stupid way you want to set it up. If you really want to die today, I'll be happy to oblige you." I shrugged. "Of course, I'm not dumb enough not to know that you'll have a sniper out in the brush to save your neck when the time comes, but I'll play your game anyway. Your boy will have to shoot damn' straight and fast to keep me from taking you down with me."

"No sniper." Bennett was being very honorable now. He looked around. "You heard me, men. This is between Helm and me, and I want no misguided help from anyone, is that understood?" He gave it a little time to sink in; then he said, "Very well. Now let's see if we can agree on the details of this remarkably foolish business. . . ."

Ten minutes later we were walking together side by side far out in the big muddy field; and I knew how the old-timers had felt stepping out into that dusty Western street . . . but of course they hadn't. I'd done some research on the subject once, back when I was in another line of work, and I'd found no evidence anywhere that the formal walk-down of the Western movies had ever occurred in real life. It's a myth, a latter-day invention like the *buscadero* belt of the legendary two-gun killer, and that holster-thong that every movie gunman ties around his thigh before heading for the big showdown. Real old-time Western holsters were flimsy things hanging loose on sagging cartridge belts, flapping wildly when the cowboy rode the kinks out of his bronc in the morning.

It took two hands to draw a gun back in those days, one to pull it and the other to hold down the ill-fitting leather pouch so you could wrench the weapon free. Just as I was going to have to use two hands here, because my fancy little secret-agent holster was made for clipping on conveniently and ditching quickly, not for staying solidly in place while the piece was being drawn. Well, at least it would get my left arm out of the way. I once knew a man who got excited, shooting to the left from a cross draw as I intended to, and blew off his own left elbow.

The ground was soggy underfoot; Bennett was getting his shiny leather boots muddy. It annoyed him and made him want to get the thing over with.

"Pick a likely spot, Helm," he said. "A man can't always choose where he dies, but you have the privilege today, within limits."

"I think we're far enough from the cars," I said, turning to face him. "Wave your hand at your boy when you're ready."

The signal to draw and fire was to be a blast on the Audi's horn. The stillness was what got you, up here. I remembered it from last time. No birds singing, no squirrels chattering in the trees. Just an endless, cold, silent land under a low gray sky. The land of my ancestors, and I'd trade it in for sunny New Mexico any day in the week and twice on Sunday. Facing Bennett, I watched him raise his arm. It was a damn' silly business, of course, but men have died in crazier ways in crazier places. But what was his edge, what had made him suddenly so brave and eager? Could he really be that good? If so, Mrs. Helm's little boy was in real trouble. Then his arm came down, and I remembered the odd way his shirt had bunched under the armpit as he raised it, and I knew. . . .

The man on the horn gave us a short three count, and sent the musical notes wavering through the Arctic air—well, the barely sub-Arctic air. I made the smart right pivot necessary to align my weapon with the target as it was holstered. Simultaneously, I put both hands to my left hip to grasp the holster with one and the butt of the .38 with the other. Yanking out the weapon, I fired as it came clear.

280

Trick shooting, not seeing the sights, not seeing the gun, even; not seeing anything but the oval of the face that was my mark. Wishing the bullet home; and if you do it right, with enough concentration, you can toss a marble into the air and hit it with the pellet from a BB gun held at the hip. It seems like magic. Just how it works, nobody's ever told me, but it works.

That is, it works if you're in practice. I wasn't. I hadn't been to the Ranch for a while, and they don't drill you on that kind of instinct shooting, anyway. They think one-handed marksmanship should have gone out with Aaron Burr, even though he did a pretty good job on Alexander Hamilton; and they want you to see the gun barrel, at least, if not the sights. I felt the muzzle blast sting my left hand, still holding down the empty holster. I felt the sharp recoil of the lightweight little monster of a weapon, and I knew I'd missed. *Concentrate, you stupid bastard! You've got to THINK that slug home, remember?*

But I couldn't help being aware that Bennett's hand had gone smoothly back for the FBI rig—he'd prepared himself, earlier, by taking off his jacket to expose it, just as I'd tucked in my sweater to make sure it didn't get in my way. Bennett had swept the gun out of the holster and was swinging it up to bear, and his left hand was coming up to meet and steady it. He was good, all right, and there wasn't a way in the world he could possibly miss me at this range with that firm two-hand grip, but he faltered. . . .

He faltered, I realized, because my first bullet had just cracked past his ear. His *ear*; and I wasn't supposed to be aiming that high! Didn't I know that in a situation like this, with speed all-important, I was supposed to snap my shot at the largest target, the chest? All the rules said so. He'd counted on it, as he'd counted on the bullet-proof vest I'd spotted at the last moment—I'd noticed earlier that he'd seemed a little thick and clumsy in the body, but I'd just put it down to advancing years and a hearty appetite. It

281

had been the secret source of his courage; but now he knew I'd caught on. Kevlar around the ribs wouldn't protect him from a slug in the face. It shook his confidence, and his hand. His shot went wide.

The Smith & Wesson kicked back at me a second time, in the vicious way of a light weapon used with heavy loads. All the psychic target-finding instruments were calibrated now, and all the psychic connections were good; and something happened to Bennett's jaw. A hair low. Wish the next one up a bit—and the hole appeared below the right eye, and one between the eyes, and one in the top of the head as he bowed forward slowly, like a tree. His dying hand squeezed off a second shot that came nowhere near me as he fell facedown in front of me. It's only on TV that they're hurled backwards across the landscape by the impact of one lousy little .38 slug, or even several of them.

I stood there for a long moment looking down at him, feeling some satisfaction as you always do upon the completion of a job, even a dirty one. I know, humanitarian regret is the fashion, but I'm not a very fashionable guy. Slowly, I became aware of the fact that nobody had come forward, either to compliment me or curse me. I saw that they were all gathered about something on the ground beside the distant Audi: a small, blue-clad figure. I realized where Bennett's last, blind, wild shot had gone. . . .

CHAPTER 28

THE death of a small blonde girl and an American bureaucrat in the far north of Sweden didn't get as much publicity as I'd expected, perhaps due to the energetic efforts of Cousin Olaf, so my family mission wasn't a total failure, even though I'd lost the subject I was supposed to be protecting. Even the Nordic peace demonstration that had escalated into incendiary violence was ignored by the U.S. papers I picked up in Chicago's Midway Airport. They had their own big story.

I don't know what it is about America. Hundreds die from AIDS yearly, and the number is rising. Fifty thousand get smashed up fatally on the nation's highways. The cancer deaths number, I believe, in the millions. Hardly anyone cares. But just let a small bunch of people—well, fifty in this case—get grabbed by an even smaller bunch with guns and held for ransom, and you can hardly find the weather or the stock market reports because of the way this dreadful national crisis monopolizes our TV screens and the columns of our daily press. Perhaps I'm callous, but I can't help feeling that the reaction is out of proportion to the stimulus. If you expend all your emotional resources on a mere fifty people, how can you cope with the multitudes starving in the Sahara?

I read up on it while riding on another plane, smaller than the monster flying machine that had brought me back across the ocean. I was now heading north over Wisconsin towards the upper peninsula of Michigan, a state which, in case you're not up on your geography, is split in two by the Great Lakes. Why they didn't give the upper chunk to Wisconsin, to which it's attached, instead of to lower Michigan, to which it isn't, I have no idea, but state lines often don't make much sense. One of the papers I'd bought had an alphabetical list of the hostages. I found there three people I knew, at least by name: *Janet Rebecca Beilstein, businesswoman; Arthur McGillivray Borden, government employee; Emil Franz Jernegan, tennis professional.*

Except that the text explained that Emil Jernegan, the young athlete Beilstein was supposed to have run off with,

283

was no longer with the others. He had been killed four days ago in a particularly brutal manner and left for the police to find. Actually, a phone call had let them know where to pick up the body, by a dirt road in western Pennsylvania. A multistate search in that part of the country had turned up no clues to where the other prisoners were being held. Obviously the kidnappers had taken Jernegan far from their hideout before executing him to let Washington know that they meant business and would kill again if driven to it—that they would slaughter the whole group if they were crowded by nosy policemen, or if their demands were not met.

Apparently, they were Central American revolutionaries who'd been impressed by the strange U.S. hostage syndrome. If it was so easy to turn the great nation to the north into a quivering mass of jelly, one would be foolish not to take advantage of the phenomenon, señor. Therefore, they had systematically abducted an adequate number of suitable victims, not so important nationally that their vanishing would trigger immediate and hysterical law-enforcement activity, but not so unimportant that their danger could be ignored. I noted that the specimen chosen for sacrifice, Jernegan, was the least prominent of the prisoners, an obscure young country club employee who'd been taken in the first place merely to provide cover for Mrs. Beilstein's disappearance. Clearly they weren't going to waste any of the more valuable hostages until they had to, waste being the operative word.

The organization called itself the PLCV. Their leader had been arrested and imprisoned, they said, by the reactionary fascist politico currently oppressing the downtrodden citizens of their country with U.S. approval and assistance. The PLCV demanded that the U.S. employ its influence to effect their hero's release and that of the brave patriot fighters arrested with him. They further demanded withdrawal of all American support for that deformed megalomaniac politician, the dictator-criminal who had the affrontery to call himself *el presidente*. . . .

We landed in the town of Houghton, a little ways out the Keweenaw Peninsula that sticks up into Lake Superior. You would kind of expect a bunch of Latin American terrorists to pick some desolate scenery near the Mexican border, as close to home as possible, in which to hide their prison camp; but these people hadn't chosen badly. That part of Michigan is still one of the less-civilized parts of the U.S., with logging the primary industry, according to the thumbnail sketch I'd been given when I reported to Washington by phone from northern Sweden and was told to haul my ass westward soonest. Doug Barnett, director pro tem, speaking. When I asked what the hell was in Houghton, I was told to disregard the Mont Ripley Ski Area, and Michigan Tech University, and concentrate first on the airport. When I had that made, I should transfer my attention to the hospital.

"He asked for you," Doug said. "If you hurry, maybe you'll make it in time."

It was cold and raining when I got off the plane. The man waiting for me had only one hand, and there were scars on his face. I'd worked with him once, before he got damaged trying to defuse a homemade whizbang that had one more booby-trap circuit than he'd figured. I tried for the name and got it: Martinson. Greg Martinson.

"This way," he said. "I've got a car waiting."

The windows were steamed up, except where the defroster made a clear spot in front, so I didn't get much of a view of Houghton, Michigan. It was a rental car, not arranged for the handicapped, but he'd clamped a little knob onto the wheel, and did all right one-handed. He dumped me in front of the hospital entrance.

"Room 29, second floor," he said.

"Thanks for the ride, Oscar," I said, to let him know I

285

remembered. Oscar was the name he'd worked under at the time.

He grinned faintly. "We old retired crips didn't do too badly, while you kept the healthy young squirts chasing you all over Europe." His grin faded. "You'd better hurry. They said time could be getting kind of short."

But naturally, having raced across the whole Atlantic Ocean and half the United States of America at barely subsonic speeds, upon reaching my destination, I found myself sitting on a hard bench going nowhere for the best part of an hour. When that grim nurse said no visitors, she meant no visitors.

There were two guards. Fedder was one; and if Fedder was there, Rasmussen would be somewhere around because they hunted together. Fedder had the roving brief, wandering around the corridors casually to see if anything or anybody was moving in on his subject. Standing by the door conspicuously, holding down the decoy spot, was a man with a patch over one eye whose name I didn't know. We nodded to each other; but we'd shared no missions, and he didn't look like the talkative type, so I didn't bother him. I just sat on my bench, reflecting that Mac seemed to have drafted every old agency warrior for the job, including some retired for physical disability—men whose loyalty to him was unquestioned. The bright young recruits who had yet to prove themselves, he'd left to Bennett.

Occasional white coats went in and out of the room, male and female. I saw a wheelchair roll by in the main hall to my left and paid it little attention; after all, this was a hospital. Then I looked again before it went out of sight and got quickly to my feet.

"Hey, Ricardo!" I called. "What the hell are you doing here?"

There were two men with the chair; small, dark-faced men in neat dark suits. They whirled at my call, and their hands went under their coats. I kept my own hands in plain sight. The young man in the chair swung it around and rolled it towards me.

"Matthew, amigo! I did not see you sitting there. . . . It is all right, muchachos, he is a friend." He grinned at me as I came up. "Although there were times in the past when that was not a certainty. But you must address me properly."

"Yes, Mr. President. Certainly, Your Excellency."

"I joke. To you I am Ricardo, always. Anyway, it is not a state visit; I am here incognito. Mr. Richard James, at your service." His smile faded, and he glanced towards the door of the room in front of which I had been waiting. "How does it go in there?"

"For God's sake, this is a hospital, man. Do you expect them to tell you how a patient is doing?" I grimaced. "I gather that you're a mean sonofabitch these days, Your Excellency. A megalomaniac, reactionary, fascist, dictator-criminal, according to what I read. Who's the guy you've got in pokey that they want out so badly?"

Ricardo Jimenez, president of Costa Verde, smiled thinly. "You are getting soft, Matthew. Unlike them, you refrain from making reference to my handicap." He patted his useless legs. "And the man I have in prison is the man I have to thank for it. You must remember him."

When I'd met him, Ricardo Jimenez had been the exiled scion of a political family trying to fight his way back into his country. We'd spent some time in the jungles together, back when another man had occupied the big presidential chair in Santa Rosalia. The nation had been a police state then—Ricardo had changed that, later—and he'd had some painful experiences with its prison system, of which the damaged legs were one reminder. He had others.

"Armando Rael?" I said, surprised. "I thought you finally managed to run him to hell out of there."

"He ran, yes, when his soldiers would no longer fight for him, but he is back as leader of *El Partido de la Lib-*

287

*eracion de Costa Verde*. PLCV. The Liberation Party of Costa Verde. He had Communist backing up to a point.''

''What are the Communists doing, backing that reactionary bastard?''

''They will support anyone who will forward their program of chaos and disruption. However, when Rael's clumsy coup failed, the reds washed their hands of the enterprise. Some of his remaining Costa Verde supporters, who dislike my reform policies and hope to get rich, or richer, if he wins, thought up this plan for achieving his freedom. It might have succeeded, since I could not have resisted much pressure from your country, but the man in that room, your superior, spoiled their plans. I do not know the details, no one will talk, but the hostages have been freed and most of the kidnappers are dead. The news will be on your television and in your newspapers this evening; it was withheld while certain principals were being traced. However, we were informed in Santa Rosalia, and I thought it only fitting that I should fly up here and pay my respects to the gentleman who has for the second time contributed so much to the welfare of my country, this time at great cost to himself.''

It was the first time to my knowledge that the head of a state, even the fairly young head of a fairly small state, had seen fit to thank us for our work in person. Looking at him, I realized that he wasn't so young any longer. The crippling injuries, and the responsibilities of his political office, had matured him.

I asked, ''What will you do with Rael now, shoot him?''

Ricardo Jimenez shook his head regretfully. ''For any other man, I would call the firing squad immediately. But not for the man who put me into this chair. It would be said I was taking a personal revenge on my predecessor in office, and I cannot afford that. I will hold him until his followers disperse, and then I will banish him, sparing his life in my usual magnanimous fashion. To try again, perhaps, but . . ."

He stopped, looking towards the door of Room 29. Three people had come out. The two men in white coats and stethoscopes went on down the hall. A tall woman remained; a slender, handsome, middle-aged lady in a gray slacks suit. Her dark hair was pulled back severely from her face; but it was the strong kind of face that could stand such treatment. She seemed to be looking for somebody; then she saw me and started towards me, but stopped abruptly and buried her face in her hands, swaying. The sentry with the eyepatch and Ricardo's bodyguards all moved towards her, but I beat them to her. After a moment she drew a ragged breath and raised her head to look at me, dry-eyed. She seemed steady again, so I released her.

"Sorry," she said. "You're Helm, aren't you?"

"And you're Beilstein, and that takes care of the formalities." I hesitated. "How is it in there?"

"It is very good in there."

I looked at her sharply. "I thought . . ."

She shook her head quickly. "It just hit me, the reaction to all that waiting. No, they say he will make it now, with luck." She shook her head almost angrily. "Dammit, Helm, who the hell did he think he was, Sir Galahad or somebody? No woman wants a man to die for her. At least this woman doesn't!"

I grinned. "But even though you feel obliged to go on record saying you disapprove, you'll always cherish the fact that he was willing, won't you?"

She drew a long breath. "Yes, damn you, and it makes me ashamed of myself. Go on in. He wants to hear all about your European adventures."

"How bad is it?"

"He was shot in the chest; but now that he has . . . has turned the corner, they think he will be all right."

There were more questions to be asked. How Mac had

managed to tease the kidnappers into taking him in the first place. How he'd set up the communications that had enabled his team of veterans, crippled and whole, to trace him. How the liberation had been accomplished. How he'd got himself shot at the last minute, apparently making some kind of a sacrifice play to save his lady from harm. And in addition, there were things to be done, like making a promised telephone call to Spud Meiklejohn of the *Miami Tribune*, and sending a wedding present to Amy Barnett—Doug had mentioned in passing that his daughter and the new boyfriend were making it official. But all that could wait.

I went in and made my mission report to the chief of my agency.

## CHAPTER 29

IT was a small ship carrying fewer than two hundred passengers. I boarded it in Helsinki, which my parents had called Helsingfors; but that was back in the days when Swedish was in and Finnish was out, in Finland. I found my cabin, a small two-berth cubicle that reminded me painfully of the one on the larger cross-Baltic ferry that I'd shared with Karin Segerby. That had been a couple of weeks ago now, and since then I'd flown the Atlantic twice, so taking a boat from Helsinki to Leningrad, which had been called St. Petersburg when my folks were kids, was really no big deal, except that I always get nervous near Russia, let alone in Russia. But this trip was cleared at both ends, and I was supposed to encounter no difficulties whatever.

When I entered the cabin, there was somebody lying on the bunk to my right; but it wasn't Karin Segerby. . . . You could say it was a tragic fluke, a wild pistol bullet finding a target at that range; but there are no flukes when you're dealing with firearms. You're supposed to know that they can kill at crazy distances. You're supposed to have more sense than to play idiot gunfight games where uninvolved folks can get hurt—and the fact that I'd told her to stay behind the car and keep her head down didn't do much for my sense of guilt.

I let the cabin door close behind me. "Good afternoon," I said to the man with whom I was to share the cabin for the night's run.

"Good afternoon, sir," he said, sitting up. He was fully clothed except for his jacket. He was a thin, pale, little man in his forties with thinning brown hair, wearing a vest and a necktie, the knot of which he had pulled down a little. He said, "I hope you don't mind that I picked this bed. I can move if you wish, sir."

He was being very polite because he had just been released from a U.S. prison and wanted to stay that way. It had taken considerable work to get him out. Mac had disapproved.

"You are being sentimental, Eric," he had said, but he hadn't said it very loudly, for the simple reason that he wasn't strong enough yet, although he'd been declared out of danger.

I said, "Look who's talking about sentimental. At least I don't have a bullet in my ribs." He smiled faintly. He'd done a job he should have left to younger men, but he'd survived it. Now he was feeling pretty good about it; good enough that he could be kidded about it. I went on: "Sentiment or not, I want some trading material. It shouldn't take much. What they've got can't be worth much to them now that the phony Astrid Land—Astrid Watrous—is

291

dead." I wondered what her real name had been; but I'd never know.

"I will see what arrangements can be made," Mac said. He changed the subject. "Your activities have brought us some mild remonstrances from Stockholm, but we can deal with them. Fortunately your distant relative, Baron Stjernhjelm, seems to be a man of some influence." He hesitated. "I gather the installation at Laxfors is not really concerned with communications. Do we know its true function?"

I said, "I know what Olaf told me. He said that it was actually a development of the system we use to detect foreign submarines along our own shores. Naturally, the Russians wanted it out of commission so they could continue their underwater activities unhampered. But the true nature of the facility had not been made public for security reasons, and also because anything built with American assistance is met with suspicion over there, these days. We have a reputation as saber-rattlers and warmongers, I'm afraid."

"Totally unjustified, of course," Mac said without expression.

"Of course, sir," I said. "But with eight people dead in a protest demonstration, the whole thing had to become public. Actually, Laxfors came out of it pretty well. The Swedes' ancient dislike of the Russians is considerably stronger than their more recent fear of America; and the whole country has been very much upset by the Soviet submarine penetrations of their waters. Anything and anybody helping to combat this kind of trespassing will meet with reluctant approval even if it involves Yankee expertise. The fact that Soviet agents were using the peace demonstration for purposes of sabotage, and had in fact helped to incite it, didn't raise the Muscovite stock any. So Laxfors and everybody concerned with it came out smelling of

292

roses, which is why they're not very mad at me over there. Just a little mad.''

Mrs. Beilstein rose from her chair in the corner, in the decisive way I'd come to recognize. "That is enough. Now you'd better let him rest."

"Yes, ma'am."

She hesitated uncharacteristically. "Oh, Matt. Could I ask you a question before you go?" When I nodded, she said, "That Bennett man, who'd made such a point of fair play. If he won your . . . your shootout, or whatever you called it, how could he expect to keep his body armor a secret afterwards? I mean, if you hit him, as you probably would. There'd be a hole in his clothes but no wound. They'd all know he'd cheated."

I grinned. "You must be thinking of the Boy Scouts of America, Mrs. Beilstein. What makes you think Bennett would keep his Kevlar vest a secret from those cynical young characters? He'd boast about it; it would be a great big joke, and they'd all have a good laugh at the tough old pro, me, who let himself be conned into a romantic pistol-to-pistol showdown with a guy wearing bulletproof BVDs."

She shook her head. "I see that I still have things to learn."

As I reached for the doorknob, Mac spoke behind me: "Eric."

"Yes, sir?"

"You were on the ground. You saw the installation. Do you really believe that submarine-detection story?"

"Of course, sir," I said. "I always believe everything I'm told. When it's diplomatic to do so."

"To be sure," Mac said. "When you come tomorrow I will let you know what I've been able to arrange for you."

He'd got me my trading material, the pale little man now sharing my cabin on the Leningrad ferry. We had dinner served in the cabin, and breakfast, according to instructions. After landing, still following instructions, I left him on board and took the standard guided tour of Leningrad. The Russians just love showing you monuments and memorials. I returned to the ship shortly before sailing time that evening.

There was a certain amount of suspense as I knocked on the door of the same cabin, wondering if our elaborate diplomatic arrangements had worked. A feminine voice said something in Finnish that I didn't catch, and wouldn't have understood anyway. I assumed I'd been given permission to enter, and did. The door sighed shut behind me; they use strong closing devices on those ships so there won't be a lot of slamming in a seaway.

The middle-aged man was gone. His place had been taken by a young woman. The first thing I noticed was the mass of very fair, very fine hair, loosely wound about her head. Then she turned to face me directly, and I saw the striking brown eyes.

"I am sorry, I thought it was the Finnish steward."

"Miss Land?" I said.

The shocking thing was how close they'd come. Well, I suppose with a population close to three hundred million, you should be able to find a pretty good match for just about anybody; and if the double you chose was bright enough and a good enough actress, and had some opportunity to study the person she was supposed to become and practice the impersonation, you could wind up with a resemblance that was quite breathtaking. Even the voice, with its accent, was very nearly the way I remembered it.

"Yes, I am Astrid Land," said the real Astrid Land. "And you must be Matthew Helm, the man to whom I owe . . ."

"Never mind owe," I said.

She laughed softly. "He rescues me from an endless gray hell, years and years of it, and says never mind. Listen, we are getting under way. It's really happening. I've been trying not to let myself believe it was going to happen, so I would not be too shattered when it turned out to be just another of their cruel tricks." She looked up at me, and licked her lips. "Nobody else seemed to care; my parents could get no help at all. Why did you do it, go to all that trouble, for a girl you'd never met?"

"It's a long story," I said.

"We have time," she said.